CAUGHT IN THE UNDERTOW

Book 2 in the Poppy Mason Series

C E de Gzell

BRIGHT STREET PRESS

Published: 2026 by Bright Street Press, New South Wales, Australia

ISBN: 9781764069120 - Paperback Edition
ISBN: 9781764069137 - eBook Edition

Cover design: Belinda Mark, Mac Magic Creative Designs

Editor: Kelly Rigby, Write with Kelly

For healthcare workers—
for all that we endure and sacrifice in the service of our communities

Caught in the Undertow is a gritty contemporary fiction novel set in a fictional hospital, The Bennelong, and includes graphic descriptions of medical procedures and traumatic events. It also includes graphic sexual activity. Readers who may be sensitive to these elements should consider this before beginning to read. This book is written in Australian English. You may find unfamiliar spelling used or slang words from the local vernacular.

Medical Hierarchy

Intern

Resident Medical Officer (RMO, or Resident)

Senior Resident Medical Officer (SRMO)

Registrar (includes both unaccredited, junior, and advanced trainees)

Fellow

Consultant

Chapter 1

Sunday, 19th January, 2020

A trail of water snaked down Poppy's back as a warm breeze lifted her damp honey-blonde hair off her forehead. She and Will were sitting on their towels watching the ocean. They had wanted to get a surf in early before the heat and humidity became oppressive. There had been just enough chill in the water for it to be refreshing, but despite the perfect conditions, Poppy's mood was low. She stared dully out to sea.

'Do you want some?' Will nudged her shoulder. Poppy shielded her eyes from the glare to look into his. Water was dripping off his wet blonde curls and creating rivulets over the contours of his cheeks. He didn't seem bothered by it and let the drips fall rather than wiping them away.

God, I love his face… those freckles across his nose and cheeks, even when it's a bit pink and peeling from sunburn. And those pillowy lips that kiss so well. He's my home.

These thoughts didn't lift her spirits. 'Thanks,' she said, taking the proffered bottle of water.

Will searched Poppy's eyes. 'What are you thinking?'

'How much I love it here. You know, us here, surfing together,' Poppy said. The water was so blue and bright, it almost hurt to look at. She swallowed a mouthful of water, spilling some down her chin which she wiped with the back of her hand. A waft of bacon smell from the barbeque outside the Bronte Surf Lifesaving Club came past on the wind and her stomach grumbled.

'Me too. But what else?' He nudged her again. 'I know you.'

A smile lifted her lips briefly. He did. 'I'm just going to miss you,' Poppy replied softly, looking out at the ocean rather than at Will. She recapped the bottle and passed it back as he wrapped an arm around her shoulders. Leaning into his embrace, she relished his touch.

Will was heading to Dubbo in the afternoon to do a country Anaesthetics rotation as part of his Senior Resident Medical Officer (SRMO) critical care year.

'Babe, it'll only be a couple of weeks at a time. We'll be fine.' He squeezed her arm, crushing her to his chest, enveloping her in the comfort of his citrusy aftershave. With the salt from the ocean, it reminded her of a margarita.

Poppy mumbled an affirmation but couldn't quite shift the anxiety. She was about to start her Resident Medical Officer (RMO) year tomorrow, still at The Bennelong Hospital, and whilst she was excited to no longer be an intern, she knew that being separated from Will would make life harder than he was making it out to be. He'd been such an important support for her this past year.

Sensing her uncertainty, he added, 'And you'll still have Gemma and Lucas.'

'I know. I'm good.' She patted the hand draped around her shoulders.

'And it's only two weeks until I come for the first visit and you'll be busy starting Respiratory. It'll fly by.' His voice was upbeat; he was probably looking forward to his new challenge and stepping up in Anaesthetics.

She resolved to be more positive. 'I'm sure you're right.'

'Come on,' he said, standing up and shaking his towel free of sand. 'Let's get some food and then I'll go home and pack.'

He offered a hand to pull her up and a sudden hot breeze barrelled through, particles of sand scraping her ankles and calves like sharp needles. Will had already grabbed both surfboards and was loping quickly up the hot sand toward the car.

Poppy turned back to the ocean and took one last look at the surf. She hoped this year would bring her closer to deciding on a specialty path. Maybe the term will be good, and the people nice…

Two seagulls squawked loudly nearby, drawing her attention with their fight over a discarded piece of sausage. Will was already placing the boards on the roof of the car, so Poppy wrapped the towel around her waist and hurried to meet him.

The sandstone façade of the hospital entrance loomed ahead. Poppy could feel the sweat building all over her body, even on the tip of her nose, and found herself routinely wiping the clear, pinecone-like beads away. The last thing she needed for her first day as a Resident was to turn up looking like she'd just come out of a sauna, hair frizzled and stuck to her temples.

Gemma slipped an arm around Poppy's waist. 'God, we were green last year, weren't we?'

'I know, right?' Poppy murmured, leaning into her friend.

It had been a full year since they had started work as interns and so much had happened. Gemma and Lucas were still strong but no closer to getting engaged, much to Gemma's disappointment. Poppy met Will on her first day, but stuffed things up early on. Whilst they were stuck in the friendzone, she had an unfulfilling fling with Joshua Hunter, a Medical Registrar who proceeded to make her life miserable after she and Will finally got together. Josh's face floated into Poppy's mind and she stepped out of Gemma's embrace.

'What's up?' Gemma asked.

Poppy looked up to the stained glass windows and then down to her feet. 'I just hope I don't run into Josh too much.'

Gemma crossed her arms over her chest. 'You remember how I said to deal with him?' She didn't wait for an answer. 'You push back. Call him out when he puts you down. That's the only way to deal with a bully.'

Poppy wasn't sure she could do that.

'Hey, wait up,' Lucas called out. 'Here you go.' He handed them each a coffee from Campos then disposed of the cup carrier into the nearby bin.

'Thanks, Luc.' Poppy was grateful for the distraction. Thoughts of Josh banished when she took that first delicious sip of her latte, savouring the velvety warmth despite the heat.

Gemma kissed Lucas unashamedly on the lips, then took a sip and groaned. 'Just what I needed.'

'Alright, peeps,' Poppy said, as they arrived at the lifts at the end of the entrance hall, 'We're going to have a good day and meet at the entrance. Family dinner tonight?'

'Definitely,' agreed Gemma.

Lucas nodded and gave Gemma a quick kiss on the cheek. 'Have a good one, ladies.'

He turned down the corridor toward the Cardiology wing and Gemma and Poppy headed up in the lifts. Gemma got off on the seventh floor for Surgical Oncology, while Poppy took the lift all the way to the eleventh floor. As she ascended the last few floors on her own, a flutter of anxiety began to rise in her chest. Who would her Registrar be? She really hoped she didn't have to work with Dr Anderson…

Dr Anderson was a Respiratory Physician and the head of junior doctor training. Poppy had inadvertently made her an enemy last year when she'd petitioned the hospital to provide more support and safer work hours for the junior staff, after a colleague had committed suicide. At the time, she thought Dr Anderson would be on her side, but instead she actively discouraged change until her hand was forced by media scrutiny.

Head up, Poppy. You can do this. No one is going to stop you. Not Josh or Dr Anderson.

She raised her chin, exited the lift, and walked down to the Respiratory ward.

Poppy walked confidently to the nurses' station, about halfway down the ward, and pushed herself forward towards a group of nurses, her voice catching as she introduced herself.

'Hi, I'm Poppy. One of the new Residents this term.' Her heart felt like it had launched itself up into her throat, the pounding was so powerful and loud in her ears. Every new term was like this.

The oldest of the group, a woman with closely cropped grey-blonde hair, spoke first. 'I'm Susan, the Nurse Unit Manager. Welcome.'

Poppy returned her smile, hoping no-one noticed the slight wobble of her chin.

'I'll show you where everyone is meeting.' Susan smoothed her uniform top over her middle and led Poppy around the corner, pointing out a meeting room where only one person was seated, chewing at his fingernails and jiggling his foot.

Poppy entered the room and walked over to the sole occupant. 'Hi, I'm Poppy.'

'Alex. One of the new interns.' He leapt to his feet and Poppy had to step back to look into his face. He stuck out his hand as if to shake, then suddenly changed his mind, pulling it back and tucking it into his armpit. 'Sorry, I've got to stop biting my nails, it's a filthy habit.'

Poor guy, she thought, giving him a reassuring smile, it's hard being an intern. 'I'm nervous too, and I've been here a year.'

'Glad it's not just me. But, seriously, is it an okay place?' He looked so young and scared, bent at the waist like he was trying to collapse his tall frame into a smaller and more disposable package. Was that how she looked last year?

'It's been good, generally,' Poppy said. 'You'll be fine. Where have you come from?'

'I did medicine in Newcastle.'

'Me too!'

Alex visibly relaxed, lengthening his frame back to full height. 'Really? Cool.' He grinned for the first time.

Two women filed into the room.

'Welcome. I'm Maria,' the first said. She was average height with mousy-brown hair and a long fringe that brushed up against unfashionable eighties glasses. Her boxy, brown pinstripe suit hung loosely, further disguising her body. Poppy wondered if it was intentional or whether she just had no fashion sense. 'And this is Olivia.' She pointed to the more fashionable woman behind her. She was not unattractive, maybe a little plain with her dark hair up in a simple ponytail. 'You must be Alex and Poppy.'

'Hi,' they both replied.

'I'm the senior Registrar. Alex, you'll be with me on Team B and Poppy, you and Olivia will be on Team A.'

Poppy's innards clenched at Maria's words – *please don't let Dr Anderson be on Team A* – but she somehow summoned a smile for Olivia, whose perfectly defined bubblegum-pink lips lifted briefly in response.

'Each team has two consultants,' Maria continued. 'Team A is Professor Pilson and Associate Professor Benjamin.'

Yes-yes, yes-yes, yes! Poppy did an internal happy dance and her guts relaxed.

'Team B is Dr Anderson and Dr Springer. We also have a Fellow from Turkey whose name is Adnan, but he will mainly be in clinics with the Consultants, so you're unlikely to see him much.'

Maria went on to explain how the term was structured. There was a weekly team meeting on Mondays at ten o'clock with an education component followed by the Registrar's case presentations, to be critiqued by the consultants, then the major teaching ward round.

Almost as soon as Maria had finished her explanation, the consultants began to arrive. One of them, Poppy guessed him to be in his seventies, was tall with white hair, and a snowy short beard. He was wearing a dark charcoal suit with a white coat and colourful bow tie. His name, Professor Brian Pilson, was embroidered in red stitching over the breast pocket of the white coat. He was carrying a cake box, which he placed on the table then opened, revealing a delicious-looking ricotta cheesecake.

'I'll get the knife and plates,' said Maria, clearly not surprised at all by this gesture.

Poppy was shocked. Was it someone's birthday, or did they always welcome the newbies with a cake? She looked over at Alex, who shrugged.

At this moment, Dr Anderson sauntered into the room, immaculately groomed as always, in a seashell-pink shift dress and suit jacket, her lustrous chestnut hair in a bun, a few intentionally loose waves framing her face.

'Cheesecake again, Brian?' Dr Anderson's porcelain skin barely moved as she spoke. Not a crease or wrinkle in sight.

'But it's the best cheesecake, Katrina,' Prof Pilson said with a slight chuckle, unfazed by Dr Anderson's snippy tone. He reminded Poppy of Dumbledore. All that was missing was the half-moon spectacles perched on the end of his nose, and the elaborate, sparkly robes. She warmed to him instantly.

Dr Anderson's eyes roved the room. Upon spotting Poppy, they briefly lingered and Poppy thought she detected the faintest of scowls, but maybe she imagined it, before her eyes moved on to Olivia and Alex. Dr Anderson walked over and introduced herself to them as the two remaining Consultants and the Fellow entered the room.

Once the cake was cut and divvied up, they all took a chair and, after basic introductions, Prof Pilson turned to the group and asked what cultural activity they had done in the last week. Behind him, Dr Anderson noticeably rolled her eyes. Clearly, there was no love lost between them.

Poppy had to admit it was weird. Most of the time the Consultants barely spoke to the junior doctors, apart from asking them to order tests. They certainly didn't converse about what they did in their private time or show interest in getting to know them as humans.

'I went to a Sydney Symphony concert,' Adnan, the Turkish Fellow said as crumbly bits of cheesecake fell from the corner of his mouth.

'Lovely, what were they playing?' Prof Pilson asked.

'Beethoven. Conducted by Simone Young. It was excellent.'

'Wonderful. I myself went to the Opera to see The Merry Widow. It was very exciting. What about the rest of you?' Prof Pilson asked, taking in the assembled group.

His question was met with silence. Alex shuffled slightly in his chair.

Maria mentioned she was reading last year's Miles Franklin Award winner and Prof Pilson was very interested in her thoughts as he had also read it. Poppy was thoroughly fascinated. It was so unexpected and completely foreign to anything she'd previously encountered here at The Bennelong. It was like they were at a garden party, making conversation over hor d'oeuvres and sparkling wine. There was none of the cutthroat, testosterone-driven environment Poppy was used to.

'Who's presenting today, Maria?' Prof Pilson asked when only the cheesecake crumbs were left.

'I've got a journal article to discuss, and then two cases from the ward.'

'Excellent, let's clear away, and get started,' Prof Pilson said as he placed his empty paper plate on the spare seat beside him.

Maria dutifully brought around a bin for the rubbish and Poppy hopped up and collected some plates.

Once Maria had her laptop plugged into the AV system, and the lights were dimmed, she started her presentation. It was on a journal article about a novel coronavirus which had been reported as spreading quickly in

Wuhan, China. The article detailed the respiratory effects, which appeared to be rapid and devastating. Poppy was fascinated as she'd seen a few articles about it in the paper, but those articles hadn't really provided much detail on the effects of the virus on the body.

'So, Maria, do you think this virus could spread beyond China? Or will it stay relatively contained, like SARS and swine flu?' Prof Pilson asked when she'd finished.

'I think it could spread. Case numbers look like they're going up exponentially. And, I guess, with China, you never know if the situation isn't worse than what they're reporting.'

'But didn't they just announce a lockdown in Wuhan?' Prof Benjamin asked.

Poppy noticed him properly for the first time. He was short and had one of those rodent-type faces, with eyes a little too close together and a weak chin.

'Yes, I believe they did.' Prof Pilson paused and rubbed his beard before continuing. 'But I agree with Maria. There is a significant risk here. Wuhan is a big industrial area and having just completed the Christmas period, there is a lot of travel in and out of all regions in China. This could easily spread to other parts of the world. And with a major industrial section of China going into lockdown, that will also likely have flow-on effects to the availability of products and trade. This could get really interesting in the next month or so. Thank you, Maria. Watch this space. Now the cases?'

Poppy wondered if Prof Pilson was right. Could this virus suddenly spread quickly throughout the world with devastating effects? Her throat caught and her heart rate kicked up.

But maybe it would just be like swine flu. That had stayed contained and never spread as predicted.

It's all going to be fine. This is the beginning of a great year. Will and I will get through this Dubbo separation, I'll learn more medicine and become more confident. Maybe I'll even find the specialty that's right for me? It's going to be awesome!

Chapter 2

'This is Margaret,' Maria introduced the patient she had led into the meeting room. The older woman shuffled in, her slippers scuffing on the linoleum flooring, a tatty pink robe hanging limply over her old-fashioned white cotton nightie. Poppy thought she looked nervous. It must be very daunting sitting in front of a group of doctors like a prized pig.

'Good morning, Margaret. Thank you for joining us,' Prof Pilson said.

Like she had a choice or really understood what she was walking into, Poppy thought.

'Hi,' she replied, her voice breaking nervously.

'Margaret is sixty-four and presented with shortness of breath on exertion and a productive cough.'

'Thank you, Maria.' Prof Pilson took in the group and Poppy instinctively tensed. 'Olivia, could you please examine Margaret?'

Olivia stood and moved to the front of the room. Unlike Poppy, she didn't appear at all nervous. 'Hi Margaret, my name is Olivia. Do you mind if I examine you?'

'That would be fine.'

Poppy watched as Olivia systematically performed a respiratory examination, which included taking her pulse, checking her fingers for clubbing and peripheral signs of anaemia, percussing and listening to her chest. She was soaking it all up and storing the actions away for when she might be called upon to do a respiratory case.

When Olivia had finished, she thanked Margaret and escorted her from the room quickly. Upon her return, she stood in front of the seat Margaret had just vacated and Prof Pilson began the oral examination.

'Is there anything else you'd like to know or examine, Olivia?' He steepled his fingers in front of his chin.

'I'd like to know her oxygen saturation, and her temperature. I'd also like to complete a cardiovascular examination and perform spirometry.' Olivia's back was straight, her hands loosely clasped in front of her.

Professor Pilson provided some additional details then asked Olivia to present her findings.

Olivia looked down at her shoes briefly before starting her presentation. She was clearly formulating her response, but Poppy was impressed how quickly she began.

'Sixty-four-year-old woman with dyspnoea and productive cough in sinus rhythm, heart rate ninety-five beats per minute, with decreased oxygen saturation, clubbed fingers, and shallow breathing, with coarse crackles at both lung bases. There were no signs to indicate pleural effusion or consolidation.' Olivia closed her mouth, waiting for Prof's next question.

'What additional investigations would you perform?' asked Prof Pilson.

'Blood gas, sputum culture, full blood count, C-reactive protein, and a chest X-ray.'

'The blood gas shows normal pH and a PaO_2 of 72mmHg. The sputum culture is negative, and the chest X-ray shows bronchial dilatation. What's your differential diagnosis?' His steepled index fingers tapped twice and then stopped while he waited for Olivia's answer.

Poppy was impressed with how Olivia presented under pressure. When Maria had introduced them, she'd explained Olivia was a junior Registrar who hadn't yet sat the Physician's exam. She was only a year or two ahead of Poppy, but her confidence suggested she was further along in her training.

Once Olivia was unable to answer a question, Prof Pilson moved on to Maria. She was an advanced trainee finishing her physician's training in Respiratory Medicine, so Poppy was keen to hear her assessment. Maria was quiet but definitive in her answers and Prof nodded his head in agreement. When he was satisfied, he made some generalised comments about the management of bronchiectasis to the room and then asked to move on to the next case. Poppy hurriedly took down some notes on her phone before the next patient arrived.

This time, Prof Pilson asked Adnan to examine the patient and Poppy noticed Olivia's shoulders visibly soften. She must be relieved not to have to go again.

Fair enough, I wouldn't want to be examined in front of the whole Respiratory department on the first day.

This patient had a pleural effusion and when Adnan percussed the chest, Prof Pilson asked Poppy and Alex to come close to the patient to appreciate the dullness that indicated fluid filling the space between the lungs and the chest wall.

'Do you hear the dullness?' Prof asked.

'Yes,' Poppy said excitedly. She'd never seen this demonstrated before.

'Now, Poppy, before you sit down,' Prof Pilson stopped her in her tracks. 'What are some common causes of pleural effusion?'

Oh shit! She couldn't believe he was asking her on her first day, in front of everyone. *Causes of pleural effusions… causes of pleural effusions…*

That familiar wave of heat rushed up Poppy's neck, and she felt all eyes in the room boring into her as she tried to form a coherent answer.

'Um… pneumonia, heart failure, malignant effusion, and…' Her mind drew a blank. Damn. She was sure she'd missed at least one other cause. 'Sorry, that's all I can think of.'

'That's okay, well done,' Prof Pilson said.

Poppy couldn't help sneaking a look at Dr Anderson. Her eyes were cold, her face mask-like and Poppy's blush deepened. She must do Botox. No one her age could have such a wrinkle-free complexion. She started to step forward, assuming she was out of the firing line. But Prof Pilson wasn't done with her.

'What are the common symptoms associated with a pleural effusion?'

This was easier.

'Shortness of breath… cough… and maybe pleurisy,' Poppy finished confidently.

'Good. Also, orthopnoea, hypoxia, tachycardia – particularly if associated with PE – and fever, if associated with infection.'

Poppy nodded but weren't these all signs rather than symptoms?

Prof Pilson steepled his fingers and tapped them in front of his nose. 'How does one characterise the different types of pleural effusion?'

Poppy's eyes drifted upward, hoping for some long, filed-away kernel of information from medical school. Different types of pleural effusion? Her eyes met Alex's and saw him chewing his fingernails again with a panicked expression, probably worried he'd be next in the firing line.

Aren't they all just fluid in the pleural cavity?

'Um…' she stalled. 'Sorry, I can't remember.'

'That's okay, that was a tough one. There are both exudative and transudative types. Exudative is more commonly associated with infection and malignancy, and transudative types are more common in patients with heart failure and liver cirrhosis. Good, you can relax now.'

Poppy exhaled her held breath and quietly returned to her seat, head down. She had completely forgotten about exudative versus transudative types of effusion. It was like a long distant memory from one lecture in medical school. The proverbial needle in the haystack. She might have to dig out her respiratory notes from med school so she wouldn't look so stupid next time.

After the meeting they headed straight into the teaching ward round. When this finished, Olivia headed off to other wards with Prof Pilson to see consults and Poppy trundled the portable computer back toward the nurses' station. She was left with a long list of jobs and it was already lunchtime. As soon as she sat down, she was immediately flanked by two nurses.

'Can you resite cannulas in beds four and fifteen?' It was the shorter of the two nurses. 'Their midday antibiotics are overdue.'

She hadn't managed to tick off a single job from the round and was already being diverted. But Poppy knew how important it was to start off on the right foot with the nurses. Making friends early on was essential for a good term. If they liked you, they'd protect you when you were busy and actively help you out. If not, they'd make your life hell.

'Sure. I'm Poppy, by the way,' she said brightly to the nurse leaning over her.

'Are you going to do the cannulas?' she asked brusquely.

'Just give me one sec to get my jobs written down, then I'll get right on it. Can you please give me the code for the drug and equipment room?'

'Yep. 7-2-6-0.'

'Brilliant. Thanks,' Poppy said, again infusing as much warmth into her voice as she could muster, but both nurses were already zeroing in on Alex, who was heading up the ward after his round.

Poppy quickly scribbled her jobs on her printed ward list and folded and tucked it into her work pants. The nurses had written a jobs list for Alex and Poppy on the whiteboard, so Poppy pulled her list back out and added the extra jobs before finally tucking it away again. In the equipment room she gathered what she would need for the first cannula, tucked a loose strand of hair behind her ear, and headed down the ward. So far, her first day was a mixed bag and she was determined that it be more of a success than not.

The first patient was a woman in her seventies with pneumonia, called Hazel Brooks. On the ward round, Poppy had felt a bit sorry for her. She had looked so tiny and frail in the big hospital bed and she'd seemed overwhelmed by the crowd around her.

'Hi Hazel, my name is Poppy. I'm the new Resident on the ward. How are you feeling?'

'I'm so tired,' Hazel gasped between laboured breaths.

'I'm so sorry. Now I just need to put in a new needle for the antibiotics, hopefully they'll make you feel better soon.'

'Oh no, I hate all these needles.' Hazel pulled up the sheets and clutched them tightly.

'I know,' Poppy said soothingly. 'It's not much fun is it. Let's have a look and see if we can find a good vein.'

After assessing both arms, Poppy's confidence started to drop. Hazel had ropey, snaking veins that rolled around to the slightest touch. Her skin was paper-thin with fading, deep purple bruises haphazardly along her arms. Poppy knew from experience that this was going to be tricky. She picked the least rolling one in Hazel's left arm and got her kit ready. Then she fastened the tourniquet and carefully cleaned Hazel's dry, bruised skin, and took a deep breath, psyching herself up.

You can do this, Pop, you've done hundreds, this will be a cinch.

'Okay, Hazel, sharp pain now,' Poppy said as she inserted the cannula through Hazel's fragile skin and into her ropey old vein. Blood filled the flashback chamber and Poppy tried to advance the needle further into the vein but it rolled away and the vein blew. Damn, she thought, as blood seeped into the surrounding tissues, the bruise building and spreading.

'I'm sorry, Hazel, this one hasn't worked.' She retracted the needle and held some gauze over the site to staunch the bleeding, the colourful tourniquet now hanging limply at her elbow. Its brightness mocking her.

'Let me just hold this for a moment then I'll have another go.'

'Ow, that's hurting,' Hazel whimpered.

'I'm sorry, honey. It won't be long. I just need to stop the bleeding.' Poppy used the back of her gloved hand to wipe a tendril of hair off her forehead. She didn't like hurting people, particularly old ladies. It was now Poppy remembered that Hazel was on anticoagulants, so she'd have to compress the wound for longer. Her list of jobs began spreading in her mind, like the bruise beneath her fingers. If she couldn't get through these simple cannulas, she was going to be here forever. Her bladder took this moment to insist that it, too, needed attention. She should have ducked to the loo at the end of the round, before the nurses had managed to corner her.

Hazel moaned in pain, bringing Poppy's focus back to the tiny woman in the bed. She checked to make sure the bleeding had finally stopped then bandaged that site and searched her right arm again for another suitable vein to try. Luckily, she'd brought two sets with her, a benefit of having a year's worth of experience on her side.

Please let this one work.

'Okay, Hazel, here we go again. Sting now.'

Poppy inserted the needle with confidence. The blood flashed and she inserted further, bracing the vein with her left hand (being careful not to stab herself) to prevent the roll. She successfully completed the cannulation and breathed a quiet sigh of relief.

'There we go, Hazel,' she said brightly as she dressed the cannula and flushed it with saline. 'Hopefully this will last longer than the last one.'

'I hope so too.'

Poppy gave Hazel's shoulder a light squeeze and left her bed bay. One successful task done. Now she just needed the rest of the day to go as smoothly.

She erased "IVC Bed 4" off the nurses' board, discarded her sharps and mess, and started the process again. The second cannula was for a young patient with cystic fibrosis who thankfully had perfect young veins, and whose cannula went in easily on the first attempt. By the time she'd tidied up again and erased "IVC Bed 15" from the board, Olivia was back from consults and wanted to go over the job list with Poppy. It was now after one o'clock. Poppy was thirsty, feeling dizzy from hunger, and desperately needed to pee. But she sat next to Olivia at the nurses' station without complaint, and they went over the jobs to perform, and the results to chase. Some they were able to tick off together, but after twenty minutes the list was still fairly extensive.

Olivia then left to eat lunch before going to see more consults, leaving Poppy to "the list". No sooner had Olivia left, then the nurses swarmed again. Wanting Poppy to re-chart medications which were due to expire, chart IV fluids, and there was now another cannula to do.

Poppy slouched in her chair. How she wished it was home time. The day had started so well, with cake and interesting conversation, and now she was exhausted and swamped. And so incredibly hungry. What she wouldn't give for some of that cheesecake now.

But enough of the self-pity. Poppy took a deep breath and wearily rose to her feet. 'Let me duck to the loo and I'll be right with you,' she said to no nurse in particular.

You got this. Let's kick some arse.

Right after she peed.

By three o'clock she had done all the most important jobs, placated and befriended a couple of the nurses (Melanie and Susan), and decided it was time to break for lunch. She caught the lift down to the cafeteria but could have cried when she entered and saw the empty bain-maries.

'What can I get you, love?' the server asked as Poppy searched the empty shelves and the lonely wilting cheese sandwich in its plastic container.

'You've finished lunch service?' Poppy asked, hoping there might be something out the back.

'Yep. Finishes at two-thirty.'

She walked quickly out the front entrance of the hospital and up the street to the first café on the corner, where she bought a sandwich and a Coke Zero. At an outdoor table she ate quickly before grabbing a crappy (but hot) coffee on the way back to the ward to finish "the list". While she'd been eating, she thought about the journal article Maria had presented. Again, she wondered if this would end up like SARS and be a flash in the pan. There was a faint buzz in the back of her brain, like a fly vibrating against a window. What if it was something more?

Chapter 3

That determination to finish her list of jobs evaporated two hours later when she decided everything left could wait for tomorrow. Her head was buzzing and she was exhausted, but at least the day was over. Lucas had texted earlier to say he was doing an overtime shift, so she raced to the front entrance to meet Gemma, remembering at least she had dinner with her best friend to keep her upright.

'Sorry, sorry,' Poppy said, jogging up to where Gemma was waiting near the ED Ambulance bay.

Gemma looked up from her phone. 'It's okay, don't blow a gasket.'

Poppy gave Gemma a hug and they began the walk home. On the way they filled each other in on their respective days. Gemma was working for four Consultants, who all mainly did breast cancer and melanoma surgery, one Registrar, and a Fellow.

'Dave, my Reg, seems okay. He was pretty chatty and we spent the morning rounding, and seeing patients,' Gemma said.

'That sounds promising.'

'Yeah, I think so. He gave me the low-down on the week. Tomorrow, I'll be in theatres in the morning and probably sorting the ward in the arvo.'

'And what about the boss you met?'

'Dr Patchett.' Gemma's voice dropped at his name. 'He was very tall, and pretty old. He didn't say too much, and only rounded for about fifteen minutes with a very cursory glance at the wounds and drains... I'm not sure I'm going to gel there.'

'Sounds like you've already formed an opinion,' Poppy said, laughing.

'You know me,' Gemma smiled. Poppy hugged her around the shoulders, and they walked on.

Gemma and Poppy had been friends since they first met in the dorms in medical school when they bonded over their mutual lust for Ryan Gosling. Gemma was statuesque with short brown hair, unusual green eyes, and what many said was a resting bitch face. Poppy knew she didn't mean to give off the impression that she disliked or looked down on you, it was just that she was quick to judge, and her own insecurity around new people often came across as arrogance. She'd been dating Lucas, their other flatmate, since early in their first year and to Poppy, they were family.

'What about you, Pop?'

'Gosh, where to start?' Poppy sidestepped a puddle of what looked like spilt milkshake and Gemma did the same. At least it wasn't a used condom. 'The morning started great. Our weekly meeting came with cake and conversation.'

'Wait, what?' Gemma reached out a hand to stop Poppy. 'Did you say cake?'

'Yep. Prof Pilson brought it, but apparently it's a weekly thing. There's a roster and everything.' Poppy resumed walking.

'Nice!'

'I know!'

'What was the conversation about? Get to know you stuff?' Gemma weaved around a woman with a pram.

'Nope.' Poppy grinned at her friend. 'It was about culture. Prof Pilson asked about what cultural activities we'd done on the weekend.'

'O-kay... that's… different.' She raised a skeptical eyebrow.

'Actually, it was really nice.'

'Was Dr Anderson there?' This time Gemma side-eyed her.

'Yeah, there were some death stares, but she basically ignored me,' Poppy replied. *Thank God.* 'I got asked about causes of pleural effusions. I think I got about three right, but he didn't push me too hard, thankfully. Pilson seems really nice. He's gotta be in his seventies, but the whole morning he was a real gentleman, very respectful, always with a kind tone when he was questioning, and sweet with the patients.'

They turned the corner, only a block from home now.

'But I didn't get lunch until three,' Poppy moaned. 'It was pretty full-on. I think Mondays, because of the morning meeting, will be a bit of a shit fight. But hopefully the rest of the week will be better.'

'What about your Reg?' asked Gemma.

'Olivia. She's a junior Reg. It's too early to tell, we didn't spend a huge amount of time together. Do you know how Lucas went?'

'I ducked down to his ward on my way out. He seems happy. He has the same team you had last year, so that's pretty cool. You liked them.'

'Yeah, good bosses. And who's his Reg?'

Gemma took a beat to answer. 'Miriam. She was there when I went down. She's absolutely gorgeous!'

'Really?' Poppy scrutinised her friend's face.

A deep frown line creased Gemma's forehead. 'Yeah. I guess I'll hear more about her later.'

'You're not worried, are you?' Poppy was surprised at the tension in her friend's body.

'No, don't be silly,' Gemma said. But Poppy got the distinct impression she was.

'Did you hear from Will today?' Gemma asked later, when they'd finished their makeshift meal of toasted sandwiches on the couch.

'No, but I wasn't expecting to. He said he was likely to be in theatres all day. We're going to speak at seven thirty.'

'I wonder how he's going? Say hi from me.'

A butterfly fluttered against the inside of Poppy's ribcage in anticipation of talking to Will. She'd been so busy and overwhelmed during the day, she'd barely considered him, but now all she wanted was to hear his voice and see his face.

Poppy made herself comfortable on her bed and eagerly grabbed for her phone when it rang at the appointed time. Will's face came on the screen.

'Hi, beautiful,' he said.

Poppy felt a wave of love at his words. 'Hi, hon, it's so good to see you. How was your day?'

'You first.'

Poppy told him all about her day, the people she'd met, and how exhausted she was.

'What about you?' she asked when she'd finished.

'Pretty good, too. I spent all day in theatres from about seven this morning until about six, as I was expecting. Got to do two of the inductions, which was good. The Anaesthetist was okay. A bit gruff but not mean.'

'What was the list?'

'All day Ortho.'

'Were the Orthopods fly-in-fly-out?'

'Yeah. Just the one guy. Flies in for two days a month.'

Something in Will's tone made Poppy ask, 'Was he okay?'

Will wiped his hand through his curls and sighed. 'A bit of a dick. Lots of swearing and having a go at his Reg. But barely even acknowledged us.'

'Why are surgeons all such dicks?' Poppy shook her head.

'Egos.'

'Yeah…' Poppy sighed.

Will moved closer to the camera. 'Anyway, let's not waste any more time talking about dickheads.'

'What do you want to talk about?' Poppy asked coquettishly.

'How beautiful you are, and how much I miss you already.'

Poppy smiled and could see her right-sided dimple flickering into view in her small image in the corner of her screen, dwarfed by Will's central one. 'I miss you too.'

They stared at each other with goofy smiles for a while before Poppy asked how the accommodation was. He'd only arrived in Dubbo the night before and this was the first chance they'd had to talk.

'So, I'm sharing with one of the Med Reg's. A guy called Brendan. I met him last year. He's okay.'

'That's good. And the house?'

'We're on the hospital grounds, out the back. It's a bunch of old brick houses. Pretty basic, but clean.'

They talked more about their upcoming weeks and when they were nearing the end of their conversation, Poppy said, 'I can't believe it's going to be two whole weeks until we see each other.' Today had felt like a week in itself!

'I know. I don't think we've spent that long apart since even before we started dating properly.'

Poppy's head dropped. 'I know, don't make me depressed.'

'Don't worry, hon, we'll get through it. And we'll talk every day.' His voice was as soothing as her mum's homemade biscuits. 'I love you, Poppy.'

'I love you too, Will.'

Even though Will had told Poppy he loved her about three months into their relationship, she still loved hearing it, and while he was the first to make himself vulnerable, she soon followed. Now saying "I love you" felt completely natural.

'Well, I'm desperate for a shower, so I'd better go. Got another early start tomorrow.' Will stood up and started walking, making the camera jerk and picture blur slightly.

'Okay. Love you. Sleep well.'

'You too, beautiful. Have a good day tomorrow. Say hi to Gem and Luc for me.'

Poppy pressed the red disconnect button. She was putting on a brave face for Will, but she already missed him. They'd been together for about nine months, and for the last six they'd basically lived together. They'd spend at least four or five nights a week together – at his place or hers – only really sleeping apart if one of them was doing an overtime shift. His stint in Dubbo was going to be tough.

Poppy woke up feeling no better than when she went to sleep. The late January humidity cloyed her skin and she slept fitfully. It didn't help that she missed Will. She'd gotten used to the feeling of his body curved into her back as they slept entwined. She felt sticky and dragged herself out of bed and stumbled to the bathroom, where a lukewarm shower helped revive her.

Lucas was eating breakfast at the table when Poppy approached. 'Morning, Luc.'

Gemma was nowhere to be seen, probably left early to get to theatres on time.

'Morning.' He didn't look up from what he was reading on his iPad.

'How was yesterday?' Poppy asked, putting bread in the toaster and turning the kettle on.

Now he looked towards Poppy in the kitchen. 'Good. You were right, the bosses are nice.' He spooned cereal into his mouth with a slight slurp.

'Yeah, it's a good term. And I heard Miriam is very pretty,' Poppy said with a cheeky grin, knowing she was pushing Lucas's buttons.

He blushed and coughed, aspirating some of his food. 'Yeah, she's nice looking.'

Poppy couldn't remember seeing Lucas blush before. Jeez, this woman must be a knock-out.

They headed over to Cuckoo Callay on their way in to work, the traffic noise drowning out any chance of conversation. Lucas waited outside while Poppy went in to order.

'Hi Stace,' she greeted the new barista when it was her turn. *This city*, by Sam Fischer was playing through the speakers in the café.

'Hey, Poppy, what can I make for you today?'

'Two large lattes, one sugar each. Thanks.'

'Coming right up.'

Poppy moved to the side to wait and watch Stacey work. Jason had moved on a few months ago, no one really knowing where or why, and Stacey had taken over. She was quintessential Newtown: more body art than spare skin, nose ring, endless ear piercings and cuffs, and her platinum blond hair with dark roots was ruthlessly parted and gelled flat to her head. She wore a white, *wife-beater* singlet, her black bra straps protruding, and loose boyfriend jeans with rolled cuffs, and brogues without socks. Her latte art was taken very seriously, even for takeaways, and she soon produced a swan on one coffee and a triple heart on the other. Stacey made sure Poppy saw her spectacular artwork before covering them with takeaway lids.

'Oh Stace, that's amazing.' Poppy picked up the two cups and wished they were sitting down to drink so she could appreciate the design more.

'I aim to please. Don't be a stranger,' Stacey said before returning her attention to her pastel green retro commercial coffee machine, her mind already on the next order.

'Oh God, that's good,' Lucas said, taking his first sip. 'That woman is a genius.'

'She sure is.' Poppy felt the warmth penetrate all the way to her extremities, and the last of her exhaustion fell away. Once they turned off King Street and made their way through Camperdown Memorial Rest Park, the noise and bustle eased and Poppy could hear the birds in the trees and the wind shuffling the leaves, like cards in a deck.

'I spent a bit of time with Josh yesterday in the cath lab,' Lucas said as he took a sip of his coffee.

Poppy's gait faltered and she almost choked on the milk foam. She knew Lucas really disliked Josh and was waiting for the next thing out of his mouth to be negative.

'He surprised me by not being a massive dick.'

'Really?' Poppy said cautiously.

'He remembered my name for the first time and even gave me a bit of teaching.'

Poppy raised a single eyebrow. 'Very unlike him.'

'My thoughts as well.'

'And he didn't use it as an opportunity to put me down?' Poppy's innards instinctively clenched as she waited for his answer.

'No,' Lucas shook his head. 'Didn't mention you once.'

Poppy couldn't help it, she was shocked. Josh might be drop-dead gorgeous, but he was also a supercilious bastard and a total know-it-all. Their brief, lusty fling had been all about him – what he wanted, when he wanted it. Things had fizzled around his specialty exams, but when Josh found out she'd started dating Will, he'd been a total jackass. Basically putting her down at every opportunity.

'Well, that's new for him,' Poppy said, downing the last long sip of her coffee as they veered down a side street on their shortcut to the hospital. Tiny terraces and workers cottages jostled for space in narrow streets barely wide enough for one car to get through. They had to make their way around patches of dog poo and mothers with prams, out enjoying an early walk, so their conversation stalled again.

I wonder if that means Josh has finally decided to move on? I hope he stops making things so difficult every time we see each other or when I have to talk to him about a consult. It is getting exhausting and it drives Will nuts. Fingers crossed!

She waved goodbye to Lucas at the lifts, feeling upbeat and ready for the day ahead. When the lift doors opened, smokey blue eyes met hers and Poppy froze, her coffee cup halfway to her mouth.

'Are you getting in?' Joshua Hunter asked, a muscle flickering in his cheek.

Poppy almost tripped over her feet getting into the lift. Had she just conjured him into existence? She stood slightly in front of him, exquisitely conscious of how close he was. As she took a deep breath, trying to calm her racing heart, his aftershave mingled with the coffee that was still halfway to her mouth and the familiarity of it triggered signals in her brain. A fleeting image of his strong arms and naked torso sprung to mind and heat ripped through her body. Thank goodness she was standing in front of him so he might not notice her discomfort. Her right hand shook, threatening to spill coffee foam out of the spout in the lid.

The lift dinged and the doors opened on the ninth floor. 'Excuse me,' Josh said as he moved past her to get out. Poppy kept her eyes down, but her arm tingled where he brushed past her. As he strode confidently away from the lift and the doors were just beginning to close, her eyes lingered on his back and drifted down to his butt. It was at that moment that he turned, catching her checking him out. He smirked and Poppy reached forward and punched the "close door" button. She could hear his barking laugh when the doors finally closed on her flaming face. Why had she fallen into that trap?

On the eleventh floor she took a moment to compose herself after she exited the lift. She couldn't arrive on the ward as she was, it would be too mortifying.

Come on, Poppy, deep breaths.

She took the last few sips of her coffee and threw the cup into the bin as she walked toward the ward. At the nurses' station she said a cheerful hello to Melanie and Susan.

'So how are you ladies this morning?' Poppy asked forcing herself to be upbeat. They didn't know what had just transpired in the lift.

'Okay,' Melanie said. Susan smiled briefly but didn't pass comment.

'How's the ward this morning, any dramas overnight?'

'Mrs Brooks died,' Melanie answered.

'What? Hazel?' Poppy asked, a hand flying up to her face as bubbles of acid from her coffee rose up her chest. 'What happened?'

'She took a turn for the worse. The night Registrar thought she might have had a stroke. ICU wouldn't take her. She died around four o'clock.'

'I can't believe it.' Poppy thought back to the interactions she had with Hazel yesterday, her small bird-like body so frail in the big hospital bed.

'Yeah, she was a sweetie,' Melanie agreed. Poppy stood still staring blankly at the noticeboard behind their heads.

'Are you okay?' Susan asked, a look of concern on her face.

Poppy registered the question and went to say "yes" but found the words caught in her throat. She nodded instead.

'She was old, Poppy. There was nothing they could do.'

'It's just a shock. I spent a bit of time with her yesterday. I just... wasn't expecting it, I guess.' Poppy appreciated Susan's attempt to reassure her, but she excused herself and went to the tearoom to put away her bag and collect her thoughts. Looking down as she closed the locker door, she saw that her hands were shaking slightly.

It's not your fault. Hazel was old and frail. There was nothing you could have done.

She headed back to the nurses' station to get to work, determined to keep moving forward and not dwell on Hazel's death. Despite being a doctor for a year, she was still not used to the emotions that bubbled to the surface when a patient she'd cared for died. Somehow, it was always a shock and unexpected, even if they were a cancer patient towards the end of their journey. Each time the surprise hit her and then the grief from her sister's suicide would leak out of the box she'd hidden it in, deep down inside. Ready to engulf her in sadness once more.

But not today. Today Poppy actively turned a corner in her mind, shut the door on Lulu, and focused on the jobs left over from yesterday. She checked to see if a few results had come in and updated some patient records, determinedly keeping her attention on work.

At some point Alex arrived, his long frame towering over her seated position. 'Hi, Poppy.'

She looked up from her computer and strained her neck to meet his eyes. 'Morning, Alex. How was your first day yesterday? Sorry I didn't get time to check in with you.'

'That's okay. It was full-on, but Maria was great. We basically just worked together all day.'

'That's good.' Maybe Olivia will be like that today, Poppy thought hopefully.

'Yeah, she's amazing.'

'Good. Well, if you have any problems or need help with cannulas, or whatever, I'm here too.'

'Thanks, Poppy.' He smiled and she had to admit he seemed more confident than yesterday. 'I'm sure I'll need your help sooner or later. Here comes Maria, I'd better go put my stuff away.' He raised his hand in a brief wave and hurried toward the tearoom.

He seems like a good egg. Eager and nervous. Probably not dissimilar to what I was like last year.

'Excuse me, Poppy?' She lifted her head to a male nurse she hadn't met yesterday. 'I'm Terry.'

'Hi Terry, what can I do for you?'

'Can you put a cannula in bed six? The night Resident didn't get to it, and we haven't been able to give his eight o'clock antibiotics.'

'No problem.' She finished what she was doing then gathered supplies from the equipment room before heading down to bed six.

'Morning, Mr Tucker. I'm Poppy. We met briefly yesterday. I'm the new Resident.'

'This food is terrible. What are you going to do about it, girlie?' Mr Tucker said gruffly, a bit of scrambled egg stuck in the corner of his mouth.

'I'm sorry, Mr Tucker. I'm not sure there's much I can do about that. But I can put in a new cannula so you can have your morning antibiotics.'

'Not much you can do?' he shouted, the scrambled egg flying from the corner of his mouth.

Worried the nurses would think she'd upset him, a blush rose up Poppy's neck and sweat prickled her armpits.

'This place is a joke. Terrible food, terrible staff. I've got private health insurance, why am I in a four-bed room with these fuckers?'

Poppy took a step back, momentarily shocked by the swearing. 'Mr Tucker, I'm sorry, you're obviously upset, and—'

'What's going on here?' Terry asked, pulling back the curtain and entering Mr Tucker's bay. Poppy's blush deepened further. 'Are you upsetting Dr Mason and causing a ruckus?'

'This place is crap, and you know it,' Mr Tucker said, jostling on the bed, his scrawny legs making his hospital gown flap.

'Now, now, Mr Tucker. If you don't calm down and let Dr Mason put in a new needle for your antibiotics, we might have to let Prof Pilson know you're abusing the staff and other patients. Then who knows what will happen.'

Mr Tucker huffed and puffed, opening and closing his mouth like a goldfish, but Poppy could see his bluster blowing off with the threat of repercussion.

'Right. I'm going to stay here and make sure you behave while Dr Mason puts your needle in.'

'Oh, alright,' Mr Tucker said resignedly, his legs finally still and his hands now loose in his lap.

Finally, Poppy was able to approach the bed. Her hands were shaking under the scrutiny of both the patient and Terry. *Please let his veins be good.* She had to get this cannula in first go. The last thing she needed was to start the day with a patient making a complaint, or everyone thinking she's useless.

Thankfully, despite his advanced age, he had one good looking vein and luck was in Poppy's favour. When she'd finished, she tidied up quickly and rushed out of the bay. Terry found her back in the equipment room. He started to say something but Poppy rushed in first, wanting to explain.

'Thank you for saving me in there. He just went off about the food as soon as I walked in. I'm so sorry.'

'No sweat. He can be a bit of a nasty old bugger at times. Really picks on the female staff. My fault. I should have warned you.'

'Thanks, Terry, I really appreciate your help.'

'No worries.'

Poppy got a good look at him as he lingered in the equipment room, gathering some supplies. He was tall and rake thin. She thought he must be a smoker as he had a lot of facial lines, particularly around his mouth. His hair was a scraggly blonde-grey and he looked late fifties, but maybe smoking and other substances were making him look older than his actual age.

Talking about then seeing Josh was a bad start to the day, but looking incompetent in front of the nurses wasn't doing anything to improve it. As Terry left the equipment room, Poppy leant on the bench and placed her head in her hands. She already wanted to hide and the day had barely started.

Chapter 4

The rest of Poppy's first week in Respiratory medicine was filled with learning the ropes, getting to know her colleagues and teaching Alex. It had given Poppy a real buzz teaching someone else and was a confidence boosting reminder of how much she had learnt in the last twelve months. But it hadn't all been smooth sailing. She'd had a rough morning preparing patients for bronchoscopy on Wednesday, culminating in a dressing-down from Olivia whom Poppy had failed to bond with so far. There was something closed-off about her. Poppy wasn't sure if it was introspection or snobbery.

By the time the weekend arrived, Poppy was exhausted and starting to feel lonely. She and Will had been talking daily but it wasn't the same as physically sharing the same space. There had been moments in their conversations where Poppy found herself holding things back or curating what they discussed. This sudden gap between them only became more obvious over the weekend when they missed each other's calls and when they finally spoke Poppy had detected irritation in Will's tone. It left Poppy wondering if the physical distance was forcing a backward step in their relationship to a time where things were more uncertain.

Monday. The morning meeting again. This time Poppy was prepared. She came to work with multiple snack packs in her bag, a 700ml water bottle, and the expectation of a long day. Team A was on-call again today, but it was Prof Benjamin rather than Prof Pilson. Dr Anderson was in charge of cake, according to the roster, and Poppy was very interested to see what she would bring after her derision last week of Prof Pilson's choice. Maybe some hideous vegan concoction?

She headed to the ward with a good attitude and quickly printed a patient list, checked with the nurses how the patients had been over the weekend, and even put in a cannula before heading to the meeting. She watched from a slight distance as Dr Anderson entered the meeting room with a cake box. It was placed on the table at the front, beside the plates, paper towels, and cake knife Poppy had brought in from the tearoom. When the lid was raised, Poppy leaned in to see a delicate looking hazelnut and meringue layer cake. It looked divine. Poppy's mouth watered in anticipation and she was very grateful when it was her turn to receive a slice.

Poppy savoured her first bite, appreciating the light hazelnut sponge, the layer of hazelnut mousse, and then the burst of chocolate meringue. *Heaven.* As she scraped the last morsel from the plate, she resisted licking her finger to rustle up the little crumbs of meringue that had escaped. She shouldn't be surprised by Dr Anderson's offering; everything that woman did was considered. Of course, her cake choice was as meticulous as her appearance.

'That was utterly divine, thank you Katrina,' Prof Pilson complimented her.

'Yes, quite delicious,' said Prof Benjamin, licking the last morsels off his fork as the others also offered their thanks to Dr Anderson, who demurely accepted.

They moved on to the meeting and Olivia presented another journal article about the novel coronavirus. This paper continued on from the one Maria had presented last week. It looked at the pattern of symptoms and duration of illness in patients in Italy. Poppy had been keeping an eye on the related news over the weekend, and Italy was now emerging as a hotspot. The case numbers had soared in the past week, particularly around Lombardy in the North.

'As you can see in this table,' Olivia referred to the table on the PowerPoint slide, 'whilst the majority of deaths reported in this cohort are in elderly patients, it is interesting to see such large numbers of patients in their forties to sixties being hospitalised. Obviously, that's quite different from other seasonal, flu-like respiratory illnesses.'

'Yes. Surprising,' Prof Pilson agreed. 'What do you think of that table with the world-wide location of reported cases?' He referred to one of the previous tables Olivia had presented.

'You mean the proximity to the animal and seafood market in China?'

'Yes, do they think this is a virus that has made the leap transmitting from animal to human?'

'I understand it is one of the purported theories, but it is not discussed in this article and I think there's still so much we don't know,' Olivia said carefully. 'It's too early to jump to any conclusions.'

'I agree,' Prof Pilson weighed in. 'Thank you, Olivia.'

This led to a general discussion about the media reports in the last week and the escalation of cases worldwide, whilst Olivia kept trying to bring the attention back to the salient points of the article. Poppy could see she was starting to get frustrated but also understood the fear building within the group. The virus had dominated the news in the previous week and Poppy had found herself constantly seeking out more information. She had felt alone in her anxiety but now she saw the situation was gradually reaching everyone around her. Sticky tentacles of fear reaching out and latching on to more and more people as the case numbers rose. Linking them all together unseen.

In the end, it was Dr Anderson who tried to restore some order to the room and suggested they wrap up and move on to the case presentations. Poppy was actually thankful. If someone had asked her only a few months ago if she could picture being appreciative of anything to do with Dr Anderson, she would have laughed in their face. Two surprises in one day.

They ran through one case from the ward fairly quickly. There'd been too much discussion about the coronavirus and it was rapidly approaching the end of the traditional lunch hour. Whilst half of her mind had been engaged in the present, the other half had been ruminating on this new virus. She wondered when the first case would be reported in Sydney.

What if it comes here? What will we do? Is there even a plan yet?

An hour or so of rounding later, Poppy stifled a yawn. She'd gone well past the sugar high from the cake and now her lids and limbs were heavy – she could picture herself curling up on one of the empty beds for a snooze.

Prof Pilson maintained his joviality with the patients and had spent time chatting with each of them and trying to engage Prof Benjamin, who Poppy could clearly see was bored and itching to move on to consults with Olivia. He kept checking his watch in a not-so-subtle way. Luckily when Prof Benjamin failed to be drawn into discussion, Prof Pilson moved on to question Olivia, leaving Poppy to type in the notes, and granting her mind the freedom to wander. Finally, they made it to the last bed.

Olivia and Prof Benjamin left to see consults and Prof Pilson bid them adieu, allowing Poppy to return to the nurses' station. Unlike last week, she was not immediately ambushed by the nurses. She decided to take the opportunity to go to the loo and grab a drink and protein bar.

Poppy spent the next couple of hours doing the chores the nurses needed sorting and ordering or chasing results from the ward round. The protein bar sustained her until she eventually had time for a proper break around three o'clock.

She took her lunch down to the Residents' Lounge, sat down and started to eat. Concentrating on her sandwich, she didn't pay attention to the news on TV until there was an emergency press conference called with the Prime Minister, Scott Morrison. Poppy paused, her Vegemite sandwich halfway to her mouth, as she watched the Prime Minister announce that all travellers from China were now banned from entry into the country.

'Holy shit,' Poppy murmured once Scott Morrison had finished speaking. They were calling it a "worldwide pandemic" and using the term COVID-19 to describe the virus. This was huge. She checked her emails to see if Melissa or Dr Anderson had emailed anything yet about the evolving crisis. Nothing. Heart racing, she group texted Will, Gemma, and Lucas.

> Did u guys see the news? PM banned international travellers from China!

She waited to see if any of them were free to respond while she finished off her sandwich, thinking to herself that the government needed to go one step further and ground all non-essential entry into the country. It would be a huge step – unprecedented and with significant economic ramifications – but with Australia being an island a long way away from the growing epicentres in the northern hemisphere, this would contain the case numbers to the local community. They could keep things manageable from a medical perspective and hopefully avoid the frightening scenes coming out of Lombardy and elsewhere.

While she was contemplating various scenarios and waiting for the others to get back to her, Olivia texted.

> Need you to meet me on the ward. Just admitted suspected COVID case.

Poppy's stomach dropped, then a wave of nausea rushed up her body. Her brain began a tug-of-war with one part wanting to freak out and sit on the floor- unable to move or manage complex thought- and the other trying to hold things together.

Come on, this is your job. You can do this.

She looked at her hand, still frozen, holding her phone.

'Come on, Poppy.' This time she said it out loud to the silent room. She forced her limbs to move, put her phone in her pocket, scrunched her rubbish and tossed it in the bin, and made her way back to the ward. She needed to pull herself together before those lift doors opened on level eleven.

Poppy met Olivia at the nurses' station with a façade of calm. Olivia was there with Susan, the Nurse Unit Manager, Terry, and Melanie, who were just coming onto the afternoon shift. There was a hush over the group, masking the underlying tension.

'So, we need to get him up to the ward quickly and get him into the negative pressure isolation room,' instructed Olivia.

'We've moved a patient out of there and cleaned it, so it's ready.' Susan had her hands clasped tightly in front of her, and Poppy wondered if it was to stop them shaking.

'And we need very clear signage and education to ensure all staff entering the room use disposable gloves, gowns, and masks, and appropriate hand hygiene.' Oliva sounded calm, but she had to be alarmed internally, surely!

'How bad are his symptoms?' Susan asked.

'Not too bad at present. Oxygen by mask only. Chest X-ray is clear. That's why he's coming here and not ICU at this stage.'

'When will we get the COVID result?' Melanie asked, her voice quiet, and almost breathless. Poppy was wondering the same thing and nodded.

'Probably tonight. And the lab has been instructed to contact the Medical Registrar on this evening. I'll handover to them to chase it up.'

'But Prof Benjamin thinks it's COVID?' Poppy finally joined in. Her body was tense and tight like a coiled spring ready to fire. She didn't want him to be right. She didn't want this to be COVID. It was too scary and her body and brain were fighting each other.

'Yes. The patient works in China and returned to see family. Timeframe, location, and symptoms fit.'

Mel and Terry recoiled like a punch had been thrown. Clearly, they were frightened of this information, too. But how was Olivia so calm, like she could have been discussing your run-of-the-mill pneumonia case?

'What about his family? Are they being tested and do we need to exclude them until then?' Poppy asked.

'Actually, we have to exclude all visitors until he returns a negative test.' This was from Susan.

It was almost too much to bear. A crack was forming in her heart. Small right now, but if too much more weight was added, it was going to fissure more deeply and Poppy didn't know if she would cope.

Before Poppy could comment, Melanie said, 'Jesus, how are we going to explain that?'

Poppy and Terry were nodding fervently and looking at Olivia.

Olivia's shoulders stiffened as her body became even more upright. Poppy noticed a slight pinkness forming around her cheeks. 'This is going to be hard for everyone, but we just need to do our best to minimise any chance of further transmission.' She pushed back her chair and stood up.

Poppy and Mel's eyes caught and Mel raised her eyebrows. The crispness of Olivia's demeanour suddenly reminded Poppy of Dr Anderson. She wondered if she was cold-hearted and lacking in empathy, or just afraid and putting on a good front?

'Let's get ready.' Susan addressed Melanie and Terry. 'Let's make sure our supplies outside the room are well stocked. I'll print up some COVID signage and instructions too. I'll also check with the Director of Nursing for a Department of Health update and guidelines. But, Terry and Melanie, we need to ensure minimum exposure to staff. So, only one nurse with one back-up on each shift to enter the room. We will need to manage tea breaks.'

Melanie nodded.

'Let's get ready and then call to get him up and ensure the porter is in gown, gloves, and mask,' Susan concluded before Melanie and Terry scarpered.

Once they left, Olivia sat down again, the colour fading from her cheeks. She explained the treatment plan to Poppy, which was essentially supportive with close monitoring for deterioration. Poppy was impressed she continued to maintain her detached, professional manner. Olivia was not a senior registrar, rather someone who was only a couple of years further along than Poppy. It was her first term in Respiratory and she was the first to admit a likely COVID case, but she appeared completely confident. Like this was just any old admission, and not a complete game-changer that had the whole world scratching their skulls and panicking. Could she really be this calm?

Once she finished, Poppy took a chance and shared her feelings. 'This is really scary.'

'No, it's just an infectious patient,' Olivia said firmly. 'We need to do our job as we would any other infectious patient.'

Poppy felt like she'd had her hand slapped and pursed her lips to stop herself saying anything more.

Maybe she's just trying to convince herself? If not, she's either extremely stoic, or crazy.

After a flurry of activity and preparation of the negative pressure room, Terry called up for the patient. Susan had secured the Department of Health guidelines and printed them out and had a quick meeting with all the evening shift nurses in the tearoom.

'These are the current hygiene requirements,' Susan informed them before reading out the information. 'I'll need the senior on the evening to go through this with the night staff at handover please.'

'What about disposal of the PPE?' one of the nurses asked.

'We've put a clinical waste bin just outside the patient's room for doffing your PPE as you leave. The donning station is in the corridor, before you head into the alcove. They are clearly signed.'

Poppy had been listening intently from the nurses' station, and whilst no one had openly expressed their fear, like she had with Olivia, she was pretty confident most were scared. You could hear it in the sudden intakes of breaths and the restless bodies shifting in their seats. The group disbanded as the patient was wheeled around from the staff lifts.

The porter, an older guy called Frank, looked a sight in a long-sleeved disposable blue gown, stretched tight over his bulging belly. Poppy could see the sweat dripping down the sides of his face under his face shield, and the visible part of skin above his mask was flushed.

'Where are we heading, folks?' Frank asked Terry, who'd come out of the tearoom to meet them.

'Follow me,' Terry said, leading them down the hall. The rest of the nursing staff were peering from the tearoom or milling in the nurses' station with Olivia and Poppy. It was like the scene of a car accident, where everyone slowed down to take a look as they passed, turning their heads like a Mexican wave.

Poppy had been distracted by Frank's appearance and only now her gaze drifted down to the patient in the bed. He was an Asian male; Poppy guessed he was in his fifties, and he was breathing faster than normal but didn't look too distressed. The oxygen being delivered by the portable oxygen tank lying beside him was obviously doing its job for now. Poppy secretly crossed her fingers behind her back and hoped things wouldn't get worse.

Poppy and Olivia followed them down the corridor. They watched from outside the room as Frank and Terry got the patient, Mr Chen, settled. Terry then did a set of obs from the portable machine, which would now remain in the room to avoid the risk of transmitting the infection to others. Poppy noticed someone, probably Susan, had hung a bright red COVID label off the obs machine. Once Terry finished, he left the room, removing his gown, gloves, and mask in the small vestibule outside, and placing them in the bin provided. Poppy and Olivia removed their stethoscopes and phones and placed them on the trolley next to the doffing station in the corridor. They gowned up, adding their masks, face shields, and gloves, before entering the room.

The smell of hospital-grade bleach was overpowering, despite the mask and shield. They must have used a whole bottle in here, getting ready.

'How are you, Mr Chen?' Olivia asked.

'Alright,' he said.

'This is my resident, Dr Mason.'

'Hi,' Poppy said as Mr Chen nodded toward her.

'I'm just going to listen to your chest again,' Olivia said as she lifted the cheap stethoscope hanging from the obs machine. It too, had a red COVID label hanging from it. Terry had informed them his temperature was mildly elevated at 37.9 degrees, and his oxygen saturation was slightly reduced at 94% on 6L of oxygen.

'His chest is still clear,' Olivia told Poppy. 'We'll leave you to rest now, Mr Chen, but staff will continue to check on you during the evening and they'll let you know when the COVID result comes back. But if you feel your breathing is becoming more difficult at any stage, please press the buzzer.'

Mr Chen nodded, still quite calm, and Olivia ushered Poppy out of the room.

They removed their PPE as Terry had, collected their belongings and headed back to the nurses' station where Poppy typed some notes into the patient's electronic medical record.

'He's still stable,' Olivia said to Terry, who had come to stand in front of them at the counter. 'I'm just going to handover to the evening Med Reg.'

'I'll call the lab and get an ETA for the result,' Poppy said.

'Good idea,' Olivia replied.

As soon as they'd finished their calls, Olivia was gone again. Just like this was any other case.

Mel stuck her head out of the equipment room, waving Poppy over then ducking back inside. Poppy joined her and Terry, who shut the door behind her.

'So, what do we think?' Mel asked them, conspiratorially.

'It's a bit scary, isn't it?' Poppy said hesitantly.

'Yes!' Terry agreed. 'But I guess it was bound to happen sooner or later.'

They nodded agreement. Poppy looked down at her hands, twisting her stethoscope into a knot.

'Olivia seemed all a bit too calm for my liking as well.' Mel voiced Poppy's concerns.

She looked up, her stethoscope forgotten. 'How can she be so blase` about this?'

'False bravado, I think,' said Terry.

'No one as junior as she is could think this was nothing to be concerned about,' Mel added.

Terry nodded, looking down at his feet, then lifted his eyes. Poppy thought she detected a hint of steel in them. 'It's the quiet ones you've got to worry about. She's probably putting on this brave front, thinking that's what's expected of her, and bottling up all her own fear and anxiety.'

Mel pulled a face. 'Which means she's gonna blow like a top.'

'Maybe. We'll need to keep an eye on her,' Terry responded, his jaw clenching.

Poppy was reluctant to say anything. She agreed, but she didn't want to back-stab Olivia when her opinion of her was still fragmented.

'Look, Poppy, if things go pear-shaped with Olivia, you come find us, okay?' Terry put a reassuring hand on Poppy's shoulder.

'Thanks, guys,' Poppy said, hoping their concerns were exaggerated. 'Well, I think I'll head off now. Good luck for tonight.'

'Thanks Poppy, we'll be fine,' said Mel, 'we're old hands.'

Terry smiled affectionately at Mel. Poppy thought he probably tolerated Mel like she was a brash younger sister. She left them to it and headed off, keen to get as far away from the ward as possible.

'Wow, first COVID case. How are you feeling?' Will asked when they were FaceTiming.

Poppy had her laptop open on her lap rather than struggling with the small screen of her phone. 'Pretty anxious. I came straight home and had a hot shower and put my clothes into the wash.'

'Good idea. The seriousness of this COVID situation hasn't even reached here yet. Neither staff, nor patients are really talking about it.'

'I guess they're far enough away from the major cities, it just hasn't penetrated yet.'

'Yeah, I think so.' Will's expression was serious. 'It'll hit eventually. Hey, I found something when I was googling today. It's called "worldometer". Just google it now.'

'Okay,' Poppy said, googling on her phone so that she didn't lose Will's face on the laptop. 'Yep, got it. Oh, I see, you get COVID cases by country.'

'Yeah, and if you click on individual countries, you get more detail.'

Poppy bit her lower lip. 'Jeez, look at Italy.' The graph showed an exponentially rising curve of new COVID cases.

'I know. Frightening.'

Poppy looked back at Will's face, her phone forgotten in her lap. 'I think that's what scares me most – the risk of the system getting overwhelmed and not being able to do anything. I really don't want us to get to that point.'

'Yeah, I hope we don't.' Concern was etched into Will's usually wrinkle-free forehead. Even though he wasn't facing COVID in Dubbo, he was worried for her.

'The government needs to close the borders,' she told him.

'I agree. Easiest way to stem the tide.' Will shrugged, like he didn't think they would go through with it.

Their conversation didn't really move from discussions of the crisis, so Poppy felt defeated by the time they hung up. She tried to improve her mood before she went to sleep by doing a guided meditation on her Calm app but still slept poorly. This horrible feeling that things were going to get a lot worse plagued her.

Chapter 5

'Mr Chen's COVID test came back positive, as expected,' Olivia said when Poppy met her on the ward in the morning. Poppy hadn't slept well and had rushed to be there on time. Her hair was already coming loose from her bun and her shirt was threatening to come untucked from her skirt.

'Okay—'

'And we had two more come in overnight,' Olivia added before Poppy could ask how Mr Chen was. 'One's an Asian female, in the second isolation room, next to Mr Chen, and the other case is an elderly Caucasian man who's returned from an overseas cruise.'

'Oh, yeah, I saw in the paper on the weekend that a number of passengers were infected.'

'Yes, but they've let them all go home, fools. So I suspect we'll see people turn up in the hospitals. He's ventilated in ICU.'

'That doesn't sound good.' Poppy frowned.

Olivia shrugged. 'We'd better get started on rounds.'

'Yes, of course.' Poppy offered a tight smile of solidarity, noting again that Olivia was crisp and well turned-out, like the biggest global medical crisis wasn't suddenly in their backyard.

Outside Mr Chen's room, Olivia updated Poppy. 'He deteriorated in the evening with decreasing oxygen saturation and was placed on humidified high-flow nasal prong therapy, HFNP, around midnight. So far his oxygen sats are holding in the low nineties.'

They donned their PPE with masks and shields and entered the room.

'Hi, Mr Chen, how are you feeling this morning?' Olivia asked.

'Oh-kay,' he said between rapid breaths.

Poppy didn't think he looked okay. His skin had a funny, greenish-grey tinge, his hair hung limply on his forehead, and there were beads of sweat at his temples. He looked wrung out.

'How're you finding the machine?' Olivia asked.

Again, he took a few quick breaths before he answered. 'Tired.'

'Alright, well, I'm going to have a listen to your chest again.'

This time he just nodded, rather than wasting the energy to talk.

Olivia placed the earpieces of the room's stethoscope in her ears. 'Can you lean forward for me? Poppy will help you.'

Poppy quickly moved to the bedside and helped him off the pillows then held him forward so Olivia could listen to the back of his chest.

'Now, try and slow your breathing if you can.'

Poppy's shield fogged up with her own breathing. Her mask must not be completely sealed, but she could not adjust it until they finished with Mr Chen, so she continued, her view clouding intermittently.

What if I breathe in the virus because my mask isn't sealed correctly? I'm so close to him right now. Jesus, what if I get COVID?

Panic rose rapidly in Poppy's chest. Already hot from all the PPE, she was now sweating heavily. She turned her head away from Mr Chen and focused on the wall, while trying to hold her breath. *Please hurry up and finish!*

'You can lean back now,' said Olivia. 'I'm just going to listen to your heart.'

Poppy eased him back on the pillows and stepped towards the door, the panic easing somewhat, her scalp itchy from sweat and heat.

Olivia clasped her gloved hands in front of her. 'Mr Chen, your lungs aren't as clear today, so I want to get a CT. I'm worried you're getting tired on the high flow oxygen. Meaning that whilst it's helping, you're still expending a lot of energy to breathe. I'm going to get Poppy to do a blood gas and we'll see how that's looking, then I'll come back and have another chat. Do you have any questions?'

Mr Chen shook his head. Poppy thought he looked too tired to care.

When Poppy had doffed her PPE and cleaned her hands with the hand sanitizer, she stepped into the corridor. Away from the vestibule outside Mr Chen's room, she allowed herself to take a deep breath in. Her nose was assaulted with the smell of bleach but she didn't care. Hopefully it would kill any viral particles that might have made their way inside her mucosa. The background hum of voices and equipment slowly returned, and with it came Olivia's voice.

'Are you coming?' Olivia was a little further along the hallway, waiting for her.

Poppy didn't need to be a genius to see her frustration.

At the nurses' station, Olivia described his examination so Poppy could type it into his electronic record.

'There weren't any coarse crackles but he's not moving much air. I'll order the CT if you do a quick blood gas. I think he's heading for a tube.'

'He looks exhausted.'

'Agreed.'

Poppy went off to the equipment room. Her anxiety levels started to escalate as she gathered the equipment needed to perform the blood gas. It was a painful procedure for the patient, and whilst she'd done several of them in the last twelve months, she still wasn't particularly confident. The added heat of PPE would just add to the sweat and stress. Poppy took a few steadying breaths and squeezed the metal bridge of her mask across her nose and cheeks to better seal it, before heading back down the corridor and donning the rest of her PPE. This time, taking extra care to ensure every step was done properly and effectively. She refused to get COVID. Will wouldn't be able to fly down to visit her this weekend if that happened.

When she entered his room, Mr Chen was sitting bolt upright, breathing rapidly and staring vacantly into space.

'Hi, Mr Chen. I've just come back to do that blood test.'

His eyes flicked toward her, but he didn't speak. Poppy pulled over the chair, its plastic legs scraping across the linoleum floor, and sat at his bedside. She felt for his radial pulse. It was strong and fast. His slim build would make it easier as there were less soft tissues to dig through to hit the radial artery. Poppy let her shoulders relax and inserted the needle and syringe perpendicularly to the skin, in the gap between her two fingers, and Mr Chen didn't even flinch. She'd hit the spot and the prepared syringe rapidly filled with arterial blood. She withdrew the needle and quickly applied firm pressure for a minute before taping some gauze over the insertion site.

There was a blood gas machine in the sleep lab at the end of the ward. Poppy took the syringe, scanned the patient's barcode from the sticky label and inserted the syringe into the machine for analysis. She tore off the printed results to take back for Olivia.

Unfortunately, it wasn't good news. Mr Chen's pH was 7.29 and his PaO2 was 58mmHg. Even with her limited respiratory physiology knowledge from medical school, Poppy knew these results were bad and indicated respiratory acidosis.

'Right. No time for CT. He needs a tube. I'll ring ICU.'

Olivia relayed the essential details to the ICU Registrar. Once she'd put down the phone, she said, 'He'll be up quickly, but I don't want to go far in case he crashes before he gets here.'

Poppy dragged a computer-on-wheels (fondly called COWs) to the area outside Mr Chen's room and together, they stood watch. They reviewed overnight notes and test results, but Poppy kept casting her eyes back into Mr Chen's room, making sure his chest kept inflating.

Please don't crash before the ICU Registrar gets here.

She didn't want to have to rush to put on PPE and then get flustered and do it wrong, further increasing her chances of getting COVID. And she wasn't even sure what to do if he crashed before the ICU Registrar got here. Could Olivia manage to intubate him?

Oh god, what if she expects me to do it?

Thankfully, the ICU Registrar was there within ten minutes and then the porters arrived within thirty, and Mr Chen was wheeled off the ward before he deteriorated any further.

As the bed rolled around the corner, out of sight, Olivia was already moving on.

'Right let's see the new one next.'

Not even a moment's reprieve before they were donning PPE again for the next patient.

Good luck, Mr Chen.

Poppy imagined crossing her fingers. Both that Mr Chen would survive, but also for this next patient. She hoped they weren't as sick as he was.

Mrs Li was in her sixties and had a positive test in the community forty-eight hours previously after returning from visiting relatives in China. Initially her symptoms had been mild, and she'd been isolating at home. But overnight she had become breathless, and her temperature had spiked to greater than 39°C. The ED admission note documented a clear chest on admission and good oxygen saturations. She'd been trialled on humidified high flow nasal prong therapy, or HFNP, in ED and had a good response. Upon stabilisation of her respiratory rate, she'd been transferred to the ward.

Poppy took and held a breath as she entered the room, expecting to see a tired, tachypnoeic patient like Mr Chen. Pleasingly, Mrs Li looked okay and her respiratory rate was only mildly above normal at twenty per minute.

'Mrs Li, my name is Olivia, and this is Poppy. We're you're doctors.'

'Hello,' she replied in heavily accented English.

'How good is your English?' Olivia asked.

'So-so.'

'How are you feeling this morning?' Olivia spoke more slowly, this time.

'So-so.'

'Not having trouble breathing?'

'Not like last night.'

'That's good. Can I listen to your chest?' Olivia held up the stethoscope and pulled the ear tubes apart before placing the earpieces in her ears.

'Okay.'

'Can you sit forward for me?'

Poppy took a step toward the bed, expecting to help Mrs Li up off the pillows, but she was not needed.

She was repeating the same words a lot, Poppy noticed. Maybe her English wasn't that good? If that's the case, she might not report a change in her symptoms, not having the language to explain things. Poppy would come back and check on her later, just in case she worsened and no-one noticed.

'Chest is clear,' Olivia said to Poppy, who acknowledged this with a nod. There was nothing else of note on the cursory examination and they soon exited Mrs Li's room.

Mr Chen might be out of her control, but Poppy breathed a little easier knowing Mrs Li was stable right now and she would check on her later to ensure she stayed that way. The coiled spring that had been loitering in Poppy's chest since she arrived at work loosened a fraction.

Next, it was down to ICU to see the other overnight admission. Poppy hadn't spent much time in ICU yet. She'd occasionally come to see a patient with her Registrar or Consultant and always found it intimidating. It was so quiet. Lacking the hustle and bustle and general noise of the wards. All the machines beeping away quietly. To Poppy, it seemed like an exclusive club where membership required some personal nomination from an existing member. The staff kept to themselves, and Poppy felt they eyed her in an assessing way. The only ICU staff member whom she'd ever found to be open and remotely welcoming was Sangeetha, the lovely Sri Lankan ICU Registrar she'd spent time with in ED last year.

Olivia seemed not to have the same anxieties about ICU that Poppy had, and strode confidently into the unit, and straight to the centre staff console.

'Hi,' she said to the first staff member she came across. 'Can you tell us which bed Mr Barnes is in?'

'Bed three,' the staff member said, without turning around to see who had spoken to her.

'Thank you,' Poppy said as Olivia strode off, not even a backward glance to ensure Poppy was following.

Outside bed three was a PPE donning/doffing station and Poppy noticed that whilst all the other glass sliding doors to the ICU beds were open, this one was closed. She also realised it was the corner room, as far away from the other rooms as possible and had an empty room on each side of it.

'Are you the Respiratory team?' A nurse in dark blue scrubs with bright red glasses asked as they started putting on their PPE.

'Yes,' said Olivia at the same time as Poppy said, 'I love those glasses.'

Olivia frowned at Poppy and asked, 'How is he?'

'I don't know if you know, but he was on that cruise ship, that has an outbreak?'

Both Olivia and Poppy nodded.

'His test on the ship was negative, but he became acutely unwell yesterday and repeat test in ED was positive. They couldn't stabilise him in ED and so he was intubated and transferred—'

'Has he had inotropes to maintain his blood pressure?' Olivia interrupted.

The nurse flinched a little, and Poppy didn't blame her, Olivia's manner was brusque. 'Yes. And this morning's bloods show his renal function is worsening. Radiology wouldn't take him for a CT chest, but his mobile X-ray looks bad. He's had dexamethasone to reduce inflammation but he's still deteriorating. The Consultant's going to liaise with colleagues in Italy to see if any other treatments have been effective in their cases. But it's not looking good.'

'Thank you,' Olivia turned her back on the nurse. 'Poppy, let's have a look at him.'

Really? What more can we do, if the ICU Consultant is phoning a friend? We're just junior doctors.

Not that she said this. Poppy simply followed Olivia into the room then watched from as close to the closed glass doors as she could get away with as Olivia listened to the front of the patient's chest. There were so many lines trailing from his body, which was splayed out like a butterfly that had been pinned to a cork board. When Olivia was finished and they'd removed their PPE, Poppy asked Olivia to wait a moment while she returned to the nurse with the red glasses. Seeing the man lying there, so vulnerable and alone, and watching Olivia examine him in this perfunctory way shifted something inside Poppy.

'Sorry,' Poppy said to the nurse. 'We just wanted to know if you had a next of kin contact, and whether anyone has spoken with them?'

'Yeah, the Reg has done that. They know things are pretty dicey.'

Poppy nodded but then thought of something else. 'Will they be able to come and say goodbye if things continue to get worse?'

'No. No visitors for COVID positive patients.' With the mask and shield on, Poppy couldn't read the nurse's expression. Did she care how traumatising this would be for his family?

'God, that must be hard.'

'Yes, I imagine it is,' the nurse mused.

Poppy found the calm acceptance difficult. Imagine being blocked from seeing and holding a parent as they lay dying. It was horrible. Thoughts of Lulu flashed into her head. That harrowing visit to her school after her suicide… How Poppy wished with her whole heart that she could have said goodbye, held her in her arms, patted her hair and breathed her in, one last time.

Olivia was looking pointedly at her watch, so Poppy joined her, head low, and together they walked out of the ICU. Whilst she could see the rationale behind the government and Health Department's closing of borders and limiting visitors to COVID patients, it was clear to Poppy that this action was also a failure of a doctor's role to provide humane care. Denying humans that close and personal contact with family during their most vulnerable moments was almost a form of torture and she had to wonder what effect cutting people off from their loved ones at such a critical time might have on their mental health and well-being.

In the lift, as they were heading back to the ward, Poppy's and Olivia's phones beeped with messages at the same time. Poppy took her phone out of her pocket and then glanced at Olivia. It was a message from the Administration unit to all medical staff that there would be an emergency meeting at lunch to discuss the COVID situation and all medical staff were encouraged to attend. Poppy was itching to discuss the message but Olivia remained impassive and unreadable.

She held her tongue but her mind was whirring to what was going to happen and how the start of COVID admissions might change the hospital, the staffing, or maybe even the hours of work. Would she need to work longer hours? Would others need to help out, as they had seen in Italy, where even Orthopaedic surgeons were suddenly assessing COVID patients. What about cancer patients – could their treatment continue if they got COVID? Her mind cascaded down multiple avenues as the possibilities increased.

'We'll need to be quick on the round if we're going to get there in an hour.'

'We can do it,' Poppy said confidently. She would hurry Olivia along or promise to come back later to follow up on jobs if she had to. There was no way she was going to miss this meeting.

Chapter 6

When the lift doors opened on level eleven, Poppy and Olivia set off at a brisk pace. Poppy grabbed a portable workstation, while Olivia continued to the bottom end of the ward, furthest from the lifts. Olivia was swift. There were no kind words, just rapid efficiency. Despite not knowing what Olivia was thinking, she obviously wanted to make the meeting too. They finished with five minutes to spare before the emergency meeting was due to start. Poppy had a list of jobs to do but there was a palpable level of anticipation about the meeting. The list could wait. Even the nurses didn't hassle her to do any cannulas or chart any medications when she wheeled the workstation back.

'Hi,' Poppy said as Alex emerged from the equipment room.

'How are you doing? I've heard about the COVID cases.'

'Yeah. Crazy. Lots to tell you. Are you going down to the meeting?'

Alex shut the equipment room door behind him. 'Let's go. By the way, I did a cannula for you.'

Poppy turned to face Alex as they walked. 'Thanks, that's amazing.'

'Susan and Terry told me all about what was happening, and I thought it was the least I could do to help out.' Alex blushed slightly as he said this. 'And anyway, you've been so great to me.'

Poppy laughed. 'I've hardly done anything.'

'Not true. Anyway, tell me about the cases,' Alex said as he pressed the call button for the elevator.

Poppy filled him in as they made their way down to the lecture theatre. They joined a growing herd of other doctors heading in the same direction.

The lecture theatre had two hundred seats, and by the time the meeting started, every one was filled. People were sitting and standing in the aisles, and it was three deep at the back of the auditorium. Poppy thought about what a fire hazard it was as she scanned the room looking for Gemma and Lucas. Her gaze settled on Joshua Hunter before quickly continuing on, her cheeks aflame as the awkward elevator ride rose in her mind. Next she met Paul Humphries' eyes and she smiled, Josh receding to the back of her mind. He'd been one of her Registrars in ED last year. He smiled back and waved. Poppy noticed he was in his usual uniform of dark dress pants, white button-down shirt, and colourful tourniquet around his neck, ready to attack someone's veins at the blink of an eye. She laughed quietly at the image. Steph was sitting next to him, and he elbowed her and pointed up to where Poppy was sitting. Poppy watched with a chuckle as Steph's facial expressions changed from initial annoyance to a big grin when she finally caught on. Poppy had missed her ED family. She hadn't seen much of them in the last six months or so. Steph made a phone gesture with her hand and Poppy nodded. She pulled out her phone with the intention of texting Steph just as Dr Anderson took the podium.

'Thank you everyone for making time to be here at short notice. We are recording this for those who can't make it.' Even in a crisis meeting, Dr Anderson managed to look chic. Today she was in a figure-hugging, navy-blue dress and matching suede heels with a flower on the strap, and her lips were painted a deep plum colour in striking contrast to her porcelain skin.

'I'm sure you're all aware now of the emerging worldwide crisis around the novel COVID-19 virus. Most of you will not yet be aware, but we now have a few COVID-positive patients in the hospital.'

A sudden rise in noise saw Dr Anderson pause. People let out small noises in shock, feet and bodies shuffling.

'The government has banned travellers from China and will likely soon impose additional measures. We have been working closely with the Department of Health and will immediately be instituting new COVID-safe policies. You will all receive an email today with links to the policy and it is mandatory that you read this today.' Her gaze swept the room to make her point. 'In addition, you must all receive education on the appropriate use and application of personal protective equipment, or PPE. You will be emailed with your session details.'

A strand of her normally immaculately groomed chestnut hair fell loose from her low chignon, and Poppy noticed there were dark smudges beneath her eyes. She looked tired.

'As this crisis unfolds there will be regular updates via email and links via Mediweb to updated policies. It is likely that there will soon be changes to staffing and wards, and you may have your rotations, shifts, or duties changed at short notice. Please understand we are all doing our best to keep you and your patients safe in this difficult, and unprecedented time.'

Did her voice just catch?

There was significantly more murmuring and Poppy heard a couple of the doctors sitting next to her say to each other, 'Change of rotations, what does that mean?'

'From tomorrow morning, all staff will need to be screened upon entry to the hospital. This will involve a temperature check and mandatory questions around symptoms of fever, cough, shortness of breath, runny nose, or exposure to a COVID-positive person. Additional hand hygiene stations will be added around the hospital. We will continue to do our best to keep you all up to date with the latest information or changes.' She paused again and Poppy noticed her shoulders rise. 'Now I will answer some questions.'

There was a clamouring of noise as multiple people tried to shout out questions at once.

'One at a time please,' Dr Anderson pleaded. 'John?'

One of the senior physicians stood up. 'Thank you, Katrina. Will we also be performing COVID testing of at-risk staff?'

'An excellent question, John. We suspect so, but the exact details haven't been finalised yet. In the meantime, if a staff member has symptoms – including fever, cough, runny nose, or shortness of breath, and they've been in contact with a known positive case – they need to present to ED.'

Another doctor stood and asked how many cases were currently in the hospital.

Dr Anderson's voice remained even this time. 'Three with one suspected in ED.'

Poppy heard someone say, 'Oh my God.' She turned to try to see where it had come from, but in the sea of people, she couldn't be sure.

'Will we make a single COVID ward or convert a section of ICU?' someone asked, half standing up.

'Yes, that is likely to happen before the end of the week.'

'What about surgery?' someone else asked.

'There's a lot of discussion in the Department of Health on this issue at present. We will update you as soon as we have more information.'

'But will elective surgery continue?' the surgeon in scrubs asked again, sounding more frustrated.

'At this stage, yes, but there may be some restrictions around the types of surgery.'

'What does that mean?' Poppy could hear the annoyance in the man's voice. He was getting louder each time he spoke.

'Well, certain surgeries or procedures that lead to increased exposure to respiratory secretions may have limitations imposed. And it's likely that trying to avoid surgery in COVID-positive patients will be encouraged.' Dr Anderson shifted her weight between her feet. Poppy had never seen her look this uncomfortable.

'So, we just pack it in?'

Poppy was staring now, along with everyone else. This guy had worked himself up. He was flushing and stroking a hand through his hair, his scrub cap scrunched in his opposite hand.

Poppy watched Dr Anderson take a breath and pause before answering. It was clear she was trying to stay calm. 'We'll likely have more information by the end of the week, and we will liaise directly with all surgical departments. Now, that's all we have time for today. Please read these and check your work email accounts daily. Thank you.'

Dr Anderson immediately stepped down from the podium and walked briskly off the stage and out the bottom exit. Several people rushed down to follow her out, clearly wanting to engage her with more questions. Knowing her as she did, Poppy suspected she would freeze them out and hole up in her office. But if she was honest with herself, Poppy was in awe of how Dr Anderson had delivered difficult information to a large and potentially hostile audience with calm efficiency. As much as she wanted this to fuel her mistrust of her, she had to accept that maybe Dr Anderson wasn't all bad (just about seventy percent).

Alex and Poppy were deep in the center of the seats so were slow to make their way out of the auditorium.

'It sounds like Maria will be admitting that new case today,' Poppy said to him.

'Yeah, it does, doesn't it? I haven't seen her for an hour or so, she's probably been in ED.'

They walked in silence for a while.

'Is it about now you wished you hadn't got Respiratory first term?' Poppy asked.

Alex choked out a laugh, 'Absolutely.'

She joined in but the levity didn't last as the impact of the meeting sunk in and they both became quiet once more.

Poppy's phone gave an email notification ping, and she opened two emails from the medical training unit. The first stating she would have to read and acknowledge the COVID-safe policy document, and the second allocating her to a PPE session that afternoon in ICU.

Poppy looked around Alex's arm as he opened his email. 'You've got this afternoon too.'

'Yeah.'

'Makes sense, I guess. Most exposed and at risk first, then filter out.'

Alex's eyes were down. 'Makes me feel a bit like cannon fodder.'

Poppy watched closely as he pushed his glasses up on his nose and then pulled at his shirt collar as if it was choking him.

Despite Alex's serious tone, Poppy couldn't help but let out a nervous laugh. Alex was right, if anyone was going to get infected, it would be them, or the nurses caring for the positive patients. The fever of anticipation was there and it sent a body-wracking shiver through Poppy. An image of rows and rows of dead bodies lined up at the hospital sprung to mind and she pushed it away. Alex looked scared and Poppy felt for him. He was just an intern and she needed to be brave for his sake.

'Hey, we're a team,' Poppy said, squeezing his arm. He smiled briefly in reply, but Poppy noticed it didn't quite reach his eyes.

That night Poppy lay awake in bed, tossing and turning, getting tangled in the sheets. It wasn't just the heat, which had increased in the late afternoon, propelled by a hot northerly wind, but also the fear of COVID. She and her flatmates had been virtually glued to the television all evening watching the news, which was becoming almost like a horror story. The reports suggested that almost ten thousand people were now infected in China and the situation in the Lombardy region in Italy was distressing. Poppy couldn't imagine having so many sick patients needing to be intubated but not enough ventilators and having to choose who would get one and who wouldn't. She really hoped it wouldn't come to that in Australia.

A kernel of fear she reserved for her own safety. She hadn't told Gemma, Lucas, or Will, but she was still anxious about this morning when her mask was not sealed properly and she was so close to Mr Chen's face, holding him up. Her PPE session that afternoon in ICU had identified a better mask for her face shape and she hoped she wouldn't be in that position again, but "what if" thoughts still pestered her. Although she'd not vocalised this to Gemma and Lucas, she had made a point of keeping more than a metre of distance from them and sitting separately to them. She'd never forgive herself if she got infected and then passed the virus on to them.

The next day, Wednesday, Poppy's team were back on-call with Prof Pilson, and there were now six COVID-positive cases in the hospital, three on the ward, and three in ICU. Poppy should have started the morning prepping the bronchoscopy list patients for Prof Pilson. But at the last minute yesterday it had been cancelled by the administration. They were anxious about any procedures that could increase staff exposure to infected respiratory secretions. So, she was on the ward when Olivia arrived.

'Hi, how are you?' Poppy asked, surprised by how fresh and wrinkle-free Olivia looked when she was feeling haggard after an anxious night of little sleep.

'Fine thanks. The ward patients have been stable overnight. Mrs Li is holding her own, but Mr Barnes died.'

'Oh, God, that's awful.' Poppy reflexively lifted a hand towards her face before remembering she was not supposed to touch them.

'He did look pretty cactus yesterday. It's not really a surprise.'

Poppy was taken aback at Olivia's insensitivity and found she didn't know how to respond.

'Anyway, I need to see some urgent admissions. You start rounding, you can catch me up after lunch.' Olivia left the nurses' station, leaving Poppy staring after her.

She wants me to start rounding on the COVID cases by myself? This isn't right. She's the Registrar, I'm just a Resident, I shouldn't be seeing the sickest patients on my own, we should be seeing them together!

Except it was too late for Poppy to confront Olivia about rounding together, she'd already left the ward.

'Morning.' Alex shuffled towards Poppy and she thought he looked as fearful as he had yesterday.

'Did you hear?' Melanie asked, approaching them from the tea room. 'First COVID death last night.'

'Yeah, Mr Barnes,' Poppy said in a defeated tone. 'It's very sad. I feel sorry for his family, not being able to see him.'

'Me too, it seems cruel.' Melanie put a gloved hand on her hip, her head tilted at an angle, her eyes distant.

Poppy noticed Alex hadn't said anything. 'Are you okay?'

He glanced up briefly, then back down into his lap. 'I'm just a bit nervous. We've got a couple of positive patients now. And... I don't know, I just feel a bit out of my depth.'

'I get it.' Poppy was itching to put a hand on his arm but waited until he met her eyes. 'We're all out of our depth. The whole world is. We just need to stick together and do what we can. Okay?'

Poppy watched him lope off with his head almost high, down toward the bottom half of the ward that was now restricted to COVID-positive patients. She hadn't been confident enough to confront Olivia and she felt ashamed of herself.

Melanie clearly hadn't seen the sudden shift in Poppy's body language. 'I'm impressed, Poppy. Confident attitude today.'

‘Fake it ‘til you make it,’ she replied, feeling even more like a fraud, and scuttled off to put her stuff away. She was the fake one. How could she be telling Alex everything was okay when she felt like the world was crumbling and her Registrar was abandoning her? Was that really going to help him? Would it help her? Maybe...

Maybe confidence, even if it is false and hollow, will keep me moving forward doing this job when the risk to me, and by extension, Gemma and Lucas, is so high. In which case, I have to be brave and keep faking it. Head up, young person, you got this.

She had a feeling it was going to be another big day.

‘Olivia left me to round on the COVID patients on my own this morning,’ Poppy complained to Will on FaceTime that evening. ‘And while I acted confident for Alex and the nurses, my legs were shaking the whole time.’

‘I’m sorry you were scared. Olivia shouldn’t be leaving you to round by yourself. Not under normal circumstances, but especially not now.’ Will’s face was creased with rising anger. It soothed Poppy, knowing that her expectations weren’t out of whack. Just knowing she could confide in someone, even if he wasn’t here and couldn’t do anything to change her situation, at least she could tell him how she really felt. Despite how close she was to Gemma and Lucas, she didn’t want to scare them with her concerns, and she didn’t want them to start fearing being around her because she had nowhere else to go. Her plan was to keep physically distancing herself and hope like hell that they didn’t get infected.

‘But it’s not all faking, Pop. You do have an inner confidence, don’t forget that. Just think about last year for a sec.’ His voice became more animated. ‘You were an intern. How many interns do you think would have had the guts to stand up and fight for what they believed in, and not rolled over when the hospital said no?’

He didn’t wait for an answer, but kept steaming ahead, ‘I can tell you... none. What you never realise about yourself is just how amazing you are. And it’s just one of the reasons why I love you so much!’ He let out a loud exhalation.

Poppy chuckled, embarrassed by the compliment. 'Oh, honey, thank you. What about Dubbo?' Are they catching up to the rest of the world yet?'

'Well yes, and no. People are talking about COVID-19 now, but more from a conspiracy theory point of view.'

'What? You must be kidding.' Poppy sat up on her bed and crossed her legs, pulling her iPad into her lap.

'I'm not. The media is very parochial, so they're just reporting heavily on the side of this being chemical warfare out of China.'

'No!' Poppy said, incredulous. 'That's crazy. People don't really believe that, do they?'

'Yes—'

'But that's ridiculous. What about all the cases and tragedy out of Italy?'

He shrugged. 'It gets a mention. But the focus is really on fear of China.'

'I don't know how I could live with that.'

'I guess it's a lesson in diplomacy.' Poppy noticed Will's surroundings for the first time. He was sitting in a chair and she could see a door behind him. She assumed he was in his room, maybe sitting at a desk and using his laptop or iPad.

'You're a better man than me, Will Charles.' Poppy relaxed back into her pillows, her irritation subsiding, a cool breeze ruffling her curtains.

Will's face came closer to the camera and his voice dropped. 'Now, let's stop talking shop. I'm missing you so bad. Today, during a hernia repair, I was thinking about your honey-coloured hair, and the way that dimple on your right cheek flickers when your smile is starting to take off... and the way your perfume smells when I kiss your neck.'

Heat bloomed in Poppy's groin. 'Tell me more.' She could only see his face, but she started picturing him with his shirt off.

'I started to think about all the things I want to do to you this weekend.'

The image of Will sharpened – he was at the beach, water was snaking its way down his chest, toward that soft hair trailing from his belly button and disappearing into his board shorts. Poppy could almost imagine tugging the tie on his shorts, him growing hard beneath her hand…

'I can't wait to see you, too.' Her voice was a little breathless.

'Not long now.'

Too long, she thought, suddenly very horny. 'What time does your flight get in on Friday?' Could she wait until Friday for sex?

'I've got Friday off so I've moved my flight to tomorrow night. I think I'll probably get to your place by about eight-thirty.'

Yay! Her clit throbbed against her underwear at the thought of the sex that would happen tomorrow night. A further flush of warmth spread through her in anticipation. 'That is the best surprise ever!'

'And there's that dimple I've missed.'

Poppy saw the familiar crinkle in the corner of his eyes and her breath caught. She put her hand to the screen, desperate to touch him. After feeling space growing between them with missed calls and miscommunication, it was really nice to feel that tug of desire again.

When the call ended, Poppy touched herself, recalling the image of Will at the beach. Her fingertips found her clitoris and she stroked gently at first, her body sinking deeper into the cushions, her iPad forgotten on the covers beside her. She pushed off her pyjama shorts and undies, licked the tip of her finger and returned to making tiny circles on her clit, feeling it pulse against her fingertip. Imagining the firm length of Will's dick as she released it from his boardies, she eased a finger inside herself, spreading and raising her legs for better access. A soft moan escaped her wet lips and she bit herself when she added a second finger. Thrusting harder and more deeply now as she pictured Will entering her from behind, the full length of him up against her cervix and rubbing her G-spot over and over again. Poppy moaned as she came hard and fast, her body jerking, her fingers slowing, enjoying her orgasm until the jerking stopped.

She lay on the bed, her pants still off, thinking about the last two weeks. So much had happened that it felt like longer. Even after her release, she was still desperate to kiss Will's lips and feel his reassuring arms around her. She missed the way her head fit neatly under his chin when she hugged him or leaned on his chest, and that citrus yet salty taste to his skin, particularly after a surf. And even though she had just satisfied herself, she was desperately looking forward to real-life sex tomorrow night.

Chapter 7

Each step toward the hospital the next morning was a countdown to seeing Will that evening. Poppy's ponytail bounced and she hummed *High Hopes*, by Panic at the Disco as she walked. A sense of lightness prevailed, her thoughts only on her reunion with Will.

The hospital was transformed overnight. Access was restricted to two entrances and Poppy dutifully queued for the mandatory COVID screening. Her temperature was checked via infrared camera, and she had to sign in to the hospital via a QR code and answer questions around potential COVID symptoms or exposure. Masks were being provided at the screening station as the Department of Health had instituted mandatory use of masks by all staff and visitors as of that morning (not just for COVID patients). Hand hygiene stations had been disseminated en masse. There were freestanding hands-free units in thoroughfares and hundreds of them nailed to the walls. You couldn't walk more than ten metres without encountering at least two of them. Not that Poppy saw anyone using them on her way to the lifts. However, Poppy used one after touching the lift call button, thinking back on her hand hygiene session from yesterday.

Doctors normally wash and clean their hands a lot, but now they would need to do it after every single touch with any surface. Poppy had already noticed her hands being drier the last couple of days. Things were going to get worse. She made a mental note to buy some hand cream on the way home.

The other email Poppy had read that morning at breakfast was from Victoria Hennessy, cancelling their PACMEN (Pastoral care and mentorship committee) meeting for tomorrow. The hospital had mandated no face-to-face meetings for the time being due to the evolving situation. Victoria had postponed the meeting until next Friday in order for an IT platform, Zoom, to be set-up that would enable a virtual meeting. Poppy worried the delay was a sign that all their progress was now going to be sidelined and brushed aside by the COVID drama. She obviously didn't want to downplay COVID in any way, but she also didn't want to give the hospital administrators an excuse to slip back into their old ways. Dr Anderson might conveniently forget everything that happened last year. Poppy's brows knitted together. PACMEN, the mentoring and pastoral care initiative, had been the one real achievement she, Will, and Tarryn had made from petitioning the hospital for better conditions and more support of the junior doctors after Surgical Registrar, Tim Pan, had committed suicide.

She was pondering this when Alex came beside her. 'Hey, Poppy, did you see the press conference this morning?'

'No, what press conference?' Poppy wondered what the latest COVID update was as she typed her password into the computer she was sitting at.

Alex's covered face leant in closer to better get Poppy's attention. 'ScoMo. They've closed the borders—'

Still focusing on the computer in front of her, Poppy cut in. 'Well, that's good.' Hopefully that would make a difference.

'There's more. No travel in or out of Australia. Gladys followed up with no non-essential travel within NSW.' He was still leaning as close as possible to Poppy without touching her, desperate for her attention.

'Wait, what?' Poppy finally turned toward him as her pulse quickened and her feet felt nailed in place. 'What does that mean?'

Please don't tell me that Will won't be able to come visit. Please, not that.

Poppy could hear the overhead fluorescent lights buzzing, or was that the ringing in her ears? Her scalp was hot, her head pounding and the harsh light felt like a spotlight.

Alex eased back in his chair. 'Essentially, we're all supposed to limit our movements. They don't want it spreading out of the city.'

The noise, the light, everything was crowding around Poppy, pinning her in place and pegging her in. Her heart was beating so fast now that her head was spinning. It was like being on the carousel – turning, always turning.

'Are you alright?' Alex's voice rose an octave, but Poppy barely heard him.

She dropped her head between her knees, worried she was going to faint.

Alex stood up so suddenly, his chair rolled back and smacked into the filing cabinet behind them. He hovered close but had taken a step back from her. Poppy could feel the anxiety radiating from him. 'Can I get you something? A glass of water? Should I call for help? Do you feel ill?'

Poppy didn't respond. She was taking deep breaths, trying to slow her heart rate and calm her thoughts. A paper cup of water appeared near her legs and she reached out, lifted her head slowly so it didn't spin again, lowered her mask fractionally, and gratefully took a sip. The coldness helped slow her heart rate and dampen her emotions.

'It's okay, I'm not sick,' Poppy said when she finally sat upright and saw the fear in Alex's eyes. 'Will was supposed to be coming for the weekend. I guess this means he won't be.'

'Oh… I'm sorry, Poppy.' Alex pulled the chair back over and sat down once more.

'Thanks. I might just see if I can call him.' Poppy hauled herself up and walked back down to the elevator bank.

The call went straight through to message-bank. She rested a hand on the glass window while she waited for Will's greeting to finish. 'You've reached Will Charles, I'm not available to take your call right now, please leave me a message after the tone.'

Her head rested on her arm, her voice low, struggling to hold back tears. 'Hi hon, it's me. I've just heard they've closed the borders and are only allowing essential travel within NSW. Better check to see if your flight's been cancelled. And call me back, okay?'

Poppy then looked up the Rex airline flight information.

'Damn it!' Will's flight was cancelled. She couldn't believe this. How fast everything had come undone. Her heart was no longer pounding but an ache had formed in her chest and the threat of tears continued. She raised her head to look out the large floor-to-ceiling windows to the view across the helipad and out over the city. The beautiful, clear skies would normally make her feel happy, but not today. The lightness and buoyancy she felt this morning had evaporated. She stared at the gorgeous day and felt trapped behind the glass, no way for the beauty to penetrate and cheer her up.

'Poppy... Poppy...'

Her name finally penetrated her synapses and Poppy turned from the frozen beauty to see Olivia bearing down on her, looking cranky, a deep scowl line between her eyebrows.

'Sorry,' Poppy said morosely.

'Come on. We've got lots of patients to see.' She turned on her heels, clicking her fingers in Poppy's direction, and headed back to the ward. Poppy bowed her head like an admonished dog and slowly followed in her master's wake.

Poppy's day was long, busy, and the cloud that hung around her head after speaking with Alex in the morning, never shifted. She reviewed patients, put in cannulas, and followed Olivia around taking notes. But it was a struggle to look interested, and she did not engage in the usual group chats at the nurses' station. She kept her head down and counted the hours until home time.

Finally, about six o'clock, as Poppy was listlessly lying on her bed, Will called.

'Oh, crap,' Will said by way of greeting when she answered. 'I've just heard your message. And there's texts from the airline. My flight's definitely cancelled. I'm not coming…'

Poppy put the phone down to wipe away the tears that had sprung and were threatening to engulf her. It was hard to believe she had been so happy last night and this morning.

'Poppy did you hear me? I'm not coming. Poppy are you there?' Will's voice sounded more agitated.

She picked the phone up again and gulped out, 'I know.' Her tears were rapidly turning to sobs, snot threatening to drip from her nose in a most indelicate way. She put her phone in her lap to blow her nose again with a trumpet-like noise.

Will's tone softened. 'Hey, hon. It's okay. It's not forever. I'm sure this is just going to be for a couple of weeks, just to avoid it spreading.'

He was being reassuring, but Poppy still felt dejected. 'I hope so.' She sniffed loudly and tried to slow her tears.

'I love you, Poppy. I wish I was on my way to you now, but it'll be okay. We'll see each other as soon as we can.'

'I know. I just miss you so much.'

'I miss you too. We're going to be okay,' he reassured again.

They talked for a bit longer, but there wasn't a lot to say. The situation sucked, and nothing they could say would make it better. After shedding some more tears on the bed, she joined Gemma and Lucas in the lounge room. Her brain continued to process Will's words. He was right, this was just a small blip on their journey. A week or two extra of being apart. In the grand scheme of things, it was minor and they'd survived worse last year.

She woke the following morning with a headache and a general dullness and took her time getting out of bed. For the first time since she started as an intern, she really didn't want to go to work. Last night she'd come to the conclusion that Olivia wasn't the nicest person to work with and the lingering anxiety around catching COVID meant Poppy wasn't even excited to learn new things. All learning was really on hold at the moment, anyway. They were all just in survival mode. It dawned on her that there was nothing to look forward to. No set event in the near future to keep her going.

'Hey, at least it's Friday,' Gemma offered over breakfast.

'I guess.' She dropped her spoon and it bounced off the edge of the bowl, flipping onto the table, splattering milk and a few rice bubbles in its wake.

Gemma reached out a hand to touch Poppy's. 'I know I'm no substitute for Will, but as Luc is working tonight, why don't we go out together? I'm up for anything!' It was uncharacteristically positive for Gemma.

Poppy looked at her friend's happy face and swallowed her negativity. 'Okay, let's do something. But what?' She discreetly moved her hand back from under Gemma's, remembering her desire to avoid contact, just in case.

'Well, they haven't shut restaurants yet, there's just mandatory QR code check-ins, so why don't we go somewhere nice for dinner?'

If she couldn't be with Will, that did sound like a good option. And with the way things were changing at the moment, they might close restaurants altogether soon.

'Sure,' Poppy agreed. She did appreciate Gemma's care.

'Great.'

Once she'd left the room, Poppy's face fell again. Before dinner, she would have to get through work, and that was the last place she wanted to go.

Poppy was putting the final touches on her makeup when her phone started ringing. It was Will on FaceTime. His face swam into view and Poppy felt her pulse quicken.

'Good morning, beautiful,' he said. 'I just wanted to check in with you before you went to work.'

'Thanks, hon. I've been feeling so miserable overnight but seeing you does make me feel a bit better.'

'I love you, babe, and like I said last night, this isn't forever... it's one weekend.'

'Yeah, I know. I just didn't realise being apart would be so hard, you know?' She pushed her lips into a smile, stepping away from the mirror, knowing she needed to reassure him.

'But it's only hard because we love each other, so that's a good thing, right?'

Poppy nodded. 'I guess that's a glass half-full way of looking at it.' And a tiny laugh escaped, her mood lifting slightly.

'Well, you've never been a glass half-empty kind of gal.'

'Except when Lulu died.' She regretted it as soon as it was out of her mouth. If he'd been sitting next to her, she would have reached out to touch him, to reassure him that it was a mistake.

'Whoa... This is nothing like when Lulu died.' Will was visibly shocked, his body recoiling backward on the screen. His reaction was the impetus Poppy needed to snap out of this funk.

'You're right, of course,' she replied hurriedly, not wanting to scare him.

'Seriously, Poppy. Now you've got me worried.'

'No, no... I'm just being silly.' She was trying to back pedal. *Why did you say that?*

'Okay.' Will's expression was still concerned. There was a scowl line between his eyes and his jaw was clenched. She knew he'd be balling at least one of his hands into a fist, even though she couldn't see it on the screen.

'Look, Gemma offered to do something with me tonight, so I'm sure I'll feel better after that.' Poppy inserted as much enthusiasm into her voice as she could muster.

'I'm sure you will.' But the tension in his face was still there. She felt bad for worrying him, especially when he was so far away and there was nothing he could do for her.

'Well, I'd better go,' Poppy said. 'But, I'll be fine. I promise.' Poppy made a kiss face at the camera then ended the call.

Will was right, she was being silly and morose. It was almost infantile. Come on, she chided herself, you're an adult. *Get a grip.*

'Morning,' Poppy greeted the nurses and Alex on the Respiratory ward.

'You're looking cheerier today,' Mel said.

Poppy instantly felt the familiar heat begin to rush up her neck, knowing she hadn't hidden her mood yesterday. 'Sorry I was a bit down yesterday,' she said awkwardly.

'That's okay, chook. I know you were looking forward to your weekend with Will.' Mel squeezed her shoulder reassuringly.

'Yeah,' Poppy sighed. 'But what can you do, right? Anyway, any dramas overnight?'

'No, everyone is pretty stable.'

'Any new COVID's?'

'Two. One here, one in ICU.'

'Cheers.' Poppy put her stuff away and then started looking up the new patient files.

Olivia sauntered in over fifteen minutes later. 'It's just us this morning, Poppy,' she said by way of greeting.

'Is Prof Pilson coming later to round?' She thought it was unusual that he wouldn't do the round first thing in the morning, but maybe he had a busy private clinic.

'No.' Olivia's reply was short.

Poppy wasn't sure how to interpret that, not knowing whether Olivia was angry at her, Prof, or something else entirely.

'So, two new overnight,' Olivia continued, and she gave Poppy the history, which was starting to feel all too familiar. In some ways that was good – the initial fear had eased, but the oppression of wearing full PPE for long periods of the day was also becoming something Poppy had begun to dread. She'd already noticed a couple of zits on her chin from the humidity of the mask, and she was just starting to develop a crack in the corner of her lips.

Great. Not only do I feel shit, but I look shit, too.

They rounded for a few hours and then Olivia called Prof Pilson to update him. Poppy surreptitiously listened to Olivia's side of the conversation while tapping away on her keyboard.

'Will do. Thanks, Prof,' Olivia said. 'I'll let you know if anything changes.'

Poppy couldn't help staring at her as she ended the call.

'What?' Olivia asked in a snarky tone.

'Sorry, I was just wondering why Prof wasn't, at least, coming to see the new patients?'

'I'm not sure that's really your business, Poppy. Why don't you just concentrate on putting those blood requests in. And Prof wants a sputum culture on bed twelve.' With that, Olivia stood up and left the ward.

Poppy was left with her mouth agape at Olivia's bitchiness. Whilst Poppy hadn't felt a real camaraderie with her Reg, there'd been no animosity either. This was new.

Terry had been nearby and sat in the seat Olivia vacated. 'What was that about?'

'I don't know. I just asked why Prof Pilson wasn't coming to do a round.'

'She was a bit harsh, I thought.'

'It was weird, wasn't it?' Poppy was hoping for reassurance.

'Definitely.' Terry leaned back in the chair and brought the pencil toward his mouth, then put it down when it hit his mask. He'd clearly forgotten it was on.

'I don't get it. It feels like I'm missing something.'

'Maybe. Hard to tell what's going on in Olivia's mind.' In lieu of chewing his pencil, he jogged his leg up and down. 'Anyway, try to put it behind you.' He gave Poppy's shoulder a pat as he stood up.

Poppy didn't see Olivia again for the rest of the day. She was left to do the work alone, as was becoming the norm, without even a phone call to check in. By four o'clock, she was starting to flag and figured she'd better fill Olivia in on the patients before the end of the day. She called, but Olivia didn't answer, so she sent a text.

Hi Olivia. I just wanted to update you on the ward. Thx, P

Maria and Alex were at the nurses' station chatting and finishing their work. While Poppy waited for a response from Olivia, she moved over to join them.

'What do you think, Poppy?' Maria asked.

Poppy hadn't been paying attention to what they were saying. 'About…?

'How it's going with the COVID cases.'

Poppy was flattered that Maria was interested in her opinion. It wasn't common that Registrars asked their juniors what they thought about anything. Generally it was a one-way direction of imparting knowledge. 'With the increasing numbers, I'm not sure that they should be on the same ward as non-COVID patients.'

'I agree. We've already had one non-COVID patient catch the virus on the ward. I've been discussing it with Dr Anderson, and I think that by next week we'll have a dedicated COVID ward.'

'What about the ICU?' Alex asked.

'Yes, that will have to separate as well. There'll have to be further changes in ED too, and maybe even a ward for suspected cases whilst they're waiting for confirmation.'

‘Makes sense,’ Poppy said, resting her tired arms on the counter in front of where Alex and Maria were sitting at a computer terminal.

There was a pause before Maria asked, ‘How are you going with Olivia?’

Poppy faltered. Maria remained focused on typing notes and her body language was non-threatening, but Poppy didn’t know her well enough to be sure she could be one hundred percent honest.

‘It’s been a steep learning curve. I mean, COVID, right?’ She inclined her head on an angle then paused. ‘It’s still all so new. But Olivia is very confident. She seems to be taking it all in her stride.’ Poppy hoped that was diplomatic enough.

‘That’s good. Well, let me know if you need help, okay?’ At this point, Maria looked up and locked eyes with her. Poppy felt a silent communication pass between them. Maybe the nurses had informed her that Olivia was basically abandoning her every day. She felt instantly reassured that Maria would be there for her if needed.

‘Thanks, Maria.’ Poppy nodded her head slightly, acknowledging that she’d taken this on board.

‘You’re very welcome. In fact, we’re really lucky to have you and Alex this term. You’re both fantastic.’ With that, Maria lightened the mood again. If only she was Poppy’s Reg.

A ping from her phone told her Olivia had texted back.

> What’s the update?

Poppy inhaled and reminded herself that you couldn’t tell tone from a text, and the beauty of texting was the brevity. She sent a text back with the salient test results and clinical status of the patients and got the kind of reply she should have expected…

> Tx

Poppy said goodbye to everyone for the weekend, grabbed her bag from the lockers and headed out. Despite Olivia and her moods, she was feeling better than she had in the morning.

Chapter 8

Gemma had chosen a bistro everyone had been raving about in Rozelle. It wasn't too far away and, in addition to the scrumptious food, it had an equally mouth-watering cocktail menu which Poppy was keen to try. At home, Poppy headed straight for a hot shower after putting her clothes on a quick hot cycle in the washing machine. This was her new routine after arriving home from the hospital.

They zhuzhed themselves up with strappy heels and skimpy dresses – Gemma towering over Poppy – slipped on sparkly earrings, and sprayed themselves with their respective favourite scents.

Taking in her friend's outfit, Poppy said, 'You look amaze-balls. Way too good for Luc!'

Gemma laughed and wrapped her arm around Poppy. 'You're crazy.'

Poppy knew Gemma felt she was out of her league with Lucas, which was probably why she was so anxious about his new Registrar, Miriam. Gemma may not be movie-screen beautiful, but she was striking – tall, great cheek bones, and piercing eyes. Her smiles were rare but intoxicating, the way her whole face transformed and softened.

'We better motor, the Uber's out front.' Gemma dragged Poppy by the hand before she could say more and offered her a mask.

The driver wound them through the back streets of Annandale and Lilyfield before making it to the Bistro in Rozelle. Poppy enjoyed looking at all the workers' cottages tight up against each other and the narrow streets bustling with cars and people. They'd been living in the inner west for over a year now since moving down from Newcastle at the end of medical school, and Poppy really loved it. It was such a vibrant place to live. Maybe a bit far from the beaches for Will, but there was always so much happening. Poppy preferred it to the sedate suburban North Shore (or "north snore" depending on your point of view) where she'd boarded for high school.

The bistro was nestled next to one of the familiar Rozelle gastropubs and was the "up and coming" French pick. Gemma and Poppy shuffled in under the navy and white striped awning and were quickly and efficiently ushered to their table.

'There's not many tables,' Poppy pointed out, as she removed her mask.

'I think it's the new COVID regulations. Something about number of occupants per square metre.'

'Oh.'

Poppy was keen to put the past forty-eight hours behind her and after perusing the drinks menu, ordered a French martini.

'Ooh, that sounds good,' Gemma said as the waitress took Poppy's order. 'I'll get one too.'

'So, this place is nice.' Poppy settled back into her comfortable chair as the waitress left and picked up her menu again.

With so few customers it didn't take long for the waitress to return with their drinks and once they'd taken large sips of their deliciously pink and frothy martinis, Poppy let out an audible sigh of contentment. 'So, what's happening with Luc and Miriam?'

Gemma frowned. 'Honestly, he can't stop gushing about her. Every day he gets home from work and it's, "Miriam this, and Miriam that." It's starting to piss me off.' She'd been subconsciously twisting her cloth napkin on the edge of the table and when she finished talking, she stopped and looked at Poppy, her eyes large and imploring.

'Hmm,' Poppy said noncommittally, taking another sip of her drink. She had a feeling Gemma was itching to say more.

'Deep down, I know he's not in love with her,' Gemma went on quickly. 'But he's obviously enamoured, and that combined with my family's ongoing pressure on the marriage front, I'm about to tear my hair out.'

'So, nothing new there, hey?'

'No. We haven't even had a recent discussion about marriage. I'm worried maybe it's off the table.'

'No, surely not.' Poppy leaned forward, shocked.

'Well, it could be. I don't even feel I can bring it up anymore. The last time I did, we barely spoke to each other for two days.' Gemma returned to twisting the napkin. 'It's a complete stall.'

'Oh, Gem. I'm sorry, hon.' Poppy reached across the table and squeezed Gemma's hand, forcing her to stop twisting the napkin. She hated seeing her friend so upset.

'Thanks, Pop.' She gave Poppy a weak smile.

I wish Lucas would pull his finger out and get his act together. They are clearly in love and Lucas needs to talk this through with Gemma – either he wants to get married but not yet, or he never wants to get married. Either way, he should tell her how he feels! He can be so stubborn, and all this digging his heels in is just hurting Gemma. It's not fair.

Before Poppy could try to reassure or distract Gemma, the waitress returned to take their orders. After the interruption, Poppy decided distraction was the better option. 'So, what's happening in the world of Surgical Oncology?'

Gemma brightened and relaxed back into her seat for the first time since they'd arrived. 'It's been pretty good, actually. I've been in theatre a lot and getting to do the closures on my own. My Registrar, Dave, has been teaching me different suturing techniques, so that's awesome.'

'And what about that boss you don't like?'

'Prof Patchett? Yeah, he's a pig. Such a misogynist. You know he keeps calling me "sweetie." And if I'm with them on a list, he's like, "oh, sweetie, can you run along and get us coffees?" Or, "oh, sweetie, can you please pick up lunch." Honestly, I want to knee him in the balls most of the time.'

Poppy cackled. She could picture Gemma doing just that. He should watch out.

'Anyway, it's mainly good, and I like the other bosses, so I just have to bite my tongue and put up with it. But I tell you, if he pats me on the head or the bum, that's it, all bets are off.'

'Stop!' Poppy said cackling again, and a little snort escaping. 'You're going to make me pee my pants.'

That made Gemma chortle too, but they had to quickly reign in their levity as their meals arrived.

'Ooh, that looks gorgeous,' Poppy said as Gemma took a pic of her plate to show Lucas later.

'Yeah, almost too pretty to eat.'

'Nah,' Poppy said, tucking in. The martinis were giving Poppy a warm glow and she felt unencumbered by anxiety. The food was delicious, she loved her friend, and life – despite COVID and Will being away – was good.

When they got home, a little worse for wear, Poppy pulled out her phone and saw she'd missed multiple texts from Will. Poppy read them slowly, the words swimming in and out of focus. It was hard for her to absorb them, so she decided she'd look at them in more depth in the morning. She texted back.

Home. Gd nte. Had fn. (heart emoji)

Then she poured a tall glass of water and lumbered to her room, spilling her drink as she went.

The weekend stretched out before Poppy as she rolled over in bed and felt the empty space where Will should have been. The immediacy of jackhammers thundering in her head and a wave of nausea kept further thoughts of Will at bay. She shut her eyes, breathed deeply, and counted slowly to twenty, trying to avoid vomiting.

After slow progress to the bathroom, plenty of water and Panadol, she took up residency on the couch and tried to call Will.

'Hi, you've reached Will Charles. I'm not available to take your call right now. Please leave a message after the tone.'

'Hi, it's just me, checking in. Call me when you're free. Love you.'

Poppy turned on the TV, looking for something suitable to pass some time until she regained some fortitude. She settled on an old *Friday Night Lights* episode and lay down, cradling her water glass. She had a thing for Taylor Kitsch and could quite happily watch him with his shirt off all day.

Eventually Gemma emerged from her room.

'Morning,' Poppy called from the couch, raising an arm in a sort of wave.

'Blergh,' Gemma replied, poking out her tongue.

'Luc still asleep?'

'Nope. I think maybe he went to the gym.'

'You up for a greasy brekkie?'

'Just give me a few minutes,' Gemma said, making herself comfortable on the second couch.

By the end of the *Friday Night Lights* episode, Poppy's hangover was begging for sustenance. She looked to Gemma who groaned. 'You want me to move, don't you?'

Poppy grinned. 'Yep. Let's get dressed and head up the street.'

By the time they had caffeinated, fed their bellies, and taken a slow lap around the park, Lucas was home and playing a video game.

'You two look like death warmed up.' He looked up briefly from his game.

'Hey!' Poppy said as Gemma said, 'Harsh.'

'I assure you, we look far superior to our appearances from a couple of hours ago,' Poppy added, using her "posh" voice.

'Well, that's not comforting,' Lucas chuckled as Poppy threw a cushion at him.

'Argh. You made me die.' He turned off his game and looked at both of them. 'What are we going to do today?'

'I vote for very little,' Poppy said, raising her hand.

'I second that vote,' Gemma added, raising hers.

'What about the beach?' Lucas suggested.

'Too much effort,' said Gemma.

'Too much sun,' said Poppy.

'You two are no fun.' Lucas stood up, tucking the game controller away under the TV.

'I vote for *Friday Night Lights* marathon,' suggested Poppy, clapping her hands.

'Yes!' agreed Gemma enthusiastically.

'Nup, can't do it. Fine, I guess I'll have to make my own fun.' Lucas walked over and kissed Gemma's cheek, briefly resting a hand on her hip, then turned to go into their room.

Before Poppy queued up the next episode, she checked her phone again. There was still no message from Will.

What was he doing? He couldn't still be asleep, it was almost midday. Maybe he went out with friends and his phone was in his pocket? Sometimes he did that and when it's on silent he doesn't feel it vibrate.

Yeah, that's probably it. I'm sure he'll call later. And it's not like I'm doing anything exciting.

Poppy pressed play on the remote while Gemma fossicked in the pantry for snacks. 'Hmm. We've only got nuts.' She banged the pantry door shut.

Upon seeing Lucas removing the juice from the fridge, she purred. 'Hey baby, do you think you could get us some snacks while you're out?'

'I'm going to the beach with mates. We'll probably go to the pub afterwards. I'm not going to be back for hours.'

Gemma pouted, her eyes downcast. Really trying it on.

Lucas laughed and kissed her head. 'How about I quickly duck out and get you ladies some provisions. But after that you're on your own.'

'Thanks, baby.' Gemma kissed his lips and hugged him tightly.

'Thanks, Luc. That's awesome,' added Poppy, leaning over the back of the couch.

He returned shortly with a bag full of chips, lolly snakes, M & Ms, and ingredients for nachos.

'You really are a prince among men,' said Poppy, already opening the lolly snakes.

'I thought you'd be hungry later, and hopefully capable of cooking without setting fire to the apartment.'

'No guarantees.' Poppy laughed.

They nursed their hangovers with junk food and TV throughout the day. Finally in the afternoon, Will texted.

> Sorry, was at the Zoo with some of the others. Only just saw your text.

The three dots appeared immediately, suggesting he would text more, so Poppy waited. Sure enough, another text appeared shortly afterward.

> Still out. I'll call you when I'm in later tonight. (heart emoji)

Poppy turned the phone over and focused on the TV again but found she could no longer follow the storyline.

'Everything okay?' Gemma asked, a purple lolly snake dangling from the corner of her mouth.

Poppy sighed loudly and sat up. 'It's hard being apart. We barely get time to talk to each other during the week, and now we're out at different times. We keep missing each other. And after looking forward to him coming down and then not seeing each other, it's disappointing not to even talk properly, you know?'

'I'm sure it is.'

They sat in silence for a while, Gemma focusing back on the TV and Poppy staring blankly, lost in thought. She'd been so miserable when she first found out that Will wouldn't be able to visit, but then the evening out with Gemma had cheered her up. Now she felt down again. Part of her wondered if Will was having more fun being away from her. Was she the only one upset they were separated?

By the time Will called late in the evening, Poppy had showered and even tidied her room. She'd just been debating whether to call him when the FaceTime jingle started. *Finally.*

Will's face swam into view and the first words out of Poppy's mouth were, 'Oh, baby, I miss you so much.' A tear escaped her eye and she quickly swiped it away, sure it was the overly sentimental consequence of a hangover and poor sleep.

'Me too.' He lifted a hand to touch the screen and Poppy breathed easier seeing that he missed her too. 'Tell me about your big night with Gemma? You were obviously out late.'

Maybe he has some FOMO, too.

Poppy proceeded to recount last night's events. 'And today, Gemma and I just chilled on the couch. What about you? What did you get up to last night? And how was the zoo?'

Will talked about people Poppy did not know, and she found herself getting lost in his face, her hangover concentration poor. As he was coming to the end of his retelling, she tried to focus but kept imagining peeling off his T-shirt and running her fingertips over his smooth chest, breathing in his citrus and salt scent.

'Hey,' she interrupted him. 'I'm feeling a bit horny. How do you feel about taking things to a new level?' Poppy arched an eyebrow, conscious of the heat pulsing in her pants. She bit her lip nervously.

'Oh, okay.' Will's eyes shone with excitement, and he sat up straighter. 'What did you have in mind?'

'I really want to touch myself. Where would you like me to put my hands?'

'Jesus, Poppy, I'm already getting hard... How about you take off your top?'

Poppy put the phone down and tried to rest it on the pillow so he could see her as she slowly removed her clothes.

'I can't see, I think the phone has fallen down.'

Poppy looked back at the pillow as she was lifting her pyjama top over her head and saw the phone had, indeed, tipped over. She tried to secure it better with a tube of pawpaw ointment to stop it sliding down. 'How's that?'

'Ah, that's good. I so want to kiss those tits.'

Poppy massaged them and tweaked her nipples, jutting her hips forward. 'What's next?'

'Pants off, and touch your clit,' he commanded.

Ooh, I like it when he takes control.

'I thought you'd never ask.' She hurriedly stripped off her trackies and undies and knelt on the bed close to the phone so Will could see as she touched her clit. 'How's this?'

Poppy's excitement was building and she watched Will's face while she touched herself.

His breath was shallow as he said, 'Put a finger in.'

'In here?' she asked playfully, picking up the phone and showing Will her vagina.

'Yes,' he said with a groan of desire.

She couldn't see what he was doing, only his face was visible, but she was enjoying showing him parts of herself.

'If you insist.' She kneeled above the phone as she inserted first one, then two fingers. She was so wet, they were sliding easily in and out, and her breaths were getting shallower. 'Oh, that's nice, oh... oh...'

Just as Poppy was reaching climax, she heard Will call out. 'What?... Wait...'

Suddenly the line went dead. Any desire Poppy felt disappeared and was replaced by crushing embarrassment.

Did someone walk in at Will's end?

Omigod, what if they saw my vagina.

Fuck!

Poppy rapidly threw her clothes back on. Will had still not rung back so she texted.

What happened? What's going on?

The three dots appeared and Poppy sat, glued to her phone, waiting for Will's response. But the dots disappeared again. Poppy kept waiting, her anxiety levels rising. She began pacing the floor. What was going on? Why was he not calling back?

She hit the call button again. The phone rang out.

'This is ridiculous,' she shouted.

Gemma knocked on the door. 'Everything alright?'

Poppy stormed to the door and flung it open, her hair flying out from her face with the created breeze. She explained to Gemma what had happened but when she came to the end of the story, Gemma suddenly burst into laughter, her eyes watering as she slapped her thigh.

'Omigod, that's … that's hilarious.'

Poppy stared at her, aghast. 'Gemma!'

But as she watched her friend laughing her arse off, now doubled over in glee, she suddenly saw the hilarity of the situation. The corners of her mouth twitched, the knot in her stomach loosened, and then her own laughter escaped. They laughed until they cried, slapping each other's arms, and eventually ended up on the floor, breathless.

When they'd finally calmed down, Poppy looked at Gemma, who still had a tear sliding down her cheek. 'What do you think happened?'

'I guess someone probably walked in.'

'Yeah, but why hasn't he texted or called?'

'It won't have anything to do with you. He's probably just pissed off at his flatmate and having a go at him.'

Just as Gemma finished saying this, Poppy's phone rang. She raced over to the bed and accepted the FaceTime, vaguely aware that Gemma had quietly left and shut the door.

Will's face came into view, his expression sour and his jaw clenched.

'Fuck,' he said.

'What happened?' Poppy asked.

'Fucking Brendan... he walked in... didn't even knock. I'm so pissed off! I can't believe it.' He was practically shouting by the time he finished.

Poppy didn't think she'd ever seen Will so angry. Immediately her own anger and embarrassment dissolved as she realised she needed to calm him down.

'Hey, look, it's okay,' she said in a soothing tone.

'No, Poppy, it's not okay. He saw you.'

'Yeah, well, there's nothing we can do about that now, and honestly how much can he actually have seen, it must have been only seconds.'

'He saw enough... Of both of us.'

'Look, I know it's embarrassing – for all of us – but you know, it's also kind of funny.' She smiled at him. Not like before, gently now.

His shoulders relaxed and his jaw softened. 'Funny, huh?'

'Yeah, ridiculous.'

Will smiled briefly in response. 'Maybe tomorrow it might be funny, but not yet.'

'Okay.'

'And let's put a pause on the phone sex.'

'If you want,' Poppy said, disappointed. 'It was fun though.'

'You were hot!'

It was not the first time Poppy had seen Will angry. He'd been angry at her last year when he found out she'd had a fling with Joshua Hunter before they'd started dating. He'd ghosted her for almost a week and been slow to forgive her when he'd finally heard her out. She didn't envy Brendan right now.

Chapter 9

Monday, 3rd February, 2020

When she was walking back in the front entrance of The Bennelong on Monday morning, her phone dinged multiple times with email alerts, as did Gemma's. They whipped them out and began reading as they walked to the lifts. As Poppy and Maria had predicted, the wards were changing. The Respiratory ward was now a purely COVID ward and designated the red ward. The ward directly below was now the suspected COVID ward and designated orange. Cardiothoracic ICU was now COVID ICU, as was the Neurosurgical ICU. The hospital was putting all elective surgery on hold and overtime shifts were changing. And Poppy's heart sunk as she read the final email.

> '... The government this morning announced an official six-week lockdown in Sydney. We are expecting to prolong term 1 and delay the change of terms...'

A six-week lockdown? Six weeks!

'Oh fuck, Poppy, I'm so sorry.' Poppy barely heard Gemma for the blood pounding in her ears as she digested this information.

How am I going to survive six weeks? I was thinking in terms of two or three weeks, tops.

'This fucking sucks!' Poppy's voice was raised. She quickly looked over her shoulder, remembering where she was.

Be professional, for fuck's sake.

'Yep, hon, it does. I want to hug you.' Gemma commiserated.

'Better not.' Poppy looked to the ceiling briefly but there was nothing there to help her. 'I'll be okay,' she reassured Gemma when they separated to go to different wards.

Gemma nodded. 'Text me later, okay.'

Poppy arrived at the back entrance to the ward via the staff lifts feeling despondent. Not only would she not see Will for ages, but she would now be wearing full PPE basically all day, and only removing it to leave the ward to see the few non-COVID Respiratory cases that would be placed on random other wards, or to take a break. Poppy felt a tingle of dread, knowing her skin would not appreciate the added humidity. It also meant extra overtime shifts as the hospital wanted to ensure there was a minimum of crossover of staff to reduce the likelihood of spreading the virus to other wards and staff. In fact, they'd added an extra overtime shift already, with Poppy set to cover both the orange and red wards tonight.

After putting her stuff away and changing into scrubs, Poppy donned her gown, mask, goggles, and gloves, and took a seat at the nurses' station to look at the patient details and wait for Olivia. They currently had twelve COVID patients on the ward and eight more in ICU. But as the case numbers were rising around Sydney, Poppy expected those numbers to steadily climb over the next few weeks.

Olivia and Prof Benjamin arrived together and Poppy found it slightly comical watching Olivia correct Prof Benjamin's PPE donning technique. A nurse was assigned the donning and doffing station and each person had to be signed off in and out of the ward to ensure correct technique, but Poppy could hear Olivia's frustration as she kept saying to Prof Benjamin, 'No, that's not right, Prof. You'll have to start again.'

She really is ballsy. I don't know that I could correct my boss so brusquely.

By the time they made it to the nurses' station, Poppy thought she could see steam coming from Olivia's ears and sweat forming on Prof Benjamin's brow.

'Morning, Prof,' Poppy said.

'Good morning, Poppy, let's get started, shall we?'

Poppy grabbed a portable workstation and they made their way to the bottom of the ward. Now that the entire ward was COVID, in some ways things were easier. The gown, mask, and goggles remained on the entire time, just the gloves changed between patients if they had touched them or their surroundings. As Poppy was in charge of the portable computer, she kept hers on throughout the round.

Three of the twelve patients on the ward were on HFNP and were grouped together in a four-bed bay close to the nurses' station as the most vulnerable group.

'Mrs Park looks pretty tired,' Prof said quietly just outside the bed bay, clasping his gloved hands in front of him. 'Let's do a blood gas and get a CT chest. But I'd have a low threshold for an ICU review.'

'Okay,' Olivia replied as Poppy made a note in her record.

The rest were pretty stable. They'd been giving everyone steroids and remdesivir in the last week but Poppy wasn't sure yet if it was really making a difference or if some people were just sicker than others. The sickest in ICU were being nursed prone, like they were doing in Italy. It was pretty scary to watch them turn a patient onto their stomach with all the lines going in and out of their bodies. Multiple staff were needed and it had to be done very slowly to avoid the lines getting caught or tangled. Thankfully, they hadn't decided on trying proning on the ward yet. Poppy hoped they kept that just in ICU. She didn't want to be responsible for accidentally unplugging someone's ventilator, or ripping out an arterial line.

'You stay here, Poppy, and sort Mrs Park. I'll take Prof to orange ward and ICU.'

Poppy put the CT order on the system and then got her equipment ready for the blood gas. Mrs Park was a forty-five-year-old mother of two who had likely caught the virus from her parents, one of whom had died last week. Her husband and kids were not allowed to visit, and she hadn't even been able to say goodbye to her dad before he died. Poppy felt very sad for her but tried to put some cheer into her voice when she went back into the bed bay.

'Mrs Park, I'm Poppy, we met on the round. How are you feeling?'

'Low-sy,' she replied over two drawn-out syllables between breaths, the low hum of the non-invasive ventilation machine whirring in the background, almost louder than Mrs Park's voice.

'I'm so sorry. We're going to get the CT soon, but first I'm going to take some blood from the artery in your wrist to see how your oxygen levels are going. You've had it done before, but it is a bit painful,' Poppy warned. She noticed how grey her skin was looking and the deep purple bruises on her arms from previous cannulas and injections. 'I'll try to be as gentle as possible.'

With her equipment prepared she sat next to the bed, feeling Mrs Park's pulse near the wrist. Thank goodness she was slim. But her pulse was pretty weak.

How she hated doing blood gases. *Well, there's no one else, Poppy, so just get on with it.*

She unsheathed her needle, drawing the small syringe back 1ml. If she did it correctly, the arterial blood would quickly fill that space without having to be drawn up. As the needle slipped easily through the tissues, a tiny bleb of blood filled the chamber and then stopped.

Damn, venous blood.

Poppy's own pulse and blood pressure started to rise as Mrs Park groaned in pain.

Calm down, try repositioning and see if you get it.

'I'm sorry, Mrs Park.' She dug the needle deeper into the soft tissues of the wrist and toward her middle finger. There was a sudden pop of pressure as the blood rapidly filled the chamber of the syringe and kept pushing the plunger upward.

Phew, Poppy thought as she quickly withdrew the needle and immediately applied strong pressure to the wrist to staunch the arterial bleeding.

'Do you want me to take that?' Sylvie, one of the nurses, offered as she passed.

Poppy allowed Sylvie to slip a gloved hand under hers to take over the compression so she could take the blood to the analyser.

Once the machine had done its thing, Poppy looked at the printout of the blood analysis. She knew the arterial blood was contaminated with a small amount of venous blood but wasn't sure how to interpret the results properly. Best to wait until Olivia was back from ICU. So, she recorded the result, stated the contamination and her plan to review it with Olivia, then got on with her other jobs.

When Olivia got back to the ward, an hour or so later, smelling enticingly of coffee even through her PPE, Mrs Park was off at CT. Before Poppy could update Olivia on the blood gas result, Olivia started whinging about Prof Benjamin. Poppy hadn't heard Olivia be rude about one of the Consultants before and was taken aback.

'Honestly, the man lacks skill or spine. He's just so... mediocre.'

'Do you think so?' Poppy was unable to stop the surprised furrow from forming between her brows.

'Absolutely,' Olivia said brashly.

'He seems okay to me.'

'Hmph.' Olivia was clearly not impressed with Poppy's assessment either.

Olivia seemed so different now to how she was in the first few weeks of the term. Sure, she'd never been warm and fuzzy, but she'd been professional and polite. Now she was arrogantly bagging out her boss to Poppy at the nurses' station, where everyone could hear. Poppy had no idea what was going on, but before she could change the subject, Olivia's phone rang.

Moments later they were hurriedly doffing their PPE, racing down the stairs to Radiology, donning again, and bustling into the CT where Mrs Park was being resuscitated. The Radiology and ICU staff were panting under their PPE and Olivia and Poppy were just in time to watch them deliver the last shock and round of adrenaline before they called time of death. Poppy felt dread form a rock in her stomach. Was this her fault? She had never had the opportunity to ask Olivia about the blood gas results.

Olivia sidled up to the ICU and Radiology Registrars, and Poppy stayed close to her side.

'What happened?' Olivia asked.

'She crashed in the scanner, that's what happened!' snapped the Radiology Registrar. 'She was completely unstable, you never should have sent her down! We're not set-up to deal with sick COVID patients! You should have just ordered a mobile chest X-ray!'

Poppy could see the veins in his neck dilate as he yelled his frustration at Olivia.

'She was fine on the ward, wasn't she, Poppy?' Olivia turned toward her and removed herself from the firing line.

'Well, I didn't see her leave the ward.' A blush added to the heat under Poppy's PPE.

'What?' Olivia's eyebrows had almost disappeared, they were so elevated above her mask, and Poppy cringed. 'You should always check a patient like that before the porters take them.' Despite the mask and goggles, there was no mistaking the look of absolute disdain that she gave Poppy.

'I'm sorry, I was with another patient.'

'Always prioritise the sickest patient, Poppy. It's like the first rule.'

And where were you, then Olivia? How were you prioritising Mrs Park when you were up the street enjoying a coffee?

No, she would not pass the buck. Olivia was right, she should have been keeping a closer eye on Mrs Park after the blood gas. Or maybe called Olivia with the result and asked her what to do?

The Radiology Registrar threw his arms up in the air and stormed off back to the reporting room, shoving his PPE into the designated bin on the way, almost knocking it over.

Her cold eyes still fixed on Poppy, Olivia asked, 'What was the blood gas like?'

Poppy's voice came out shakily. 'I was going to discuss it with you. It was contaminated with a bit of venous blood, so I had trouble interpreting it,' She couldn't meet Olivia's hard stare.

The ICU Registrar was still there and had the patient's record open on a tablet and passed it over to Olivia. 'Despite the venous contamination, the patient was clearly sick.'

'Jesus, Poppy, you should have called me immediately,' Olivia snapped.

Poppy wanted the floor to swallow her whole. She'd never before made a mistake that had resulted in a patient's death. She swallowed to stop the tears that were threatening to fall.

'I'm sorry.' The wretchedness she felt was like a physical pain.

How could I have been so stupid? Maybe if I had called Olivia, instead of waiting for her to come back, Mrs Park might still be alive.

'Clearly, I can't expect you to do even the simplest things on your own.' Olivia snapped as she stormed off down the hall. 'Come on, we need to update Prof Benjamin, and then *you* can call the family.'

Poppy bit her lip hard and sucked a breath in through her teeth, her body trembling as she hung her head and followed in Olivia's angry wake. Fuck, how much would she give for Will to be here right now, putting his arms around her and telling her everything was going to be okay. Because of her mask and shield, she couldn't even wipe the snot that was starting to trickle from her nose. All she could do was to try to snort it back up.

'Stop snivelling,' Olivia commanded, clicking her fingers. 'Come on and hurry up.'

Poppy trudged along behind Olivia's rapid gait, ashamed. She'd been feeling pretty confident lately, especially with helping Alex out, but now she realised how little she still knew. Whilst the ICU Registrar said the blood gas clearly showed how sick Mrs Park was, she still didn't really get it. And clearly Olivia was in no mind to teach her how to interpret them. If Maria was around, she'd ask her, but she hadn't even seen her today. She'd just have to look it up later so she could do better next time.

Back on the wards with a new set of PPE, Olivia directed Poppy to call the patient's husband while she updated the nurses and Prof Benjamin. Poppy's hands were shaking as she entered the mobile number. She held her breath, silently willing it to go to voicemail as the number rang.

'Hello,' a male voice answered.

Poppy took a steadying breath. 'Hello, is that Mr Park?'

'Yes.'

'Hi. My name is Dr Mason. I'm the Resident looking after your wife—'

'Is everything alright?' he interrupted before Poppy could continue.

'Actually, I'm afraid it's not, Mr Park. Your wife... she was really unwell this morning... and we were getting another CT scan... and...' Poppy paused here, not really sure what to say next. Should she come right out and say, "your wife has died?" Or "your wife has passed?" Her brain was starting to flip out with indecision and she was vaguely aware that Mr Park was saying something on the phone and Olivia was staring at her, making a wind-it-up hand gesture.

'Hello, are you still there?' Mr Park asked.

Poppy's brain kicked back in. 'Yes... yes. I'm sorry to be the one to tell you this, Mr Park, but your wife stopped breathing. The team resuscitated her for a considerable time but at no stage did she start breathing independently again. I'm so sorry.'

'What? What does that mean?'

'I'm sorry, Mr Park, but your wife has died.'

Fuck, was that too blunt?

'She died?'

'Yes, I'm so sorry.' Poppy was absently jiggling her leg up and down now, and it was starting to judder the desktop. Olivia nudged her in the ribs as Poppy could hear Mr Park crying on the other end of the phone. A surprisingly loud howl made Poppy pull the phone away from her ear and Olivia again did the wide-eyed, wrap-it-up hand gesture at Poppy.

'Mr Park?' Poppy softly asked.

'Y-es,' he answered between sobs.

'I'm so sorry. Do you have any questions?'

'Can I come and see her?'

Poppy's heart sunk further. 'I'm so sorry, but as she was COVID-positive, we can't allow that.' She couldn't believe she was having to say such a thing to a grieving husband, but then she remembered the technology the hospital was about to use for meetings.

'Maybe we could arrange a Zoom call so you could see her face and say goodbye that way?' Poppy said, feeling proud of her quick thinking.

'What's Zoom?'

'It's an online platform that allows video calls. You can do it from your phone if we can get the staff to send you a link. It might take a bit of time but let me see if I can arrange it.'

Poppy ignored Olivia's single arched eyebrow and decided she would make it her mission to sort this out for Mr Park. It was the least she could do, considering her role in Mrs Park's death. She took down his email address and promised to be back in touch before ending the call.

Chapter 10

'You shouldn't promise things you can't deliver,' Olivia said as soon as she had hung up.

'It can't be that hard, surely.'

Olivia said nothing and Poppy imagined she was pursing her lips behind her mask.

'Will Mrs Park's body come back here or go straight down to the morgue?' she asked.

Olivia ignored her.

When Poppy realised Olivia wasn't going to answer, she went to look for Susan. Poppy knocked on her office door, but didn't enter, expecting that Susan wouldn't be in full PPE.

'Hi Poppy, I heard about Mrs Park. How are you?' Susan asked as she opened the door and stepped back to create a space between them, wearing a mask only as Poppy expected.

Poppy was comforted by her concern. 'I've certainly had better days. Do you know if her body will come back here, or go straight to the morgue? I want to try to arrange a video call for the husband to say goodbye.'

'That's a good idea. She'll go straight to the morgue, I suspect.'

'Okay.'

'That poor family,' she said as Poppy was about to return to the nurses' station.

She stopped in her tracks. *Does she blame me, too?* But there was no scowl or anger in her face.

'Yes, it's truly awful,' Poppy said, the rock now a boulder inside her.

The staff in the morgue had received Mrs Park but were not keen on the idea of the Zoom call.

'That's not really something for us,' the technician started to say, but Poppy rushed in.

'I understand you've not done this before, but this man has just lost his wife. His kids have lost their mother and their grandfather, all in the space of a week. They haven't been able to hug them goodbye, or—'

'But it's not—'

'They haven't even seen their bodies to know it's real,' Poppy interrupted passionately. 'Don't you think we should try to do this? It might really help them say goodbye.'

'Okay, okay. I'm not a monster... But I don't even know how to start setting that up.'

Poppy raised a clenched fist in triumph. 'If I come down and do it all, can you just help me with the body?'

'I suppose,' he said begrudgingly.

'Thank you!' Poppy clapped her hands together when she put down the phone, the boulder shifting slightly.

Poppy went back to Susan and explained the dilemma. Together, they decided to use one of the iPads the hospital had given them for family calls, and IT helped talk them through setting up Zoom. Poppy wanted to high-five Susan at their achievement, but they were appropriately distanced 1.5 metres apart, so she mimed it instead.

Susan said, 'How about this?' She lifted her elbow up and Poppy got the message. They elbow-bumped. It was close enough.

Poppy may have facilitated an earlier death for Mrs Park by not being vigilant enough, but at least she could give her husband some closure. She knew that if she was in his shoes, that's what she'd want.

An hour later, Poppy navigated down to the bowels of the hospital and found the barely identified morgue amongst the rabbit warren of tunnels and exposed services. Her ID badge didn't immediately allow her access, so she pressed the intercom.

'Yes?' a weirdly disconnected voice crackled through.

'Hi, it's Poppy, I'm a Resident. I'm meeting Tran, the technician.'

There was static and Poppy was just thinking she'd have to repeat herself when a metallic lock release sounded, and the automatic doors opened inward.

Once out of the spooky, barely lit tunnels, the overly bright fluorescent lights, humming gently overhead felt reassuring. In fact, apart from the smell of bleach and formaldehyde, this area was very similar to the rest of the hospital. At the end of a small anteroom there were a few chairs and a reception desk behind Perspex. The desk was unattended and after waiting a polite minute or two for the voice on the intercom to emerge, Poppy had no choice but to ring the bell on the counter and wait.

She checked the time, noting she still had five minutes until the scheduled Zoom call. At glacial speed, a stooped older woman with thick spectacles eventually shuffled into the reception area.

She slowly raised her head toward Poppy. 'Yes?'

'I'm here to meet Tran.'

'And you are?'

'Poppy. I'm a Resident.' She tapped her foot in frustration at having to go through this again. Hadn't this woman just spoken with her on the intercom?

'ID please?'

Poppy held her ID badge up to the Perspex and the woman leaned forward to peer at it with her coke-bottle glasses, and then up at Poppy's face. Poppy was shifting from foot to foot now, eager to get through the door.

'You'll need to sign the visitors book.' The lady passed it through the Perspex opening and Poppy dutifully signed it and handed it back.

Poppy thought it odd that the process to enter the morgue was more rigorous than to enter the wards, but she held her tongue. It was time for the Zoom call and she was just desperate to get there and set up so she didn't keep Mr Park waiting too long.

Finally, Poppy was given instructions, shown the PPE equipment, and buzzed through. She didn't really know what to expect, but behind the entrance, the morgue was divided into two halves. On the right lay the autopsy suites, which were predominantly empty and stacked with equipment since all autopsies were now done centrally at the coroner's in Glebe. The left side held the body drawers, and here Poppy found Tran waiting for her in full PPE with a single drawer open and a body still covered by a sheet.

Poppy got straight to the task of setting up the iPad and opening the Zoom meeting. She checked again that the camera and audio were working, then waited for Mr Park to join. Thankfully, the WIFI in the basement was still good.

The tear-stained face of a forty-something Chinese man filled the screen.

'Mr Park?'

'Yes,' said with an intake of breath as he clearly tried to prevent himself from sobbing.

'I'm Poppy. We spoke earlier.'

'Yes.'

'So, I just wanted to make sure you're happy to proceed. That you want to see your wife?'

'Yes… Yes, please. I want to say goodbye.'

'Okay. In a moment, Tran is going to pull back the sheet so you can see your wife. I'll hold the camera so it will be just you and her. When you're ready to finish, please let me know.'

'Okay.'

'Are you ready now?'

'Yes. Yes, I'm ready.'

Poppy held the iPad over the body and Tran gently removed the sheet down to Mrs Park's shoulders. Poppy could hear Mr Park sobbing, and the murmuring of words spoken in Mandarin. After a few minutes, the words stopped. Some minutes after that, as Poppy was thinking about her upcoming overtime shift, all sound had stopped.

Maybe there's an issue with the WIFI connection?

Tran had left once he'd pulled down the sheet, so Poppy held her breath and lifted the iPad so she could see the screen. The video link appeared to still be active, but Mr Park had gone.

What should she do – wait, or just end the call?

'Mr Park?' Poppy called out and waited. She tried again more loudly. 'Mr Park?'

Poppy felt the stillness of complete solitude, and the hairs on the back of her neck became erect in a wave up to her skull.

She was jiggling from foot to foot and biting her lower lip.

Should I end the call?

As she was about to press the red "Leave Meeting" button, Mr Park came back into view, accompanied by his two children. Little girls in neat dresses, their hair brushed straight with midline parts and thick fringes.

Poppy felt her breath catch in her throat. 'Mr Park, I thought you had gone.'

'I want my kids to say goodbye to Mummy.'

'Are you sure?' Poppy asked, her breathing becoming shallower.

'I'm sure,' he said resolutely, his jaw clenched and his chin jutting forward.

'Okay, kids. My name is Poppy, and I'm a doctor. Do you know what has happened to your Mummy today?' She kept her tone even while she waited for them to answer.

'She died,' said the older girl, tears already coursing down her cheeks.

'Yes, that's right. And I'm so sorry that this has happened to you all.' Poppy paused before continuing, a lump in her throat making it hard to swallow. 'Do you want to see Mummy to say goodbye?'

Again, the older girl responded, staring defiantly at Poppy. 'Yes.'

Poppy looked at Mr Park and he nodded. 'I'm going to turn the screen so you can see Mummy.'

As the family became obscured from Poppy's view she heard screaming and turned the screen back to see the smaller child cradled in her father's arms, crying loudly and pounding his chest with her little fists. The older girl still held Poppy's gaze, but her chin and lower lip were wobbling. Was it the right thing to do? Should she have said no to the kids seeing their mother?

'Is that enough?' she implored Mr Park.

'Yes.'

'Okay, I'm going to end the call now. The staff will be in touch about arrangements. I'm so sorry for your loss.'

'Thank you, Dr Mason.'

Her legs were unsteady when she ended the call. She looked for a seat, but there were none, so she put a hand against the closed body drawers to steady herself. Had she compounded her earlier mistake, and helped traumatise two little girls even more than they already were?

An hour into her overtime shift, Poppy received a call.

'Hello, this is Poppy.'

'Are you the COVID Resident?'

'Yes.'

'It's Tran, from the morgue. We've got a deceased patient with a pacemaker. He's COVID-positive and the funeral guys won't take him until the pacemaker's removed.'

Poppy paused, wondering if he was going to make it clear what he wanted from her. But Tran said nothing further.

'I'm not sure how this involves me.'

'Usually, the Palliative Care Resident removes them, but because he's COVID-positive, he said to call you.'

'Oh.' Poppy's stomach dropped.

'Yeah, so if you could come down and cut it out, that'd be great. The funeral guys have gone to get dinner, so you've got about half an hour or so.'

Tran hung up, leaving Poppy still holding the phone to her ear. Her heart rate had kicked up and sweat started to prickle her scalp. The ever-present PPE now a hot box. She'd never removed a pacemaker before and she was stuck. Bolted to the chair and floor in her hot box suit.

Someone was tapping her shoulder and she turned slowly, still mired in her uncertainty of how to proceed.

'Poppy, are you okay? Sylvie asked in her quiet voice, muffled further by the mask and shield. Before COVID hit, Sylvie had been a petite, quiet Japanese woman in her thirties. Now with PPE shrouding her, she'd become a ghost, silently sneaking up on Poppy when she wasn't expecting it,

'Oh, Sylvie. Yes, I'm fine.'

Sylvie sat down and watched her, obviously unconvinced. 'What's wrong?'

'The morgue guy just called me. He wants me to come down and take out a pacemaker.' Was the PPE choking her? Blood was pounding in her head and her breaths were tight and short.

Is this a panic attack?

Sylvie's hands were in her lap and she continued to watch her. 'You've not done that before?'

'No.' A sudden wave of relief swept through her body.

Weird that admitting my incompetence makes me feel better.

'Why don't you ring the Registrar? They might know.'

'Good idea. Thanks, Sylvie.' Her body was her own again, moving into action to look up the overtime roster. When she read the name listed, however, her stomach dropped again and she mumbled the word, "shit," under her breath. A brief nod to self-pity before forcing her fingers to hit the number saved in her phone.

'Yes?' the voice on the other end of the line was curt. Why did he behave this way, Poppy wondered.

She pursed her lips then said, 'Hi Josh, it's Poppy.'

'Yes, there's this thing called caller-ID. Maybe you've heard of it?' His voice dripped with disdain.

Poppy envisioned punching him in the face. Instead, she let him have his jibe and proceeded cordially, her innards clenched in a protective mechanism. She had to be ready for whatever putdown he was going to give her next.

'So, I'm the COVID Resident and I just received a call from the morgue asking me to come down and remove a pacemaker.'

'And?'

He sure wasn't going to make this easy for her.

'Well, I've never seen or done that before, so I was just wondering if you could help me?'

There was a pause. Poppy felt the hairs on the back of her neck tingle for the second time that day. Surely, he'd have to help her?

'Honestly, Poppy, your ineptitude never ceases to surprise me. This is not climbing Everest. Take a scalpel, make a cut, and pull it out. Even you could manage that.' He laughed and then hung up.

Fuck! She wanted to scream.

What the fuck did I ever see in that prick? He is the most arrogant, self-satisfied arsehole that ever lived!

Blood was pounding in her neck. Okay, calm down. She made herself take five slow breaths in and out, her eyes closed, picturing the freckles across Will's nose and trying to block out Josh's laugh. Then she went to the supply closet to see if she could find a scalpel.

She was on her knees rummaging through the bottom shelves when Sylvie came in.

'What are you looking for?'

Poppy sat back on her haunches and looked up. 'Do we have any scalpel kits?'

'I'm not sure... But if we did, they'd be over here near the dressing packs and suture cutters. Let me see.' Sylvie started looking herself while Poppy hauled herself up from the floor.

'Yep, you're in luck.' She passed Poppy a scalpel kit.

'Thanks, Sylvie, you're a lifesaver... or a death-saver, depending on your perspective.' Poppy said with a quick chuckle. Sylvie didn't laugh in return and dropped her head fractionally. 'I'm sorry. That was crass.'

'That's okay,' Sylvie said, leaving the room.

Poppy worried she had offended Syvlie. She didn't know her as well as Mel and Terry, who were chatty. Mel, in particular, was positively boisterous at times. If Poppy had to use a word to describe Sylvie, it would be demure. Poppy looked down at her feet, adding "insensitive" to the list of her infractions for the day. It wasn't as gut-wrenching as her other mistakes but it didn't make her feel any better about herself.

As much as she was loathe to admit it, Josh was right. This wasn't the big deal she was making it inside her head. This person was already dead, she couldn't inflict more pain on them, even if she wasn't very skilled. As he said, it comes down to making a cut and removing a device. Surely she could manage that and not add any further mistakes to her day.

Poppy hadn't paid much attention to Tran the first time she'd been in the morgue. She'd been too anxious about being ready on time for Mr Park. This time, as he led her down the corridor to the autopsy suite, she studied him and wondered what type of person did this job. He was in PPE, so there wasn't much of his body to see. She knew he was Vietnamese based on his Christian name, but she couldn't predict his age based on the little she could see of his face. How did he become a morgue technician, and what do morgue technicians do apart from move bodies into and out of drawers?

The patient was already on the autopsy table, covered by a sheet.

'Are you good on your own?' Tran was already turning to leave, his blue plastic gown rustling amongst his legs, his white knee-high gumboots visible below the hem.

He didn't wait for an answer and Poppy heard the soft close of another set of doors and then oppressive silence. The knowledge that she was surrounded by dead people weighed heavily. A cold shiver ran through her body.

Pull yourself together, Poppy.

She placed her scalpel kit on the side of the table and pulled the sheet down to the patient's abdomen. Poppy skimmed his face briefly, noticing the deep lines that age had etched, and the abundant grey hairs peeking out of his nose and ears, then looked at his chest wall for which side the pacemaker box was located. A visible rectangular bulge elevated the skin on the left side, and she moved closer and opened the scalpel kit. Poppy felt the edges of the pacemaker box and made a 4cm vertical incision just laterally. It was then she realised she hadn't thought to bring forceps or retractors.

Bugger, she'd just have to use her fingers. She pushed her fingers under the skin and tried to probe around the pacemaker box. Eventually, she'd managed to create a channel around the perimeter of the box and was able to try to grasp it. The first time, her fingers slipped straight off. *Ugh.*

She tried again. This time her grip held, and she gently tried to move the box toward the incision. Poppy found she could manipulate it only about five millimetres or so. More pressure and Poppy was able to wiggle it up and down until one edge was poking out. She stopped and took a breath, not realising she'd been holding it. Spreading her legs apart and bending her knees slightly, Poppy tightened her grip once more and pulled and wiggled harder. Now the box was half-out and Poppy was able to grab the wires that snaked from the box, down through the vein and directly into the heart.

Poppy kept the palm of her hand on top of the box to help with leverage, and pulled the wires towards herself, bracing with her legs. The wires pulled taut but didn't move.

'Hunh,' Poppy said out loud to the empty room. She wasn't expecting that.

She blew inside her face shield to try to move a sweaty hair out of her field of vision, braced her legs, engaged her core, and pulled again with as much force as she could muster.

Startled by sudden clapping behind her, Poppy turned quickly, immediately releasing the pacemaker box.

'Jeez. I know you're not the best Resident around, but I honestly thought you'd be able to do this on your own.'

Joshua Hunter. Leaning laconically against the door frame with one leg crossed over the other.

Chapter 11

If Poppy wasn't already bright red and sweaty from straining under the PPE, she'd have blushed in anger.

Fuck this.

'Fine, Josh. Let's see you do it.' She placed a hand on her hip and stepped back from the edge of the autopsy table.

He raised an eyebrow, before finally relenting. 'Okay.'

Poppy stepped back further from the table as Josh moved into position. She watched as he slid his hand over the box, grabbed the wires, just as she had, and yanked. Again, the wires pulled taut but remained fixed in situ.

Suck it! You couldn't do any better!

Poppy heard him mutter, "Damn," under his breath.

'What was that?' she asked sweetly.

He ignored her sarcasm. 'I think we might need to try together. This is really stuck in there. I want you to slide your hand under the box and then we can pull at the same time.'

As much as she wanted to tell him to do it by himself, she couldn't bring herself to be that unprofessional. 'Fine,' Poppy muttered holding back the desire to knee him in the balls.

She moved closer to Josh and angled herself just behind his right shoulder so that she could reach in with her right hand. Their bodies were now in contact and Poppy was acutely aware of her breasts imprinting on his back. She was keen to get this over with quickly despite the aphrodisiac smell of his spicy aftershave.

'Okay, on 3. 1... 2... 3.' Josh said with them pulling together at the same time.

Still no joy.

'My hand slipped off at the last second. I think I need to be closer,' Poppy said.

'You go in front.' Josh stepped back, their eyes locking briefly before Poppy averted hers. His blue eyes at odds with his chestnut hair and tanned skin made her stomach flip-flop and her skin tingle. She didn't want to feel like this and she certainly didn't want him to know he still had any effect on her.

They repositioned themselves, and now Poppy couldn't help thinking about Josh's groin against her hip.

'Alright, are you ready?' Josh checked.

'Yes.'

'1... 2... 3.'

They yanked in unison, the wires released at speed, and Poppy fell back into Josh as they came hurtling out. They ended up on the floor, Poppy in Josh's lap, the pacemaker leads still clasped in Poppy's hand, and bloody trails on the ceiling and their shields.

Josh started laughing. Poppy turned to look at him and despite their history, she couldn't help but laugh too. Who would have thought she would end up on the floor of the morgue, in Josh's lap, covered in sticky, congealed blood. They were still in a tangle on the floor, laughing when Tran entered.

'What the hell happened?' he asked, taking in the blood trail on the ceiling.

Poppy hurriedly got up.

'Hi mate,' Josh responded casually. 'We had some trouble removing it. Sorry about the blood.'

'What should we do with the device?' Poppy asked, trying to restore some semblance of professionalism.

'There's the bag,' Tran responded, pointing to the nearby bench.

'Oh, thanks. Is that all I need to do?' Poppy asked.

'Yeah, you can go,' he said, grumpily, his eyes still stuck on the ceiling, probably wondering how he was going to get the blood off.

Poppy hurriedly doffed her PPE and was quick-stepping toward the reception doors when she felt Josh's presence at her heels.

'So, that was actually quite fun,' Josh said to Poppy as the doors swung toward them.

Poppy didn't turn around but kept walking.

'Wait up,' Josh said, taking hold of her upper arm.

'What, Josh? What do you want?' Poppy crossed her arms on her chest and took a step back from him. 'To put me down some more?'

Josh wiped his forehead, looked down at his shoes, then back at Poppy. 'You're right. I've been a complete prick. I'm sorry.'

Josh apologising? That was new. But Poppy wasn't going to let him off that easily. She turned to keep walking. 'Okay. See-ya.'

He caught up and tried again, grabbing her arm. 'Poppy, wait.'

She shrugged out of his grip but stopped and waited. He looked at his feet again, but not long enough to make Poppy interject.

'Sorry is not enough, I know. And excuses are not enough. But you did hurt me last year at the ball.'

'What?' Poppy said shrilly.

He can't be serious!

'I thought we had something going, and then you just blew me off.'

She blew him off? In what reality did that happen? He kept her at a distance and used her as his booty-buddy. Poppy watched his face, looking for signs of disingenuity, but he looked sincere and sad. She was suddenly wrong-footed. Was she the bad guy in his mind?

'Umm.'

'I guess it's no excuse, but that's why I've been so mean. I'm sorry.'

'Well... I'm sorry too.' This conversation was not going how she expected. 'I thought you didn't have real feelings for me.'

'No Poppy, you're wrong. I did.' He leaned toward her, running a finger down her arm. 'I do...'

Poppy couldn't help but shiver. 'Josh, I'm with Will now.'

'Oh.' His head dropped like he understood, but he was still leaning in toward her. Crowding her space with heat and that spicy aroma of his aftershave that excited her, involuntarily.

She shook her head briefly. What the fuck? Why wasn't he stopping? As Poppy's brain was reeling, trying to piece together these mixed messages, Josh began nuzzling her neck.

'Seriously?!' Poppy pushed Josh firmly in the chest. 'I just told you I'm with Will and your response is to kiss my neck?'

Josh shrugged and walked off down the darkened tunnel toward the lifts.

Argh! Poppy felt like tearing her hair out. What the hell was wrong with him?

Poppy couldn't wait until tomorrow to tell Gemma about this. There was no signal down in the basement, so she took a lift up to ground and called Gemma from the passage down to medical admin which she knew would be deserted at this time of day.

She took off her mask and leant against the wall.

'What's up?' Gemma asked by way of greeting.

'You are not going to believe what just happened!'

'What?'

Poppy paced up and down the darkened corridor while she filled Gemma in on Josh's behaviour right up to the point where he nuzzled her neck and she pushed him away. When she finished the retelling, she exhaled loudly, stopping in the middle of the corridor. She leant back against the wall, tipping her chin to the ceiling. In a quieter voice, she asked her friend, 'When will he stop being able to manipulate me?'

'I don't know, hon.'

The line was quiet while Poppy thought. She was embarrassed that she'd let him unsettle her again. It stoked the anger and resentment that had been lurking inside her every time he'd belittled her in the last year. Heat whipped through her. 'I'm just so furious right now. Argh!' Poppy half-screamed, then quickly turned around, remembering where she was. Luckily the corridor remained deserted.

'Take a breath,' Gemma suggested. 'Look, Josh is a complete dick and not worth your time. With everything that happened last year, he doesn't deserve to breathe the same air as you.'

'Mmm.' She needed this. Needed the reminder not to waste her energy on Josh.

'You've got to put it aside and go finish your shift.'

Poppy took another deep breath. 'Okay.'

'Go get 'em, girl.'

'Thanks, Gem.'

Poppy had the distinct vision of herself wearing an Akubra hat, a bandana tied around her neck and a short denim skirt, riding a mechanical bull, one arm raised in the air like a proper rodeo rider. Yes, she could do this, if necessary she would have to rope in Josh and show him who was really the boss. If he could manipulate her, maybe she could manipulate him too. If he was honest when he said he still had feelings for her, then maybe she should use that to her advantage next time she had to interact with him. It would be a nice change to see him wrong-footed for once.

Poppy returned to the ward still feeling on edge. Luckily there were menial tasks, also known as "scut work," to keep her occupied for another hour as her anger fizzled out. She re-charted fluids and medications, checked blood results, re-sited cannulas, and checked chest tube outputs.

Terry sidled up to her when her eyes were glued to the computer, scanning blood results for abnormalities.

'Poppy, can you please have a look at the new chap in bed five? He's really itchy and looks like he's getting a rash.'

'I'll just finish this and I'll be there in a sec.'

'Thanks.'

Once she'd finished logging all the blood results, she opened the patient file on bed five. He'd come up from ED when Poppy had been down in the morgue wrestling with Josh, so she knew nothing about him. The best information was usually to be found in the Medical Registrar's notes, so that's the entry she opened. She was jolted by his age as she read the first line.

"Twenty-two-year-old with community-confirmed COVID…"

Twenty-two? That was only two years younger than she was. Now she wanted to know why he was in hospital instead of still in the community, so she quickly read on. More words and phrases jumped out at her.

"High fevers >39 deg." "Sudden shortness of breath." "Profound weakness."

When she finished reading the entry, Poppy slumped back in her chair. Gosh, only twenty-two and sick enough with COVID to be admitted. This was a frightening wake-up call and Poppy's brain was oscillating between a glue-like sluggishness and frizzing with rapid thoughts. The one most frequent thought, like a pinball hitting a slingshot, was "twenty-two." Pushing back from the chair and standing up, Poppy walked down to bed five, wondering if she would find a pale and sickly underweight twenty-two-year-old when she walked through the door.

'Hi Justin, I'm Poppy, the Resident on the ward.' She introduced herself, seeing immediately how incorrect her prediction was. He was pale, but not a sickly weedy adult, but a robust, muscular one.

He was on the high flow humidified nasal oxygen and the machine hummed in the background. Poppy watched him take two quick breaths, his broad chest expanding and pushing his sheet and blanket up, before responding. "Hello," he said before quicky taking another breath.

'Terry said you were itchy?'

He nodded. His dark brown hair slick with sweat and flattened in patches to his head.

'When did it start?'

Two breaths again before an answer. 'Just now.'

Poppy approached the bed. 'Can I have a look at your skin to check for a rash?'

There was nodding again. He was conserving his energy appropriately but it was a marker of how sick he was that he couldn't easily speak in long sentences and phrases. Poppy pulled over the obs machine which had been loitering in the corner of the room and found the torch tucked away in the basket. She turned it on and pointed it at her hand to make sure it worked, knowing the batteries in them were often flat when you wanted to use them. Once she was beside him, he pushed his covers down to his legs.

'I'll check your arms first and your legs and then your chest and back.'

She ran the torchlight down each arm and leg and sure enough there was a fine, lace-like rash with a few scratch marks where he'd been itching. There were no big red bumps and nothing on his legs.

'Can I sit you up so I can undo your gown and check your chest and back?'

Justin nodded again and grabbed the side rails in an attempt to pull himself off the pillows, but he was too weak and flopped back down, landing heavily against the bed.

'How about I help you.' Poppy slipped an arm under his shoulders. 'On three. One… two… three.' Once sitting up, she undid the bow at his neck and let the gown slide forwards. Both his chest and back were muscly and toned. He obviously was normally very fit, so the inability to pull himself off the bed was a real concern. The rash was also on his chest and back and looked the same as the arms.

'I'll help you back down,' Poppy said after re-tying the gown. He shut his eyes in exhaustion. 'Do you know if they gave you any strong painkillers in the ambulance or ED, like morphine or fentanyl?'

Justin opened his eyes and nodded.

'It could be that. I'll check your chart, but morphine can commonly cause a rash like this. It's very itchy but should settle over the next twelve hours. I'll chart you an antihistamine to ease the itching.'

He blinked at her then took another two breaths. Poppy waited, knowing that he was going to say something more.

'I guess that means… I wouldn't make a good… junkie.'

The extra words brought on a coughing fit and Poppy instinctively put a hand on his arm. When he settled, he slumped deeper into the pillows, his eyes shut for a moment, but Poppy waited. He gave her a lopsided smile when he'd recovered.

'It's a good line. But probably would have had more impact if you could say it in one go.' She gave his arm a pat with her gloved hand.

A brief laugh-like sound came from his mouth and Poppy worried it would send him into another coughing fit, but he gripped the bed and took two more furious breaths before relaxing.

She patted his arm once more. 'You rest. I'll get Terry to bring you the antihistamine. Hopefully, it will ease the itch for you, and I'll put a note in that you're allergic to morphine.'

Justin gave her a final nod and lopsided smile before she left the room and removed and replaced her gloves. Poppy sent a silent wish to fate that he would turn the corner.

'Hey,' she said to one of the Residents when she peeked her head into the Residents' Lounge for a break later. Poppy was glad Josh wasn't there. She may have talked herself up after calling Gemma, but her bravado was waning and she didn't really relish another interaction with him right now.

'What's happening?' Poppy asked of the news that was on the TV.

'Mayhem, death, fear.'

Poppy didn't like his tone. Too dismissive. 'Can you turn it up?'

As she listened in, it was clear that things in Italy were no better, and now the outbreaks in London and New York were spiralling out of control. There were reports of multiple refrigerated trucks being used as temporary morgues as hospital capacities were overrun. The images from New York were particularly eerie. The "city that never sleeps" was suddenly deserted, streets empty apart from trucks and ambulances banked up and around the hospitals. The bubbling of fear caught in her throat, like the sensation of being sucked into a rip.

Poppy remembered the first time she was caught in a rip. It was a hot summer's day in Newcastle. One moment she was swimming with her friends, enjoying the sun and salty water, the next she was suddenly drifting away from them, pulled by an invisible undertow. Her heart thrashed against her chest as fear rose and she started paddling in earnest. Only, her friends got further and further away. With her distress skyrocketing, she quickly became fatigued from the effort to paddle and go nowhere. Her legs were dragging her down, her arms on fire. It was terrifying. The complete lack of any ability to change her situation and the realisation that she was in serious trouble.

Luckily it was a patrolled beach, and sob of relief caught in her throat when a lifeguard paddled out to pull her, heavy-limbed, onto a longboard. When her embarrassed, breathless body plopped onto the sand, friends anxiously swarmed around her as she panted her thanks to the lifeguard.

It was a wake-up call to the brevity of life amongst the enormity of nature. She had learnt that day that control was an illusion. When you realise that, the ensuant fear can be overwhelming. Poppy could see it happening now. Fear. Spreading and multiplying as the human race saw how woefully out of their depth they were against this new virus.

As she sat in the Residents' Lounge thinking about the rip and COVID, she realised how irrelevant her encounter with Josh had been. There were far more important things happening right now here in this hospital and elsewhere in the world. Certainly more important than her wounded pride.

When she went to handover that evening it was the first time since the new COVID staffing changes had come into effect. Last year the mentoring committee Poppy helped establish had made inroads and positive changes to support the junior staff but the same could not be said of the rostering committee. The ongoing squabbling had meant very little was achieved. In fact, they had only managed to hire two additional Medical Registrars, despite the original plan for at least five, one additional Surgical Registrar, and three additional Residents. There had been no changes to the way terms and rostering were managed. Now that the Health Department had effectively put a hold on all elective surgery, a number of Interns, Residents, and Registrars doing Surgical and Anaesthetic terms had been redeployed to help in ICU, ED, and on the wards. It meant the COVID wards now had their own Resident and Registrar overnight, in addition to the usual night staff.

As the handover was concluding and Poppy was heading to the door, she heard the Night Registrar for the COVID ward mutter, 'Night gathers and now my watch begins,' under his breath.

Poppy didn't recognise him and wondered if he was one of the Surgical Registrars. 'Is that from *Game of Thrones*?' she asked.

'Yeah, the night watchmen. It feels a bit surreal, like I'm battling an enemy I can't see, and I've just got to hold the ward until the morning and try to keep them all alive.'

'It sounds pretty scary when you say it like that.'

His eyes darted around the room, over her head, and finally landed on hers. 'To be honest, it feels pretty scary.' He ran a hand through his hair and looked down at his feet.

This Registrar was at least two to three years more experienced than her, and somehow it felt like the table had flipped. Someone who would normally be so confident and testosterone-fuelled now needed her to reassure him. 'They're all pretty stable right now. I think it'll be okay.'

‘I hope you’re right,’ he said as he walked past her with his head bowed.

When Poppy made it home and to bed, she thought back to what the Night Registrar had said and its implications. The world really was going to pot. Surgeons, normally such arrogant cowboys were suddenly fearful and completely out of their depth. How was she doing okay? Her anxiety was still there, lapping at her ankles, but she didn’t feel overwhelmed. Should she be freaking out too?

Chapter 12

Every day there were press conferences updating the public on COVID numbers across the state and, it seemed, additional changes within the hospital. COVID cover had changed to twelve-hour day and night teams in shifts. Gemma had been redeployed to COVID cover due to the new elective surgery ban and she was now on day shifts for the rest of the week on the orange ward. She'd only received notification that morning and was currently in a state of flux.

'Fuck this, fuck them!' she raged, pacing the kitchen. The space was small so it only took her two strides to reach the sink before she turned and took another two back to the fridge.

'It's not that bad,' Poppy placated, her hands in the air, her voice soft and low.

'It is that bad, Poppy. I was really enjoying my term and now I have to cover COVID wards for God knows how long.'

'Well, we might get to hang out, that could be fun.' She gave up trying to stop Gemma pacing and went around the other side of the kitchen bench and sat on a stool.

'And what if I get COVID? What if we all get COVID?' Gemma continued, ignoring Poppy's comment. Poppy found it interesting that she didn't seem that worried about getting COVID when it was just Poppy coming into contact with positive patients. It irked, but right now her friend needed reassurance.

Poppy clapped her hands. 'Hey.' This stopped Gemma's pacing. 'You need to calm down. It's going to be okay.'

Gemma took a deep breath. 'I'm freaking out, aren't I?'

Poppy shrugged. 'Yep, you kind of are.'

'Okay, I'm calm,' Gemma said after a couple more breaths and a vigorous shake of her upper body.

Poppy also had to do twelve-hour shifts and was on days until Thursday but would then move to nights on Friday. She felt a lurch in her stomach at the prospect of night shifts again, knowing how dislocating they were, but said nothing. It was a policy between them that only one of them could freak out at any one time.

'With this new lockdown, we'd better go to the shops on the way home and stock up.'

'Good idea.'

Lucas joined them, a towel wrapped around his waist, his blonde hair wet from the shower. He grabbed a piece of (now cold) toast from Gemma's plate and took a bite. 'Cold.'

'You snooze, you lose.' Poppy laughed. 'Hey, have you had any changes to your term or shifts?'

'Nothing yet, still status quo.'

'You're lucky,' Poppy said, noticing Gemma's pursed lips.

With the lockdown in Sydney, the Premier had encouraged people to work from home and prevented all non-essential travel. The trio noticed immediate changes as they strolled to work with the streets virtually deserted and most businesses shut or serving takeaway only.

'This is so weird,' Poppy commented to Stacey at Cuckoo Callay as she passed their coffees through the window.

'Yeah, I know. The boss sent everyone home this morning except me and one cook.'

'Really?' Poppy's mouth hung open.

'Yeah. We're all just waiting to see if we'll still have a job tomorrow. And if we'll get paid.'

'Shit, Stace, I'm… that's… I'm sorry,' Poppy stammered hopelessly. 'I'll have my fingers crossed for you.'

Poppy had been so focused on the impact of COVID on her life, her friends, and patients, she hadn't really had time to think about the broader community. She was suddenly grateful she had secure employment. Stacey and so many others didn't have that safety net.

Stacey nodded but said no more. Poppy stood awkwardly for a moment. She thought about what she'd said. It wasn't enough to convey her concern, but while she saw Stacey most days, they weren't exactly friends, and she was worried anything else would just sound false, or insincere.

Once on the red ward, Poppy headed to the donning/doffing station, deposited her things in a locker, placed her mobile in a snap lock bag, and began the ritual donning of PPE.

When she reached the nurse's station Mel was standing there, looking worn down. 'Morning, Poppy,' she said flatly.

'Hey, what's up?' Poppy asked.

Mel sighed audibly. 'A couple of deaths overnight.'

'Who?' Poppy wasn't sure she wanted to know. Her innards clenched and she braced herself for the answer.

'Beds five and ten.'

'Bed five?' That wasn't possible. 'Not Justin?' she croaked. 'The twenty-two-year-old?'

Mel nodded.

But he was so young, so robust. She just had a joke with him only yesterday. Poppy was overcome by a wave of nausea. Was she going to vomit? She put a hand to her stomach.

'Are you okay?' Mel asked, noticing her hunched state.

The acrid taste of partially digested coffee hit the back of Poppy's throat but she swallowed it back down and stood up. 'Yeah, just a bit shocked. Justin was so, so…'

'Young?' Mel put a hand on Poppy's shoulder and waited. 'He was. This whole thing isn't fair.'

Mel was right. This wasn't fair. Life wasn't fair. COVID was like roulette – where was the ball going to land? Whose time on the planet was up? It didn't have any rhyme or reason.

'He didn't even have any underlying medical conditions,' Poppy eventually said.

'No.'

'Did he even make it to ICU?'

'No. He crashed really suddenly. Everyone was shaken.'

This time Poppy didn't even reply. Maybe Gemma was right to be so agitated. If Justin, strong, fit, Justin, could die from COVID, then so could she. They were all on the front line. They could get COVID at any point. Who knew if the precautions they were taking would be enough? How could she, or any of them, keep doing this?

'Fuck,' she muttered.

'Yep. Fuckity, fuck.' Mel agreed.

An internal struggle was being waged inside Poppy. The professional, honourable part of her that wanted to carry on and do the job she was paid to do. And the anxiety-prone young adult that was feeling completely overwhelmed, who wanted to run and hide in a darkened room where no one would find her.

Olivia's arrival on the ward ended the struggle before there was a clear winner.

'Okay, just us again this morning,' she said, breaking Poppy's internal crisis.

It took Poppy a beat to add this information to the shit-show that was taking place inside her.

'What?' she asked somewhat incredulously. Prof Pilson was not coming in, *again*? Patients were dying, and they were on their own?

'Close your mouth, Poppy, and don't make a scene. Even behind a shield, that's unbecoming.'

Poppy reflexively shut her mouth, her lips forming a thin line. *How did she know my mouth was open?*

'Let's see who's new, shall we? We'll start with them first.' Olivia pulled over a mobile workstation, trying to propel Poppy forwards into the working routine.

Poppy was so overwrought, she couldn't let it slide this time. 'Wait, sorry, I don't understand. Why isn't Prof Pilson coming in to the hospital? It's been more than a week, and—'

'Stop!' Olivia slammed the keyboard down. Her eyes were cold and betrayed some deeper emotion, Poppy couldn't quite put her finger on. 'Let's just get on with it.'

Poppy wanted to say more. She wanted to ask why the Consultant, who was required to see all new admissions within twenty-four hours, wasn't fronting up to the hospital. Why were they being abandoned, unsupervised to fend for themselves when they were so out of their depth? But Olivia had fixed Poppy with a stare that was, she now realised, part fury and part fear. Poppy was worried if she did ask these questions and demand answers, Olivia just might crack. Maybe she was only just holding it together, herself. Projecting an outward efficiency but silently freaking the fuck out?

Poppy waited a beat and then relented. 'Okay, Olivia, let's start.'

She focused on what was expected of her and the professional veneer was reapplied to her facial features while a wet blanket was laid over her simmering internal crisis.

Their round of the ward lasted until around one o'clock. But for once, at least, they were a team. Poppy and Olivia moved patient to patient, and jobs were done as they went before moving on to the next patient. By the time they made it back to the donning and doffing station, Poppy was relieved to remove all her PPE. There was sweat down her back and her face was slick with a sheen of moisture. She took her bag from her locker and wiped her face on a sports towel she'd stowed in there, before putting some paw-paw ointment to the cracks in the corners of her lips. The one on the left was bad – she noticed some blood on her fingertip as she pulled it away, along with the accompanying sting that sent a shiver and a stabbing pain into her jaw. A crust was forming at the edges. She really needed this break from the PPE and decided she would go outside for some fresh air and to get something to eat.

When Poppy emerged into the sunlight she stopped and turned her face toward the sun, just like flowers do, closing her eyes. She relished the warmth on her skin, the light breeze gently fluttering her hair at the nape of her neck. All thoughts paused as she enjoyed this moment and listened to the lorikeets and mynas in the trees chattering away. When a cloud passed in front of the sun, the sudden shade cooled the vestiges of sweat on her body, sending a shiver down her back, and reminding her to move on.

As Poppy walked up the street, looking for an open café to buy a sandwich from, she texted Gemma and Lucas to see if they were free for lunch.

Lucas: Already ate

Gemma: Me too & btw I hate this shit

Poppy chuckled. It wasn't that she wanted her best friend to suffer that made her laugh, it was more a version of comic relief. Gemma was now in the same boat she was, so she was no longer alone. And Gemma's dry "call-it-like-it-is" attitude, took some of the edge off Poppy's anxiety.

The bakery café was open, but Poppy had to order and pay at the door and wait on the pavement for her order. A bag of food was subsequently thrust at her through the small opening in the door about five minutes later, a look of fear on the server's face.

'Thanks,' Poppy said, but her smile died when the door was slid shut in her face. She coloured as she backed away and almost ran into Alex and Maria.

'Don't worry, Poppy,' Maria said. 'There's a lot of people who are scared to catch COVID from hospital staff.'

'Really?'

'Yes, they don't realise how many precautions we're taking to avoid that, and there's starting to be a lot of hysteria in the media. If you're okay to wait for us, it'd be nice to eat together.'

'Yeah,' Alex added eagerly. 'Can you wait for us?'

'Sure. That'd be great.' This was exactly what she needed, fresh air and friendship.

Once they were back in the garden off the side of the hospital and unwrapping their lunches, Maria asked, 'So, how are things going?'

'Alright, I guess.'

Maria studied her with an intensity that made her look away.

'Poppy,' Maria started tentatively, 'I know you don't know me well, and I'm sorry we haven't had a chance to properly get to know each other with all the COVID craziness, but I want you to know that you can talk to me. You can be honest. Things are pretty effed up.'

Poppy looked up and the faintest of chuckles unexpectedly fell from her lips. Maria was so earnest, she couldn't even say the word "fuck" out loud. Her shoulders relaxed fractionally and she took a deep breath. Maria was genuine and trustworthy, and when Poppy looked from her to Alex, she realised that he had gained confidence and was more relaxed. How had their roles reversed in such a short space of time?

'Well, maybe they aren't so okay. Last night, a twenty-two-year-old died. Twenty-two! And Prof Pilson hasn't stepped foot in the hospital for more than a week... and I thought Olivia was cold and unfeeling but now I'm worried she's on the verge of a breakdown... and what if we get COVID? If a healthy twenty-two-year-old can die, so could we. And I'm oscillating between just doing the work and completely freaking out and feeling alone.' Once she started talking, the words tumbled from Poppy's lips, gaining pace as her deepest fears were exposed.

Maria put a hand on Poppy's leg briefly. 'Yes, it can be overwhelming, can't it?'

Poppy swallowed hard. At least Maria hadn't denied her fears.

'Let's talk things through,' Maria suggested. 'I know that helps me when I feel out of my depth.'

'Okay.' Feeling reassured, Poppy remembered her sandwich and took a bite, glad to let her talk. For the first time in a while she felt supported; someone senior was in charge and knew what to do to keep them all safe.

'Let's start with the deaths. I agree, it's very sobering. But remember, we are in full PPE, we are taking every precaution to prevent us catching it too. One thing I've started doing, apart from wearing scrubs, is having a shower before I change back into my clothes to go home at the end of the day. It probably isn't doing anything, but it makes me feel a bit safer.'

'Me too,' Alex chimed in, nodding and looking from Maria to Poppy.

'Yeah. Okay, I might do that too,' Poppy said, feeling a slight loosening of the knots inside her.

Maria had been holding her sandwich in her lap but brought it toward her mouth when she asked, 'Tell me a bit more about Prof Pilson.' There was a loud crunch when she bit through her sourdough crust.

'Each day, Olivia just brushes it off saying we're on our own.' Poppy had finished her sandwich now and took a gulp of her Coke Zero.

Maria swallowed, dropping her sandwich back down to her lap. 'What about Prof Benjamin?'

'He's been in, it's just Prof Pilson.'

Now it was Maria's sandwich that was forgotten. 'And she hasn't said why he's not coming in?'

'No. And every time I've pushed it, she's jumped down my throat.'

Maria picked up her sandwich once more and took and swallowed a bite while she considered things. 'Leave that one with me. But has he been available by phone?'

'Yes,' Poppy admitted. 'We call after rounds and when a patient is deteriorating.'

'Good.' Maria squeezed the last morsel of her sandwich in her mouth and wiped her fingers on the paper napkin then placed it in the sandwich bag and scrunched it into a ball. 'Now what about Olivia, you mentioned you were concerned?'

Poppy felt the sting of guilt and tried to back-pedal. 'It's nothing really,' she said, fixating on the Coke bottle cap in her hands. 'It's probably just me. I can't read her very well and I don't think we have the best rapport.' Heat rose into her cheeks. 'Olivia's very confident,' she added.

'Well, leave that with me too, if that's okay. But I think we should maybe find a way for at least the four of us to check in more regularly with each other. We've been very isolated and I don't think that's helping any of us.'

'That would be good,' Poppy replied, looking up, the knots loosening further.

The conversation moved on to other things and by the time Poppy returned to the ward and donned her PPE again, she felt more settled. There was still a support system there for her, she'd just needed to engage it.

Chapter 13

Poppy waited for Gemma at the front entrance after work. The breeze whipped strips of bark shavings from the nearby flower bed into a dance, and dust caught in her eye. She was just trying to clear it when Gemma strode out the front entrance. Her long legs covered the distance quickly, her crossover satchel slapping her thigh.

'How'd you go?' Poppy asked when Gemma linked an arm through hers. They strode off, Gemma shortening her stride length automatically.

'Bored out of my brain. And all the protocols! Let's not talk about it, I'm too hangry!'

Poppy squeezed her friend's upper arm, and they trudged along up the street to the small local supermarket on the way home.

At least they were changed out of scrubs and not getting filthy looks from everyone in the shops, but the level of fear was still noticeable. A few days ago, very few people were wearing masks in public. Now everyone was masked, and some were also wearing gloves.

'Fuck, no pasta,' Gemma said to Poppy as they wandered the aisles.

'No flour either,' Poppy added, pushing the trolley along slowly, one of its wheels whizzing independently from the others, slowing the whole process.

Now that they were stuck on twelve-hour shifts, they weren't going to have much time for meal prep, so they headed to the ready-made meals and added as many as they could scrounge to the trolley. Yoghurts were well-stocked but there were no eggs and most of the cheeses were empty.

'This is so weird,' Poppy declared looking at the empty aisles. 'I've never seen anything like it.'

'Yeah, look, I'm going to race forward to get toilet paper, you keep adding whatever you can,' Gemma said, and her long legs hastened down the aisle.

Poppy haphazardly added whatever she thought could be useful, but most of their usual staples were out of stock. As she was turning into the last aisle, she heard raised voices.

'That's mine,' Gemma said loudly, pulling a large pack of toilet paper towards her as a lady on the other end tugged back, grunting with effort.

Poppy stopped in her tracks, taking in the scene before her. Two grown women having a tug-of-war over the last packet of loo paper! Gemma was tall, but the other lady was large, and Gemma was being dragged forwards each time her opponent tugged.

'Bitch,' the large lady called as her grip failed on the plastic and Gemma staggered back with the sudden lightened load.

The large lady now bent low and rammed into Gemma with her bulk, like a bull ramming a gate. Gemma, who was already off balance, easily slammed back into the floor, hitting her head, the wind rushing out in an audible, 'Ooof...' and the toilet paper fell loose by her side.

Poppy ran towards her as the large lady scooped up her trophy and shuffled rapidly toward the checkouts. 'Shit, are you okay?' She abandoned the trolley and knelt over her friend.

'Fuck,' Gemma replied as she sat up, running a hand to the back of her head and seeing a touch of blood on her fingers as she inspected them.

'Let me see.' Poppy moved behind her and parted her hair, checking for a scalp laceration, knowing how much they could bleed. 'It's okay, no laceration. It'll be fine.'

'Fuck,' Gemma said again, her hand instinctively cradling her head.

Poppy pulled her to her feet. Somehow in the kerfuffle, Gemma's shirt had ripped at the pocket, but aside from that, the frizzed hair, and the bruise to her noggin and her pride, she was okay.

They wandered back over to where Poppy had left the trolley and looked in. 'Jesus, someone's nicked some stuff out of here while I was helping you.'

'Fuck... Newtown.' Gemma shook her head at the incredulity of the situation. 'Let's just get this stuff and go. These people are crazy!'

Poppy nodded, then wrapped an arm around her friend, who was walking slowly. 'You're not wrong.'

They staggered home, defeated.

'Dinner's hot,' Lucas called from the couch. 'It's on the—' He stopped when he took in their appearance. 'Jesus, what happened to you two?' He put his bowl of food on the coffee table and made his way over to them, taking the shopping bags out of Gemma's hands and placing them on the bench.

'What happened?' he asked again, worry etched into his face.

Gemma shook her head. 'The shops are fucking nuts.'

Lucas began rubbing her back.

'Yeah, it's like a war out there. Lots of shelves are bare and people are nasty,' Poppy added.

Gemma tentatively touched her head again. 'There was one last packet of toilet paper, and I grabbed it and was turning to walk away, when this lady came out of nowhere and tried to steal it out of my hands. I was so shocked, but I wasn't going to let go, so I pulled back—'

'And then it was on!' Poppy chimed in excitedly. 'And let's just say, Gemma was as tall as her opponent was wide.' She couldn't help the grin that formed.

'So, there was tugging back and forth until she lost her grip—'

'And called Gem a bitch.'

'Yes, and as she let go, I stumbled back—'

'And then she tackled her to the ground!' Poppy said, stealing the punch line.

'And I dropped the loo paper as I hit my head, and she grabbed it and scurried away.'

'Fuck me, are you okay? Did you lose consciousness?' Lucas asked, turning Gemma so he could look at her eyes.

Gemma gently removed his hand from her chin. Holding onto it, she said, 'I'm okay. I promise. No concussion. Just dented head and dented pride.'

‘Come over to the couch and sit down. I’ll get you dinner and an ice pack,’ Lucas said as he kissed Gemma lightly on the lips.

Lucas handed her a bowl of food and ice pack for her head and Poppy looked at them and thought of Will. She really needed to hear his voice.

‘I’m just going to eat in my room and see if I can call Will,’ she said, but they were lost in each other and it barely registered.

She recounted the story again for Will, and he, too, was shocked. ‘It was so weird. And not just the supermarket. The streets were so deserted today and when I got lunch, they didn’t really want to serve me in scrubs. I felt so uncomfortable. It’s like a switch has been flicked and everyone is suddenly scared of each other and only out for themselves.’

‘Yeah,’ Will sighed, scraping his curls off his face. ‘I guess we can do that. And instead of banding together to fight a common enemy, the enemy is invisible. Anyone could have it. So, it’s isolating and that can make people mean and selfish, I guess.’

‘It’s sad.’ Poppy frowned.

Will put a hand up to the camera, like he wanted to touch her. ‘I wish I was there with you.’

Poppy mirrored him. ‘Me too.’

With Poppy’s focus on the supermarket fight and the changes around them, she forgot to tell Will about Josh making a pass at her the previous evening. It wasn’t because she was intentionally keeping it a secret, she had simply forgotten about it when so many other overwhelming things had happened since they last spoke. The memory resurfaced when she was getting ready to sleep and she resolved to tell him next time they spoke. Keeping secret her brief relationship with Josh from Will last year had almost cost her the chance to have something serious develop with Will. She wouldn’t make that mistake again.

Over the next couple of days, Gemma found a routine with the COVID cover and the longer shifts, but Poppy noticed how attentive Lucas remained toward her. Because their shifts were longer and Lucas was still rocked by the supermarket fight, he was doing daily runs to the bigger supermarket in Leichardt to try to get toilet paper and other essentials, and cooking for them. Thankfully he finally managed to buy an eight roll pack on the day they completely ran out of tissues and loo paper. They had been discussing stealing from work and were grateful they didn't need to go to such extraordinary lengths.

Who would have thought that people would stock up on toilet paper more than food! Gemma's fight at the supermarket wasn't the only one, with the top news story featuring fights breaking out in other supermarkets and convenience stores as the toilet paper crisis deepened. Supermarkets had even resorted to hiring extra security and only allowing customers to buy one milk product and one toilet paper package (when it was in stock). It really was a crazy time.

Friday arrived and Poppy slept in as long as she could, knowing she was starting three night shifts that evening, eight until eight. She only woke fully at about eleven after waking earlier and reading before falling back to sleep. She had some breakfast but wanted to have a bath before her PACMEN Zoom at midday, so she set an alarm to make sure she got out in time. This was the first meeting of the new year due to the cancellation of their regular meetings when COVID hit. All junior doctor education sessions had also been cancelled and social distancing and increased workloads were putting additional strain on the workforce. Poppy was worried staff mental health could hit a new crisis point and she wanted to brainstorm what they could do to protect each other.

When her alarm sounded, she pulled herself out of the tub, towel-dried, and wandered into her room to boot up her laptop. She clicked the link on the email but hadn't realised she would need to download and install the Zoom app before connecting to the meeting.

'Shit,' she muttered, realising too late that the bath was probably a luxury she didn't have time for. Her frustration increased further when she had to find her password to approve the app installation and she flapped over to her tiny modular desk, wrenched open the top drawer and fossicked through loose staples, rubber bands, pens, and note pads for the purple sticky note stuck to the side with the password on it.

Poppy glanced at the time as she punched in the password with her right index finger. 'Fuckity fuck.' It was 12:01pm.

Finally, the app started downloading and Poppy raced back to her chest of drawers, flinging drawers open and grabbing undies, bra, T-shirt, and shorts and throwing them on the bed before running back to the laptop now perched on the edge of her desk.

Yay, she thought as she saw the app had finally completed installation. Poppy clicked the "Join meeting" link and the Zoom box opened just as the secured edge of her towel, which had been loosening as she ran to the chest of drawers and back, finally released and Poppy's towel fell to the ground, exposing her from the navel up for all the participants to see.

'Fuck!' she said out loud as she reached down to grab the towel and cover herself as quickly as possible. 'Sorry,' she shouted, flustered, as she fumbled with the mousepad to click off the video and microphone, whilst keeping her barely covered body below the camera.

She heard Dr Hennessy say, 'It looks like some of us are having some technical difficulties,' as she hurriedly threw on her clothes and went back to her laptop. This time she was too embarrassed to click on the video and just turned on the microphone.

'Well, most of us are on now,' Dr Hennessy continued.

Poppy debated whether she should apologise again but decided it would just draw further attention to her gaffe.

'Right, let's get started. Thanks everyone for joining. Given the current COVID situation, I thought it was really important that we meet and regroup. Obviously face-to-face meetings are now off the agenda for some time, so Zoom is the platform the hospital has decided to proceed with. I think it's quite good, from what I can tell, and the audio and video is very clear… '

Oh great, clear as crystal view of my tits for all to see!

'For housekeeping, I'll ask that everyone keep your microphones on mute unless you're speaking so we avoid background issues. And videos on if possible.'

The participants all did as instructed, and Poppy immediately blushed.

'Excellent, thank you,' Dr Hennessy said, nodding on the camera. 'Given all the COVID related changes in the hospital, I thought it might be worth adding a reminder about the counselling availability with Henry, although he will move to Zoom sessions, when we send out the mentor/mentee questionnaires for this year's allocations.'

Poppy saw multiple nodding heads on the gallery view.

'Sorry, excuse me Dr Hennessy,' Poppy interrupted, turning her microphone back on.

'Go ahead, Poppy.'

'Does that mean all meetings and teaching is now moving online?'

'Grand rounds will probably resume next week via Zoom, but unfortunately junior doctor teaching remains suspended at present.'

'What?' one of the other Residents exclaimed and Poppy noticed some others shifting or recoiling on their video feeds. Poppy knew the junior doctor education sessions, which usually ran weekly, allowed not just an opportunity for them to learn, but also a social outlet for them to connect and support each other.

'Yes. Hopefully it's only temporary. I'm sure Dr Anderson and her team are looking at ways of incorporating Zoom. Certainly, multidisciplinary team meetings will start up again via Zoom in most instances.'

'It's me again, sorry,' Poppy interjected. She needed to find a way to press the importance of supporting the junior staff without putting Dr Hennessy or any of the other Consultants on the call off.

'That's okay, continue.'

'I'm just concerned that the junior staff are now very isolated with all these changes, not just from access to teaching, but even within their own teams. With social distancing and PPE and changes to terms and shifts, I'm worried that the mental health of junior staff is even more at risk.'

Dr Hennessy nodded, along with some of the others on the screen. 'I hear you, Poppy. But we are rather hamstrung at the moment. Do you have any specific ideas that might help, aside from Henry's counselling sessions?'

'Maybe, if we can't offer teaching, we can offer some other check-in system? Just for the junior staff?'

'What were you thinking?'

'Maybe a Zoom session in the teaching timeslot, to touch base, and just for residents and interns. Leave it open for people to talk and connect.' Poppy didn't really know whether anyone would join but did know that she was feeling lost and alone. And if she was, other people would be, too.

'Let me discuss that with Dr Anderson and we'll see if we can set something up in the teaching period and if Henry can be there.'

'Thanks.' Poppy turned her microphone off and sat back. She knew she could trust Dr Hennessy and that she wasn't just giving her lip service. Her suggestion would be taken seriously and she would think of a way to advocate for it and implement it.

'Well, if there's no other issues, we might close the meeting. Melissa will send out the questionnaires today. We'll meet again in two weeks to review them, and I'll be in touch regarding junior staff check-in.'

As soon as the meeting closed, Poppy's mobile rang. It was Dr Hennessy. Poppy could feel the blush returning, and for the first time since Dr Hennessy became her mentor last year, she was anxious to accept the call, not sure if she would face some formal repercussion for flashing an entire meeting.

As soon as the line connected, Poppy apologised again. 'I'm so sorry, Victoria.'

'Don't sweat it, Poppy. Hardly anyone was logged on and it was so quick, a real blink and you miss it moment,' Dr Hennessy reassured her.

'Well... I don't know what to say.'

'It's okay. I just wanted to check in with you. How are things? You're obviously in the thick of it, doing Respiratory?'

'Yes. Up and down, I guess. My anxiety around COVID is fluctuating- some moments I'm feeling scared about catching it, other moments it's starting to feel routine.'

'That makes sense. When you're busy, you're just focused on the tasks at hand. It's only in the quieter moments that the enormity of the situation sinks in.'

'Exactly! How about you?'

'I'm good. We're starting to work a process of moving patient appointments to Zoom to reduce visitors to the hospital, so that's been logistically challenging, but the last week or so there have been a lot of face-to-face cancellations anyway, as people don't want to come into the hospital. So I think patients will accept Zoom appointments.'

'Yes, the fear in the community is really obvious now,' Poppy said before filling Dr Hennessy in on the toilet paper fight and the suspicion at the café.

'I'm looking forward to meeting Gemma one of these days,' she said, laughing at the supermarket fight.

'I think you'll like her. In some ways she's a bit like Dr Pearce.' Harriet Pearce had been one of Poppy's first Consultants in the ED when she started as an intern last year. Poppy's first impression was that she was spiky and abrupt, but she had found over the term that she was a fair and good teacher, and quietly supportive.

'Then I'll definitely like her.'

When Poppy got off the phone, she still felt awkward about her Zoom nudity and bereft about the COVID situation, so she rang her mum, hoping for some emotional bolstering. Recalling the incident for her mum, Poppy didn't know if she wanted to laugh or cry.

'Mum, I was naked, and everyone could see me!'

'Oh, no, darling—'

'I'm mortified.'

'Yes, I can understand that.'

Poppy huffed. Her mum was usually so good at cheering her up and making her feel better when something embarrassing happened. But so far, this exchange wasn't going the way she'd hoped.

'Well, at least you have a beautiful body, darling.'

'Argh, great, so now I'll be remembered as the Resident with the hot rack who was naked on that meeting one time.'

'There are worse things,' her mother said.

Silence descended and Poppy picked at the towel that was still flung on the bed. It was old and thin in patches, she really should replace it.

'Well, you can't go back in time, so you just have to try to put it behind you and move on. What are you doing for the weekend?' her mum said brightly, obviously trying to change the subject.

'Unfortunately, I'm on night shifts, starting tonight.'

'Oh, that doesn't sound like fun.'

'No, it won't be.' Poppy was being childish and petulant now, still picking at the towel.

'Do you get some time off after the nights finish?' Her mum was trying hard to connect to Poppy but that was proving more difficult than usual.

Normally, Poppy filled her in on life in Sydney and her mum did the same with life in Orange. There was usually some quip about her dad, and Poppy would feel comforted and safe, like she did as a child. But that was not happening today. It was only serving to accentuate her current fears and shortcomings.

'Just a couple of days.'

'Well, maybe you could do something nice then? Have something to look forward to.'

'Mum, Sydney is in lockdown.' Her mother really didn't get it. 'No unnecessary travel and stay at home orders. You can't even exercise more than five kilometres from home, so the beach is out too.'

'I didn't realise it was that restrictive.' Her voice had gone from bright and upbeat to quiet and low. 'Maybe you could do some baking? Or learn a new skill, like knitting?'

'Seriously, Mum?' This was pointless. It's like they were in two different worlds. But this was the first time they'd spoken since the COVID outbreak started. It wasn't really fair to dump this disconnection on her mother.

Poppy attempted a brighter tone. 'I'd better go. Send my love to Dad.'

'Okay, stay well. Love you.'

'You too.'

When she got off the phone her skin was almost itching, like she wasn't comfortable within herself. Partly, she felt bad for not being nicer to her mum, but she also had an ongoing sense of unease that hadn't lifted since the first COVID patient was admitted. Going into night shifts brought its own anxieties and she needed to find some way of distracting herself and settling down before she went to work.

Chapter 14

Poppy was cooking dinner when Lucas got home.

'Hey,' Poppy said, turning around briefly from the stove top, as he walked in the door.

'That smells good.' Lucas came up beside her and sniffed the air above the pan.

'Yeah, thought I'd make it early and then you and Gem can reheat it when she gets home later.'

He walked around the other side of the bench and placed his bag on the counter. 'Thanks.'

'No worries. You've been doing a lot of the cooking lately.' Poppy turned the heat off and scraped the pan with a spoon, portioning out her dinner into a bowl and leaving the rest to cool on the stove.

Lucas sat with Poppy at the dining table while she ate. He was tapping his foot, like he was nervous about something.

'What's up?' she asked.

'I want to discuss something with you, but I need you to keep it secret from Gemma. Can you do that?'

His gaze was intense and he'd stopped tapping his foot. Poppy scowled, her mind immediately jumping to the gorgeous Miriam and something unforgivable. 'It depends on what it is.' She tried to keep her tone neutral in case she was completely off base.

'It's not bad,' Lucas reassured her, seeing her icy stare. 'But it needs to be between us.'

She relaxed fractionally, her food forgotten. She was curious. What could it be? 'Well, tell me what it is? We don't normally keep secrets from each other.'

'I know, but... I want to get a ring and ask her to marry me.' A grin broke out on Lucas' face, making him look at least five years younger.

'Oh my god!' Poppy dropped her spoon from where she had been absently holding it and wrapped her arms around her friend. 'Luc, that's awesome! I'm stoked for you both!'

He hugged her back. 'Thanks, Poppy.'

'Of course, I can keep that a secret!' She released him but kept a hand on his shoulder.

'So, I've been looking at rings online and I was thinking something like this—'

He opened his phone and showed her a picture of a pear-cut emerald with two smaller pear-shaped diamonds set perpendicular to the emerald in a platinum band.

Poppy's jaw dropped. 'Wow! Luc, that's spectacular.' *And super expensive.*

'What do you think, honestly?' he asked with a nervous pursing of his lips. 'Do you think she'll like it?'

Poppy analysed the ring and thought about her response. She and Gemma had often talked about rings and what they liked when they were browsing shops in the city, and she knew Gemma had envisaged a simpler round diamond design. But she wondered whether that reflected Gemma's concern over what she thought Lucas might spend, rather than her heart's desire. Poppy was also cognisant that Lucas had put a lot of thought and effort into this and she didn't want to hurt his feelings. She wanted to do the right thing by both her friends.

'Luc, it's a stunning ring. The emerald will really suit her.'

'Yeah, that's what I thought, too. Really bring out the colour in her eyes,' he said, staring down at the picture on his screen.

'But maybe white gold instead of platinum?' Poppy ventured, tentatively.

He looked back up to Poppy, his eyes wide open. 'You think?'

Poppy nodded enthusiastically, relieved. 'Well, they both grey over time, but platinum looks darker.'

He nodded again, looking back down at the phone. 'That's a good thought, thanks. But... you think a design like this… she'll like it?'

Should she tell him what Gemma said she wanted?

Poppy stalled for time by looking at the picture again. She hoped this wasn't the wrong choice. 'I can't speak for her. But I think it would look lovely on her.' *Fingers crossed.*

'Thanks, Poppy.' He was visibly relieved and at the sight of his boyish grin, she wanted to hug him again. She refrained, one big hug would be enough for Luc.

Poppy sipped her drink. Another thought occurred to her. 'How are you going to get it with stores shut?'

'Well, so far I've just been looking at designs. Now that I think this is the way to go, I'll start emailing jewellers and go from there. I probably can't buy anything or do a romantic proposal until after lockdown anyway, but I can do all the research.'

'That's great, Luc. What changed your mind?' She had to ask – he'd been so stubbornly against taking this next step for years.

'COVID.' He sat back in his chair, his phone on the table, his eyes narrowing and looking at the wall. Then he turned toward Poppy. 'All this craziness just brought home how short life can be. You know? What are we waiting for? We love each other and we want to spend our lives together, and I would die without her. So, I just needed to get past my own bullshit, really.'

Poppy laughed, 'Oh, Luc, this is just the best news ever!' She launched out of her chair to hug him again as he said thank you into her hair.

This was the lift that Poppy needed. Something to look forward to and hold onto. A positive reminder that life would prevail and they would get through this storm that was COVID-19.

When Poppy was getting ready to head into work, the reality of Gemma and Lucas getting engaged sunk in. Would she have to move out? As amazing as this news was, it would change their dynamic forever. She was going to try to FaceTime Will from work later, but she wasn't sure she should talk to him about it yet, despite desperately wanting to. Maybe she should wait until it was official?

The giddy excitement of Lucas' news had morphed into another anxiety to add to her plate and a further feeling of displacement. She trudged toward work as the sun was setting, her footfalls heavy. There'd been no time to check the roster and see who the Night COVID Registrar was. She hoped it wasn't Olivia, they could use a break from each other.

As Poppy was in the middle of her PPE donning, a familiar voice said, 'Looks like it's just the two of us.'

Oh, no. Joshua Hunter. Poppy was glad she had already put on her mask and shield so he wouldn't see her mouth, *Fuck*.

'You're on COVID nights too?'

'Yep, all weekend.' He was getting his disposable blue gown on and looking down at what he was doing, but Poppy was sure she saw him smirk. He was enjoying this. Enjoying revving her up, again. Poppy thought back to their recent encounter after the morgue and her determination not to be manipulated by him anymore. If anything, she should use any overtures of lust or feelings against him.

Poppy jutted her chin and kept her tone disinterested. 'Okay.'

She finished donning in silence and then headed down to the nurses' station to handover from the dayshift team. Gemma had been assigned to cover Poppy until she returned from nights, so Poppy said 'Hi,' then subtly raised her eyebrows and pointed her head behind her, indicating Josh, who was just heading up the ward.

'No,' Gemma said under her breath and Poppy arched her brows in response.

When Olivia saw Josh, she practically beamed. 'Hi, Josh!'

Olivia walked right up to Josh, so close they were almost touching, forcing Poppy slightly off to the side to avoid touching either of them. Even with the mask and shield, it was obvious that Olivia had the hots for Josh.

'Olivia,' Josh responded neutrally. Looking down at the printed list Gemma handed him, he said, 'So, what have you ladies got for us tonight?'

When Gemma passed a duplicate list to Poppy, she raised her eyebrows pointedly. Olivia ran them through each of the cases and Poppy added extra notes to her sheet.

When they'd finished, Olivia clearly wanted to prolong her time with Josh. 'It's such a shame about this weekend.' She closed the space between them again. 'I was really looking forward to it.'

Poppy started to inch closer to Gemma, wanting to distance herself from the two of them, but she was also interested in Josh's response.

'Yes, it is. But with the lockdown, we probably had to cancel anyway.'

'Oh... yes. Maybe you're right.' Olivia's voice clearly conveyed her disappointment.

'Well, Poppy and I need to handover with the orange ward, too. So, thank you ladies, see you later.' Josh held out his list, attempting to usher Poppy toward him and out of the ward.

Despite the mask and shield, Poppy noticed Olivia's brows knit together as she gave her what looked like a death stare. Poppy was stunned; Olivia and Josh seeing each other? She gave Gemma big round open eyes of surprise as she said goodbye and followed Josh back down the ward to doff her PPE and head to the orange, suspected COVID ward, to do it all again.

Handover was straightforward and after they farewelled the day team, they sat at the nurses' station to review and plan the start of their night.

'It looks like there's a few scut jobs on both wards and one sick patient to review upstairs on red ward. Why don't you get started with the scut here, then you can meet me up there?'

'Okay,' Poppy replied gratefully, thinking she could dawdle down here for a while and reduce the time she had to be in close proximity to Josh.

'Bye,' Josh called as he sauntered down the ward.

Poppy was introducing herself to the nurses and putting her page number on the whiteboard when she felt her mobile vibrate in her pocket. She pulled it out and saw there was a text from Gemma. The face recognition wouldn't work with the mask and shield, and she had trouble even tapping in her passcode through the plastic snap-lock bag. Eventually, all the numbers were accepted, and she could open Gemma's message.

Gemma: WTF- is Olivia screwing Josh now?

Poppy sat down and slowly typed through the plastic:

IDK, maybe? Frightening!

Gemma: Yeah! She's a real bitch, btw. They deserve each other!

Poppy: Quite possibly. So, not a fan, then?

Gemma: Not remotely. She swanned in late, treated me like the shit on her shoes, and barely lifted a finger all day.

Poppy: Any of the Consultants come in?

Gemma: Benjamin. He was ok. Good luck, hon! (Fingers crossed emoji) Keep your distance!

Poppy: (heart emoji)

The first night, Poppy was tied in knots, constantly suspicious and on guard around Joshua, waiting to be bullied, belittled, or for some form of inappropriate physical contact. But to her immense surprise, he remained friendly without being overly familiar. Professional and respectful. And, as opposed to Olivia who would issue directives then leave Poppy to do the work, Josh and Poppy worked as a team throughout the night and took breaks together. But his behaviour frustrated Poppy as she knew she could not trust or rely on it.

At their first break, a few hours into their shift, Poppy wanted to call Will, so she took her protein bar to one of the on-call rooms next to the Residents' lounge.

'Hey! God, I miss you,' Will said once they'd connected.

'Oh, Will, I miss you too,' Poppy said, sadly.

'How's the night shift starting?'

'Okay, but I don't have much time, and a lot to tell you.' Before Will could respond, she kept going, knowing that her pager could go off any moment. She was sitting on the edge of the bed, leaning forward towards her phone. 'Firstly, I had the most mortifying experience today on the PACMEN Zoom.'

'Why, what happened?' Will asked, a furrow of concern appearing between his eyebrows.

Poppy told him about the nudity and Will laughed, and his face relaxed.

'Oh, honey, that's even worse than our pathetic attempt at phone sex.'

'I know! That was one person, who doesn't even know me. This was my colleagues in a professional setting where I want to be taken seriously... What is it with me and devices – I think I'm jinxed!'

Will laughed and he looked happier in that moment than he had in the last few weeks. 'Did Dr Hennessy say anything?'

Poppy had taken a bite of her protein bar and had to swallow before replying. 'No, she was really good about it, but I feel so ashamed.'

'It'll be okay, I'm sure barely anyone saw, and they'll forget about it soon enough. COVID is keeping everyone very busy where you are, and very bored where I am.' The animation on his face that had been there only moments before disappeared in the blink of an eye.

'Really?'

'Yeah. All the fly-in-fly-out surgeons can't come, so very little surgery is happening. The only anaesthetics I'm really doing now is Obstetrics. They've got me helping in ICU and ED a bit just to pass the time.'

'I'm sorry, hon, that does suck. Gemma feels the same, being relegated to COVID cover and missing her surgery term.'

'I have even less to complain about than Gemma. I've got it way easier here than in Sydney right now.' He pushed his lips into a smile but Poppy could tell that it was forced.

'True.'

Will wiped his curls from his face and leant forward towards the phone. 'Anyway, you said you had lots to say, and I interrupted you to have a whinge. What else were you going to tell me?'

Poppy lifted her head, her eyes darting to the closed door and she brought her phone closer to her face so she could talk quietly. 'Guess who's the Reg for nights?'

'Who?' He raised an eyebrow with interest.

'Josh,' Poppy whispered, chewing her bottom lip, nervously, worried about Will's reaction.

'Fuck,' Will said, visibly clenching his jaw. Poppy had told him what had transpired in the morgue, and his already low opinion of Josh took a further precipitous drop.

'And what's even more strange was Olivia's behaviour around him at handover – she was flirty. I think they might be seeing each other.'

'Hunh.' He rubbed his chin and the stubble made a crackling sound across the line. 'Maybe that explains her progressively cold demeanour towards you? You did say she was nicer at the beginning of the term.'

'Yeah, you might be right. Maybe Josh has been shit-talking me?' Poppy brightened at the thought. For some reason, it was more acceptable for her that Olivia dislike her because of Josh, rather than because Poppy was in some way unlikeable.

'I wouldn't put it past him. How's he been so far?' His brow furrowed again.

'Surprisingly okay, but I'm on my guard.'

'Good, keep your distance.'

'I will. I'd better get back to it.' Poppy sat up straighter and her eyes darted to the door again. 'I don't know when we'll get to talk next. Maybe I'll try you just before I leave for work tomorrow night?'

'Let's try for then. I have no idea where or what I'm doing day to day now, but I'll text you as well. Just keep your phone on silent when you're sleeping.'

'I will. I love you.'

Will paused like he wanted to say more. Poppy saw the furrow return to his brow. 'I love you. Be safe.'

The way he said it had Poppy wondering if he was holding something back. He ended the call before she could ask and she sat there on the bed watching her now black phone screen, her protein bar forgotten in her right hand. Will had a long-seated dislike of Josh and Poppy wondered again if there was more to it than just what had transpired between her and Josh last year.

She stood, placed her phone back in her pocket, the ziplock bag it would return to when she went back into PPE curled below it, and took another bite of her bar. Putting thoughts of Josh out of her head for now, she thought only of Will. It was nice to see his face and hear his voice. They were finding it harder to connect with the altered shift times, and that would likely get worse in the next few weeks. She was determined to focus on the simple happiness it gave her to see and talk to him just now.

'You look happy,' Josh said as Poppy came back into the Residents' lounge, the protein bar between her teeth. 'Talk to lover boy?'

And there it is.

She glowered at him but didn't respond. Instead, she sat on one of the couches, away from him, and they watched TV in silence until both their pages chirped simultaneously around fifteen minutes later.

'5613?' Josh asked, picking his up and reading the extension number on the screen.

Poppy detached hers from her hip. 'Yep, same.'

'I'll call.' He picked up the closest handset and dialled the extension.

'It's Josh, the COVID Registrar,' he said as Poppy watched him, wondering why the nurses had paged them simultaneously.

'Okay... And his BP?... Yes, she's with me... We'll be right up.'

'What's the story?' Poppy asked as he put down the phone.

'Sick patient on the orange ward. COVID swab just came back positive, and they want him reviewed before they call the porters to transfer him to red ward.'

'Why'd they page us both?'

'There's also some scut work on orange.'

'Oh.' Poppy gathered the bar wrapper and tossed it into the nearby bin as she stood and headed for the door. Josh turned the TV off and was only a step behind her. She probably imagined it, but she almost thought she could feel his warm breath on her neck.

She reached the door first and held it open for him to exit before her. That way she could keep an eye on him. As he headed down the corridor, Poppy stopped, causing Josh to turn back.

'I'll meet you there. I'll just duck to the ladies first.' She was thinking about giving herself some extra space from Josh, but also about how difficult it was to go to the bathroom, take a drink, or even wipe your face whilst in PPE. It might be a couple of hours before she'd get another break.

When she made it to orange ward in her PPE, she saw the list of jobs written on the whiteboard and got to work. It was mindless really. Cannulas, recharting fluids, doing timed bloods or observations. Her mind wandered. First, she thought of Will and how much she missed him. His sandy blonde hair, always a bit unruly around his ears, which often crackled to her touch from built up saltwater, the citrus scent of his aftershave, and his calming presence. Then her mind flipped to the comparison with Josh. His arrogance and insouciance, how she felt tied in knots around him, and how he constantly played games with her.

Lost in her thoughts, Poppy had not noticed Josh approach the nurses' station where she was currently sitting in front of a computer.

'Poppy,' the sound of his voice broke her reverie. 'Would you grab supplies for bloods and coags, and join me at bed five?'

She quickly turned her head away, hoping he didn't see her blush and know she was thinking of him. But she needn't have worried, he had already returned to the closed curtains around bed five's bay.

When she pulled back the curtain a short moment later, balancing the kidney dish with supplies in her left hand, she gave an audible gasp and almost dropped the dish. The patient, a man in his sixties, whom she was expecting to be short of breath and in respiratory distress like all the other deteriorating COVID patients she'd seen so far, was mildly short of breath, but the thing that Poppy wasn't prepared for was that he was very swollen and covered in bruises. His skin was tight and shiny and there was bleeding around his cannula site and clear fluid was seeping from his swollen legs. She'd never seen anything like it.

It took her a moment to pull herself together as Josh calmly continued to talk to him. Poppy finally registered what he was saying and made her way to the side of the bed.

'... I suspect you have some complications of the infection. In some people, the virus can go on to cause problems with other organs, such as the heart, kidneys, and liver. We need to take some bloods and get a chest X-ray and ECG. We may need to do some other tests as well, but that's what we are going to start with. I'm concerned that your blood is not clotting as it should. If the blood tests confirm that, we will need to give you some clotting factors to see if we can stop you bleeding.'

He had been all business as he imparted this information. Keeping his attention on the patient, his gloved hands clasped in front of him. When he paused, the patient nodded.

'Okay, we're going to get things started, but then we'll get you transferred to ICU. You may need more intervention and assistance than we can manage on a general ward. Do you have any questions?'

Poppy had been distracted, listening to Josh talking, and feeling her own blood pressure rising with the seriousness of the situation. She was impressed with how calm Josh was, but he hadn't made it clear to the patient just how critical things were. Poppy had made the leap and recognised that this was likely to be congestive cardiac failure with disseminated intravascular coagulation (or DIC), and with the patient actively bleeding, DIC even without heart failure had a high mortality rate. Add the heart failure and COVID and this was dire.

Poppy gently placed the tourniquet around the patient's swollen arm as he replied that he didn't have any questions.

Josh nodded. 'I'll go talk to ICU. Dr Mason will do the blood tests and we'll arrange a portable chest X-ray. Are you married, or have a next of kin I can call?'

'Wife,' the patient muttered.

Poppy prodded his arm, looking for a vein.

'I'll give her a call, too, and let her know what's happening,' Josh said as he left the cubicle, closing the curtain again behind him.

Each time Poppy prodded his swollen tissues, searching for a vein, a faint purplish wheal would develop just under the delicate skin surface. She was mentally crossing her fingers and toes, hoping with all her might that she'd get the vein first go and get bloods off quickly. If her fingertips were causing this kind of bruising, she was worried what the tourniquet might be doing. She breathed out some of the pent-up tension as the venous blood filled the first tube, but once she released the tourniquet, she breathed in sharply again at the thick, purple bruise that looked almost like stretch marks under the indentation of the tourniquet. There were even a few droplets of blood forming on the skin surface.

Fuck, she'd never seen anything like this!

Poppy found some facial towels beside the bed and gently, using her left hand, tapped them to the breaks in the skin, not wanting to push too hard, whilst she held the venepuncture site with gauze in her right.

She heard a groan, and Poppy turned her attention back to the patient's face. His chin had slumped to his chest. Had he stopped breathing? Her heart rate skittered.

'Shit!' Poppy dropped his arm and shook his shoulder. 'Sir, sir, can you hear me?'

Her eyes searched for the emergency button as her blood pressure rose, blood hammered in her ears, and a surge of adrenaline coursed through her body.

There it is.

She punched the emergency button then lowered the head of the patient's bed so he was flat, and tilted his head back to clear his airway and listen for breath sounds. There weren't any, so she stood on the chair she had just vacated, leaned over the bed, threaded the fingers of her right hand through those of her left, straightened and locked her elbows, and began chest compressions just as Josh and two nurses entered the cubicle.

'What happened?' Josh asked.

'Stopped... breathing,' Poppy puffed out as she continued her rapid compressions, trying to do two compressions every second. The heat and sweat had completely fogged up her shield so she couldn't see clearly, but she continued her compressions, a tightness forming in her shoulders, and her own breathing becoming more rapid.

Poppy heard the heavy clunking of the arrest trolley that one of the nurses wheeled in. Then the sound of a drawer being opened and things being pushed around. She assumed it was Josh fossicking for a Guedel's airway, knowing it would take the arrest team more time than usual to reach them as they would have to don PPE to enter the ward. She willed herself to keep going, despite already starting to tire.

'Keep going, Poppy,' Josh said, as if he had been reading her mind.

Through the haze of her shield, she saw Josh hand-bagging with oxygen as the nurses hooked up ECG leads and the pads for the defibrillator. Poppy was still compressing, and felt like she wanted to vomit from the effort as the pain in her shoulders and upper arms screamed with each downward compression.

'Stop for a moment,' Josh said and then looked at the rhythm on the screen. Poppy took a welcome break, standing upright on the chair and easing the tension in her lower back. As the fog on her shield cleared, she looked down at the patient's chest which now had a purply-black bruise where she had been doing compressions. There was even bleeding around the Guedel's tube. A trickle of blood spilling onto his chin.

Did they have any chance of saving him?

The ICU staff and arrest team finally walked in as Josh said, 'PEA. Give adrenaline.'

'What have we got?' the ICU Registrar asked as his shield intermittently fogged and cleared from his breathing and glasses. Josh gave the background as the Anaesthetic Registrar took over the airway and one of the ICU nurses relieved Poppy of the compressions.

Poppy shuffled back out of the way, breathing heavily.

The ICU Registrar took over the lead and Josh moved to the side of the bed, closer to Poppy.

'Okay, hold compressions again. Let's reassess the rhythm.'

Poppy looked on as the monitor continued to show a flat line with occasional little blips that weren't quite heartbeats. She knew, in her gut, that this was most likely unrecoverable. Converting a non-shockable rhythm to a shockable one was highly unlikely. Mentally knowing the person in front of you, who only moments before had been upright and speaking, was about to die was very different from accepting it. In that moment, as the ICU Registrar said, 'Give another round of adrenaline please,' Poppy could not take her eyes off the screen, willing it to return a normal heartbeat.

Josh delivered the adrenaline through the cannula, having already drawn it up. Once it was in the line, the ICU Registrar said, 'Continue compressions.'

Poppy's breathing was slowing, but her insides remained tightly clenched, as was her jaw. After what felt like hours, but in reality was only another ten minutes, the ICU Registrar called time of death.

Poppy breathed in sharply. She took in his swollen body splayed out on the bed, a tube sticking out of his mouth, all the leads and wires still attached to his chest, and the forgotten tourniquet limp around his arm. The bruising and swelling made his body look like one that had come from a car accident and it seemed completely incongruous with COVID. Since starting work as a doctor, she'd participated in maybe eight arrest teams. Only one had been successful. Each time she felt the loss in her body, like a kick to the solar plexus. She hung her head and slowly filed out of the cubicle with the other doctors, saying a silent farewell to the patient in her mind.

'So, DIC as a complication of COVID?' the ICU Registrar asked Josh while they stood in the corridor. His voice was low, but Poppy could hear the hint of excitement.

'That's what I was thinking. We didn't even get a chance to send the bloods off. He deteriorated too quickly.'

'I think that's the worst DIC I've ever seen.' The ICU Registrar bounced on the balls of his feet, making his excitement even more evident. It irked Poppy.

'Me too,' Josh replied.

Poppy was still behind them, observing.

'Could be worth writing up as a case report. You should send the bloods.'

Couldn't they at least give it a few minutes before they thought of ways his death could advance their careers? Poppy's brows knitted and she hastened past them, back toward the nurses' station, not wanting to hear any more.

When Josh joined her after the ICU Registrar and his team left, he said, 'Hey, still send those bloods off.'

She couldn't look at him. It was so morbid, this side of medicine. This desire to compete and score goals at a time like this. Poppy didn't want to be a part of it. She didn't trust herself to speak, so she placed the bag of blood tubes on the bench in front of them and turned to walk down the corridor.

'Where are you going?' Josh asked with a hint of surprise in his tone.

She didn't turn back but said over her shoulder, 'I'm just going to re-gown after that, before I start the paperwork.' She didn't mention the bloods. Of course, she would do as she was asked, but she didn't have to be happy about it.

'Wait. Good idea,' Josh said, striding to catch up with her.

As they were stripping their blue gowns and throwing everything in the doffing station bin at the end of the ward before the lifts, Josh said, 'That was crazy, wasn't it?'

Poppy could see he was excited too. His face animated and his eyes lifting to the ceiling, lost in thought. He then leaned back against the wall, in no hurry to regown.

'It was awful.'

Poppy wet a facial wipe and wiped her face clean of the sweat. She squeezed it out, wet it again, and then held the cool, wet cloth against her face as she bent over the sink. It cooled her down quickly. When she was done, she scrunched it in a ball and threw it in the bin. There were comfortable chairs facing the darkened window just to the side of the lifts. She slumped into one and heard Josh sink into the next. It was a while before either spoke again.

'Every arrest is awful, but that was like a horror show. I think I'm going to be seeing that in my dreams,' Poppy eventually admitted, her head in her hands.

Instead of making her feel like a child, Poppy was surprised when Josh concurred. 'I've seen a lot of weird shit in the last four years, but that tops the list.' She looked up at him to check he was being serious and was relieved to see him leaning forward and looking at his folded hands.

They were quiet again for a few more minutes before Poppy resolved it was time to get back to work. 'What should I put as cause of death on the death certificate?'

He held a hand across his jaw, tapping his index finger as he thought. 'I think we list COVID as the primary cause, then secondary DIC and secondary heart failure as additional causes.'

'Alright.' Poppy dragged her heavy limbs out of the chair and proceeded to start the donning process again. Her adrenaline surge had completely dissipated, and she felt weary. Her legs were like lead, her head had started to buzz, and she wanted nothing more than to crawl into bed and sleep for hours. That feeling wasn't helped by the minimal lighting on the wards. It was quite different from ED where most of the lights blazed twenty-four hours a day. On the wards there was often only one light on in the nurses' station, and nurses carried a torch when reviewing patients, trying to protect the patients' sleep as much as possible.

Back at the nurses' station, Josh picked up the phone to call the next of kin and Poppy started the death certificate and her documentation of the arrest in the patient's electronic medical record. She also sent off the bloods she'd taken, her annoyance having cooled. But she couldn't help listening in as Josh spoke with the patient's wife and was surprised again by how gentle and thoughtful he was. Poppy could hear the wife crying and Josh waited patiently, allowing her time to express her grief.

Why did he occasionally behave like a good guy?

It was too confusing. Sometimes it was easy to hate him, and at other times, like right now, she'd forget what a prick he could be. She wished Gemma was there to slap her out of it!

Chapter 15

Once Josh was finished on the phone, he headed back up to red ward to review another patient, and Poppy continued her scut work. When she finally left orange ward and looked at the time, she was surprised to see that it was already after midnight. Night shifts were crazy like that; you could lose whole hours in what felt like minutes. She decided to hit the vending machine for some chips on her way back to red ward. Unhealthy option, she knew, but nights were all about survival.

An hour or so later they were back in the Residents' lounge. This time they each took a couch and lay down with blankets. Poppy thought about sleeping.

'You awake?' Josh asked softly.

'Yep.'

Poppy waited for Josh to say what was on his mind, but the silence became prolonged. She didn't really know what to say to him. Was he planning on asking her for more details on her relationship with Will? Her insides clenched just thinking about how awkward that would be.

Eventually, when it was clear Josh was waiting for her to speak, she asked, 'Are you and Olivia dating?'

Immediately, she regretted it. He would think that meant she cared about who he was dating. She was staring up at the ceiling, and the lights were off, so he couldn't see the blush that crept up her neck. Maybe she did care?

There was a gap of silence before he answered. 'We've been out a few times.'

Again, Poppy didn't know what to say next. Will was probably right, he was probably shit-talking her to Olivia, but he'd just deny it if she confronted him. She still had to get through another two night shifts after tonight, so she didn't want to antagonise him.

'It's not serious,' he added, almost as an afterthought.

Yeah, in *your* mind, Poppy thought. She suspected Olivia probably felt differently on the subject. Again, Poppy remained quiet.

'What about you and Will? Are things serious with you two?'

Did his voice just catch? Surely not.

'Yes, they are.' Will's face conjured in her mind and Poppy couldn't help but smile.

'He's in Dubbo at the moment, isn't he?'

Poppy risked turning her head slightly, so she could see him. He was on his back, watching the ceiling, as she had been moments ago. She rolled back and said with a sigh, 'Yes.'

'That must be hard.'

'It's not fun,' she agreed.

Poppy was worried he would say something inappropriate, like suggesting they go out again, but the silence deepened. Eventually she turned her head to look in Josh's direction and saw, with relief, that his eyes were closed. Rolling back, she closed her eyes and thought of Will as she drifted off to sleep.

The horrible beep-beep-beep and vibrate of one of their pagers shattered her sleep, what felt like moments later. A trail of drool had leaked onto Poppy's chin. Embarrassed, she swiped it with the back of her hand before Josh noticed, and reached for her pager as it continued its incessant beeping and migrated across the table with each vibration. Punching the button to turn it off, she reached her arm further out of the blanket to get the phone.

'Hi, it's Poppy,' she said quietly as she connected to the extension.

'Poppy, it's Sylvie on red ward. Sorry to bother you, but one of the patients is more breathless. Could you come and review?'

'Sure, I'll be right up.'

As Poppy put down the handset, she looked at her own phone for the time and was shocked to see it was almost 4:30am.

'What time is it?' Josh asked with his eyes closed, his skin smooth and drool-free.

'About four-thirty.'

'What's up?'

'Patient on red ward, more short of breath.'

'Okay, let's go together.' Josh threw off his blanket and sat up suddenly. His scrub top had deep creases in it and his hair was sticking out in clumps. Poppy watched him smooth it down with his right hand, and then he looked like himself again, albeit a more tired version.

'You don't have to,' Poppy said.

'We're a team. We work together.'

'Okay, thanks.' Again, Poppy was surprised. He was behaving exactly the opposite of Olivia. The cynical part of her wondered if it was just another manipulation, a way of getting her defences down so he could make another pass at her, like he had the other evening.

In red ward, they donned their PPE for what felt like the hundredth time this shift and proceeded to the nurses' station to find out which patient needed review. Once in the patient's room, Poppy immediately saw he was struggling. He was sitting up, breathing rapidly and shallowly, and responding in single words to Josh's questions.

'He's not moving much air,' Josh said as he listened to the patient's chest. When he finished the examination, he joined Poppy at the end of the bed. 'Let's do a blood gas and trial HFNP.'

'Okay.'

'Is he already on steroids?' He automatically wrapped the stethoscope around his neck.

. Then, obviously remembering about COVID, he pulled it straight back off and looked at it like it might bite him before placing it back on the obs machine in the room.

'Yeah, I checked on the way in.'

He nodded. 'I'll set up the HFNP with the nurses, if you do the blood gas?'

'Sure.' Poppy left the room to get the supplies as Josh started to explain the plan to the patient.

The blood gas was straightforward for once, and by the time Poppy came back from the analyser in the sleep lab with the printout, Josh was returning to the nurses' station. They sat down together and Josh explained the result to her. Finally, she had a framework for how to analyse them.

'We'll give him an hour and see if the oxygen sats improve.'

Poppy turned in her seat at the computer to face him. 'And if it doesn't?'

'If it doesn't, he'll need to go to ICU,' His tone was matter-of-fact.

When the hour was up his oxygen saturation hadn't picked up much.

'Mmm,' Josh said, back outside the patient's room again once they'd re-checked the readings. Poppy wondered if he was itching to rub his chin again while he thought. 'Not much change.' His oxygen saturations were still oscillating between the high eighties to early nineties.

'And he looks tired,' Poppy added noticing the patient's shoulders slump between breaths and his eyes flutter but stare vacantly in front of him.

'Yeah, I agree. I'll call ICU.'

Poppy watched and listened as Josh made the call, trying to learn from his description. It was after six now and they would need to keep a close eye on him until he went to ICU, so they stayed put until handover. Thankfully, the ICU Registrar came up promptly, agreed with Josh's assessment, and the porters had just wheeled him away when the day team arrived for handover before eight o'clock.

After showering and changing, Poppy walked bleary-eyed out of the entrance and straight into Josh's unmoving back as the bright sunlight dazzled her vision.

'Sorry,' Poppy apologised as she stepped back.

He turned to face her, the hint of a smirk tugging at the corner of his lips. 'That's okay, I was waiting for you.'

Why? Poppy thought with suspicion.

Josh must have seen the sudden change in her expression. He lifted his hands in surrender. 'It's okay. I just wanted to say thank you for a good shift.'

'Oh, okay. Well thank you too, especially for explaining the blood gases. That was really helpful.' She shifted her weight from one foot to the other.

'You're welcome.'

They stood awkwardly looking at each other, Josh's hands in his pockets, looking down at his feet then back up at Poppy, like he wanted to say more but wasn't brave enough. Then he abruptly turned and said goodbye, presumably headed for home. Poppy waited a couple of minutes, wondering what was on his mind, then set off herself.

Will and Poppy missed talking to each other that evening, but the second shift was okay. Josh remained attentive and professional, and they continued to work as a team. After a few hours, Poppy relaxed and even had moments where she found herself enjoying Josh's company. It was a quieter shift than the previous night and she and Josh had several hours in the Residents' Lounge.

They were playing pool and Josh said, 'Have you heard about the new check-in system?'

'Which one?' Poppy leant forward and took a shot.

'The QR code you have to fill out at every venue.' He walked around her to get to the white ball and Poppy was conscious of how close he came to her. They didn't touch but Poppy felt the heat from his body.

She watched him lean down to line up the shot. His shoulders strained the cotton of his scrub top. 'Not just what we have to do here?' She tried not to linger on the lines of his body.

'No. It's everywhere now. For contact tracing. So, if you've been in contact with someone who has tested positive, you get a notification.'

Poppy stopped thinking about Josh's body as she absorbed this information. 'Wow, that's going to be a massive job.'

He pocketed one of his balls and stood back up, assessing what to do next. 'Absolutely.'

Poppy thought for a moment and leant against her pool cue. 'You know, as horrible as this shit-storm is, it's actually kind of lucky it happened now, and not like, five years ago.'

'How so?' Josh asked as he leant forward to take another shot, his eyes moving from Poppy's, down to look at the balls in front of him.

'Well, the technology is just so much better, isn't it? Mobile phone and GPS data, Zoom. Five years ago, you could barely do a conference call. Now you've got perfect quality video teleconferencing with no delay or connection dropouts. And multiple different people can join the conference with no hiccups.'

'Good point.' He stood up and looked at her from across the table.

'And it enables people to work from home so much more easily.'

'The city must be a ghost town. Maybe that will be the new norm whenever this settles?'

He was still assessing her over his pool cue. Poppy wondered what his gaze meant. 'What, work from home?' she asked.

'Yeah.'

'Those city rents will plummet. It'd be much cheaper for companies to pay people to stay home rather than rent expensive office space.' Poppy walked around the table to where the white ball lay, near where Josh was standing.

'And better for the environment with less cars on the road.'

She bent to take her shot then looked back up at him, half-standing. 'True… a new tomorrow.' She rested her cue on the edge of the table. What an interesting concept. COVID could impact the future and ultimately change the way businesses practised, which could have positive secondary effects for slowing global warming.

She leant down again to line up the shot. 'So, you passed your exams last year. What's next?'

'I managed to get an advanced trainee Cardiology job here. But I got redistributed once COVID hit.'

Poppy straightened. 'How do you feel about that?' She hadn't really given any thought to what he'd been doing before he landed back in her life.

'Initially, I was furious—'

'I'll bet,' Poppy interrupted.

'But now… We're all doing what we can, I guess.' He shrugged and seemed lost in his thoughts. 'This is a once-in-a-lifetime event.'

Once-in-a-lifetime. Would it be the only one in her lifetime? The enormity of the situation kicked her anxiety up again. It was like the rev of an engine when you put the foot down on the accelerator. A sudden surge of fear. 'Let's hope so.'

'Agreed.'

'So how long do you think it's going to last?' Poppy asked, bending forwards finally to finish her shot.

'My secondment, or the pandemic?'

'Either, both?' she replied as she smacked the ball and sent it barrelling down to break up a group stuck on the side cushion.

'The secondment; hopefully only a month or so?' He began to chalk his stick. 'Maybe as long as the stay-at-home orders.'

'And the pandemic?'

'Five years,' Josh answered, deadpan.

'What?' She sat heavily on the edge of the couch behind her. 'You think that long?'

'I think if you look back at the Spanish flu, we're looking at a disrupted five years. Maybe two to three really bad years at the beginning.'

'Jesus. That's depressing.' She hoped he was wrong.

'Mmm.' He bent for his shot.

Poppy watched him in silence. She was behind him on the edge of the couch as he leant forward over the table in front of her. Her eyes roved over his butt, like they were out of her control. When he finished the shot and turned around, Poppy quickly averted her eyes, but not before she saw a smirk form at the edge of Josh's lips. Fuck, totally busted.

He brushed against her as he walked past, giving her access for her next shot. 'Sorry, I blocked you.'

'Gee, thanks.' Poppy had a crack but missed her ball and potted the white in the process. Josh lined up the black easily and won the game.

'Good game.'

'Yeah, it was fun,' Poppy said honestly.

'Shall we play again, or see what's on TV?'

'Let's watch TV,' Poppy answered, thinking it was safer than continually having his butt on display.

As they were taking spots on the couch, Poppy's foot caught in the edge of a blanket, and she awkwardly fell into Josh.

'Sorry!' she exclaimed, failing as always to contain her blush.

Josh squeezed her arms and looked into her eyes. 'That's okay.' He held contact a beat longer than was necessary, before he gave her a gentle push to right her balance.

If this were *Grey's Anatomy*, Poppy thought, we'd be pashing and tearing at each other's clothes right now. She blushed again, but thankfully Josh had turned his attention toward the TV.

He pointed the remote at the TV and some crime show came on. 'How about this?'

'Sure,' Poppy said reflexively, not paying attention. She was too busy mentally chastising herself.

What are you doing? Why are you getting turned on by the devil? Seriously, what is wrong with you?

Whatever they were watching passed by in a blur.

Chapter 16

Beep, beep, beep. Poppy's pager went off for what felt like the hundredth time the next shift. It was two o'clock and Josh and Poppy were in trouble. They'd reviewed sick patient after sick patient, and had been running between the red and orange wards all night.

'Answer it. It's okay,' Josh said as he took over chest compressions on the latest patient on red ward to code before being transferred to ICU. Not that Poppy suspected they would have fared much better there. Sangeetha was the ICU Registrar on tonight and she'd told them only one in four of the COVID patients in ICU were surviving to extubation. They just didn't have any medicines making a real impact.

Current news reports were talking about a race to create an effective vaccine. Poppy didn't know how long that would take and how effective it would be, but she knew they still needed to do more in the present. Find some drug, some antiviral, that had a hope of curtailing the illness and reducing the death rate. If not, closed borders and stay-at-home orders would not be enough to limit the spread of disease and the deluge on the hospital resources.

'Stand clear to shock,' Poppy heard Sangeetha say in her soft but clear voice as she threw her gloves in the bin in the corner of the room and shuffled to the nurses' station, slathering her hands in hand sanitizer along the way.

'Hi, it's Poppy, COVID RMO,' she said when someone picked up the extension.

'It's Luke on orange. One of the patients is more breathless.'

'How are their sats?'

'Dropping. It was over ninety on four litres of oxygen. Now it's down to mid-eighties on twelve litres.'

'Okay. We've just been working a code blue on red. I'll be down as soon as I can. Which bed?'

'Twelve.'

'See you soon.' She hung up, desperate to clean her face and wipe the sticky tendril of hair that was irritating her temple.

'What's up?' Josh asked, appearing at Poppy's side.

'Someone deteriorating on orange. Did you call it in there?'

'Yeah. Time of death, 2:07am.'

Sangeetha and the nurses came into view.

'We've got another sick one on orange,' Josh informed Sangeetha.

'Great,' Sangeetha said with a deep furrow in her brow. 'I'd better get back and check on the unit before you call me again.'

'Ciao,' Josh replied, seemingly unruffled, as always.

Fuck, he's not even sweating, Poppy thought, as a rivulet ran down her back and into her underwear.

'Why don't you go down to orange and start to review the patient.' Josh sat down in front of the computer. 'You know what to do.' He nodded at her. 'Get started and I'll be down once I've typed up this arrest. You'll still have to come back here later to do the death certificate.'

She nodded back, absorbing his confidence. 'I'll see you on orange.'

Heading toward the lifts, she was relieved to be able to remove her PPE and wipe down her face at least, before she started again.

With a kidney dish full of equipment for bloods and a blood gas, she entered bed twelve on orange in fresh PPE and saw another sick patient struggling for breath. Pale, and sweat-soaked, his grey hair hung lankly.

'Hi, Mr Hooper, my name is Dr Mason. I see you're having trouble breathing.'

Gasp, gasp, 'Yes.' A loud, hacking cough followed. When he finished coughing there was a prolonged pause, and Poppy almost dropped the kidney dish, worried he wasn't going to take another breath and would code in front of her. But as she reached his side, he took a deep, guttural breath, and collapsed back on the pillow.

Luke, the nurse, came in with an observation machine. 'How are we doing in here?'

'Great. Can you please repeat his obs? His respiratory rate is all over the place.'

'Sure thing.' He wheeled the machine around to the opposite side to Poppy and began attaching the blood pressure cuff.

'Mr Hooper, I'm going to listen to your chest quickly while Luke is doing that. But just breathe as you are. Don't take deep breaths, okay?' She inserted the earpieces of the stethoscope into her ears and picked up the diaphragm to place it on the patient's chest.

Mr Hooper nodded, a small tuft of grey hair, that wasn't plastered to his forehead, bobbed in time. Poppy was thankful he didn't try to speak again. His chest sounded empty, like no air was getting in. There was the faintest of air entry in the upper zones only.

'He's barely moving air.' She removed the earpieces and lowered the stethoscope, placing it on the end of the bed as she sat and positioned a "bluey" under the patient's arm so she could take the blood samples.

Luke told her the obs while she was drawing blood. They confirmed her suspicions that Mr Hooper was teetering on the edge.

'You want me to call it in?' he asked.

'Yes, please. Thanks.' She released the tourniquet and held a square of gauze to the wound and then taped it firmly so she could move on to the blood gas. 'Okay, I've got to take some arterial blood now, and it will hurt more.'

Poppy looked at him and saw a barely perceptible movement of his eyebrows that she took for consent and moved on.

By the time Josh, and then the arrest team arrived, Poppy was stressed. Mr Hooper was sliding rapidly off the precipice, into the abyss. She'd seen this a dozen times now, and knew that if they didn't intubate him quickly, he would arrest and die. But she hadn't wanted to try intubating him on her own. Sangeetha made that call quickly, and the Anaesthetic Registrar performed it swiftly and efficiently. Thankfully, they halted his slide for now, at least.

They stabilized him briefly, then wheeled him off the ward, ICU bound. Maybe he would be one of the lucky one in four who made it, Poppy thought, as she watched the tufts of grey hair above his pillow receding from sight.

'Right. Let's go document this one,' Josh said, removing his gloves and cleaning his hands. Poppy followed along behind him, dragging her legs.

Fuck, this sucks. There's just nothing we can do for them. When are things going to get better?

'You document your steps until we got there, and then I'll take over.' He pulled out a chair and pushed it toward her.

'She took the chair and once she'd typed up her role in the arrest she passed the keyboard to Josh and pushed her chair back so he could roll over. She looked up to the board and saw a list of scut jobs, her shoulders slumping.

She pointed to the board. 'I'll get started on that.'

Maybe doing some simple scut jobs would help. It would remind her that not all the COVID patients were dying. Some of them were doing okay and making it home.

'Okay,' Josh replied with his head down, focused on what he was doing. She watched him for a minute. He seemed able to do the work and not let it get to him. Why couldn't she be like that? For the last twelve months she had felt every death like a blow and every patient that suffered some bad complication or was in a lot of pain tore at her. If things continued this way, she might not be able to survive medicine. There had to be a way to better distance herself from the suffering. She just had to find it.

Poppy was tired and hungry. A glance at her phone and she was surprised to see it was after three-thirty. This last hour had flown by. As Poppy was recharting fluids for one of the patients, her pager beeped.

'Hi, it's Poppy, COVID RMO.'

'Hi Poppy, just wondering if you can come back to red to do the death certificate? ED want to transfer someone, so we need to clean the room once we get the patient down to the morgue.'

In all the drama with Mr Hooper and her own internal angst, she'd completely forgotten about the death certificate. 'I'm sorry.' *Bad Poppy.* 'We've just finished up with a sick patient. I'll head up.'

'Thanks. That'd be great.' She hung up.

Poppy finished charting the fluids in the patient's electronic medical record and told the nurses on orange she'd come back to finish the scut work once she'd done the death certificate.

When she was almost at the donning and doffing station, she heard Josh call out, 'Wait up, Poppy!'

She noted the urgency in his voice and turned back. He had already turned away from her and was running down the ward. Josh never ran or looked stressed.

Oh no, not another one.

Poppy ran after him. Sure enough, another patient was struggling. Poppy and Josh spent the next hour or so trying to stabilise them. Luckily, they weren't as bad as Mr Hooper, and they eventually settled on non-invasive ventilation.

When Poppy removed her gloves, she noticed the three missed pages from red ward. 'Shit.'

'What?' Josh asked, stripping his gloves and squirting the hand sanitizer on his hands and rubbing them vigorously, keeping his eyes on Poppy.

'Red ward. They want me to do the death certificate. ED want to transfer someone.'

'Look, it's after five o'clock and we haven't had a single break all night. ED can wait. Tell them you'll come as soon as you can, we need a break first.'

Poppy didn't require a lot of convincing when she could barely stand up from fatigue. However, a guilty twist settled in her chest as she returned the pages.

They headed to the Residents' Lounge for a break, but Poppy felt like she was ditching school. Worried that someone would catch them out.

'Don't worry so much, Poppy.' Josh sipped his soft drink and ate his reheated leftovers, his feet crossed on the coffee table. His whole body oozed confidence and relaxation. Would that ever be her?

Poppy rolled her shoulders back and tried to let the guilt dissipate, her stomach growling in anticipation of the sandwich she'd packed. As she leant over the table to take her first bite, the muscles in her lower back spasmed uncomfortably. She sat up straight and rubbed a fist into her back whilst she chewed.

Poppy let out a long, loud sigh after she swallowed.

'You look like you've had it,' Josh said.

Did he sound concerned?

'Yeah, I feel it. How come you look so good?' She coloured as she said it. It wasn't meant to be a compliment. 'What I mean is, why don't you look exhausted, too?'

'Oh, I'm tired, but I've been down this road more times than you. My body is better prepared for it.'

'Hmph.' Poppy chewed on in silence.

When they were throwing their rubbish away, ready to head back to red ward, another page came through to Josh's pager.

'COVID Registrar.' Josh listened to the speaker on the other end, his face giving nothing away. 'We'll be right up.'

'What's up?'

'Sangeetha wants us to help out on a code on seven.'

'Non-COVID ward?' And she wants us both?' Poppy asked, thinking she really needed to get back to red ward and do the death certificate.

'Apparently.' He stood and held the door open for her.

Poppy wasn't sure why they wanted her there as well. Presumably, they already had Sangeetha, an Anaesthetics Registrar, and the non-COVID Medical Registrar. She was barely more than a glorified dog's body – how much could she really contribute?

'What about the death certificate?'

'They want us for a reason. It can wait.' His tone was firm and clear. It didn't convey annoyance, but if she pushed it further, she suspected it would.

All Poppy could think as she matched Josh's brisk pace down the corridor, was that she hoped they understood when she eventually made it to red ward.

By the time Poppy was able to extricate herself and slog up the internal stairs to red ward, it was almost 7:30am. She arrived at the donning and doffing station short of breath, sweaty, and with greasy skin. She knew she must look haggard. The nurses had just finished handover and were filing out of the tearoom.

A male nurse she didn't know clocked her with a hard stare. 'Poppy?'

'Yes?' Pulling the last glove on, she stepped around the donning station.

He stood in front of her, blocking her way, his fists on his hips. 'I want you to know that your behaviour overnight has been completely unacceptable.'

'Uh… Sorry?' Poppy stammered, as the other nurses stopped in their tracks and turned back to watch the action.

'We have been waiting for you to do the death certificate for bed six since two o'clock.' His fists were still pressed firmly into his hips and Poppy wondered if he was going to stamp his foot. If he wasn't so angry and she wasn't so knackered, it might be comical.

'Yes, I know—'

'You need to prioritise your time better.' He was leaning forward now and if he hadn't been wearing a mask and face shield, his spit might have been flying.

Poppy took a step back, her leg hitting the metal trolley that held all the PPE. Raising her hands, she tried again to explain. 'But—'

'In the end, ED had to send up one of their Residents to do it, to make way for the patient in ED to be transferred.' He was still leaning toward her. If he had been a bigger man, it would be really threatening.

Hands still raised, she had to fight the urge to push him away from her. She swallowed and reminded herself that none of this was her fault. 'I'm sorry, but—'

'I'm not interested in excuses. You should know I will be making a complaint to your director of training.' He turned around and stormed off, his shoes squeaking on the linoleum flooring.

Poppy dropped her hands. Great, the last thing she wanted was to give Dr Anderson more ammunition against her. The nurse entered the NUM's office and closed the door forcefully. Despite her misery, Poppy wondered where Susan was.

Handover would start soon, but she couldn't stand around here, not after that dressing down. She made it one flight down the internal stairs then collapsed and started crying. Initially, she tried to contain it to quiet shudders, but the exhaustion and stress of the night caught up with her, and it quickly deteriorated into body-wracking sobs and messy snot. In her rush to leave the ward, she had forgotten to remove her PPE, and so now she discarded her snotty mask and moist face shield.

Footsteps sounded from below, and Poppy hurriedly swiped at her eyes and nose.

'Poppy?' Josh asked, coming around the corner onto the landing. 'Why are you in... Wait, what's the matter?'

'It's nothing,' Poppy stood up and turned quickly to start back up the stairs so Josh couldn't see her blotchy face.

'It's not nothing.' Josh put a hand on her shoulder, encouraging her to turn and face him again. 'What's happened?' he asked gently.

Poppy took a deep, shuddering breath, and explained her interaction with the nurse on red ward, her eyes barely meeting Josh's. She knew she wouldn't be able to hold herself together if she saw compassion in his eyes.

Josh's eyes narrowed above his mask and then he was making his way up the stairs.

'Wait, Josh, what are you going to do?' Poppy asked, suddenly even more nervous. In the past, she'd been on the receiving end of Josh's disdain and wasn't sure pissing off this nurse would improve her situation. Her jelly legs slowly followed his up the stairs.

Poppy caught up to him as he finished donning his PPE and tried again to deter him.

'Wait, Josh—'

'No,' he said, without turning around. He strode straight towards the NUM's office. Without knocking, he threw open the door.

'Is this him?' he asked Poppy, who was a few steps behind, dragging a new set of gloves over her sweaty hands with difficulty.

'Yes,' she replied faintly then dropped her eyes to the floor, scared to watch what happened next.

'Right. Now you listen to me, seeing as you didn't listen to *Dr* Mason,' Josh started, through gritted teeth. 'How dare you threaten and intimidate my Resident. Dr Mason has done nothing wrong. Nothing.'

His voice was steady and firm but not raised. Poppy relaxed enough to lift her eyes.

'All night we have raced from one sick or dying patient to another. We have not been sitting on our arses. We have been saving lives. And you have the audacity to suggest a death certificate is more important than preventing another patient from dying?'

The nurse looked from her to Josh. 'Well—'

Josh didn't step any closer but spoke over him. 'Maybe it's been so long since you had a clinical role that you've forgotten how to triage, and that the first rule is to treat the sickest, and those who can be saved first. We can't help those who are already dead, so we've been prioritising the living all night.' Josh stopped and stared down at him, still seated behind the desk. The nurse appeared to shrink in the chair.

'Well, what do you have to say to defend your appalling behaviour toward my Resident?' Poppy could almost hear Josh's teeth gnashing as he clenched them together, waiting for a response.

'I didn't know.' The nurse's voice was small, no longer the forceful presence he'd been with Poppy.

'Because you never gave her the chance to explain. You just tore strips off her.'

'Yes,' he mumbled.

'I think Dr Mason deserves an apology,' Josh demanded, still not raising his voice. Poppy's eyes widened at the demand of an apology.

'I'm sorry,' he said, briefly meeting Poppy's eyes.

Poppy nodded. She didn't trust herself to speak. This whole encounter had a weird, almost out-of-body feel to it. Josh defending her and demanding an apology was not something she would have imagined happening a few days ago. Right now, she just wanted to get handover done, go home, and collapse into bed. Her entire body felt both depleted and completely on edge.

'Well, maybe next time you could remember we are all just trying to do our best in what is a pretty fucked up situation.'

Poppy couldn't believe Josh had just sworn at a NUM. He was many things, but professional would have been high on the list.

The nurse raised his head and met their gazes squarely. 'You're right.'

'Okay, then,' Josh finished, turning around again.

At the doffing station Poppy stopped him, touching his back briefly. 'Thank you.'

She wanted to say more. To thank him for standing up for her and making the NUM realise what they'd been up against that night. But she couldn't. Something shifted inside her. The fear and distrust had suddenly gone, like it had evaporated with his act of kindness. Its absence created a new space, where questions were forming. Currently shapeless and hazy. She wasn't ready to prod them and find out what they meant.

'That's okay. I may have overdone it, but I can't stand it when people bully the juniors.'

Poppy had to bite her lip before she began laughing. The exhaustion had her on the tip of hysteria. Josh was definitely more complex than she had previously allowed for. He had previously been a real bully with her and other junior doctors. Did he not see that in himself? Or maybe, like everyone else, he could be mean when he, too, was stretched and out of his depth. Maybe it was a protective mechanism? These were things she now wanted to understand about him. But it wasn't the time. They needed to get handover done and they both needed rest.

Chapter 17

Back out in the bright sunlight, Poppy shielded her sore eyes to look up into Josh's face. Desperate to get home to bed, Poppy was about to say goodbye when he spoke.

'Right-o. I know you want to go to sleep more than anything else right now—'

'Yes, I do.' Was he about to suggest something else? There was no way she was going to agree to anything.

'But. If you do that, you'll wake up feeling even worse. Trust me.' He leaned toward her, but not in a threatening way. 'Here.' He placed his sunglasses over her ears. Because her body was strung out from exhaustion, her face tingled at the slightest touch and this gesture was suddenly intimate. 'Let's go get breakfast and sit in the sun for a bit, at least. You need to merge with daylight again.'

It wasn't just her face that tingled when he'd touched her, everything about her body was tingling. Her legs, her back, her head. Everything overly sensitive from the lack of rest. She wanted nothing more than to cocoon herself in the softness of her sheets and sleep until her body felt normal again.

'Come on. You know I'm right. You've got to stay up for a while, otherwise it'll hurt that much more later.' He bent down, trying to get her to meet his gaze.

'I'm not promising much. But I do need breakfast,' she relented.

'That's a start.'

They trudged up the street slowly. Poppy kept Josh's shades on. It helped reduce some of the sensitivity to the light. Besides, he didn't seem to be in a rush to get them back. At least the streets were quiet. They didn't have to jostle for space on the footpath, or shout to hear each other talk. Most of the cafes had "closed" signs in their windows, but a few were selling takeaway meals. Poppy was tempted to get pancakes drenched in syrup but decided it would be too difficult to manage in a takeaway container. She settled on a bacon and egg roll and a very large coffee.

Like everywhere else, the park was deserted when they sat at a bench to eat their breakfasts. They ate mostly in silence. Poppy didn't have the energy for conversation. She wondered if Josh felt the same. On the few stolen glances she took while eating, he seemed peaceful, staring off down the park, one hand on his coffee cup and one on his roll. He appeared to alternate bites and sips with ease, no drips of sauce bothering his lips or landing on his shirt. By contrast, Poppy hunkered over her roll, determined not to get sauce stains on her clothes. She used two hands and left her coffee cooling at her feet.

Like a lot of things about the last three night shifts, Poppy hadn't been expecting this. This comfortable silence. The apprehension she'd been carrying around her like a cloak had lifted. She didn't know what they were to each other and whether they'd ever be friends, but she no longer distrusted him. That, in itself, was a big step forward.

Crumpling up her paper bag, she turned to face Josh. 'You were right. I needed that.'

He was looking at her, waiting. What more was he expecting? Then his lips twitched and he pointed at her face.

Duh. She laughed as she removed the sunglasses and passed them back to him. 'And thank you for those.'

'You're welcome,' he said, putting them on and standing up. 'What are you going to do now?'

'I have no idea.'

He sipped his coffee, his expression unreadable behind the glasses. But he didn't seem to be in a hurry to leave her or to add anything further.

'And thanks. Last night was hell. But at least we were in it together.' She dropped her head to her coffee cup, examining its rim, suddenly conscious of their proximity and that she too wasn't in a rush to leave. That awareness left her feeling uneasy. Like somehow it was unfair to Will in some way.

When she looked up again, he was still watching her behind his shades. Now the silence was awkward. Was he waiting for her to say more?

Just as she was about to say goodbye, he finally spoke.

'Nights are the pits, and COVID Nights hit a new low. But I'm glad we were in it together, too.' He tilted his head slightly to the side then said, 'I'll see you around, Poppy.'

Poppy was left watching him walk further down the path away from her, more questions starting to rise from within.

The first thing she wanted to do when she reached her empty apartment was get into the shower and scrub her skin free of sweat and dirt of the last twelve or more hours. She'd been too exhausted to shower at the hospital when she changed out of scrubs. Unsure if it would worsen or ease the hypersensitivity, she tilted her face to the shower rose, allowing the water to pound her skin. Initially every drop felt like a heated needle, but eventually it eased and became more pleasurable. When she finally felt clean and her legs were so weak she was sure they couldn't hold her up for much longer, she turned off the taps and wrapped herself in her soft towel. She knew sleep was tugging at her and would soon engulf her, so she got straight into summer pj's and closed her thick curtains. There was no energy left to call Will, she'd have to do it later. Her eyes closed instantly when she rested her head on her pillow, her fan on low humming in the background, her mind already powering down.

The room was hot when she woke discombobulated a few hours later. She wasn't sure if it was night or day or even where she was. At first, she thought she might be in the on-call room or the Residents' Lounge. It was the humming fan that ultimately brought her room into focus. Her body was less tingly than it had been before her sleep but now a headache had taken hold and her throat was dry. Legs and back ached in protest when she moved to sit up. She hadn't had the capacity to put a glass of water by her bed, so she was forced to get up. Once she'd skulled a full glass of water at the kitchen sink she decided she was now awake enough to try and stay up for the rest of the day.

What do you do to fill your day when the city was in lockdown? Normally, she would swim laps at the local pool, but it was shut. A surf at the beach was also out as it would breach the 5km rule of the stay-at-home orders. It would have to be a walk. Poppy changed into exercise gear and laced up her sneakers. Scraping her hair up with her fingers, she tied it into a ponytail and went back to her room for a hat before heading out the door.

Pounding the empty pavements, she looked through the darkened windows of the closed stores. Airpods in her ears, she'd been listening to *Medicine* by Robinson and the Romantics, but decided to call Will, on the off chance he might have time to talk.

'Hi, beautiful, I've been wondering if you were okay.'

Poppy was hit by a wave of guilt. She could have messaged to say she was too tired to talk before going to bed. 'I'm sorry I didn't call. I was just wrecked.'

'I was getting worried.'

'I'm okay, I promise.' Peering into the unlit shop window in front of her, all she could see was herself. It was a faded version, though, like an old toy that had seen better days. It unnerved her and she turned away from it to continue her walk.

After a pause, Will said, 'So, how was the last couple of shifts?'

Poppy's body suddenly felt heavier as she thought back. 'Last night was horrid.' Her pace slowed and each step forward was like a step back into the shift.

'Why? What happened?' She could hear the anxiety slip into his voice.

'It was never-ending death and codes. I think it was my worst shift ever.'

'I'm so sorry, babe, that's awful.'

'Yeah.' She could hear her feet hitting the pavement and someone talking in the background at Will's end. 'At the end, the NUM on red ward yelled at me in front of everyone for not coming to do a death certificate earlier. Can you believe that?' Her voice rising as she remembered how he wouldn't let her speak to explain and just how hopeless and wrecked she had felt at the time.

'I've been there before.'

His answer surprised her. 'Really?'

'Once when I was an intern on nights, I was busy reviewing patients and couldn't get back to do a death certificate for a few hours, and I got raked over the coals.'

'That's exactly what happened to me.' She'd stopped walking without noticing.

'I think it happens quite often. And it's always because ED is backed up and want to offload an admission.'

'Anyway, Josh had a go at the NUM, and he ended up apologising.' Poppy started walking again. When silence filled her ears, Poppy continued, trying to minimise Will's reaction. 'But get this. Josh said he doesn't like it when people bully the juniors.'

'That guy is deluded. He is one of the worst offenders.'

Poppy suddenly felt sick. Guilt grabbed hold of her stomach and squeezed. 'Right?' Her voice caught at the end, knowing this was not fair to Josh. Keen to quickly move off the topic of Josh, she stood up straight, her voice steadier as she said, 'I'm so glad nights are over, and I can go back to normal shifts again.'

'You're happy about working with Olivia again?'

Poppy snorted, looking over her shoulder despite knowing no one was there. 'I wouldn't go that far... What have they got you doing today?'

'ICU. But there's only three patients, so not much to do.'

Poppy pictured him leaning back in his chair. 'You must be bored.'

'Bored stiff. I've been watching a surf comp on my phone.'

'Where?' Her thoughts veered off onto a sidetrack as she wondered what Josh was doing now. He was the only other person not working that she knew of. He was probably playing video games.

'Hawaii.'

'Wait.' Her brain caught back up. 'Is it live or a replay?'

'No, it's live.'

'How can they be doing that with COVID happening? The numbers in the US are going crazy.' This was wrong. How could they be running a surf comp, potentially exposing all those people to COVID? Surely, there would be restrictions in place.

'No idea. But at least it's keeping me entertained.'

Poppy understood that he was bored. But this was not right. Despite all the restrictions in place in Sydney, things were bad, people were dying. His attitude was more blasé than it had been previously. He'd been shocked about the locals not really understanding what a momentous event this was, and now he was nonchalant about a surfing comp. Maybe, she was just overthinking things. She was worn out and sleep-deprived, after all.

To change the subject, she made a decision to tell Will about Gemma and Lucas' likely engagement.

His voice brightened. 'That's great news.'

This was definitely a safer topic. 'It is. Gemma will be so happy. And her family can finally get off her back.' Poppy pressed the pedestrian call button then realised how dumb that was when there were barely any cars on the street. She checked in both directions and then stepped off the curb and crossed the street.

'Until they start pressuring them for grandchildren.'

'You are totally right,' she laughed. 'They will, won't they?'

'Afraid so.'

'Obviously, you can't say anything, not that you would, of course, but I've been thinking about it and I'm going to have to move out.'

'Probably. They'll want their own space.'

'Yeah.' Poppy wondered if Will would suggest they find their own place and both move out of their share arrangements. But he said nothing. There was a growing silence, the sound of Poppy's feet on the pavement the only noise.

There were muffled sounds of someone else at Will's end.

'Listen, I've got to go. I'll call you later, okay?'

He ended the call before Poppy could even say goodbye.

Her stomach had dropped in the prolonged silence, and now Poppy dragged her feet to a nearby bus stop. She sat on the bench and wondered why Will had not suggested they move in together.

Is he not that serious about me?

Then she caught herself. Don't be paranoid, she chastised. It was probably just a shock and he needs time to process it first. Still, maybe the ground beneath her feet was not as solid as she thought.

A sudden deep horn honked near her ear, startling her. Poppy turned to see a bus had pulled up next to her and the driver was motioning at her.

'Sorry,' Poppy shook her head and waved in apology, then stood up and resumed walking.

After a few more minutes lost in thought, she raised her head from the pavement and took in her surroundings to find herself all the way down at Broadway. She'd walked all through Newtown, passed Sydney University, and down to the large shopping precinct. It really felt like a ghost town. Not many cars on the roads, and none of the usual hustle and bustle from streams of people. Poppy hadn't encountered a single person, not unless you count the bus driver, who didn't even open the door. *Wow, it's like an apocalypse movie.*

Poppy double-checked there were no cars, then walked into the middle of what should have been a very busy intersection. She took several photos on her phone and then started the walk back home, stopping on the way at the closed pool in Victoria Park. The sign out front just read, "Closed until further notice." Poppy sighed, then messaged a couple of the pictures to her mum.

'Darling, is that Broadway?' Her mother asked as soon as Poppy accepted her call.

'Yes. Can you believe it?'

'I'm shocked. I mean, I've been keeping up with the news, and obviously talking with you, but those pictures are so confronting.'

'I know. It's like a movie set without a movie.'

'Or a ghost town.'

'I was standing in the middle of Parramatta Road when I took those, and there wasn't a single car or bus around.'

'I'll have to show your father when he gets home from work. He won't believe it either.'

After her mum got over the reality of Sydney in lockdown, Poppy filled her in on Gemma and Lucas' pending engagement and her discussion with Will.

'You can't read anything into that,' her mum said immediately.

'You don't think it means he doesn't want to move in together?' Poppy asked, her voice cracking at the end and making her feel like a little girl again, needing reassurance from her mum when she was left out of a group activity, or a boy she liked hadn't called the day after they'd kissed.

'Not at all. It probably hasn't even crossed his mind yet that it's a possibility. If you didn't ask him, he probably thinks you're not ready for it. Especially after you got cold feet at the beach at the beginning.'

'Mum, you know we've moved past that.'

'I know you have, darling, on the surface.' Her voice was gentler now. 'But it might have left a scar for him, is all I'm saying.'

There was silence as Poppy contemplated her mum's words. When Will had asked her if she was all in that day at the beach when she rode her first proper wave, she had hesitated. It's not that she hadn't wanted to commit to a serious relationship for the first time in her life, more that she was terrified of her heart breaking if it didn't work out. After Lulu's death, Poppy hit rock bottom. She barely got out of bed or ate for the first few months, and almost flunked out of uni. It was Gemma and Lucas who got her out of that bleak time and got her through the year at uni. But Will saw the hesitation and reacted like he'd been slapped. They were on shaky ground at the time and Poppy could see it might all slip through her fingers like the sand on the beach. As Will pulled away from her, saying, "Okay, I get the message," her frozen body finally reacted, and a guttural, "No" escaped her lips. She flung her body at his, grabbing him fiercely. She'd repeated over and over again, "No, don't go. I want this too."

Eventually, when her tears had soaked into his hair and neck, he'd turned and admitted he was scared too. But he thought she was worth the risk. They'd kissed and that longstanding fear inside Poppy shifted.

Recalling it now, Poppy had to admit to her mother. 'Maybe you're right.' Maybe her hesitation that day had left a wound. Poppy had thought it healed by now, but maybe not.

Besides, they were currently in separate cities and Lucas hadn't even proposed yet. There was plenty of time to work out where they both stood. Her pace picked up when she finished the call, her throat suddenly dry.

Finally, Poppy had company when first Lucas, and then Gemma, returned from work.

'Oh my God, Olivia is just vile,' Gemma complained after walking through the door and flinging her bag on a dining chair.

Poppy turned from the couch. 'Why, what did she do?'

Lucas turned from the stove where he was making a start on dinner.

'Well, it's pretty much like you've been saying these past few weeks. She just doesn't do the work. She does a round then buggers off, not contactable. So, I called her on it.'

Surprised, Poppy asked, 'You did?'

Over Gemma's head, she could see Lucas's brows knit together in worry.

After Gemma kissed Lucas on the top of his head, she continued. 'At the end of the round when she was listing all the jobs that needed doing, I simply said, "Which ones are you going to do?" and stared at her, waiting for a response.'

Poppy was practically hanging over the edge of the couch now, eager to hear how this boldness played out. 'What did she say?'

Affecting a snooty tone, she said, '"These are all your jobs, Gemma." So, I asked her what she would be doing whilst I was doing all of these jobs, and she said, "That's really not your business, you just need to do the work you are being paid for." And she strode off the ward.'

Poppy could picture it clearly in her mind. Gemma had nailed the snooty voice, too.

'I didn't see her again, until just before the evening handover,' Gemma continued. 'Where she proceeded to give handover like she'd been busy taking care of the patients all day. She didn't even acknowledge or check in with me. Which blew back in her face when she suggested one of the patients was stable and would be discharged tomorrow.'

'And they weren't stable?'

'No, they'd developed a likely UTI, and I'd started them on antibiotics – which I pointed out to the group – but of course she had a go at me for not informing her of this change.'

Poppy grimaced.

'But I just bit back and said I would have told her if she'd been around to tell.'

'How'd she take that?' Lucas hovered at Gemma's shoulder, his face a picture of tension.

'Not well. She said, "Gemma, I think you need to remember that you are the most junior member of the team, and as such you need to keep your Registrar informed of any changes to a patient's clinical status."'

'Please tell me you stopped antagonising her at this point?' Lucas pleaded, scraping his hand through his hair.

'Where would be the fun in that? No, I suggested that she look up the definition of "team" first. But you'll be glad to hear Maria jumped in before it could really degenerate.'

Poppy was in awe of her friend's ballsiness. If only she was that brave, she might not have needed Josh to rescue her with the male nurse that morning. Poppy probably wouldn't have pushed as hard as Gemma had with Olivia, but she could have made him listen to the events of the night instead of allowing him to continue to yell at her in front of everyone.

'You need to be careful, hon, having a knock-down, drag-out fight with a Registrar is not smart,' Lucas said.

Gemma's gaze became steely and Poppy wished she could now be invisible.

'It was barely a tiff, and frankly, I don't care about Olivia. She is a lazy, spineless cow, who gets off on pushing other people around. She has no bearing on my future.'

Lucas' jaw ticked. 'You don't know that.' He matched her steeliness. 'It's never smart to burn bridges. Medicine is a very small world. You never know who knows who, and you don't want a rumour starting that you're difficult to work with. Even if it's not from the surgeons.'

Poppy slunk lower into the couch, trying to make herself as small as possible.

'You're over-reacting, Luc.' Gemma walked out of the kitchen and collected her bag.

Lucas followed, his voice rising. 'Am I? You need to be more careful, is all I'm saying.'

Gemma stopped in her tracks and turned back to him. Whatever expression she saw on his face softened her. She reached out to take his hand. 'Okay, hon. I'll try to hold my tongue.'

'Thank you,' Luc said into her neck as they hugged.

Luc was right that Gemma had pushed things too far before and had been reprimanded. He was obviously just worried for her, but equally, Poppy was proud of her bravery. She was so wound up in her own anxiety and need to please people and make a good impression; she would never stand up for herself like that. Gemma wasn't hamstrung by the same fears.

Before Gemma went off to their room, Poppy asked. 'Hey, where's Susan this week? There was some nasty acting NUM when I finished this morning.'

'Oh, yeah, Martin, he's a dick. He's come from one of the closed surgical wards. Susan has COVID.'

'Is she okay?' Poppy's heart started racing. Maybe their precautions weren't enough.

'Terry said she's fine. She's had a high fever and a mild cough but nothing more serious at this stage.'

Not sure if she wanted to know the answer, she asked. 'Do they think she got it on the ward? She's not really clinical.'

'No, apparently, from a relative.'

'Oh, that's good. I guess it means we're doing well with the hygiene on the ward.'

Gemma sat next to her and patted her thigh. 'It does.'

'I hope she feels better soon, though. It's pretty scary. She's the first person I know who has it.'

'Me too. But they're going to make her stay off work for a full fourteen days.'

'That long?' Her friend was so nonchalant about all this. For someone who was seriously complaining about potential exposure to COVID only a few days earlier, she was now pretty unconcerned.

'They're still not sure on the incubation period, so it fits with what they're now requiring for all travellers arriving into the country – a fourteen-day quarantine.'

Poppy hadn't seen any news for a few days and wasn't aware of this change. 'That's going to be tough. How are they going to enforce it?'

Lucas walked over and sat on the other couch. 'It was on the news last night. They're setting up quarantine hotels with security guards.'

Poppy's mouth gaped. 'That sounds a bit like prison.'

'I think that's probably how it would feel. They're also upping the police presence out and about, checking whether people have valid reasons to be driving, and making sure they are obeying the 5km radius rule.'

'Gosh. You go on nights for a few days and the whole world changes.'

The other two nodded, each lost in thought. Poppy wondered how non-health care workers felt about all these rules. Did they understand why the government was making these restrictions?

It was hard to know what to say. Not only were things changing rapidly in the hospital, but every day there were new rules and regulations outside of it. Poppy couldn't keep up. Sydney now felt like a police state. Whilst there wasn't an evening curfew yet, the government had instituted multiple conditions on the population's civil liberties, at least in Sydney and Melbourne. The other states, where COVID case numbers remained low to negligible, had yet to follow such drastic measures, but Poppy suspected that would change too in the coming weeks to months.

Poppy wondered, would all these changes cause chaos and lead to people acting out against the government? Or would they trust the government was acting in their best interests? And what about people in nursing homes or those with disabilities? Were they still being allowed to see their relatives, loved ones, or carers? If not, was keeping them isolated really helping them, or could it be hurting them?

Chapter 18

After a very boring few days at home, with little to do, and no one really to talk to, Poppy was almost looking forward to returning to work on Thursday. Even if it meant working with Olivia again. She was also keen to see Alex and Maria, as the last few weeks had been very dislocating. Once she'd changed into scrubs, she went straight to the little conference room where they'd had their early Monday morning meetings. It was now the COVID handover room to avoid multiple donning/doffing of PPE for the staff coming onto shift.

'Hi, Alex,' Poppy said enthusiastically as she made her way over to him. The chairs were all set up in a circle but spaced 1.5 metres apart. They didn't need to wear full PPE in here but were still required to wear masks. Poppy sat down in the seat next to his.

Swapping his crossed legs and angling towards her, he said, 'How are you? How was nights?'

'Pretty busy and depressing. When do you do them?'

'I think the end of next week, then again a few weeks later.'

'Yeah, I saw they revised the shifts again. It's doing my head in, all these changes.' Poppy slumped in the chair. 'And there's still no clear end date to the term.'

Alex nodded, his head which had been high when she first came in, now dropping. It reminded Poppy of a cut flower slowly drooping on its stem in a vase. 'I know. It's starting to look bleak.'

'But Maria's still around, right?' Poppy hoped she hadn't got COVID or been reallocated.

He perked up a bit at the question. 'No, she's still here. I don't know how I would have coped if I didn't have Maria.'

Poppy didn't dare imagine what it could have been like if he had been partnered with Olivia. She almost shuddered.

Alex turned his attention back to Poppy. 'Did you see they moved the on-call to a week about? Prof Pilson, is on this week.'

Poppy shook her head. 'Have you seen him?'

'Who, Prof?' Alex looked confused.

'Yeah. I mean, I don't think I've seen him since the very beginning of term, before all the COVID cases started coming.'

Alex's head bobbed. 'No, I don't think I have either.'

Poppy looked around, but Olivia still had not arrived. Maria walked in the door looking more flustered than Poppy had ever seen her before. 'Maria, are you okay?' she asked.

Maria walked straight to where Alex and Poppy were sitting. 'Hi Poppy. Actually, I've got some bad news for you.'

Poppy's stomach dropped. What could it be now? Maybe they were going to send her home and she'd have to come back tonight to do more night shifts. Before Poppy could think of other disastrous revelations, Maria spoke.

'Olivia just called in sick with COVID.'

In some ways, that was actually a relief. Her stomach relaxed and her voice brightened. 'Do you know if she's okay?'

'Well, she said she's lost her taste and smell and has a mild cough, but not much else in the way of symptoms.'

'That's good, at least.' Would it be uncharitable for Poppy to wish her symptoms were worse? Not so bad that she ended up in hospital, but bad enough that she might have a more empathetic outlook on their patients in the future.

'Did she say where she thought she got it?'

'I didn't ask.' Before Poppy could respond, Maria continued. 'So, she'll be off for fourteen days. I was just on the phone with Melissa O'Brien in the training unit, but it sounds like there's a real shortage of relief staff, so there is no one who can fill in this week. I've spoken with Prof Pilson, and he's going to ask Adnan, the Fellow, to assist you on the ward this week.'

'That should be fine. I guess he'll swing by later today?' She'd not spent any time with Adnan so far, but surely he'd be more engaged and helpful than Olivia.

Maria picked up her phone, her head bent forwards towards the screen. 'I assume so. But I'll pass on any other info as it comes in. And I'll share both his and Prof Pilson's numbers so you can contact them directly if you need to.'

Poppy's phone dinged with the incoming shared contacts. 'Thanks, Maria.'

'And don't forget, you can call me too, if you need.'

'Thanks, I appreciate that. Do you know if Prof is coming to handover, or for a round at some stage today?' Poppy wanted to cross her fingers. Hopefully, now Prof Pilson would come in to support her.

Maria's attention was back facing the front of the room where the Night Registrar had taken the centre chair. Without making eye contact again, Maria said, 'He didn't mention it, sorry.'

Handover started and conversation stopped. Poppy took notes, but felt a growing sense of unease building, making it difficult to concentrate. What if Prof didn't come in and Adnan was even less enthusiastic than Olivia? Nights had been bad enough, but at least she'd had Josh, who despite his faults, was a damn good Registrar. If she had to do it all on her own, could she? Or would she fail spectacularly?

Once handover finished, Poppy donned her PPE and headed into the ward. She printed an up-to-date patient list, separated into red and orange wards, and transferred some tasks onto the new list, before texting Adnan.

Hi, it's Poppy. I understand you're covering while Olivia is sick. We've just finished handover, are you coming to do a round, or should I get started?

While she was waiting for a text back, she grabbed a COW as well as a couple of kidney dishes of equipment for cannulas, thinking she'd do them as she went, to keep the efficiency up.

After a few minutes of dawdling and talking to the nurses whilst she waited for a text back, she decided she had better just get on with it. Poppy started at the bottom of the ward, checking in with each patient on her list, examining them briefly, typing up notes, charting medications as required, and re-siting cannulas. By the time she got to the other end of the red ward, two hours had elapsed. Thankfully, the patients were all stable, but Poppy still had no reply from Adnan.

I wonder why he hasn't texted back? Clinics are shut, so it's not like he's busy seeing patients. Should I call Prof Pilson?

Poppy decided she'd complete her ward round on the orange ward, and if Adnan hadn't gotten back to her by then, she would call him. She was lucky again, that the patients were all stable on orange ward and she completed the round in an hour. Before calling Adnan, Poppy checked if any of the blood results or COVID tests were back yet. That way she would have all the information at her fingertips when she spoke with him.

The ringtone rang and rang and rang, not even diverting to message bank before it rang out. That's odd, Poppy thought. A cold chill dashed up her spine and into her scalp. She sat and stared at her list whilst the hairs on her neck continued their pilomotor reflex.

There must be a good reason. She resolved to wait a couple of minutes and then try again.

Poppy doodled a flower on the edge of her list and let her mind wander. She thought about Will and moving in with him, and when she should bring it up again. And she thought about Gemma and Lucas and how happy she was that Lucas was finally ready to marry Gemma. She couldn't wait to talk to Gemma about it and knew that the waiting was going to get tougher as time seemed to be moving at a snail's pace. Long work shifts and little to do outside of work with no clear end to the lockdown meant that it might be weeks or even months before Lucas could actually buy the ring and ask Gemma to marry him. It might be the longest secret that Poppy had ever been expected to keep, and one of the most important. She wasn't sure if she could. Especially now that there was this uncertainty about moving in with Will. Poppy really needed to talk to Gemma about it, and she couldn't do that until the engagement was official. Gemma could always be relied on to give sensible and no-frills advice. What would she say in this situation? Would she say the same as her mother – that Poppy needed to make the first step in suggesting they move in together? Or would she say that it suggested Will was not on the same page? Arghh, what was she going to do?

Her pager started its annoying buzzing, breaking her thought spiral. Her guts clenched in anticipation. Adnan had still not texted back, so she was on her own for now at least.

'Hi, it's Poppy, COVID Resident.'

'Hi, it's Seb in ED,' a familiar voice, rich and smooth, greeted her.

Poppy couldn't help the smile that somehow broke through her underlying anxiety. 'Seb, how are you?' It had been too long since they had last connected.

'I'm good, Poppy, how about you?'

She thought for a moment but answered honestly. 'It is a weird reality that we are in, but I am doing okay.'

'I'm glad to hear that.' His tone was still warm, but Poppy could tell there was underlying tension. 'Listen, I can't get a hold of Adnan and he's listed as on-call for COVID today.'

The gut-clenching returned. 'Oh. I haven't been able to get a hold of him either.'

'We've got two suspected COVID patients down here who need to be admitted. Can you come and see them?'

'Me?' Was she squeaking now?

'I don't think there is anyone else.' Before she could protest, he hurried on. 'Look, they're pretty straightforward. Neither of them are in respiratory failure, but the PCR's won't be back until tomorrow, and they need to come in. I've already given both a shot of dexamethasone and started remdesivir, so there's not really anything to add.'

Poppy tried not to sigh out loud, resigned to the fact that she had no choice, despite it not normally being a Resident's job to admit new cases from ED. 'I'll come right down. Where's your donning and doffing station, if coming from the ward?' Her foot subconsciously tapped up and down under the desk she was seated at.

'It's beside the staff lifts next to the staff entry at the back. See you soon.' He hung up before Poppy could say goodbye.

Sweat had already begun prickling her scalp. She had never seen a consult on her own before. Most of the time the Registrars did it by themselves, and only occasionally had she gone with them. And two probable COVID patients? She'd have to ring Prof Pilson directly to admit them. She hadn't even seen him for weeks, what if she made a complete arse of herself? She decided she would call Adnan one more time before heading down to ED. But the call rang out again.

Where the hell is he?

Poppy contemplated calling Maria to ask what she should do but figured Seb needed things sorted out quickly. At least she trusted Seb. He had finished his training in ED last year and was now a Consultant, so she knew her role was largely superfluous and that gave her some comfort.

Her feet guided her to the donning and doffing station, exactly where Seb said it would be, even though her mind was split between the fear of making a fool of herself and rising anger toward Adnan. As she put on her PPE, she ran through what she should do with each patient in her mind.

Number one: re-take history and perform examination.

She couldn't just rely on Seb's word, despite her faith in him.

Number two: check results and what medications have been charted.

Poppy took two deep breaths.

Number three: call Prof.

She took a final deep breath, elbowed the button to open the doors, and headed into "the snake pit".

A lingering sense of déjà vu overcame her as she walked down the acute beds section. Her ED term at the very beginning of her internship last year really had been a baptism of fire. She'd participated in some pretty intense resuscitations, most of which had been unsuccessful, she'd met both Will and Josh for the first time here and started a crusade to improve the conditions for the junior medical staff. With COVID now raging, those initial changes were slumping backwards. It would probably suit Dr Anderson, who could pretend she'd put her full support behind it, but that the climate had not been ready to institute sweeping changes.

Seb came toward her, down from the flight deck which was now rimmed with Perspex and had doors to enter and exit by. 'Thanks for coming.'

'Hi Seb, great to see you again.' Despite the full PPE, Poppy could see he looked tired and Poppy wondered for how the conditions in ED may have changed with COVID. It had always had such a team feel, but with PPE and social distancing, that might have been lost.

He nodded and his body remained tense. 'Sorry you've had to come down. The two patients are in resus one and two. Here's a COW for you to use. Just keep it outside the resus bays, though, okay?'

Poppy's eyes widened. 'When did you get computers on wheels?' Whilst they had become commonplace on most of the wards, the ED had never had any.

'As soon as COVID struck, there was *finally* enough money to justify the expense.'

Poppy folded her arms across her chest. 'Hmph, more like enough motivation.'

'Exactly. Anyway, sing out if you need anything. Just wave through the glass and I'll come out.' He was already turning away from her.

'Cheers,' she said to his retreating back. There were some other staff she could see in the flight deck but with all the PPE, she wasn't able to recognise anyone.

Poppy quickly looked at the notes and results on the patient in resus one and then headed in to see them. Her heavy steps beating a rhythm in time with her thumping heart. This patient was a man in his sixties with a background of ischaemic heart disease and diabetes. He was overweight and mildly short of breath but managing well on supplemental oxygen. He even offered Poppy a weak smile when she entered, his lips quirking upward on one side. The goofiness of it in the situation reduced some of Poppy's own anxiety. If the patient could put on a brave face, so could she.

Clasping her gloved hands in front of her, she approached the bed. 'Mr Johnson, I'm Dr Mason, one of the doctors from the Respiratory team. Can you tell me about why you've come to hospital?'

Mr Johnson told Poppy about how he had been working in his convenience store last night and then started to feel feverish.

'So, I rang my guy who does the night shift and asked if he could start a little earlier so I could go home to bed.' He grabbed onto the side rail and leaned forward to cough. Once that settled, he resumed. 'But the fever got worse, and I had a terrible headache and started coughing. But dry, no phlegm. My wife started to worry this morning and called an ambulance.'

Poppy nodded. 'Before yesterday afternoon, were you completely well?'

'Yeah. Just working as normal. It hit me suddenly around six o'clock.' He wiped a hand across his forehead where his sweat had accumulated.

Poppy then took a more detailed medical history and listened to his chest. She'd already seen that the chest X-ray on admission didn't look too bad and his blood gas had confirmed what Seb had told her; that he wasn't in respiratory failure. Definitely straightforward.

She stood back and wrapped the stethoscope over the obs machine. 'Mr Johnson. We're going to take you up to the ward in a bit.'

He grabbed the handrail and leaned toward Poppy, his expression serious. 'Am I going to die, doc?'

Poppy paused. Was he? She had no idea. She'd seen COVID patients look stable one minute and the next they could be either intubated and ventilated, or dead. She didn't want to lie to him, but she didn't want him to panic either.

'At the moment, your lungs are coping with the infection. The ED staff have given you a steroid medication to try to reduce any inflammation in your lungs, and hopefully that will help too. But the next forty-eight hours will be critical.'

'So, I could die?' Poppy could see the panic in his eyes and shifted her weight between her legs.

'We're going to take really good care of you, Mr Johnson. Try not to panic.' Poppy smiled at him but then realised that, of course, he couldn't see it behind her mask, so she squeezed his shoulder instead. 'Now, I'll be back soon. I just need to assess the other patient and talk to my Consultant.'

'Okay.' He flopped back down onto the bed.

Poppy changed her gloves and typed up her findings on the COW then went to see the other patient. This one was much the same, although female, and Poppy went through the same routine. Once she finished typing up these notes, she waved at Seb.

He stepped down from flight deck. 'How'd you go?'

'Fine. Can I come into flight deck to call my Consultant?'

'Sure, just change your gloves again.' He held the door open for her. She did as instructed and then walked past him. As soon as he shut the door the sound of machines and people evaporated. It was like being in a soundproof cube. Despite the quiet, it felt oppressive, like the walls were closing in around her, the air heavy and thick.

She walked quickly to the closest free computer and sat down. A weight settled on her chest. This was a new level of responsibility and it came with additional pressure. One that she wasn't sure she was ready for. She picked up the telephone handset but paused to take a steadying breath. When she'd finished exhaling, Poppy lifted the handset toward her head but knocked it on her face shield. On the ward, she preferred to use the eye goggles. They didn't give her as much of a headache, and they were easier to manage with phones and procedures. But down here, she'd gone with the shield, feeling safer behind it. Once repositioned, she was able to hear the dial tone and was thankful for the soundproof booth.

'Hello, it's Brian Pilson.'

Poppy's leg started to tap under the table. 'Hi Prof, its Poppy.'

'Hello, Poppy, how are you?' The rich tones of his melodious voice were instantly soothing, and Poppy's nerves reduced somewhat, her twitchy leg settling down.

'I'm okay. How are you?'

'Fantastic.' Poppy heard the faintest of chuckles. 'Maria tells me that Olivia is sick with COVID.'

'Yes.'

'And how are you getting on with Adnan?' Like the beginning of the term, when Poppy was first introduced to the Monday morning meeting, Poppy had the feeling this conversation could have taken place at a garden party, under the canopy of a tree, with a glass of chilled champagne in hand.

She shook away the mental image. 'Actually, I haven't been able to get a hold of him.'

'Really?' While he sounded surprised, he did not sound worried.

'Yes, unfortunately.' She paused waiting for him to say more. When he didn't, she continued, her leg tapping again. 'So, I was wondering if you were coming in to do a round? I've seen all the patients and just seen two new admissions in ED.' She inhaled, waiting for his response.

'Oh, no. Sorry, Poppy, I can't come in.' His voice had lost all its animation and become flat and dull. Should she ask him why?

No, that was too weird.

There must be a reason he can't come in. After a beat, she said, 'Okay. Well can I tell you about the two new admissions and then let you know about the ward patients?'

With animation once more, 'Absolutely. Please proceed.'

He's always so formal, but gentlemanly, Poppy thought. She couldn't help but like him, even when he was leaving her in the lurch. After she had filled him in on the two new admissions, she asked if he would like anything else done for them.

'No, Poppy, I think you've presented the cases well and you have things in hand. But if you could possibly check in on them later in the afternoon, just to make sure they are still stable, I would appreciate it.'

Her leg had stopped tapping and Poppy relaxed. Her first admissions and she had not embarrassed herself. 'Okay, not a problem.'

She tried to contain her pride and keep her voice professional, but inside, she was congratulating herself. *You go, girl!*

'And now, how about the existing ward patients, how are they doing?'

Poppy went through all their patients on both the red and orange wards and the results that were still pending.

'Well, if you are worried about any of their results, or any of their conditions deteriorate during the day, please feel free to give me a call at any time.'

'Thanks Prof.'

His voice was gentle, like he was soothing a child. 'Please call, even if you are not sure.'

Poppy's lips twitched. 'I will.'

She put the phone down and her smile grew. It stretched the corners of her lips so far, the crack on one side split. There was a sharp pain and she grimaced, lifting a hand to touch it. Remembering her PPE, she thought better of it. Instead, she drummed her fingers softly on the edge of the desk. Some version of a happy dance. Her Registrar was sick and the Fellow who was supposed to be covering was AWOL, but so far, she was holding it together.

Chapter 19

Typing up the admission confirmation in the patients' notes, her mind back on the job, Seb rolled up next to her; keeping his chair at a safe distance.

'How'd that go?'

She turned toward him. 'We'll admit them both to orange ward under Pilson.'

Seb relaxed. 'Great. Any luck contacting Adnan?'

Poppy shook her head. 'Not yet. I have no idea where he is. Prof didn't know either.'

'Weird. Well, if any more come in, I'll still try him first. But if I don't get a response, are you okay to come back again, if needed?'

'Sure, Seb. Maybe when this is all over, you can buy me a drink!'

He stood, pushing the chair in under the desktop. 'Of course. Once this lockdown ends, we can get the gang together for a well overdue catch-up at the Marly.'

'Can't wait!'

She thought back to her time here in the ED last year and the lovely group of people she'd worked with. It'd been too long since she'd last caught up with Steph or Lucy, and she hadn't seen Seb, Paul, or Graham properly since she'd finished her term. Occasionally she'd get to say a few quick words with them if she was in the ED, but that was rare in itself. It took some of the shine off this positive wave of feelings, knowing that she hadn't made any real effort to stay in touch. That was something she vowed to change when all this was over.

Once she'd finished her notes and stripped off her PPE at the doffing station, she checked the time on her phone and pulled her pager out of her scrub pants. She hadn't felt it vibrate, but she'd missed a few pages from red ward.

She scanned the dirty white walls around her and spotted a telephone handset on the wall near the staff lifts.

She returned the first page. 'It's Poppy.'

'Poppy, it's Terry. Bed eight isn't looking too good. Are you done in ED?'

'Just finished. I'll be up in a sec.' She was about to hang up, but remembered there was more than one missed page. 'Was that what the other pages were about too?'

'No, I think there's some scut work too.'

'Okay.' Poppy's stomach grumbled. It was already after one o'clock, and she hadn't eaten since six this morning. Or had a drink. Just as she thought that, she realised how dry her mouth was. She licked her lips to moisten them and a sharp pain stabbed through the corner of her mouth again.

Yowch!

The dry crack had fissured. After the initial intense pain, there were rivulets of electricity that continued for another minute, like the aftershocks of an earthquake. Before she donned PPE again, she'd put some more paw-paw ointment on it to prevent it getting worse. Once she'd reviewed and sorted the patient in bed eight, she would take a break and get some food. She compelled her legs forward, knowing the sooner she got to the ward, the sooner she'd be able to eat.

Up in red ward, the patient in bed eight was definitely starting to struggle. Once Poppy had examined her, she stood at the end of the bed and thought, what would Josh do? They'd worked so closely together over those night shifts and reviewed and treated so many sick COVID patients, that he was now her benchmark. Funny how complex people and situations could be. Josh who had been utterly horrible to her too many times to count, had been the best teacher she'd had so far this year. She didn't have time to indulge in thoughts of whether they were now becoming friends or not, and dragged her concentration back to the situation in front of her.

Poppy gripped the end of the bed, shifting her weight forward and relieving some of the heaviness in her legs. 'I think we may need to look at what's called non-invasive ventilation. It's like a step up from just the oxygen you're getting from the mask, but a step before we think about putting a tube down your throat and ventilating you with a machine,' she explained to the patient.

'What?' the patient gasped which, in turn, initiated a coughing fit.

'I'm sorry. I didn't mean to scare you.' *Fuck!* Poppy backtracked a bit. 'It looks like the oxygen via the mask is not enough for you at the moment. You are very breathless on the maximum amount. I will take a blood sample from the artery in your wrist to confirm that your lungs are starting to struggle.' She paused allowing the patient to digest the information. 'At this point we usually try a different mask system, called HFNP which better delivers the oxygen to your lungs. We usually do this first and hope that you stabilise, before we think about the intensive care unit.'

Finishing her spiel, she stepped back, forcing the weight back through her legs again. The patient just stared at her blankly. The sweat under her PPE increased, and a drop of sweat tracked into her lip fissure, alighting shock waves of pain again. She reached a hand out to steady herself.

I've totally buggered this up. Should I try again?

Poppy watched the patient's eyes, and they just looked glazed. Maybe not. It didn't look like she was taking anything in. 'I'll just go get the equipment I need for the blood sample and be right back.'

The blood gas result confirmed Poppy's prediction that she was heading downhill. As she sat looking at the print-out at the nurses' desk, Poppy wondered whether she should call Prof Pilson again, or should she ask Maria to review her first. There'd still been no response from Adnan, so Poppy assumed there was no point trying him again. A number of reasons for Adnan's lack of response sprang to her mind but she pushed them aside for now. There was no time to go down that rabbit hole.

'Hi Maria,' Poppy said a few minutes later, once she'd made her decision. 'Unfortunately, I haven't been able to get a hold of Adnan all day.'

'Really?' Poppy heard the ding of the lifts in the background of the call.

'Yes. I've tried several times and so has ED.'

'Are there admissions to sort out?'

'I've already seen two and spoken with Prof, so they are okay. But I've just come back to red ward and one of my patients is deteriorating. I've done an ABG, but I think she needs a trial of HFNP, and I was wondering if you might review them for me?'

'Of course! I'm so sorry, Poppy. I would have been happy to go to ED.'

'That's okay.'

'No, it's not fair on you. I'll come straight up now and see your patient on red and I'll ask switch to send any new admission calls to my pager.'

'Thanks, Maria, that's very kind of you.' How different she was from Olivia.

'Not at all, Poppy. You shouldn't have to do all this on your own. I'll see you soon.' Poppy could just make out Alex's muffled voice in the background as the phone cut out.

Maria assessed the patient with Poppy observing quietly at the end of the bed.

'Yes, she needs HFNP.' Maria turned to Poppy and looped the stethoscope over the obs machine. Her voice softened. 'Good work, Poppy. Have you hooked the machine up yourself before?'

'No, I haven't.'

Maria headed towards Poppy, her small eyes squinting with a smile. 'Let's do it together and I'll explain as we go.'

'That'd be great. Thanks, Maria.' She wasn't sure if first year Residents usually dialled up HFNP machines, but maybe by showing initiative in admitting the ED patients and making the correct assessment here, Poppy had earnt the right to learn a more advanced skill.

Once the patient was all set up and they'd watched her for a while and re-tested her oxygen saturation on a finger probe, they headed back to the nurses' station.

'Can you keep an eye on her sats?' Maria asked as she pulled out her pager which was wailing loudly.

'Yes.' Poppy nodded, taking a seat at the computer to type up the instructions.

'And can you please update Prof Pilson? I need to move on.'

‘Of course,’ Poppy replied, then hesitated. She really wanted to discuss Prof Pilson’s absence from the hospital since COVID started. But was now the best time, when they were short on staff, and Maria had been kind enough to help her out? Maybe she shouldn’t overload her just now. But would she get another chance?

In the time it took Poppy to run these thoughts through her mind, Maria had already made it to the doffing station near the staff lifts and Poppy had missed her chance anyway.

Great.

She typed up the events in the patient’s medical record then called Prof and filled him in. One of the nurses then pestered her to do the scut work and food and water was pushed further down the line. Scut work and result checking bogged her down for another couple of hours and by the time Poppy had a chance to stop and look at the clock again, it was after four o’clock.

As soon as the time registered, though, her body started to make its feelings known on the lack of hydration and food all day. Her head suddenly throbbing, her throat and lips dry as the desert, and her legs heavy and shaky. She made her way off the ward and down to the Residents’ Lounge with her lunch bag, stopping for a Coke Zero from the vending machine on the way.

Before handover, Poppy found a second opportunity to speak to Maria alone. They were on red ward and Alex had gone off to do a cannula.

‘Maria, I was hoping to talk to you about Prof Pilson.’ Poppy leaned back against the desk. ‘I know we’ve talked before, but now with Olivia off and Adnan uncontactable, I just wonder if there is a specific reason why he’s not been coming into the hospital to see the patients. I haven’t actually seen him since prior to COVID starting.’

Maria looked up from the computer. ‘Still? Not once in all the times he’s been on-call?’

Poppy shook her head.

Maria looked down for a moment, thinking. ‘Has Olivia said anything new?’

Poppy waited while one of the nurses walked past and then continued more quietly. 'No.'

'Hmm.'

Poppy let the silence grow. She wanted to know what Maria thought. Surely the hospital policy was that all new admissions needed to be seen by the admitting Consultant within a certain time period?

Eventually, Maria spoke again. 'Let me have another chat with Dr Anderson.'

Poppy pushed herself off the desk, instantly agitated. 'Really? Dr Anderson?'

'Yes, why?' Maria asked, obviously picking up on Poppy's sudden panicked tone.

'Ah… she's not my biggest fan.' She unconsciously took a step away. Maybe this hadn't been the best idea.

'What do you mean?'

Could Maria not know about all the dramas from last year and Poppy's role in it?

'Well… I was involved in petitioning the hospital for better support of the junior staff. Dr Anderson wasn't exactly a fan.' She finished quietly and cast her eyes about to make sure they were still alone.

'That was you? I had heard an intern was involved, but I didn't realise it was you.'

Was that admiration in her voice? Poppy wished they weren't in PPE. It was so hard to read people's faces and body language accurately when so much was covered. 'Guilty.'

Maria stood and nodded her head. 'Good on you. That took guts and was needed.'

I think that is admiration.

Maria continued. 'Anyway, this isn't about you, it's about Prof. And Adnan. As competent as you are, Poppy, we can't have an entire team being run solo by a first year Resident. It's not fair on you, and it's not safe. And the Consultant must see the patients, it's required.'

I thought so.

'I just don't want more reasons for Dr Anderson to hate me.'

Maria just nodded, which wasn't particularly reassuring. 'I'm just going to go into the meeting room and give her a call before handover.'

'Okay,' Poppy said, instantly wishing she hadn't raised the issue at all. There was no telling what Dr Anderson would do with the information.

Poppy was lying down on the couch at home, staring up at the ceiling watching the lights of passing cars flash overhead. The smell of steaks being cooked on their small outdoor barbeque was making her mouth water. Even though she'd eventually had lunch at around four o'clock, she was still hungry. But she couldn't compel her body to move, it was like a wrung-out dishrag, limp and probably smelly.

'So, what do *you* think's going to happen?' Gemma asked after Poppy had filled her in on her chaotic day.

'I honestly don't know. By the time Maria finished talking to Dr Anderson, it was handover. I asked her about it on the way down to theatres to get changed and she said Dr Anderson would take care of it, and we just had to wait now to see what happens.'

Gemma repositioned her legs under her on the other couch. 'Leaving Prof aside for a moment, it's pretty weird don't you think that Adnan wouldn't answer a single call or message all day?'

'Yeah, it is bizarre. I've been thinking about it all day. Maybe he's sick with COVID, too?' Poppy rolled onto her side and looked at Gemma. 'I mean he's out here without his family, so he might not be answering his phone if he's unwell.'

'Good thought.' She started picking under her fingernails to clear them of dirt. 'I could see that happening.'

'Or—'

'What?' Gemma looked up again, forgetting her nails.

'Well, this may be a bit paranoid,' she lifted one hand off the couch to stop Gemma from interrupting, 'but maybe he's flown home and not told anyone?'

Gemma leant back in the chair. 'Whoa, that's extreme.'

'You think?' Poppy asked, scrunching up her lips, suddenly uncertain.

'It sounds more like something I'd come up with.'

Poppy's lips relaxed and she raised her eyebrows. 'True.'

Back to inspecting her fingernails, Gemma continued. 'I've never met the guy, do you really think that's a possibility?'

Poppy tilted a head to the side, thinking, and then rolled back to look at the ceiling once more. 'I don't know. I just thought that if I was in Australia and my wife and kids were across the world and a global pandemic hit and I was just doing a Fellowship, so not essential, I'd probably want to just go home before there were no more flights.' She rolled onto her side, again, resting her head on her crooked arm. 'Don't you think?'

Gemma looked up. 'Actually, when you put it like that, it sounds completely reasonable. Where's he from?'

'Turkey.'

'Yep, I'd definitely want to high-tail it home. If the shit was hitting the fan, I'd want to be with my family.'

'Me too.' She was glad Gemma could understand her reasoning. The thought had nagged at her during the day when she'd been wondering about potential reasons for Adnan's silence.

'Well, either way, he'll have to respond at some stage.'

Poppy's FaceTime with Will that evening was consumed with Poppy's latest work dramas. So much so that she didn't even consider bringing up their housing situation again. It just didn't feel right. But once their call finished, she started obsessing over it again. He seemed his normal self on the call, but why was he not thinking about it?

If they were sitting together talking, Poppy would just ask him straight out what he thought about moving in together. But with the distance and the short calls, it was so much harder to judge the situation.

Why did he have to agree to go to Dubbo at the last minute?

Lying in her bed, her body thoroughly exhausted, her mind would not shut off. Everything would be so much easier if they were together. When would that be? Again, she wished she could talk to Gemma about it and get her advice, but that, too, was out of the question.

Arghh.

Sleep would not come. She pulled out a book and tried to divert her mind. But after twenty minutes, she'd read one paragraph several times. *Rushing back*, by Flume, stuck in her head as her day and thoughts about

Adnan and Prof Pilson kept circling. Clearly, reading wasn't going to get her to sleep. Her body was depleted but her mind was flying high on a trapeze. She placed the book on her bedside table and threw off the sheets, kicking them toward the end of the bed when one foot became trapped. Looking at her phone would only depress her and make her more anxious, so she got up and quietly slid open the door onto their small balcony. She tiptoed past Lucas and Gemma's room and went to the far end and leaned over the railing. The steak smell lingered but a cool breeze caressed her skin. There was no one on the street below but cars still rumbled down the side street. Poppy tried to quiet her mind by simply observing her surroundings. A lone bark broke the quietude and she searched for the source but couldn't find it. Colourful lights from an apartment across the street projected from a large wall-mounted TV and Poppy wondered what the person was watching so late at night. Slowly her brain calmed and all worries about Will, Adnan, and Dr Anderson dissipated. Sensations in her body became more urgent. The itch of a mozzie bite on her ankle. The tightness in her calves. The pain on her lip. She yawned and took a step back from the railing. Time to try for sleep again.

Chapter 20

When Poppy's alarm woke her from a deep sleep the next morning, she had to think for a few minutes to remember what day it was and whether it was morning or night. As she went to get out of the bed, her legs were tight and sore. She also had a headache. Excellent, she thought, flow on effects from yesterday.

I wonder if today will be any better?

An hour later in the handover meeting room, waiting for everyone else to arrive, she wondered if she'd be on her own again today, and whether there was any update about Adnan or Prof Pilson. Someone had put the chairs back in rows instead of a circle. They were still spaced well apart, though. As Alex entered the room, Poppy raised her hand to wave but stopped with it suspended in the air, like she was about to give him a high-five, when she saw who was directly behind him. Josh. Her hand was still stupidly in the air when moments later, he sat next to her.

'It's not primary school, Poppy. If you want to ask a question, you don't have to raise your hand.' So, Josh's superior attitude was back in place.

'What are you doing here?' Poppy asked, wrestling with her annoyance at his presence.

He'd crossed one leg over the other and his body was angled slightly away from her. 'I got the call this morning. I was told you couldn't cope on your own, so I'm here to save you, *again*.' Hostility was radiating off him.

Poppy felt heat rush up her neck and her pulse pound.

Fuck you, buddy.

'That's not what's happening,' Poppy replied through gritted teeth. She couldn't believe she had just started to trust him.

He turned toward her, like he was about to say more (probably another snide comment), but then Maria arrived at their seats.

Breathing heavily, like she'd been in a rush to get there, she kneeled on the chair in front of them. 'Good, you're here, Josh. Thanks for helping out. Poppy, you won't believe this, but Adnan finally got back to me last night. He's actually gone back to Turkey.'

Still seething over Josh's comment, Poppy couldn't muster any surprise. 'Really?' So, she'd been right last night.

Maria rocked the chair back towards them. 'I was shocked. He just left without telling anyone, apparently.'

'Mmm,' Poppy responded, coolly.

'It's pretty poor form.' Even though he was wearing a mask, Poppy knew Josh's jaw was clenched when he said this.

Maria rocked the chair back toward them again. 'I think so. I mean, look, I know it is really scary at the moment. But the least you could do is actually inform your employer, right?' Poppy had never seen Maria like this before. She was usually nice, but busy and professional. Here, she was behaving like a schoolgirl dishing the gossip.

'It would be the very least he could have done,' Josh said, now crossing his arms across his chest.

Sanctimonious prick.

'I'm sure he was worried about his family's safety.' Poppy directed her comment to Maria. She wanted to counter Josh's lack of empathy with some of her own.

'Maybe.' Maria stopped rocking the chair. 'But a phone call and email to the training unit wouldn't have been a big imposition, under the circumstances.' She sat down and draped an arm over the back to look directly at Poppy. 'Anyway, Josh is going to cover the rest of the week. We're not sure about next week, but I'll keep you updated.'

Poppy stopped seething about Josh long enough to remember to ask her about Prof Pilson. 'And what about the other matter? Is there any news there?'

Both Josh and Maria looked to Poppy.

Maria dropped her voice even though no one would know what matter Poppy was referring to. 'Not yet, I'm sorry.'

Poppy tried to be upbeat. 'Thanks, Maria.'

Josh was still looking at her, with one eyebrow raised. But before he could pester her about it, the Night Registrar took the front seat and handover began.

Poppy was back on her guard as soon as handover ended, and she and Josh started their rounds. She was just waiting for the next barb or put-down, and was twisting herself into knots in anticipation.

'Sounds like we're going to be pretty busy,' Josh said amiably, looking down at his patient list.

Poppy just stared at him. Was he being nice now? Or was he going to follow up with another putdown?

'I think we should do this ward, then if nothing urgent comes up we should get a coffee before we do orange ward. How does that sound?' He looked up from his list.

'Good, actually,' Poppy replied, shocked but appreciative. 'Yesterday, I don't think I stopped at all until about four o'clock.'

'Well, there's two of us today, so that should make it quicker and more efficient. But with twelve-hour shifts, you do need to take care of yourself as well as the patients.'

Here again was the Josh of night shifts, Poppy thought. The one who was pleasant, relaxed, and a great team player and leader.

But how can he be a bastard one minute and then completely reasonable the next? I just don't get it!

They worked steadily for an hour and a half then walked up to Campos for a coffee. Poppy treated herself to one of their delicious caramel kisses and they sat on a bench seat a bit further down the road. The sun was warm on Poppy's face, and she turned toward it as she savoured the rich caramel and warm coffee. This might be the highlight of her week, she thought.

So lost in her own head, she hadn't thought about Josh sitting so close to her on the bench until he said, 'I wish you felt as friendly toward me as you do that caramel thingy.'

Poppy turned to him, a scowl forming between her eyebrows immediately. 'Josh, I honestly don't get you. On night shifts and just now on the ward you've been awesome. Really easy to work with, a good leader and teacher, but then this morning you made me feel like an idiot in front of Alex, and don't get me started about the morgue. I just don't know where I stand with you.'

Josh just stared at her, the faintest glimmer of a smile forming at the edge of his lips.

Did he get off on making her uncomfortable?

He took a slow sip of his coffee. 'This morning I was rude, and I'm sorry. I was pretty frustrated to be called back to the wards. Yesterday I was manning the cath lab.'

'Oh, that sucks, I guess,' Poppy replied, feeling bad for him. She took another bite of her caramel kiss.

'I was hoping to get a break from COVID cover for at least a week and get back to Cardiology.'

'Fair enough. It really has been pretty shit for you, hasn't it?' She rested the treat on the paper bag in her lap, her focus on Josh, who was now staring down at his coffee cup dejectedly.

He shrugged. 'I wouldn't disagree with you. But you're right, I shouldn't have taken it out on you… I'm sorry.'

'Well, I get it now. But for the sake of my sanity, do you think we could try to be nice to each other from now on?'

'Poppy Mason, I will do my utmost to treat you with a chivalrous manner at all times.'

Now he was definitely taking the piss. She raised an eyebrow at him, archly. 'Let's not go overboard.'

Josh was true to his word and continued to behave himself. But Poppy heard nothing more from Maria regarding Prof Pilson. Josh thought it was highly inappropriate but stopped short of making any real noise of complaint. He just wanted to sail through and get back to Cardiology as soon as possible, and Poppy couldn't blame him. When an email check-in from Dr Hennessey arrived the following day, she thought it a good opportunity to discuss the situation with her mentor.

To: poppy.mason@thebennelong.com.au

From: Victoria.hennessey@thebennelong.com.au

Dear Poppy,

I wanted to check in with you and see how you were surviving this torrid time. Are you doing okay? My clinics are all telehealth now and our meetings are temporarily on pause, so I am free to talk if you want to chat one day around lunchtime? I'm keen to hear all about your experiences with COVID. Being at the very coalface, I'm sure you will have much to tell me.

All the best,

Victoria.

Poppy finally had a chance to call Victoria on Friday. Josh was watching the latest COVID update from the Premier and the Chief Medical Officer in the Residents' Lounge. She found an empty on-call room down the end of the corridor and sat on the desk chair.

'Poppy, how are you?' Victoria asked as soon as she answered the call.

'I'm okay.'

'You sound exhausted. Has it been gruelling?'

Poppy rested back against the chair. 'Yes. Long shifts, all in PPE, lots of codes. And things keep changing.'

'I can imagine it is hard to keep up.'

'It's all happening so fast, it's hard to keep on top of it all. And then my Registrar got COVID this week, so on Wednesday I was completely on my own when the Fellow had secretly left the country and not told anyone.'

She'd sat forward again, eager for Dr Hennessey's reply. Would she be shocked?

'Sorry, wait, what did you just say?' Poppy couldn't read her tone over the phone.

'I'm going too fast, sorry.'

'That's okay, but what was that about the Fellow?'

'Oh, right… So, when my Registrar got COVID, they wanted the Fellow to cover, but no one could get a hold of him, so I was on my own—'

'But what about the Consultant?' Poppy could hear the shock now.

'We-ell…' Poppy drew out the word, stalling.

'Yes?'

Now she came in with the bombshell. 'To be honest, I haven't seen Prof Pilson since before COVID. Every time he's been on-call, he hasn't come in.' Poppy sat back in the chair.

There was a pause before her reply. 'What, every time?'

'Yes. My Reg, and then me, we've just called him and told him what's happening.'

'But he hasn't physically seen any of the patients since COVID started.'

Now Poppy's leg was jiggling. 'As far as I know, that's right.'

With no word from Dr Anderson or Maria, Poppy wanted Dr Hennessey to weigh in. She'd gone beyond incredulous, now she just wanted someone senior to take the burden away. It wasn't fair that they were always on their own. The buck was supposed to stop with the Consultant.

'And the Fellow?'

'Well, he'd secretly flown home to Turkey, and hadn't told anyone. So, we'd all been calling and leaving messages without response. I had to see the new patient admissions in ED and then talk to Prof.'

'Mmm,' Dr Hennessey said quietly.

Poppy let her digest the information and then continued, her leg jiggling again. 'Anyway, I guess once he landed, he saw all the missed calls and messages and finally let someone know that he'd left. So yesterday they found someone else to cover for this week and I'm not sure what will happen next week.'

'So, just so I'm clear on this, on Wednesday you covered all the in-patients and admissions yourself, without a Registrar or Consultant?'

'Well, I talked to Prof on the phone. And late in the day, when one of the patients was deteriorating, I asked Maria, the Advanced Trainee Registrar, to review them, which she did.'

'Hmph… Is anyone doing anything about Prof Pilson?'

Now Poppy's heart rate kicked up. 'I've spoken to Maria a couple of times, and she's discussed it with Dr Anderson, but I don't know what's happening.' She bit her lip waiting for Dr Hennessey's response.

'I see… I must say, Poppy, I'm very sorry you've been placed in this position. It's unacceptable in the best of circumstances, but to be left on your own during a global pandemic, is just disgraceful.'

'Thanks, Victoria, but I'm okay.'

'Poppy, I know you are a good Resident. But you shouldn't be in this position. I will talk with Katrina Anderson and see exactly what is happening behind the scenes. This can't go on. A Consultant must see every new admission, and if Prof Pilson is not able to do that, then we need to find some alternative arrangements.' Poppy could hear the fire in her voice. 'If, for nothing else, this is exposing the hospital to potential litigation.'

'Thank you, Victoria.' A wave of relief overcame Poppy. She then changed tack. 'But what about PACMEN and the staffing?'

'I'm sorry to say that everything is on hold now. We don't have enough staff to fill all the rosters at the moment, so the additional staff have been absorbed into relief cover. And as all the meetings are on hold, PACMEN is also in hiatus.'

'But now is when people will really need support.'

'Oh, I agree, Poppy, but so far no one has taken advantage of Harry's Zoom counselling sessions. I think most people are just too busy.'

'I just don't want to see everything we've done fall by the wayside.' Poppy hung her head, her body slumping in the chair. This was not the news she wanted to hear.

Dr Hennessey's tone softened. 'I don't either, Poppy. But I think right now, whilst everything is so chaotic, we have to accept it has been sidelined. But trust me… Once we move out of lockdown, that will be the time to restart PACMEN, at a minimum.'

'Okay, good.' She looked up at the utilitarian room around her. There was no noise from the corridor beside her. It served as another reminder of the pandemic.

'And Poppy, don't lose heart.'

Even though Victoria could not see it, Poppy nodded. 'I'll try not to.' She injected some brightness into her voice and followed the rules of politeness. 'But what about you? How has your COVID experience been thus far?'

'Thank you for asking.' Poppy was immediately glad she'd made the effort. 'It's been okay. Our biggest issue has been access to a couple of the medications our patients need due to global shortages and slower transportation, and trying to convince some of the patients to come into the hospital, and others to stay away. But compared to what you're dealing with, it's been pretty easy. We've lost our two basic trainee Registrars to COVID relief, but other than that, we've been doing fine.'

'That's good.'

'You hang in there, Poppy. Let me sleuth around about Prof Pilson, and I'll get back to you.'

When the call ended, she stayed a moment longer in the room. She would have to wait for Dr Hennessey to get back to her about Prof Pilson. The ball was out of her hands and she would have to hope that between Dr Hennessey and Dr Anderson, some suitable solution would be found. She stood up, nodded to herself, and left the room. Despite nothing to do, she was relieved that at the end of this shift she would have two whole days off and all she really wanted to do was sleep and talk to Will.

Gemma was doing a fifteen-hour shift on the Saturday, so it was just Lucas and Poppy stuck in the apartment together. Poppy slept late but woke to the smell of fresh coffee and bacon. The bacon alone was enough for her to drag her depleted body out of bed.

'Oh my God, I was salivating from my bedroom!' Poppy said as she opened her bedroom door.

'Morning. Thought you could use a big breakfast.'

'You are honestly, the best man I know, Luc.'

Lucas looked over his shoulder, spatula raised in the air. 'What about Will?'

Poppy took a seat on one of the kitchen bench stools and rubbed her eyes. 'Okay, maybe tied for first place.'

Lucas laughed easily at that and placed a coffee in front of Poppy before turning back to the cooktop and the sizzling bacon alongside the eggs that he was scrambling.

Inhaling the coffee triggered a dopamine release in Poppy's brain. God coffee is so good, she thought, savouring that first mouthful. Instantly, the heavy legs and dry mouth receded to the background, as the caffeine hit her system, energising her. Now her body clicked into gear. She went around the bench and got plates and cutlery ready for Lucas to dish up.

'That was so good, Luc. Thank you,' Poppy said as she licked the last morsel off the corner of her lip.

'You're welcome. I know you've been doing it tough, so I thought this would help.' His plate was clean, and his knife and fork were neatly placed together in the centre of the plate like they were at a restaurant.

'It does, thank you.' She sat back in her chair and took a last sip of her coffee.

Lucas got up to take his plate back to the kitchen and Poppy started quietly singing to herself.

'What are you singing?' Lucas asked after stopping abruptly and turning back around with a strange look on his face.

'Just that Ariana Grande song.'

'*Thank u, next*?'

'Is that what it's called? I didn't know the name.'

'Yes. But she's not singing about how grateful she is for her bacon and eggs.' He was still holding his plate suspended in air, a crooked smile elevating one side of his face.

'She's not?' Poppy's head tilted to the side.

'No, she's singing about her ex-boyfriends. For teaching her things about love.'

'Really?' Poppy asked, one eyebrow lifting.

'Yes,' chuckled Lucas. 'Did you really think she was talking about bacon and eggs?'

Poppy looked back down at her empty plate. 'Well, I figured she must really love her breakfast. And bacon and eggs *is* great comfort food, so whatever floats your boat, I guess.'

Lucas had to put his plate back down on the table, he was laughing so hard. He slapped his thigh. 'I can't wait to tell Gemma. She's going to piss herself.'

'No! She won't let me forget it.' Poppy reached a hand out to implore Lucas but then let it drop. 'I guess it is pretty funny. I'm going to have to go listen to it again and see if you're right.'

'Bacon and eggs,' Lucas snorted as he finally picked up his plate and headed to the kitchen.

'I'll clean up,' she said, joining him in the kitchen and taking his plate. At the sink, rinsing off the tomato sauce she turned her head. 'What about you? How are things going in Cardiology? How's the lovely, Miriam?'

Lucas leaned back against the bench, the tea towel he'd used to dry his hands over his shoulder. 'Good, and good. But I didn't get to tell you, on Wednesday I ran into Josh in the cath lab.'

'Really?' Poppy stopped rinsing the cutlery.

'Yeah. And he was bizarrely nice.'

'Bizarrely nice?' Poppy waited for Lucas to say more.

'He was all chummy, and asking how I was, and then he asked after you.'

Poppy's breath caught. 'What did he say?'

Lucas scrutinised her before continuing. 'He asked how you were recovering from nights and said the two of you had a rough run, but that you'd really impressed him.' His head nodded at the end as if to imply this wasn't news to him.

If Poppy wasn't already standing against the bench she would have taken a step back. 'Impressed him? How?' It was the first public compliment Josh had ever given her and she needed to know more. Her chest felt constricted like someone had placed their hands around her ribs and was squeezing her tight.

'He just said that you two had worked really well as a team and that you'd showed great skill and a real calmness under pressure.'

There was a slight lessening of the pressure around her rib cage. 'Hmph…'

'Weird right?' Lucas placed the tea towel neatly back over the handle of the oven.

'I don't know, Luc,' she replied, looking down at her hands and seeing she'd been dripping water onto the floor. She turned back to the sink and shook them off before turning around again. 'All last year he was an absolute prick to me, and then he's been a mixture of a prick and then a pretty decent guy this year. I just can't wrap my head around it. He's like a yo-yo.'

'I think he still has a thing for you, but he's got nothing on Will,' Luc said deadpan, his eyes flat.

Poppy wasn't sure if Lucas' dislike of Josh was due to him dismissing him last year or if it was really about how he had treated her.

'I agree, Will is amazing. I think Josh just wants what he can't have or likes the chase more than the reality.' Finally returning to the sink and the job of cleaning up, Poppy turned the water back on. 'Whatever, I have no time for that. Besides, you could never be his equal in a relationship. I think he'd always want to be the victor.'

She could no longer see his face as she squirted dishwashing liquid into the sink but heard the steel in his voice. 'Yeah, I can't see him treating anyone as an equal.' It sounded to her like she might have been right in guessing his dislike stemmed more from the way Josh had treated him than her.

Their conversation paused, leaving Poppy thinking more about the comparisons and differences between Will and Josh. Whilst her hands were busy scrubbing the pan, a deep longing for Will began to gape open. She'd been so busy at work lately and their conversations had been ad hoc and short. It would be good to reconnect properly and they'd agreed to try for a long FaceTime chat later that morning.

Chapter 21

Poppy finished placing the pan and spatula on the draining board and wiped her hands on the tea towel. She was thinking about having a shower when Lucas burst back into the kitchen, his laptop under his arm.

'I've got some more news!'

'What?' Lucas had all the excitement of a little boy after riding his bike for the first time.

'I decided I couldn't wait for this lockdown to end to start making some headway with the engagement ring, so I've made some calls and spoken with a jewellery designer, and I wanted to show you the final design and the stone they've sourced for the ring. Come and have a look.' He motioned for her to come back to the dining table where he set up his laptop.

'Oh my gosh, Luc, this is so exciting!' Poppy said, almost hopping as she made her way back to the table.

He turned back to her with an impish expression. 'I know, it really is!'

Poppy placed a hand on his shoulder. 'That's great, Luc, I'm so glad you're enjoying it.'

'I am. More than I thought I would. I'm already starting to plan my proposal.'

'Ooh, do tell.' Poppy's hands came together in anticipation.

'Not yet. Let's look at these first,' he said, turning the laptop toward Poppy.

'So, here's the emerald,' he said, showing her three pictures of a pear-cut emerald with a small measurement ruler beside it in two of the pictures, and lying on someone's finger in the last photo. 'That's the salesperson's hand,' Lucas said as Poppy got to the last picture.

'Well, it's clearly not your masculine hand,' Poppy said, giving him a gentle nudge in the ribs. 'It's lovely, Luc, a really bright colour.'

'I thought so. They had a few others to show me, but one was quite pale, and the other two were so dark, they almost looked black. This was the nicest.'

'And probably the most expensive, right?'

'Yep.' He looked back at her rather than the laptop. 'I think they probably do it on purpose, you know? Like you tell them how much you want to spend and what shape etc. that you're looking for, and then they come back to you with a bunch of duds that are under your threshold, and one really nice one that's a bit over. Not so much over that you'll baulk, but enough for it to sting a bit.'

Poppy laughed. 'I'd never thought about it before, but you're probably right. It's very clever, really. Now, show me the final design.'

Lucas found an email with the drawing of the design and then turned the laptop back towards Poppy.

'Ooh, that's stunning, Luc.' It was a coloured drawing, very similar to the original photos she and Lucas had previously looked at on the internet, but instead of perpendicular smaller pear-shaped diamonds on each side of the emerald, there was now a cuff of tiny diamonds on each side, hugging the central emerald.

'I decided to go with white gold as you suggested,' he added, pointing to the band.

'She's going to love it.' Poppy clapped her hands and bounced in her seat.

'I hope so.'

Poppy sat back in the chair and grinned at Lucas. 'So, what about the proposal?'

Lucas shut the lid of the laptop. 'I was thinking about how much Gem loves Lady Gaga but also Turkish delight—'

'How are you going to connect those two?' Poppy interrupted. She couldn't think of how a proposal would come out of those two things.

'With COVID, it's not like I can take her to a Gaga concert.'

'No, sadly.'

'I thought I could make a pretend concert here at home. With lights and play the concert versions of the songs, and we could all dress up.'

Poppy's heart leapt. 'You want me there?'

'Where else will you be?' Lucas scoffed. 'We're in lockdown.'

'True.' Poppy felt sad her best friend couldn't have the most perfect proposal ever.

'I thought I'd make it like it was our plan to do something fun. And we could make her favourite drink and I'll source that delicious Turkish delight she likes from Petersham, with the Persian fairy floss. And we can play a few songs, have a few drinks, and then when it gets to *Shallow*, I could get on one knee and ask her to marry me.'

'Oh, Luc—'

'What do you think?' He was working his jaw, a clear sign of nerves.

Poppy hugged him. 'It's lovely. She'll love it.' A tear formed at the edge of her eye and her voice was suddenly husky. After the hug, she swiped at her eye and sat back in her chair. 'When do you think this will happen?'

'The jewellery store said it would take about two to three weeks to make the ring and I'll have to physically go to the store to pick it up.'

'Which, theoretically, may be beyond lockdown?'

'I don't know, Pop.' Lucas placed a hand on the top of his laptop, his fingers drumming on the lid. 'The daily updates are still sounding pretty bleak. And you know firsthand how bad it is on the wards. I think lockdown will be extended beyond the six weeks.'

'Oh, Luc, touch wood, quickly. I don't want you to jinx it.' She hurriedly tapped the chair she was sitting on. Her eyes fixed on a point on the wall in front of her as anxious bubbles simmered in her gut. Prolonging lockdown would prolong her separation from Will. The drumming of Lucas' fingers was like a train thundering down the track. Poppy could imagine the train was carrying Will. But instead of bringing them closer together it was heading away from her. She just wanted to be able to see Will again. Was that too much to ask?

Poppy sat on her bed, waiting for the clock to inch toward eleven o'clock when Will said he would FaceTime. Unconsciously, she had begun twisting the drawstring of her hoodie around her fingers and biting the corner of her lip. She desperately needed to feel close to Will right now. The uncertainty over the future, particularly with regard to moving in together, was widening the divide between them that had been growing whilst they were separated. Even though most of the time they had been able to FaceTime and see each other, it wasn't the same as being together physically.

As she was thinking about Will, Josh and that infuriating half-smirk of his popped into her head. The image was so clear. Weird, she thought, but then they had spent a lot of time together in the last week and Lucas had just brought him up in conversation. She tried to recall Will's face in order to banish Josh's from her mind. The image was slightly hazy, like his face had been blurred by a photo filter. Instead, she switched to thinking about how he made her feel. The first thoughts that sprang to mind were comfort and a sense of belonging, as well as sexual desire. Unbidden, Josh swam into focus again at the thought of sex. *Stop it!*

She gently smacked her head and noticed the hoodie drawstring was wound so tight around her finger that it was turning red at the tip. Immediately, she unravelled it and stood up to go to the kitchen and get a Coke Zero from the fridge.

She took her time, wanting to delay returning to bed and her unbidden thoughts of Josh. With her first mouthful, the fizz hit her throat with a pleasant eruption of popping. It lessened with a second mouthful as she lingered in the kitchen before heading back to her room, can in hand. The sound of *Goodbyes* by Post Malone was coming from behind Gemma and Lucas' door, and Poppy's mind instantly circled back to Josh again. She needed to get him out of her head. As she approached her own bedroom door, she heard the unmistakable tinkling of the FaceTime ringtone and quickened her pace, her heart rate instantly picking up.

By the time she plonked herself back on the bed, the call had rung out and she'd spilled Coke on her hand and bedspread.

'Damn!' she swiped at the mess and called Will back. 'Sorry, sorry,' Poppy said once Will's face swam into view. 'I dashed to the kitchen to get a drink and didn't get back fast enough.'

'That's okay. How are you?' It seemed oddly polite and formal.

Poppy was suddenly nervous. 'I'm okay, what about you?'

'Yeah, fine.' He swiped a hand through his hair. 'Bored.'

'Oh... What—' Poppy started just as Will said, 'What—'

'You go first,' Will said.

Poppy sighed. It was like they were two acquaintances rather than a couple. 'I wasn't going to say anything exciting, just wondering what you've got planned to stave off boredom for the weekend. You're not on at all, are you?'

His eyes roved the screen, not lingering on hers. 'No, not on, and there's not much to do really.' He huffed.

Poppy had to hold in a huff of her own. Her body was so drained and here he was complaining of being bored. Suddenly, their lives were on very different tracks.

'Zoo?' she suggested

'Done that.'

'Oh, yeah, of course.' Now Poppy was looking down. She knew he'd already been to the zoo. It was like she had felt she needed to suggest things to perk him up, he wasn't giving her much.

Normally their conversations were effortless. Easily flowing from one to the other, but today it was starting to feel like hard work finding a decent rhythm.

'Well, who's around that you can hang out with. Go to the pub for lunch?' she tried again.

He rubbed his eyes. 'Yeah, I guess. Pretty much everyone is around, because no one can travel back to Sydney, so there'll probably be some kind of get-together by tonight.' As an afterthought, he added, 'But I'd much rather be back home with you.'

Poppy's heart lifted, 'I'd love that too.' She put a hand up to the screen, as if to touch his face. He looked tired and as she searched his eyes, they drifted away from her. The silence lengthened but it seemed only Poppy felt the pressure to fill it. 'Lucas showed me pictures of his planned engagement ring this morning.'

'Really? That's cool.' That gave him some of his usual animation.

'He's decided not to wait for lockdown to be over, so he might even pop the question in the next few weeks if the ring comes.'

'Wow.' His head nodded but he didn't say anything further.

Poppy left an excruciating pause, hoping Will would fill it, but he didn't. What was he thinking?

Why won't he talk to me properly?

'So, it's got me thinking again about moving out.' She sat forward on the bed, bringing the phone screen closer to her face so she could study his reaction.

'Yeah?' His face was unreadable. He was nodding and bouncing in his chair, as if in time to music, but he wasn't engaging with her.

All these one-word answers were starting to grate Poppy's nerves. She rushed to fill the silence and remain positive. 'Yeah. I mean, I know there's no rush, but once it's official, I think I should start looking for somewhere else to live, don't you think?' Would he finally take the bait and mention moving in together, she wondered.

'Makes sense.'

Poppy let the silence drag, watching Will's face intently. He wasn't getting the message, maybe she should just ask him outright? She was on the verge of suggesting they move in together when he finally spoke.

'If I had to live in Dubbo for the rest of my life, I think I might shoot myself.'

Poppy recoiled from the screen. This was so unlike Will. It sounded more like something Olivia might say. It felt so wrong and jarring hearing it from Will. If Gem had said it in a flip way, Poppy would have laughed it off. But this was so out of character for Will, she became concerned.

She leant forward again and softened her voice. 'It's that bad, is it?' she asked, hoping to draw him out more.

'Yeah, it's bleak.' He scraped his hand vigorously through his hair. Poppy thought he might pull some out if he kept doing it. 'The town is a shithole, the people are so basic. I just couldn't do it.'

'I don't think I've heard you be this negative before. Has something happened?'

'No.' But he didn't meet her eyes as he said it.

'You're usually so much more upbeat.' What was going on, she wondered. Had there been something bad that happened at work, maybe?

'I'm just missing you and feeling flat, I guess. And it's hard not being able to surf. I didn't realise how much I'd miss that.' He looked up at her with a sheepish expression.

After a pause to see if Will would add more, Poppy said, 'Are you sure that's all it is?' If it wasn't directly to do with work, maybe he had a disagreement with his housemate.

'Yes. Don't worry about me, Pop. I'm just counting the days until I can hold you again.'

Offering what she hoped was a comforting smile, 'Me too.' Normally Will was the one comforting her, it was unnerving for their roles to suddenly be reversed.

Poppy couldn't bring up moving in together now. She didn't know whether it would cheer him up or create more tension. 'Are you and Brendan still getting on okay?'

'You mean after the awkward moment where he busted us attempting phone sex?' There was marginally more brightness in Will's voice.

'Yes, exactly,' Poppy replied, relieved he was closer to his usual self.

'Yeah, we're getting on okay.' His face clouded over again. 'Although, I'm not sure how faithful he's been whilst he's been here.'

'Really?' This was a surprise.

'Last weekend when we were out, he got very drunk and very physical with one of the locals. She was young, too, maybe only just over eighteen.' His eyes were shifting all over the place again.

'Did you see him with her?'

'They were basically pawing each other on the dance floor, and I did see his tongue in her mouth. But I don't know if he took it further than that. That was when I decided to call it a night.'

Jeez, he must have been really uncomfortable, he's still looking anywhere but at me.

'Gosh. Do you know his partner?'

He scrunched his lips up. 'Yeah, I do, and she's really lovely.'

'That's pretty shit. But you shouldn't let what he's done make you feel bad. You can only control your own behaviour, not someone else's.'

'I guess,' Will said, but still looked really unlike himself. It seemed odd to Poppy that he was so invested in Brendan's love life, or that it should upset him so much. But she understood how much his university girlfriend had scarred him when he found out she'd been cheating on him for months. That must be why he was taking this so badly.

Poppy could hear a knocking sound and Brendan appeared behind Will's head. He twisted around to talk to him, and when he turned back, his face was still drawn. 'I'm going to have to go, Pop. Everyone's meeting at one of the bars and Brendan is going to drive.'

Trying to cheer him up, she said, 'Well, maybe that's a good thing. He won't drink as much or get himself into trouble.'

'I guess we'll see.' He was standing up and now Poppy could only see his midzone. 'I'll be right. Got to go. Love you.' Then he shut his laptop screen.

'I love you,' Poppy said quietly to her empty room.

His abrupt ending to the call surprised her as did his whole demeanour during it. She placed her phone beside her on the bed and looked out the window, unable to shake the uneasiness about Will's state of mind. He seemed so down on the phone, it was so unlike him. Poppy worried that there was more happening than he was admitting too. She couldn't see him being this down over something at work, he was usually pretty relaxed and honest about any mistakes that might happen. What if he, too, had kissed someone else? What would that mean for them? And could that be why he was so reluctant to even hint at moving in together?

Poppy needed to distract herself, otherwise she was really going to sink into a negative thought spiral.

'Wait up, Luc?' Poppy called out. She leaned forward, placing her hands on her knees and sucked in deep gulps of air. Frizzy tendrils of hair stuck to the sides of her face, and she knew she must be as red as a beetroot. Lucas had turned back to talk to her but was annoyingly jogging on the spot.

Poppy raised her eyes to his and said, 'You know I suck at running.'

'I know, but the pool and gyms are shut, and there's nothing else we can do outside within the 5km radius,' Lucas replied, still bouncing on his feet. Poppy noticed, with further annoyance, that he was barely breaking a sweat. 'Come on, Pop, you can do this. It's only one more 'kay until we get back to the car. Now buck up, stand up, and let's keep moving.'

She looked up again to give him a death stare, but he had already turned around and started moving down the path again. Jeez he was a tough task master. Fuck, she thought, standing up straight and noticing the pull in her lower back as she did so. Her lungs were burning, and her back was aching. Running had never been one of her favourite exercises to do, but with the long shifts, lack of access to the pool, beach, or gym, she hadn't really done a lot of exercise since Will left for Dubbo, and she could feel her waning fitness in every laboured breath, jarred joints, and tight muscles as her feet continued to propel her down the path.

They were running part of the Bay Run around Haberfield. And it was a glorious afternoon – the sun was shining and there was little humidity with a slight on-shore breeze. When Poppy finally came in sight of Lucas and Gemma's car, she saw Luc leaning against it, drinking and scrolling on his phone. There was a thin sheen of sweat over his forehead, and his cheeks were a pale pink, but he didn't look like the wheezing, red-hot mess that Poppy knew she was right now. She walked the last few steps and Lucas reached behind him into the car and handed her drink bottle to her.

'Thanks.' Taking thirsty gulps, with some spilling onto her chin, Poppy rested next to Lucas on the car and looked out over the water. There were no boats out there today, no car noise behind her, and the sky had that crystal aquamarine colour, so perfect without any pollution, it took Poppy's breath away.

'What?' Lucas asked.

'I was just appreciating how beautiful it is. And how quiet. The sky is so clear right now.' Poppy pointed a hand up above her.

'Yeah, I've noticed it too when I've been out jogging,' he said before refocusing back on his phone. 'Without all the cars and trucks on the road, the air and sky are so much clearer.'

Poppy kept scanning the water. It was so lovely to be outside and not in the hospital or their apartment. She didn't want to waste it by looking at her phone like Lucas was because she didn't know when she'd next be able to do something like this.

'You ready?' Lucas asked, putting the lid back on his empty bottle and placing it in the drink holder beside the driver's seat.

Poppy nodded and went around to the passenger side to get in. Her mind drifted back toward Will again as *Happier* by Marshmello and Bastille came on the radio. He'd been so unlike himself lately. Could he be getting depressed? She knew how pervasive it could be, and with him so far away from her, both physically and mentally, she worried that there was little she could do for him.

'Hey, Luc…' She pivoted in her seat to face him as they drove along Dalhousie Street.

Not taking his eyes off the road, he responded, 'Yup?'

'Have you talked to Will much lately?' Her water bottle was resting in her lap and she started rolling it between her hands.

'Not since he went to Dubbo, why?' His eyes met hers for a moment before he turned back to the road.

'He's just been sounding more down the last few times we've talked. I'm starting to get a bit worried about him.'

'Oh?'

'Yeah. He's pretty bored in Dubbo, and there's not much to do... I wonder if maybe you could give him a call sometime. Just, you know, check in with him?' She kept her eyes down on her bottle but could feel Lucas's on her when they stopped at a red light.

'Sure, I can do that.'

'Thanks, I appreciate that.' She stopped rolling the bottle. This was good. Blokes sometimes talked blokey stuff or cajoled one another into a more positive outlook. They wouldn't openly discuss their feelings, but they had this way of skirting around the edges of something important that seemed to work at times better than when women got together and wallowed in their emotions. Poppy really hoped that a call from Lucas would help. She put her bottle in the drink holder and looked out the window, enjoying the bright colours on display and let Will loose from her mind.

Chapter 22

Monday 17th February

At handover, Monday morning, Poppy found herself not being surprised when Josh took the seat next to her.

'Hi,' he said as he sat down.

'You again?' she replied, not unkindly this time.

''Fraid so.' He crossed his legs and leaned back in the chair but this time he was angled toward, rather than away from her.

'Oh well. I guess I could do worse.' She smiled to herself under the mask.

'True,' he said without a hint of humility.

Maybe Josh wasn't as bad as she had thought. He might even be growing on her. Will had been fairly flat again on their call yesterday, and Poppy wasn't sure how to help him. She tried drawing him out in conversation without success, even suggesting he have a chat with one of his siblings, or one of his closest friends, but Will had insisted there was nothing wrong. The chasm between them was growing, and the things left unsaid were weighing more heavily on Poppy's mind. So, spending time with Josh, and the normality of ward work (even COVID ward work), currently seemed a lot easier than tackling her feelings about her relationship with Will. A relationship that only a few weeks ago had seemed so strong, now felt precarious.

Poppy and Josh fell into a routine during the week. They worked side by side, ate together, and even socialized together in the Residents' Lounge in their limited downtime. Slowly, Josh opened up more about his past. Poppy already knew he had been raised by his mother, but her insight grew when she realised how much scarring his absentee father had really caused. His whole body appeared to tense when he talked about him, and his sentences became short and delivered through progressively pursed lips. This physical reaction moved Poppy, and her own scars, that Josh himself had inflicted, began to dissolve. How could she hold against him the hurt he inflicted on her in trying to avoid being hurt by another person? Whilst his method of avoiding the heartbreak of loss was different to the one she used after Lulu, it came from the same well of despair. She suddenly realised that at their cores, they were both just desperate to avoid the pain of loss again and had built up their own walls and protection systems to avoid it.

'I was lucky, though,' Josh said as he leant forward to hit a pool shot in the Residents' Lounge one late afternoon.

'In what way?' Poppy asked, as they continued to talk about Josh's formative years.

'Well, it would have been so much worse if Mum had a parade of boyfriends in and out of the house. At least she was supportive of me and my future.'

'She sounds like a great mum.' But Poppy wondered how hard she must have worked as a single parent and whether Josh was left on his own much.

'She is.' There certainly didn't appear to be any underlying tension in Josh's face to suggest he harboured any ill-feeling towards her. He appeared relaxed and open. They had their masks in their pockets in here as they were on their own and it was such a big room. He leaned down to line up the ball and executed a perfect shot, sinking his target in the side pocket. 'And she and her brother are really close. So, I spent a lot of my childhood with my cousins. I never felt too alone.'

Uncanny that he'd basically read her mind. She looked down at the cue in her hand and felt momentarily guilty for thinking he'd been alone. How presumptuous of her. 'That's nice. I'm not really close with mine.' Maybe she was the one who'd missed out on something in childhood, not him.

'No?' He'd finished his turn and came to sit on the window ledge next to where she'd been waiting. He was watching her closely, expecting her to divulge more.

'We were in the country, and they were in the city. So, it was really a once-a-year, Christmas kind of relationship.'

'You didn't have other family in Orange?'

'My dad's sister and parents were there. But my dad's sister didn't have any kids and she was much older than him, so I don't think they were that close. My cousins are on my mum's side. But it was good to have grandparents around. They're both dead now, but when I was little we spent a lot of time with them.' Poppy hadn't thought about her paternal aunt or her grandparents in ages. There was a tug of grief thinking about her grandparents, remembering sleepovers, hot chocolates, and wrinkled but strong hands, and then it was gone.

Josh looked down at his cue. 'I only really had one grandparent in my life. I didn't have any contact on my dad's side, and my mum's father died before I was born, so I only had my mum's mother.'

'Is she still alive?' She didn't want to dwell on her own grief and was more interested in pulling together more threads of Josh's life.

He chuckled in a way Poppy had not seen him do previously. It was youthful and unpretentious. 'Yes, she is, and she's a real spitfire.' He looked back up at her, that impish grin in place. 'She's only about five foot two, but she doesn't hold back her opinions. I really enjoy her company. She gives as good as she gets.'

Poppy liked this look on Josh, it was endearing. 'It sounds like you've been raised by two strong women, then?'

'I have.' He nodded and rocked his crossed leg at the same time. She'd never seen Josh this at ease and relaxed, she was keen to one day witness Josh in his mother's and grandmother's presence.

They continued their game of pool until the ward needed them again. But Poppy thought more about what this conversation revealed about Josh's own personality. It sounded to her like he enjoyed banter. His grandmother was tough and maybe even a little tyrannical, and his mother was soft and possibly subservient to Josh's needs. Maybe the reason he often yo-yo-ed between almost cruel banter and then supportive teammate might reflect this dichotomy in his upbringing. Maybe he needed an equal partner who could help him find a happy balance between the two extremes. Soften the more cynical and cruel aspects of his personality and open him up to a more empathetic attitude toward others. For that to happen, though, Josh would need to open himself up to love and partnership. And Poppy didn't think he had the insight yet to allow that.

Several days later, Poppy was shocked by Will's appearance on FaceTime. They'd kept missing each other's calls and it was the first time they'd managed to connect. There were deep shadows under his eyes and he had more stubble than she'd ever seen before. He must not have shaved since they last talked.

'Hey, are you okay?' Poppy asked, worry creasing her brows.

'I was on last night and got called in for an epidural and then there was an emergency appendicectomy, so it was a long night.'

'What did they have you doing today?'

'Not much. Just ICU and there was one case in theatres.' He yawned on the screen.

'I guess you'll want an early night, then?' It was already nine o'clock.

'Yeah,' he yawned for a second time. 'I'm pretty beat.'

Poppy looked down at her bed and picked at a loose thread on her bedspread, rolling it between her fingers. She had still not found a good opportunity to talk about moving in together. Their conversations were becoming increasingly short and superficial and aside from her growing concern about their relationship, she remained worried about Will's mental health. Each call felt more and more like a chore, and less something she was looking forward to. Lucas had been true to his word and rung earlier in the week but had said that Will had been pretty cheerful on the call, so maybe Will was only moody with her. And if that was the case, what did that mean for them?

'Is everything okay with us?' she asked suddenly, not wanting to tiptoe around any longer.

'What do you mean?' Will's brows pulled together, his voice now with an edge to it.

'It's just that you've seemed really down and not that keen to talk to me lately. I just want to make sure that you still want to be with me?' She bit her lip, waiting for his response, her eyes searching his.

Will sighed and dropped his eyes. 'Of course I do, Poppy.' But he sounded angry rather than reassuring. He also didn't add anything further which made his statement more difficult to believe.

'I love you, Will. I just want you to come home to me. I miss you so much, and I miss us.' She could feel the tears threatening and there was a catch in her throat, stopping her from saying more.

'I do, too.' But again, to Poppy's ears Will sounded tense and testy. How could she get him to relax and open up to her?

She swallowed hard, hoping her voice wouldn't crack when she spoke. 'So, there's nothing to be worried about?'

'Now you sound paranoid. I'm not Brendan, I haven't been cheating on you—'

Her ears were ringing. 'That's not what I'm suggesting,' she interrupted. 'I'm worried about you, Will. You seem depressed.' Her voice dropped lower. 'I don't know what to do to help you from here.' She looked at Will's face on the screen, silently imploring him to talk to her. Confide in her.

But his body stiffened and his jaw set hard. 'I'm not depressed. I'm just angry.'

She sat back. This was not the response she was expecting. Trying to keep her tone level and non-threatening, she continued. 'What are you angry about?'

'You and Josh.' His breaths were coming quickly.

'Me and Josh?' Poppy's eyebrows hit the roof. 'What about me and Josh?' Now it was her turn for annoyance to creep into her tone.

'You're spending so much time with him, and I don't trust him.' His body was still tense and he was still breathing fast.

Poppy softened and had to hold in a laugh. At least this was something she could reassure him about. 'Hon, you have nothing to worry about. We're working together. Neither of us has a choice in that. He has been completely professional.' When his body showed no sign of softening to her message, she added, 'We just work together. Trust me.'

Poppy watched Will rub his hair out of his face once more. He really looked terrible. 'Sweetie, trust me. I love you. I want to be with you. In fact, I want to move in with you.' The last word caught in her throat and her guts clenched. She really hoped this would brighten him up but was dismayed when his body showed no sign of relaxing.

'What?' Why did he look like he'd been hit in the face?

Swallowing hard, her hand shaking, she continued. 'That's right, you heard me. I want us to move in together when I move out of here. I've been trying to find a way to bring it up these last few weeks, but you've just seemed so unlike yourself, I didn't know how to.' Her voice petered out toward the end like a train running out of steam.

Poppy watched on in shock as Will started to cry, his shoulders juddering and his hand covering his face.

Her chest tightened. 'Sweetie, what's the matter?' This was so unexpected. Why would the question of them moving in together make him cry? What was happening here? Blood began to pound in her ears as she watched her shaky screen, waiting for him to respond.

'I'm sorry,' Will said in between sobs, his hand still covering his face so Poppy had to lean as close as possible to her screen to make out the words.

Quietly she said, 'Sorry for what?' Her insides twisted painfully and she held her breath, waiting for his reply. What could make him this upset? It must be really bad.

'I've… I've done something stupid…' He started crying louder and Poppy found herself no longer looking at Will, but at the dirty white ceiling and 1980's track lighting above where Will was sitting. Where'd he go?

'Will?' she called out.

There was no answer, just the sound of muffled crying.

'Will, honey? Please talk to me…'

Poppy waited, blood pounding in her ears. What has he done? For the first time she wondered if he had been with someone else. She felt sick at the thought. Or could it be something to do with work? Her mind skipped through several possible scenarios, with increasing ramifications whilst she waited for him to pull himself together and talk to her. She wasn't sure which she dreaded more – something really bad at work, or a betrayal of her trust? All she could see was the dirty ceiling. When she could no longer hear him crying, she wondered if he had left the room. A brief flare of anger lit inside her then extinguished when she heard Will blow his nose. Then he picked up the phone and his face came back into view.

'What's happened?' Poppy asked gently.

In a whisper-quiet voice that Poppy strained to hear, Will said, 'I took some fentanyl from work.'

Poppy recoiled. He couldn't be serious!

His sunken eyes, ringed in purple shadow and red from tears, begged her for understanding. Whatever possible scenarios Poppy had imagined, this was not one of them. But she had to admit, it kind of made sense – the moodiness, the hollow look of his face.

'O-kay…,' Poppy said slowly, her heart pounding in her chest and sweat prickling her scalp. She tried to school her features into something neutral whilst internally her body was ringing all kinds of alarms. 'Tell me exactly what happened.'

Poppy listened as the whole story fell from Will's lips in a hurried, whisper-soft eruption. Brendan had not been the one to cheat on his girlfriend with a young local, it had been Will. When this came out Poppy wanted to scream at him. It was like he'd stabbed her in the chest with a knife, the blade piercingly hot. Her thoughts stopped momentarily as she stared at the screen.

'I'm so sorry, Poppy, I was very drunk, and she reminded me of you.'

What the fuck? Is that supposed to make me feel better about this?

Now that previous flare of irritation was starting to boil into anger. Poppy could feel her neck and cheeks heating up but she kept her jaw clenched shut, knowing she couldn't interrupt. She needed to hear the whole story.

'I was almost able to convince myself it was you.' Will explained how he kissed her on the dance floor of the only nightclub in Dubbo. It had been Brendan, not Will, who had pulled him away and taken him home before he could make the situation worse by sleeping with the girl. Ever since that night, though, his guilt and anger at himself had grown to the point of intolerability. He couldn't sleep, barely ate, and the lack of interesting work, meant long boring days stuck reliving his stupidity and obsessing over his mistake.

'And each time I saw you on FaceTime, the guilt overwhelmed me. That's why I've been avoiding your call the last few days…'

He purposely avoided me?

Poppy was winded.

Will raked his face with a free hand. So often in Anaesthetics they used only a fraction of a vial of fentanyl and discarded the rest. In Sydney, they were strict with recording and witnessing the discarded remnant vials, but in Dubbo, there was less supervision, and it had been easy for Will to pocket a partial vial as he pretended to throw it in the sharps bin.

'I kept the vial in my pocket all day, not sure what I was planning to do with it and whether I would actually use it. Instead of obsessing about what an idiot I had been, I was obsessing about whether to take the fentanyl or not. I could almost feel it as a hot stone in my side.'

You fucking idiot.

It was getting harder for Poppy to keep her face neutral as she continued to listen.

'And then I took it home with me at the end of the shift, with what I would need if I decided to use it.'

So not just the drug but at least a needle and syringe as well. Planning to take it. Planning suggests he'd thought about this before, if not acted on it. Poppy's brain was screaming now, *Fuuuuck*!

Her cheeks were on fire, not sure how much longer she could hold back. Wanting this to be over so she could hang up and scream into her pillow and let the hot, angry tears flow.

'And then you were so excited about Lucas' ring and his planned proposal. And you brought up moving out again. And I knew you wanted me to suggest we move in together, I could see it on your face. And I just couldn't. How could I suggest we move in together, when I'd cheated on you? And when I told you it was Brendan, you were so understanding. It just made me feel worse.'

Poppy saw his hand pound his chest. Did her understanding mean he was blaming her for making him feel more guilty?

'So that night, when I got back from the pub, Brendan was still out, and I came home and took it… Not all of it, just a tiny bit. And I felt nothing for a while. No guilt. No disappointment, just blissful nothingness…' His voice petered out.

Jesus. What the fuck do I do with this?

He'd stopped looking at her, his head low, his voice barely audible. 'The next morning, though, I couldn't believe what I'd done. I discarded the rest of the vial and hid the sharps container in my bag until I got to work on Monday and then discarded it at work. Poppy, I'm so ashamed. I don't know what to do.'

Now he looked at her with desperation. He needed her to forgive him. If she didn't, she knew this could be the beginning of something much bigger than kissing someone else and stealing drugs once from work. She knew she would need time to really process this, but right now, she just had to support him.

Despite her body internally protesting, she said calmly, 'It's okay, Will. We can work this all out.'

'Really?' Will asked, tears sliding down his face again and his body slumping with relief. 'You mean that?'

I don't know.

Poppy tried to detach from this and pretend she was just a doctor and he was just a patient. She let her professionalism take over and smothered her burning anger. Her voice remained gentle and even. 'I do. It will all be okay. But right now, I need you to promise me, that if you feel like using again, you'll call me. Promise me.'

His eyes widened and his hair was sticking up on the side where he'd been rubbing it. He was leaning toward the screen now and Poppy could make out spittle in the corner of his lips. It added to the slightly crazed look. 'I'm never going to do that again, Poppy, I swear.'

She could see that he was resolved never to be in this position again.

How she hoped that feeling would hold. 'Okay. But if you do, you need to call me.'

She needed him to reavow this. 'Okay, but I'm not.'

His jaw was tight once more.

Now her own anxiety crept into her voice as the professionalism slipped. 'And you don't feel like using again?' This time it came out almost as a squeak.

But Will was emphatic. 'No! One hundred percent, no.' He faltered and his voice dropped. 'You believe me, don't you?'

Poppy was shell-shocked and couldn't bring herself to say, "yes." Her body suddenly depleted from the internal struggle it'd just waged, but her heart still pinged with the look on Will's face in that moment. She nodded then tore her eyes from the screen. The abandoned thread still rested on her crossed legs and she focused on that while her mind processed all that she'd just heard. Two things she never thought Will would be capable of – cheating on her, and using drugs, and he'd done them both in one go.

She looked back up to the screen and found Will staring forlornly at her. Her body shivered, a sign that the adrenaline was dissipating. Poppy wanted to end the call so she could be alone to think, but she was anxious not to make him feel badly for fear he might use again.

'I don't want you to worry, Will. We'll find a way to sort through this. I'm glad you told me. But right now, I need to process this. How about I give you a call before I go to work in the morning? We both need to get some sleep.'

He looked fearful. 'Okay, but please call me?'

'I will. I promise.'

'I love you Poppy, and I'm really sorry.' His voice caught and he swiped at his nose.

Poppy ended the call and lay down on her bed.

She felt like she'd just aged ten years in the space of that phone call. It was bad enough that Will had kissed someone else, but that he'd stolen drugs from work – fentanyl at that – was so much worse. She didn't know what to do or how to feel about this. Staring at the ceiling for five minutes didn't enlighten her any further, either, so she ventured to the kitchen, poured herself a shot of vodka and slung it back in one go, appreciating the hot fire that slid down her oesophagus and warmed her stomach.

The lights were off in the lounge and the front door deadbolted, so Gemma and Lucas had already turned in for the night. She wouldn't tell them about this anyway. Stealing fentanyl from work was a major deal, and despite her need to offload it to someone else, Poppy was pretty sure that this needed to stay between her and Will. What the hell was she going to do now?

Chapter 23

'Are we okay?' Will asked desperately when Poppy called him on her way to work the next morning.

Did she even know the answer to that question?

Will anxiously swiped his hair off his forehead while he waited for Poppy to answer.

'I love you, Will, but there's a lot we need to discuss and work through.'

'I know. I'm so sorry, Poppy.' Another hair swipe. 'I'm sorry, I've been such a fuck-up.'

Poppy watched her screen as she walked. Her Airpods were in place and with no one else near her on the pavement, she wasn't concerned with being overheard. His face looked creased from sleep and his vulnerability last night and again now was what moved her most.

'Will, everyone makes mistakes, I get that. But this is big.' She could see him move toward the screen like he was about to interrupt. 'Let me finish.'

'Okay.'

'We're going to need to work through this. Together. And that's difficult with the distance and my long shifts.' Each step toward the hospital was like wading through a muddy field. Slow and arduous.

'I know, you're right.' Poppy noted the dejection in his voice and his slumped posture. Like he was already giving in and giving up, without even trying.

She had to pump a positive tone into her voice for Will's sake, even when her whole head felt heavy with the weight of his admission. 'So, let's talk again tonight, okay?'

'Okay. I love you, Poppy.'

'I know. Have a good day,' she said as she ended the call. She couldn't bear to say, "I love you" right now.

Poppy had not slept well and now she felt physically sick. Her thoughts kept dissecting what she saw as three issues. The first, the kissing someone else. That was the easiest. He'd been very drunk, it was stupid, and with the other bigger issues, Poppy could easily forgive this slip-up. The other two issues were far greater and could carry more serious ramifications. Will had stolen fentanyl from work!

If anyone found out, a complaint to AHPRA could be made. At best, he could have restrictions put on his medical registration. At worst, he would be deregistered as a medical practitioner and maybe even charged with a criminal offence. This frightened Poppy inordinately. The third issue was the drug use itself. Poppy never would have thought Will at risk of drug addiction. He had such a relaxed and philosophical view of things. She'd barely seen him angry, let alone distressed enough to look for an easy escape. Whilst she knew that taking drugs once didn't make him an addict, could it open the door to the possibility in the future? Should he see a counsellor now? Poppy felt completely out of her depth. Will's behaviour the last few weeks had been disturbing, but she had no idea how bad the problem really was, or how alone she would feel.

If only it had been as simple as depression.

What she feared only a day earlier would seem like a blessing compared to what she now faced. She couldn't tell anyone about it, she couldn't ask for help, and in some ways neither could Will. Asking for help would be tantamount to admitting he'd stolen and used drugs. What were they going to do?

Poppy was so distracted that she barely took anything in at handover and buggered up donning her PPE. The nurse supervising had to ask her to start again.

'Are you okay?' Josh asked when she eventually sat down at the nurses' station.

She barely turned her head to look at him when she replied. 'Yep.'

'Are you sure?' Josh persisted. 'You're not feeling sick? Feverish? Should we do a COVID swab?'

Poppy looked him in the eyes. She'd started to trust Josh this last week or two and she saw genuine concern on what she could see of his face.

'I'm not sick. Just distracted.'

'Something to do with Will?' His posture stiffened.

'Yes. But I don't want to talk about it, so let's just get started, okay?' She pulled her ward list from out of her scrub pants pocket and flattened it on the desk.

They worked as usual, side by side, but Poppy remained distracted. Half her mind was on the jobs at hand, and half was floating behind her like a half-empty helium balloon, dragging on the string. The balloon contained thoughts of Will and fentanyl and what she should do. By the time they walked up to Campos for a coffee a few hours later, Poppy still had no clear plan.

They'd walked up in silence, Josh respecting her need for space, but when they sat down with their coffees, he handed her a caramel kiss.

'I thought you could use this,' he said and then took a sip of his coffee.

Poppy looked up at him and smiled. 'That's very sweet of you.' She hadn't even noticed him buying it.

As she took a bite and a sip of her coffee, she tried to focus on the sensations and block thoughts of Will. The caramel was rich and well offset by the chewy biscuit base and the rim of dark chocolate on top. Poppy loved caramel. She loved hard caramels, Fantails, salted caramels, and dulche de leche. It was her go-to flavour of ice cream or gelato, and her first pick in a box of chocolates. It should make her feel better now. But she couldn't quite switch off her brain, and her lips turned down. She placed the half-eaten kiss down on her lap with a loud exhalation through her nose.

Josh, who'd been looking off into the distance, quietly drinking his coffee, turned toward her. 'I know you said you didn't want to talk about it. But I don't think I can go the whole twelve hours in silence.'

Poppy looked at him and then away, into the distance. 'I'm sorry, Josh. I've just got a lot on my mind.'

He rested his coffee on the side of the bench they were sitting on. 'I'm going to level with you. I don't really want to hear about you and Will. But it's clear that something is bothering you, and in order to get back to our usual cordial repartee, I need you to feel better. So, what can I do to make you feel better? I thought the caramel thingy would help, but clearly, it's not enough.'

Poppy couldn't help herself; she laughed. Trust Josh to make this about him. Stupidly, it also worked to get Poppy to stop thinking of Will and the huge hole he had dug himself.

'You really are self-centred, you know that, right?' Poppy replied when she stopped laughing.

Josh smirked in response. 'I know. But I think it's a gift.' He quirked one eyebrow up and down.

Poppy laughed harder, feeling lighter. 'Really, how so?'

'Well, thinking primarily of oneself, avoids situations like these,' Josh said, making a circle with his hand around Poppy's face. 'You can't get truly crushed by someone, if you never let them in, in the first place.'

Poppy stopped smiling. Josh had just nailed it. Will had crushed her. But he'd also loved her in a way no one else had. And she loved him too. Enough to want to help him, despite feeling completely out of her depth and on her own.

She reached a hand toward Josh and rested it lightly on his arm. 'But that's sad, Josh.' Her voice was soft. 'If you never let anyone in, you'll never be in love.'

'And this is what love looks like?' Again, he made the same circle gesture with his hand around Poppy's face.

She sat back. 'Sometimes, yeah.'

'I think I'm sparing myself, whatever this is.'

She didn't want him to think that love just hurt. 'But sometimes, it's also amazing, like flying high in the sky, or cuddled in a warm embrace, protected and safe, or burning with desire—'

'I don't need to hear that bit,' Josh interrupted quickly.

Poppy coloured. 'I just mean that, yes, when you love you open yourself up to occasional hurts and the potential for loss, but you also gain so much in the process. Before Will, I was scared to love. Like you, I kept things pretty superficial. Just sex, mainly.' Her gaze darted away from Josh. 'But now, I know that even when things are tough, I'd still want to be with Will, still want to share my journey with him. The good bits and the bad. It's all worth it.'

Poppy felt a loosening inside her. She was confident that she and Will could get through this. They would be okay.

'No.' Josh shook his head. When he turned back, the impish grin had returned. 'I'm still not convinced. You make a somewhat compelling argument, and you are smiling now, but the way you've been so down today, I'm not sure it's worth it.'

She knew he was playing with her. And for once she didn't find it manipulative, just fun. 'Well, Josh, I'll have to keep working on you,' she finished, lifting the rest of the caramel kiss to her mouth.

'Okay,' he said. Poppy was focused on her treat and didn't know how to interpret his tone. But she was lighter now than she'd started the day, and for that she was grateful.

Poppy was walking home that night and noticed the weather had turned cool. Her thin cardigan barely protecting her from the cold wind that ripped up King Street. Will and she had a lot to talk about tonight and she knew she would likely be late to bed again. Just the thought made her yawn, but the coolness forced her to quicken her heavy steps. Josh also entered her thoughts on her walk. He had opened up to her more but she wasn't sure where they stood with each other. Were they friends now? Could you ever really be friends with an ex? And what about that moment in the morgue? Had he been honest with her when he said he still had feelings for her, or was that just him playing?

'Hi, Pop,' Gemma said, giving her a hug as she walked in the door. 'I've left dinner for you on the bench.' They'd all become less anxious about physical proximity as COVID fear had receded by immersion.

'Thanks, Gem.' She hung her bag over a dining chair and walked into the kitchen.

'How was your day. Josh still behaving himself?' Poppy noticed Luc turn on the couch to watch as Gemma mentioned Josh.

'Today was fine. And Josh is fine. But I need to talk to Will, so I might just take this into my room.' Steam was still coming off the bowl, so she didn't bother zapping it in the microwave, just grabbed a fork.

'Is everything okay?' Gemma asked, a pucker forming between her brows.

'There's just a lot going on. I'll fill you in later, I promise.' Poppy said, taking her bowl to her room.

She sat at her small desk and FaceTimed through her laptop so she could have her hands free to eat.

In the middle of chewing when Will's face came on the screen, she waved instead of saying hello.

'Hi!' Will's relief was palpable. 'I'm really glad you called.'

'I'm going to eat while we talk, it's been a long day.' Poppy forked another vegetable from the bowl and shovelled it into her mouth.

'Did anything happen at work?' His scowl was worse than Gemma's.

'No, just the usual sick COVID patients, and an AWOL boss. But it was okay. I just didn't get much sleep last night.'

Poppy took a couple more mouthfuls of food and decided Will looked better. There were less shadows below his eyes, and he'd shaved and washed his hair. He must have slept better after offloading the burden of his guilt onto her.

'I'm so sorry, Poppy. For everything. I'm sorry I was a drunken idiot and kissed someone else, and I'm sorry I didn't tell you about it. But most of all, I'm sorry that I've done something totally stupid and unforgivable. I'm sure that you're worried what this means?' He was looking at her intently but waited for her to respond.

She swallowed. 'Yes, I am a bit… Have you ever taken drugs like this before?'

She wasn't even sure she wanted to hear the answer. *What if he says yes?*

There was no hesitation. 'No, never! I swear. I've only ever smoked pot. And not often, just a bit early on at uni. I haven't smoked at all since starting work.'

'So why now? And why fentanyl?' Poppy could hear the shrillness sneaking into her voice.

Will hung his head, running a hand through his loose curls. 'I don't know, Poppy. Honestly.' He looked back up at her, his eyes imploring her again to believe him. 'I know how stupid it was. How risky and potentially career-ending. I'm so sorry. I was just so stressed. I felt horrible for not telling you and guilty as hell and I couldn't see a way out. I just wanted to escape myself, I think.' His voice had been strident at the beginning but now petered out with the self-loathing admission. 'Normally when I'm stressed, I surf. Being out on the water clears my mind. It grounds me. I don't know what to say or how to make you understand. I just lost myself.'

Poppy had stopped eating, her food now congealing in the bowl. She kept looking at Will, wondering if she knew him as well as she had thought she did. This just seemed so out of character for him. Maybe it was just a moment of craziness? A moment in time where his calm rationality couldn't calculate the risks and see the potential danger? But if that was the case, what was to stop that risk-taking behaviour from occurring again, the next time something really stressful happened in his life?

'But you're normally so calm and grounded.'

'That's what therapy and surfing did for me. Before that I was a ball of stress and anxiety. Angry a lot.' He seemed to run out of steam and just stopped in this halfway zone of explanation.

Poppy knew how much Will had helped and supported her last year and felt the pressure to return that support now he needed her help. Even if this scared her more than anything had previously, she had to at least try to support him now, and hope that she'd be able to get over the personal betrayal and fear that had started to creep in when she looked at his face.

But she couldn't flat-out lie. 'I can't tell you, I understand, Will. Because I don't think I do. Not really. What you did is just so beyond what's acceptable for doctors, but also beyond what I expected for us.'

'I know. I'm so sorry, Poppy.' He started crying again, breaking Poppy's heart a little more.

'I know you're sorry. I can see that. And I want to help you...' This time it was her pushing hair off her face and taking a breath. 'The drunken kissing, whilst upsetting, doesn't bother me too much. It's something I could forgive. If you had only told me about it, instead of lying and saying it was Brendan.'

It was weird how the mind worked. Poppy didn't realise until this came out of her mouth that this lie seemed to clinch the entire problem. Blaming the cheating on someone else – had that been to test her response? It suggested planning or manipulation, just like the syringe, needle, and sharps bin. But surely, Will wasn't that guy?

'I should have told you, I know. I wanted to. But I didn't want to lose you.'

And there it was a second time – insight and manipulation. She didn't want to believe it and again she pushed it deep inside. 'Even if you told me about the fentanyl, before you actually took it, I could have helped you. But you didn't, which makes me think there's more to this than impulsivity… And I don't know what to do, Will. I have no experience with this.' She slumped back in the chair, overwhelmed by contradictory feelings.

'Neither do I,' he protested. Again, Poppy thought it sounded like he was trying to prove to her this was a once-off event.

Silence fell between them.

'What should I do, Poppy? How can I prove to you that I'll never do any of this again?'

'I don't know, Will,' she whispered. Her heart felt so heavy. She still couldn't believe this was them. 'I don't think you can prove it to me.' Not realising it, she'd also made herself smaller – shrinking down in the chair, as if folding in on herself.

'I'll do anything. I don't want to lose you.' He looked as if he was in physical pain.

It hurt Poppy in her chest to see Will this way. It had been bad enough when he had looked so depressed and she felt helpless, but now he looked broken.

He needs to speak to a professional.

The truth was obvious to her, but how to explain it to him?

She chose her words carefully. 'I don't want to lose you either, but I'm out of my depth here. And you're in Dubbo and I'm not. And that worries me. It makes you vulnerable.'

'I promise you, I'm not going to use again. It was a stupid, stupid mistake.'

Worried he might blow up at the suggestion, she brought up the elephant in the room. 'I think you need to talk to a counsellor.'

His face immediately closed off, his body stiffening on screen. 'No. I can't do that, Poppy. There's mandatory reporting.'

Why is this all on me to sort out? Why isn't he giving any suggestions?

That flame of irritation flared again. This wasn't fair to her. It was time to put her foot down. She sat up straighter and looked at him directly. 'Will, you need to talk to someone. So, who is it going to be?' Her lips as straight as the line in the sand she was demarcating.

Now it was his turn to shrink on screen. 'Can't I just talk to you?'

She huffed and blew a segment of fringe off her face. 'No, Will. My hours are terrible. And this goes beyond me.' When he wouldn't meet her eyes, she softened fractionally. 'It needs to be someone you trust, who you can be open with, and who might be able to help work through whatever issues lie underneath this.' But then she let her inner thoughts out in a metaphorical punch. 'Because I don't think anybody wakes up one morning and just takes opiates for the hell of it. IV opiates, at that. I know you feel like shit for kissing some rando, but I honestly think this must go deeper than just that.'

Silence descended again and Poppy watched and waited. She wasn't going to back down on this, for both their sakes. Will was obviously thinking about what she'd said – his eyes were down and he was rubbing his chin, a mannerism she'd noticed he did when he was trying to decide on something. So, she waited. She let the silence grow, hoping he might come to the decision voluntarily. Any counselling process would also need his buy-in to be effective, so he needed to make the decision.

Another thought occurred to her while she waited. Was there a legal requirement for her to report him to AHPRA? She knew if he had used at work, during a shift, there would be an obligation under the concern for public safety. But what about this instance? Heat rose within at the idea of reporting him herself. It was not one she wanted to entertain and would be a death sentence for their relationship. Like the idea of him planning the drug-taking and cover-up story, she pushed it deep inside her for now. To be examined at some later date.

Eventually, he looked up, his eyes clear. 'I could talk to my sister?' He raised his eyebrows, clearly hoping this was an acceptable suggestion as his sister was a Psychologist in Brisbane.

'Do you think?' It wasn't unreasonable to Poppy's mind.

'I think she can keep it to herself.' He looked relieved.

'When will you speak with her?' Poppy wanted to cross her fingers. He would need to follow through and quickly, otherwise it would get put off and lost in the weeds.

'Tomorrow. It's too late now.'

Poppy relaxed back in the chair, her body depleted like she'd just run a marathon. 'Okay.'

Despite Will's protestations that he would do anything; Poppy knew forcing the issue would likely cause separation between them. The chasm, that had been growing all term, just got a little wider. She would have to hope that when they got through all of this, they'd still be close enough to bridge the gap.

After the call ended, Poppy sat with her laptop closed in front of her and stared at the photo on the wall of her and Lulu when they were younger. It was taken two years before Lulu's death and they were both smiling with their arms around each other. Lulu looked so full of life and promise – proof that a snapshot in time was so unreliable. From that photo, you could not tell that Lulu would go on to become depressed and commit suicide. Did these last twenty-four hours completely alter the course of Poppy and Will's relationship? Did it change the fabric of what she thought was true and to be trusted about them? If Lulu had confided in her, like Will had now, could she have prevented what happened? Would this plan of counselling protect Will from further drug use? There were too many question marks for Poppy's liking. She pushed back on the chair and stood up, trudging to her bedroom door.

In the kitchen, Poppy took a tub of Ben and Jerry's fudge brownie ice cream from the freezer and a spoon from the cutlery drawer.

'It must be a big deal if you're going for the big guns,' Gemma said, taking a seat opposite Poppy on one of the barstools. 'What's going on with you and Will?'

Poppy spooned a mouthful of ice cream into her mouth, buying herself time to construct her answer. She couldn't tell Gemma about the drugs; it would be too much of a betrayal.

'Will kissed some rando a couple of weeks ago when he was wasted and then lied about it. Said his flatmate, Brendan, had done it.'

'Oh.' Gemma looked startled. She clearly hadn't been expecting this.

'Yeah.' Poppy kept her head low and spooned another mouthful, worried if she looked Gemma in the eyes, she'd divulge more.

'So, you're pissed.'

'Yup,' Poppy replied around the spoon that was wedged in her mouth.

'Fair enough,' she said, nodding, 'It was a dick thing to do.'

'Yes, it was.' Poppy shoved the spoon back into the tub so the handle was sticking up. She risked looking up at Gemma; she was resting her elbows on the bench. 'But I'm mainly pissed about the lying. He's been withdrawn and acting off. I thought he was depressed. I was getting really worried about him. I even got Luc to ring him and check in on him.' Her pitch was rising and she paused to swallow, worried she was going to cry. If she started, she wasn't sure she could stop, and if that happened, Gemma would definitely know there was more to it than just the kissing.

Gemma cocked her head to the side. 'Mmm.' She thought for a moment. 'Well, he was obviously really stressing about telling you.' Clearly Gemma didn't think the blaming it on Brendan was a big deal, but she didn't know the full picture.

Poppy pushed off the bench and retrieved the spoon. 'I know. But I'm allowed to be pissed off.' Now she was tetchy when she spooned some more ice cream into her mouth. It was her favourite flavour, but she could barely taste it.

'You are, definitely.' Gemma's eyebrows narrowed in concern. 'But you're going to forgive him, right?'

If you knew the full story, would you be asking me that? Maybe you'd be telling me to run!

Poppy looked at her friend as she thought this. She was itching to tell her and to know what she really thought. But she averted her gaze and said what she thought was expected. 'Yes… Once I've fumed for a bit.' She wasn't entirely sure it was the truth.

Gemma sat back and tapped a hand down on the bench. 'Good. Because you two are great together.'

We were.

She didn't agree, instead choosing words that were safe. 'This separation is getting really hard. And who knows when it's going to end?'

'It will end, though. You just have to hang on a bit longer.'

'I'll try,' Poppy said, her voice flat. 'But I'm not sharing any of this with you, just saying.'

Gemma giggled. 'Fair enough,' she said, coming round the kitchen bench to wrap Poppy in a hug.

Poppy had hoped that she would sleep better that night, after talking to Will again, but she didn't. She continued to obsess about things, particularly the drug use, like continuously repicking a scab so it bleeds. If you do that enough times it will leave a scar. As she alternated between reading for distraction, and then tossing and turning, she kept coming back to the fear that bothered her the most.

Was this a sign that she really didn't know Will as well as she thought she did?

Chapter 24

Josh was going to stay filling in until Olivia came back from COVID leave. When they made their now-routine trek up to Campos for a coffee, Josh asked how she was doing today.

'I'm okay. Thanks for asking.' She didn't sound convincing, even to her own ears.

'Have you sorted out whatever is going on between you and Will?' Josh kept his eyes straight ahead as they walked, so Poppy couldn't see his facial expression but she could feel his body tense beside her.

'Uh... Not yet, not really.'

'I know I said yesterday that I didn't want to hear about you and Will…' He audibly sighed. 'But if you do want a sounding board, I can give it a go.' Everything about his body language said he'd be doing it under protest.

A brief laugh escaped Poppy's lips. She couldn't help it, the idea that she would confide in Josh her relationship problems was preposterous.

As soon as she had control over her face, she said, 'Thanks, Josh. It's a thoughtful offer, but it's okay. I've got Gemma to lean on. And it will all work itself out.' She wanted this to be true.

'Well, just putting it out there, that I'm here if you need me.' With that, he stood taller and continued walking, clearly relieved that he wouldn't have to hear the gory details of whatever was happening between them.

'Thanks.'

As the day went on, Poppy became progressively more fidgety. She checked the time on the wall clocks persistently and tapped her foot wherever she happened to be standing or sitting. If she hadn't been in PPE and in the middle of a pandemic, she probably would have chewed her nails. Will finally texted in the afternoon, when Poppy and Josh were taking a break in the Residents' Lounge and she excused herself and found an empty on-call room down the corridor. She took her phone out of the snap-lock bag and looked at the text.

> Will: Just got off the phone with my sis.
>
> Poppy: Excellent. How did it go?
>
> Will: Will fill you in tonight. But I think, ok. I love you, Poppy.
>
> Poppy: (heart emoji)

Poppy waited, watching the screen to see if Will would message again. Despite what she'd said the previous evening, she was hoping he'd tell her more about it. But she had to remind herself that he was at work too. It was probably just a brief chat to set up for a bigger talk later. At least it was a start, she reminded herself, standing up and heading back to the lounge.

'Something good?' Josh asked when she returned, smiling.

'I think so.' Some of the tension left her body. Now she wasn't the only one carrying the weight of Will's news.

'Excellent. So, you're going to stop moping around and entertain me again?'

Poppy laughed, 'It's always about you.'

'But of course!' His eyes sparkled with mischief.

How funny it was that she now enjoyed his company so much. Knowing him better, she realised that most of the time he was just having a laugh, trying to get a rise out of her, badgering her. It was an attention-seeking trait. She guessed another downside of being an only child. But now that she saw it for what it was, she could banter back, and it honestly felt good right now to keep things light when so much was weighing her down. She put thoughts of Will to the back of her mind, inside a door that she shut, turning the key in the lock.

'You want entertainment?'

'Yes!' Now he was positively grinning.

Poppy felt unexpected heat shoot in her groin. She was enjoying having his attention, even when she knew she shouldn't be encouraging him. Holding his gaze fractionally longer than necessary, to really hook him in, she finished with, 'Then let's play pool.'

Poppy watched him deflate, then laugh. He had obviously expected something better than that.

'Okay, but I'm breaking,' he said, standing from the couch.

'But, of course,' she cheekily parroted back to him, picking up a pool cue from the edge of the table.

'She just listened to everything I had to say, and it was good. I'm confident I can trust her to keep it to herself,' Will said while they were FaceTiming later that night.

'That's good. I'm glad. And look, you don't have to tell me what you talk about, but I'd like to know how you think it's going, does that sound okay?' Poppy gnawed at her lower lip as she waited for his reply.

'Absolutely! I will keep you up to date. And I don't want to shut you out, that's not what this is about.' He looked neat and at ease, closer to his usual self.

'I know. I get it, it was my idea. You need to talk to someone with experience. I just want to know that you are safe, and that you have more than just me to help you.' If she kept biting her lip like this, it was going to bleed.

'I do know. And there's really no risk.' He rubbed his hand lightly through his hair. Even this gesture held less tension than it had for a while. 'It was a once-off insanity. It will never happen again, I promise.'

How many addicts have sworn the same sentiments?

The more he said that, the more he brushed it aside as if it were trivial, the more Poppy's worries returned. Her guts suddenly like the roiling waves before a tropical storm. Choppy with no sign of abating.

When they finally finished talking, Poppy was shattered. Work was draining and the emotional strain of things with Will were superimposing on her already partially depleted state. Her brain felt almost empty, like the pressure of all these thoughts and emotions had caused some sort of explosion, decimating all activity for a while. She lay on her bed and put a random playlist on, noise-cancelling headphones blocking out everything around her, immersing her in the music. Her limbs heavy on the underlying sheets, her eyes closed.

Bad Liar, by Imagine Dragons, came on and Poppy's eyes flicked open. The singer was speaking to his partner, talking about infidelity and a troubled and unsustainable relationship. Tears slowly started leaking from Poppy's eyes. She hadn't cried until now. But now she couldn't stop. They built until she curled on her side, clutching her pillow to her chest, and grieving this change to her relationship with Will. Grieving too for the horrors she had faced at work, and the sudden uncertainty about the future. When *Bad Liar* finished, *Before you go* by Lewis Capaldi started, doing nothing to ease her suffering.

Whenever sadness overwhelmed Poppy, Lulu hovered around her like some translucent force. Old feelings returned to the surface. She'd not been able to save Lulu and now the fear of losing Will to whatever this was felt too much to bear. Her heart was carved out of her body. Bloody, raw, and pulverized. Poppy lay on her bed, hollowed out, until she fell asleep, fully clothed on top of the sheets, from sheer exhaustion.

Poppy and Josh worked well together, even under pressure, as they had discovered on nights. But over the next week, before Olivia returned to work, things got even busier. There had been an outbreak of COVID at one of the local nursing homes, and consequently, all the nursing home residents were moved into the hospital. They couldn't all fit on the COVID red ward, so the Geriatrics ward had become a temporary Geriatrics COVID ward. This meant these patients became managed by two teams – the Geriatrics team who managed the day-to-day geriatrics related issues, and the Respiratory team who managed the COVID related issues. Thankfully, they didn't all get admitted at one time; the administration had some sense here and staggered the admissions, with the sickest coming first, and trickling down to the asymptomatic positive patients waiting a few days before the transfer. It also enabled a fairly equitable split between the two

Respiratory teams. But they soon found the nursing home staff were becoming positive as well.

The hospital was reaching breaking point. Full wards, sick patients, staff numbers going down as the infection spread into the workforce, and a full on-site morgue. The fissure on Poppy's mouth was so bad now that it oozed continuously. She had dressed it, but the humidity under her mask and shield kept lifting the dressing, allowing sweat to trickle back in. Intermittent pain became a new companion. Sharp shooting bursts without warning as the salt content hit the wound. Each time it happened, she would stop suddenly, desperate to touch the affected area, but would have to remind herself mentally not to touch her mask.

'Are you okay?' Josh asked at one point, when Poppy stopped suddenly whilst walking in front of him and he almost slammed directly into her back.

'I've got a fissure at the edge of my lips, which is killing me. I can't get a dressing to stay stuck over it.'

Josh paused, then said, 'At the end of this ward, I'm going to look at it, and we'll go from there.'

'Oh-kayee,' Poppy said tentatively. She didn't really like the idea of Josh examining her, it was too intimate. But she was at the point where her own ideas were failing, and she would take all the advice she could get.

Each day, Josh and Poppy left the Geri's COVID ward until last. They had found in the first few days after the change, they kept tripping over the Geri's team if they went there after the red ward, because the Geri's team rounds just went on and on. It meant they became completely inefficient, and Josh had a really hard time with inefficiency. At one point, Poppy had watched him tap his foot while waiting for the Geri's Registrar to finish examining a patient so that he and Poppy could review them. He really didn't like to be kept waiting.

Thankfully, for Poppy, on this day, their round on the Geri's ward was quick and efficient. It was around midday, so the Geri's team had probably gone off the ward to have lunch, enabling Josh and Poppy to seamlessly review patient after patient. Another blessing that none of them were deteriorating. The previous day, they had sent two to ICU and had already heard this morning that neither had survived the night. Poppy was becoming hardened to the mounting death toll. No longer did each death physically affect her like a punch to the solar plexus, she was in pure survival mode now. And she had too many of her own worries to deal with.

Aside from the oral fissure, there was obviously the problems with Will, and she had started to develop low back pain and occasional sciatica. Long shifts on her feet, not enough exercise or time off, and probably reduced nutrition were contributing. But her whole body felt old. Tired, heavy, and stiff. Because of the lack of staff, and the twelve-hour shifts, Poppy (and everyone else) was way over the number of safe work hours. But no one had complained. What could they do, really? The wards needed staff, and there was simply not enough to go around all day, every day. If you had asked Poppy last year if she thought working one-hundred-and-twenty-hour fortnights was acceptable, she would have been shocked and appalled. That was one of the concerns she had raised after Tim's suicide. But now, that was becoming standard. What she really needed was a massage, but with all the restrictions in place, it was currently impossible.

'Right,' Josh said, as Poppy uncomfortably took a seat on the edge of the examination bed in one of the respiratory clinic rooms, all of which had not been in use for the last month. 'Mask and shield off. I'll have a look.'

The surgical dressing she had applied that morning was already peeling off around the edges. She was relieved Josh was gentle when he pulled it away, and closed her eyes as he turned on the inbuilt light attached to the magnifying headset he had just pulled down over his eyes.

'This is nasty,' he said, tentatively spreading the adjacent skin to examine the depth of the fissure. 'Open your mouth, so I can check if it involves the cheek as well.'

Poppy did as instructed and wondered if her breath was okay. She was grateful he was wearing a mask. He probably couldn't smell it even if it was rancid.

'It doesn't go through to the cheek, which is good. But I think we should get one of the ENT guys or Plastics to have a look at it. I'm not sure what's the best approach, given the humidity and moisture under the mask.'

'Me either. What I've been doing clearly isn't working.'

‘I’m mates with one of the ENT Regs, I’ll give him a call and see what he’s up to today. Probably not much as they’re only allowed to do emergencies.’

Poppy listened to Josh talk with his friend. It was weird listening to someone else’s conversation like this. People’s speech and mannerisms often changed depending on who they were talking to, and that was clearly the case here. Josh, who was normally so confident, supercilious, and at times cold, became blokey, using the word “mate” often, and his voice even sounded rougher, losing the usual well-rounded diction he used with her and the other staff. It turned out that his “mate” had gone to the same selective boys’ school with him and been captain of the rugby team. He’d been studying in the library, and was quite happy for a distraction, so said he would meet them at the surgical outpatient’s clinic.

‘Bro,’ the ENT Registrar addressed Josh as he approached and gave him a gloved fist bump. He definitely had a rugby player’s physique, being taller and broader than Josh. Poppy detected dirty blonde hair peeking out of his personalised scrub cap and had to refrain from sniggering at the clichéd golf motif.

‘You’re Poppy?’ he asked after he and Josh had finished their ritual greeting. ‘I’m Matt.’

‘Hi,’ Poppy said taking a step toward him from behind Josh.

‘Alright, let’s go in here,’ he said as he unlocked one of the closest clinic room doors with his ID card.

‘I’ll wait out here for you,’ Josh said.

Poppy, who had been following along, turned back. ‘That’s okay. I can just meet you back on the ward, if you like.’

‘It’s all good. I’m just going to wait.’

Poppy tipped her head to the side. She was going to protest further that this was unnecessary, but he had his head down and was looking at his phone, so she went into the clinic room.

‘Ooh, this is nasty,’ Matt said after he’d examined Poppy, standing in front of her as she sat on the edge of the clinic room bed. He was so tall, he had to really bend down to take a good look.

'I'm finding it hard to keep a dressing on because of the humidity under the mask. The sweat just keeps lifting the edges. And the pain as the sweat hits the centre is getting worse.'

'I'll bet.' He rolled the procedure trolley he'd prepared close to him. 'This is going to hurt like a bitch, I'm sorry,' he said as he dunked some gauze into chlorhexidine and then proceeded to clean the wound. Fire ripped through Poppy's mouth and licked its way up to her brain. It was so fierce, she had to grip the edges of the examination bed, and clamp her jaw shut to prevent herself from crying out in pain. She held her breath and squeezed her eyes shut until he had finished.

'Sorry about that, I know that was rough.'

Poppy wondered how often he said that to patients, and whether he was now hardened to the pain he caused, just as she was becoming hardened to the lives they couldn't save.

'Mmm,' was all she could say as she took her first breath and tried to release her fingers from the claw-like grip they held on the bed.

'You said you'd been using paw-paw ointment?' He peered down at her face, the light from his headset blinding her briefly before he realised and flipped the light toward the ceiling.

'Yes.'

He nodded. 'Not a bad thought. Good barrier, minor antibacterial properties. But I think you need something stronger. I'm just going to put Kenacomb on it. It's got a steroid, and antifungal, and an antibacterial in it. You can keep the tube,' he said as he applied a thick layer to the centre of the fissure and then a smaller layer over the raised edges. 'But make sure you clean it first. I'll give you a bottle of chlorhex as well. And you probably need to do it at least twice a day until it starts to heal.'

Poppy took the proffered tube. 'What about dressing it?'

'He tapped his foot while he thought. 'Yeah, that is trickier with the masks. I think this one might be the best option.' He rummaged in a cupboard full of different dressings. 'It's got a central non-stick pad, and a fairly strong adhesive on the edge...' He looked down at it doubtfully. 'But I'm not sure any of them will stay on for a whole shift. Here's a bunch to get you started. Just text me when you need some more, or if they aren't working. Josh can give you my number. And if it looks like it's getting infected, call me straight away. We don't want to take you to theatre, it might ruin your smile,' he finished cheerfully.

Poppy attempted a smile in response, but it was a weak effort. 'Thank you. And thanks for your help, I appreciate it.'

'No problem. It was probably the highlight of my day!' He offered her his hand to help her off the bed. They left the clinic room and met up with Josh in the corridor; he still had his head down, looking at his phone.

'All good?' Josh asked as they approached, sliding his phone into his pocket.

'Yep. Give her my number, bro, so she can call me for more supplies.' He waved and headed back to the library.

Josh noticed her hands full of antiseptic, ointment, and dressings. 'Do you want me to carry some of that for you?'

'Thanks.' She offloaded the dressings to him. 'Can we drop these up to my locker before we get lunch?'

'Sure.'

They walked in silence for a while, before Josh said, 'Do you know you're limping?'

'What?' Poppy looked down at her feet mid-step and almost tripped over. Josh put out a steadying hand. 'Yeah, mild but there. Left side.'

'Oh. I hadn't noticed.' Poppy blushed. First the mouth, and now this – Josh was going to think she was falling apart. 'But I have been having some sciatic pain,' she admitted quietly, sounding even closer to one of their geriatric patients.

'Really?'

She was quick to explain. 'Yeah. I think it's just an accumulation of everything, you know?'

'It sounds like you need a break.'

'In an ideal world.' Poppy laughed humourlessly. 'But at some point I'd love to get a massage, at least.'

'Might help.' Josh handed over the supplies so she could store them in her locker and then went to retrieve his lunch from his own.

Shit, my body is completely falling apart!

It's like she was becoming middle-aged and yet she was only twenty-four. Josh must think she was either a hypochondriac or just a decrepit weirdo. She hid her face in her locker for a moment before pulling her lunch out when he asked if she was coming.

For once, the rest of the shift was fairly light, and Poppy sat down with Gemma and Lucas when she got home after reheating the dinner they had made.

'So, what's new with you two?' She took a bite of the noodle dish in her hands and then winced with pain from the side of her mouth.

'Not much,' Gemma replied. Lucas was rubbing her shoulder while focusing on the TV. 'They've got me helping on Labour ward this week, which is awesome. Finally, I'm doing something I enjoy again. What's wrong with your face?'

Poppy had winced when she chewed. 'Fissure. It's been getting worse. Josh and then one of the ENT Regs looked at it for me today and gave me some cream and stuff. It was awkward... That's great about obstetrics, Gem. Are they short on staff?'

'Everyone is,' Luc chimed in, still focused on the TV. 'Even we are down in Cardiology.'

'What – more COVID in the staff?' Poppy had thought the COVID cases in staff were mainly restricted to those frontline workers exposed on a daily basis.

Lucas nodded and drew his attention away from the TV. 'Mainly community transmission, though.'

'Aren't people obeying the stay-at-home orders?'

'No,' Gemma said. 'I guess you've been so busy, you probably haven't been keeping up with the news and the press conferences.'

'No, not really.' She dropped her eyes back to her bowl, not wanting Gemma's penetrating gaze on her when it wasn't just COVID keeping her busy and away from the news. She was afraid Gemma would see through her to the turmoil brewing beneath the surface.

Thankfully, Gemma didn't notice anything was wrong. 'Yeah, the police are having real trouble enforcing the rules. There have been a few localised skirmishes between police and civilians, and I think they are reaching record numbers of fines issued for breaking the rules.'

Poppy looked back up, raising her eyebrows. 'Wow.'

'But some of the civil liberties groups are trying to mount a class action to quash the fines,' Lucas added, reaching to his glass to take a sip of wine.

'Sounds like I'm really out of the loop.'

They all turned their attention back to the TV and Poppy resumed eating. It sounded like a lot had changed in the community.

I wonder where all this is heading?

She couldn't imagine a civil uprising occurring in Sydney, but two months ago she couldn't imagine a global pandemic like the Spanish Flu, either, so what would she know?

When she took her bowl back to the kitchen, Gemma said, 'Hey, why are you limping?'

'Josh noticed it too, today. I've got some sciatica. My back's been really sore lately, I think from all the long shifts on my feet and the lack of exercise.'

'That's no good. Maybe you should see my cousin.'

'Which one?' Poppy asked, unsure where Gemma was heading with this. She knew none of Gemma's family were doctors or physios.

'Jane, the massage therapist.'

'Oh… yeah. I'd kill for a massage at the moment.'

'Do you want me to set something up?' Gemma picked up her phone that had been beside her on the couch.

'Won't that be completely breaking the rules?' Poppy was at the kitchen now and had placed her bowl on the bench while they continued their conversation.

'Yeah, but when everyone is breaking the rules for no good reason, why can't you break them for a good one?' She looked down at her phone again. 'I'm texting her now.'

Poppy laughed. She loved Gemma's mind sometimes. Generally, Gemma was a stickler for the rules. But on the odd occasion she thought the rule was stupid or it was already being bent or broken by others, she was quite comfortable breaking it herself.

Gemma's phone dinged. 'Are you off this weekend?' she asked, reading the message that had just come in.

'Yep, then Josh and I go back to nights again. I think they are just trying to keep us as a team now until Olivia is back.'

Gemma nodded. 'That's brutal. I'll see if I can set something up for Saturday.' Her head bent down again toward her phone and Poppy continued to the sink to rinse her bowl and place them in the dishwasher. 'And I'll make sure she knows she has to wear a mask.'

'That'd be great.' A massage would be bliss.

Almost as an afterthought, Gemma raised her head. 'Oh, and Luc said we were going to try to have a pretend Gaga concert this Saturday night. Did he tell you?'

Poppy looked behind Gemma at Lucas, who had his eyebrows raised. She knew exactly what this meant but was surprised things had moved so quickly while she'd been busy with Will.

'He mentioned something about it,' she said as casually as possible.

Lucas's face returned to a neutral expression as Gemma turned back to kiss him quickly on the cheek.

'Yeah, I can't wait. I reckon we can make it really fun. We'll have to strategize outfits.'

'For sure,' Poppy said, still in the kitchen, one hand resting on the benchtop.

Abruptly, Gemma stood up and came over to the kitchen bench. She lowered her voice. 'How are things with Will? We haven't really had time to talk about that for a few days, and you've been spending a lot of time FaceTiming each other.'

Poppy's eyes darted to Lucas', knowing even with Gemma's voice low, he would be able to hear. His attention was glued to the TV, but it was obvious he was listening. There was an underlying desire to unburden herself and tell Gemma exactly what was really happening. She wanted her friend's advice and reassurance that she was making the right choices. But she knew she couldn't do that to Will.

Forcing herself to meet Gemma's gaze, she said, 'Improving.'

'Sounds like you're still a bit frosty?'

Again, Poppy considered her choice of words. 'Maybe a little.'

It was better that Gemma thought she was holding back her forgiveness, rather than becoming suspicious that there was more to the situation than Poppy was letting on. She could be relentless if she thought you were holding back.

'Maybe the massage will help you let it go?' Gemma asked, hopefully.

'Maybe,' Poppy said as she left the kitchen.

Could her pain be a psychosomatic symptom, she wondered. Wouldn't it be amazing if something as simple as a massage could rid her of the anxieties about Will, the ones that kept her stomach roiling and her muscles spasming? Poppy would gladly break the COVID restrictions if that was the case.

Chapter 25

Poppy limped toward the end of the week, physically and emotionally. At least she had the pseudo-concert and the massage to look forward to before the horror of more night shifts. She'd managed to chat to Lucas alone when Gemma was doing an overtime shift and they had decided on their plans for the concert and Lucas' proposal. Poppy had even had a squizz at the ring. It was so exquisite, she couldn't hold back a few tears. She was so happy for them and amazed that she was going to get to take a part in it.

Will was still talking to his sister every day and looking bright and cheerful again when they FaceTimed. But as he returned more and more each day to his normal state, Poppy felt herself hollow out. She couldn't escape the fear that this might not be a one-off event. Or her newest fear; how would she feel about him when they were finally face-to-face in the same city again? Would she be able to collapse into his arms, and kiss him like all was forgiven and forgotten? Or had something between them been irrevocably lost?

In addition, she'd still heard nothing from Victoria or Dr Anderson regarding Prof Pilson. Would he ever come back to work? Working with Josh, she was less anxious about his absence as she'd seen first-hand what a good and competent doctor he was, and knew the patients were well cared for. But surely, they must make some kind of decision soon?

On Saturday morning, Poppy and Gemma stood in front of Gemma's open wardrobe. Gemma was pulling out skirts and tops and holding them up to herself, or Poppy, in front of the mirror in various different combinations and chatting excitedly.

'What about this for you?' Gemma said, holding up a strapless, black-and-white asymmetrical mini dress with a bustier top. The pattern was geometric, and Poppy knew it looked great on Gemma, but wasn't convinced it would look good on her shorter and bustier frame.

'I'm not sure,' Poppy admitted, scrunching up her face.

'Just try it on, and let's see,' Gemma cajoled.

Poppy quickly stripped down to her bra and undies and shimmied into the dress. She and Gemma had been living together for so long, they had no self-consciousness around each other. Once the dress was on, Poppy stood back to get a better view in the full-length mirror. Gemma was looking up and down Poppy's body, a frown line between her eyes.

'Um,' Gemma said. 'It's the right look, very Gaga... but there's something off... I can't quite put my finger on it.'

Poppy meanwhile was surprised it looked as good as it did. Her boobs weren't overflowing the bustier, and the asymmetry at the base wasn't too low for her small frame.

'I've got it! It needs red. I think we use really bright red lipstick and go crazy on the eye makeup. And I've got just the earrings,' Gemma said, rushing over to the chest of drawers and rummaging through her jewellery cases to find what she was looking for. 'These!' she proclaimed, holding up a pair of large red earrings with a smaller circle at the top and a larger circle below. 'Put them on.'

Poppy did as she was told.

'Now, imagine bright red lipstick and over-exaggerated eyes.' Gemma swept her fingers up beyond Poppy's eyes and then looked back at their reflection in the mirror.

'Yep, I think you've nailed it.' Poppy loved seeing her friend so excited. Neither of them had had any fun since that night out at the beginning of the term, and she knew this was going to be really special. It was so great that Gemma was really embracing the idea.

Turning away from the mirror, Poppy asked, 'What about you?'

Gemma flicked through some clothes again, then pulled out a micro miniskirt which would accentuate her long legs and a silver sequined top. She held them in front of her. 'What about this?'

'Not Gaga enough,' Poppy replied, taking over the search through the clothes. She was looking for something that had some green, wanting to tie in the emerald in the ring, she knew was coming out of the box later tonight. Despite Gemma's green eyes, she had little in the way of green tones in her wardrobe. Unsatisfied, Poppy stepped back, a hand to her chin, thinking.

'Hang on.' She went back to her own wardrobe and fossicked until she found what she was looking for. 'What about this? With that skirt.' Poppy pointed to the skirt Gemma had placed on the bed with the silver top.

Gemma picked up the skirt and held it up and Poppy held the top up while they both looked in the mirror and considered it. The top was one that Poppy had bought on a whim but never worn, realising once she got home that it was a bit too tight for her chest. It was a shimmering dark green and silver. Not sequins so much as a metallic material, that sparkled in different light or over the contours of your body. Because Gemma was taller, it left a band of flesh visible, and as her chest was smaller, it smoothed over her physique better, looking snug without straining.

'It's ace. Thanks, Poppy.'

'And some silver glitter on your temples?' Poppy suggested.

'Absolutely!'

Poppy smiled. Gemma was going to look awesome, when the moment arrived. 'Now that we've got us sorted out, what are we going to do with Luc?'

'I heard that!' Luc called out from the lounge area where he had been hiding since their operation began. 'I'll have you know that I am quite capable of sorting myself out, thank you very much!'

Poppy looked at Gemma and raised her eyebrows, and they both giggled quietly.

'I heard that, too!'

'Then you should stop eavesdropping,' Gemma said, heading back into the lounge room with Poppy on her heels. 'So, what is your plan, then?' Gemma, with hands on hips, towered over his crossed-legged position on the floor.

'It's a surprise,' Lucas said calmly, pausing his video game, the faintest smirk pulling at the corner of his lips.

'Not even a hint?' Gemma pestered.

'No.'

Gemma folded her arms and continued to look down on him, her stare intense, but he would not relent. So, she flounced off, back into their room, Poppy on her heels once more.

Once back in their room, Poppy whispered, 'What do you think?'

Gemma did an exaggerated eye roll. 'I don't know. I have no idea what he's planning to wear, and it's not like he's been out shopping, like ever!'

'But he might have bought something online,' Poppy suggested.

'I suppose,' Gemma said petulantly. 'I just hope whatever it is, it's good.' She flopped onto hers and Lucas' bed, pulling a cushion over her chest.

'I'm sure he'll make an effort. Remember, it was his idea.'

She didn't want Gemma to worry and she had to squeeze her nails into the palm of her hand to prevent herself from smiling. If she smiled, Gemma would surely realise there was more afoot and she was worried that she, unlike Luc, would crack under her intense gaze. Lucas had already shown her what he was planning to wear and had secretly stashed it in her wardrobe to avoid Gemma coming across it too early.

'Well, I'd better get out of this and get ready to head off to meet Jane.'

Gemma looked at her watch. 'You'd better motor. It'll probably take you half an hour to get there.'

She turned back. 'Even with less traffic on the road?'

Gemma sat up. 'You're right. It could be as quick as fifteen minutes.'

Poppy's feet were rooted to the spot as a thought arose. 'What should I say if the cops pull me over?' Maybe this was a bad decision.

'Just explain that you are a doctor and you're heading to St George for a shift in the ED.'

Had Gemma already thought this up herself? Had she secretly visited her family and not told her?

'And what if they ask to see my ID badge and realise it says The Bennelong instead of St George?'

Gemma twisted her lips to the side. 'Cross your fingers and toes that they're not that observant or hold your finger over the hospital name.'

'I don't know, Gem. Now, you've got me worried.' Maybe she should cancel.

Gemma stood and placed her hands on Poppy's shoulders. 'Trust me, it'll be okay. You need this.' She herded her toward her own bedroom. 'Off you go, it's time to get ready.'

Her voice sounded more like a preschool teacher than her friend. Poppy could picture her addressing her children in this voice in the future.

'Okay,' Poppy acquiesced, and closed the door behind her.

Gemma's cousin, Jane's place was in the Shire, bordering on the Royal National Park. They were in an upstairs room, looking out over the bush with the windows open. Poppy got comfortable on the massage table, down to her underwear with the large towel placed over her body. Jane started gently but soon found the muscles that were tight in Poppy's lower back and pelvis. Poppy focused on breathing through her pain.

When she finished working on Poppy's lower back, she rubbed some Tiger Balm into the sore spots. The cold fire of the tiger balm in her tight muscles combined with the soft breeze like champagne bubbles caressing Poppy's skin was surprisingly relaxing. The occasional squawk of a cockatoo or low warble of a currawong interspersed with the cheerful twitter of passing lorikeets made it a distinctly Australian setting. The Vietnamese sounding music, whilst not in keeping with the other sounds, was still soothing and somehow wasn't discordant.

Despite Gemma's prior strong words to her cousin, Jane was not wearing a mask. When Poppy was on her back and Jane was massaging her shoulders and neck, her sour coffee breath washed over Poppy, who caught a faint whiff of it despite her own mask in place. But it was the one sour note of the experience. As the massage came to an end, Jane whispered in her ear that she would give Poppy ten minutes to rest in place. Poppy had reached a state of semi-consciousness and let her mind slip, enjoying the warm breeze on her skin, and the birds twittering. Will briefly came to mind, but her relaxed state enabled her to let him go, without dwelling. Josh, too, was recalled, causing Poppy to stir momentarily from her deep ease, and this time she had to try more consciously to let her mind drift back to thoughtlessness. Finally, she was at peace, her mind rested, her body rested.

Then the timer brought her focus back to the present and she blinked herself into consciousness.

Born this way was blaring from the speakers, and all three of them were dancing, the girls shouting out the words, their arms reaching to the ceiling. Even Lucas was thrashing around, dressed in his silver and black shiny checked pants and his sheer black top. He even had silver sunglasses that weirdly reminded Poppy of Dame Edna Everage's. Lucas had set up a coloured LED light display which was flashing across the ceiling and the walls, the rest of the apartment lights off, and they'd moved one of the couches out of the lounge room, so they had space to dance and go crazy. Lucas had even found an old concert of Gaga's that he'd downloaded and was playing on the TV with the sound off, so it really felt like they were at a concert.

When the song ended, Lucas paused his playlist. 'Break time. We need to top up our drinks.' He headed to the kitchen.

'I'm having the best time!' Gemma exclaimed, as they both caught their breath.

'Me too!'

'Ladies,' Lucas said, handing them each a fresh margarita, poured from the jug he had made earlier.

'Thanks,' they both said in unison and took big gulps from their glasses, Poppy spilling a bit on her chin in her enthusiasm.

'So good,' Poppy said as she wiped away the stickiness. She flopped back onto the remaining couch and a fraction more drink spilt over the rim. Her already sticky finger swiped it and then she sucked off the sweet and salty lime flavour.

Lucas joined them and they drank quietly, savouring the break and watching the concert images on the screen. But as soon as their drinks were drained, Lucas whipped them back to the kitchen and restarted the playlist.

Just Dance was up next, and the intensity of their dancing resumed where they had left off. As soon as it finished, the music slowed and a lone guitar began as *Shallow* started. Poppy knew what was coming and she gently eased her body away from Gemma and Lucas. When Gaga got to the chorus

Lucas reached for Gemma's hand. She turned toward him and as her eyes met his, he knelt down on one knee. Poppy watched, a tear forming as Gemma's free hand flew to her chest, understanding what was about to happen.

'Gemma Louise Winstead, I have loved you for a very long time and I have been a fool to keep resisting this next step. I don't want to live a second of my life without you and I want to share every moment of your life. I don't want to wait any longer. So, Gemma, would you do me the honour of becoming my wife?'

From his pocket, Lucas took out the emerald and diamond ring and held it up toward her.

Gemma was already crying. 'Yes. Yes, of course I'll be your wife,' she squealed and, not missing a beat, Lucas slipped the ring on her finger, where it fit perfectly.

The two embraced, Gemma crying into Lucas' shoulder, and Poppy watched on, silent tears of joy cascading down her face and smearing her elaborate makeup. Gaga sang on in the background and they slowly started dancing, their bodies clinging to each other. It was beautiful to witness, and Poppy stayed quietly on the periphery, not wanting to insert herself into this moment which was just for them. When the song finished, they kissed, slowly, and Poppy turned toward the kitchen.

She started to walk in that direction, but Gemma reached out a hand to her, breaking their kiss. 'Wait, Poppy, don't go.'

The couple separated and both put their arms around Poppy bringing her into their embrace. Feeling overwhelmed by the love in the room, Poppy mumbled 'Congratulations' into their bodies and they all hugged and cried at the same time. Eventually one of them laughed, breaking the intensity of the moment, and soon they were all laughing.

Poppy stepped back, wiping her eyes and smearing her makeup more. 'Let me take some pictures of you two.'

'Okay,' Lucas said.

They'd already taken pictures earlier, of them all dressed up in their Gaga outfits, and of them drinking margaritas. Now Gemma and Lucas embraced, holding Gemma's newly adorned finger toward the camera, all ecstatic smiles.

'Now I'm going to take some of the ring,' Poppy said, zooming in on Gemma's finger.

'And what about me kneeling?' Lucas asked.

'Yeah,' Gemma said, positioning herself and outstretching her hand again toward Lucas, her eyes on his, not watching the camera.

'Got it,' Poppy said confidently.

'Let's ring our parents,' Gemma said excitedly when they'd finished taking all the pictures they wanted.

Poppy retreated to her bedroom to let them enjoy their calls. Will was expecting her to FaceTime once the proposal had taken place. Once she'd shut the door, she went and sat cross-legged on her bed, pulling a pillow into her lap and leaning back on the remaining one. Her heart rate had been elevated when the proposal and the emotions were flooding her system, but now it slowed. She thought she'd be excited to share this news with Will, and before the last few weeks she would have rushed to get into her room so she could call and fill him in. Now she sat staring at the wall in front of her. It wasn't that she was not happy for Gemma and Lucas – she was over the moon for them. But there was so much uncertainty in her own future, it was like a cloud of mozzies buzzing around her head. She knew one of them could sting her at any moment, but she could not see them to kill them, and the waiting for the inevitable was torturous. With things so much in a state of flux with Will, she might end up moving out on her own. She didn't even know if they would still be together in a few months' time. Suddenly, as Gemma and Lucas's path moved solidly forward, hers was floundering on the spot.

Chapter 26

'How'd it go?' Will asked as soon as their call connected. His eyes were bright and Poppy could see the excitement on his face. He even rubbed his hands together, waiting for her response.

Poppy pushed her suddenly darkened mood down and tried to match Will's. 'It was great, Gemma had no idea. It was like in the movies, and we all cried and hugged.'

'Wow, that's exciting for them.' He nodded his head in time with his words and a brief image of a Jack-in-the-box head fluttered through Poppy's mind.

'It is.' A pause ensued and Poppy's mind wandered and her eyes left the screen. Again, she thought how Gemma and Lucas were moving forward with their relationship and their lives, but she and Will had somehow moved backwards. Could they get past this point?

'You're frowning.' Suddenly Will looked fearful.

'Am I?' Poppy asked, trying to consciously rearrange her face once more.

Will crossed his arms across his chest. His voice became hard, the words clipped. 'Yes… You're still not convinced about me and the drugs being a one-off, are you?'

'I want to be, Will.' She swallowed down the anxiety before saying, 'But how can I be sure?'

Now his voice was raised. 'You know me, Poppy. You know the person I am. Do you think I'd want to take drugs?'

Poppy shrunk back from her screen. 'No, I wouldn't, but that doesn't change the fact that you did,' she finished almost in a whisper.

Will exhaled heavily and this time when he spoke, his voice was softer. 'Poppy, I love you. I was an idiot who made multiple mistakes and I'm sorry. I'm sorry I kissed someone else. I'm sorry I lied and wasn't honest with you about it. I'm sorry I got so freaked about it that I did something unforgivable. I would take every one of those stupid decisions back if I could. I would fly to Sydney if I could and hold you tight so you could see how much I mean what I say for yourself. I'll keep talking to my sister and I do anything else you ask to convince you that this is not an ongoing problem. But if you can't get past it, then everything I do will never be enough.'

'I want to forgive you, Will, I do…'

'But you don't.' The phone shifted and she was looking at the ceiling. She thought she could hear heavy breathing in the background.

'Will, please pick up the phone. I'm still here and I want this. I'm just so anxious about what all of it could mean for us, for our future—'

His face was back onscreen. 'And what do you think it means?' He spoke through clenched teeth, his anger barely contained.

Poppy had only seen Will this angry once before, when he confronted her and Josh on the dance floor at the Residents' Ball last year, when he thought she was having an affair with him. Poppy knew that whatever she said next could be crucial to them either repairing this damage or breaking it further.

She swallowed, tears springing from her eyes and falling down her cheeks. 'I'm worried it means I don't know you as well as I thought I did. I was ready to move in with you, and now—'

'Now you want to break up with me?' Will's voice rose and cracked on that last word.

Do I?

Breaking up hadn't yet entered her mind, she'd been focused on uncertainty and fear, she hadn't even contemplated breaking up, yet. But she needed time to herself to digest the idea and pick it apart. Instead of talking about breaking up, she simply said, 'I love you.'

Poppy watched Will furiously wipe a tear from his cheek. 'But you don't know if we have a future anymore?'

She couldn't answer, because that was exactly what she was worried about. How could she admit that and hurt the one person she loved more than anyone else?

'Don't worry, your silence is your answer.'

Before she could say anything, Will disconnected the call, and Poppy dropped her phone on her bed. She choked out a sob and flopped back on the bed before rolling onto her side and cradling a pillow, wishing she could make the pain and uncertainty go away. Burying her face deep into the pillow, she let the tears come. If there was a way to go forwards or backwards in time she would take it right now, rather than having to endure this and knowing there was nothing she could do in this moment to make it better.

Night shifts loomed and whilst Poppy's back and mouth felt better, her soul felt worse. Will had not returned her calls and she'd resorted to sending a long email, which also remained unanswered. It would be she and Josh on nights again and Poppy was comforted by that. They had a routine and a way they worked together down pat now, so she didn't have the anxiety of being on with someone she didn't know. But she worried about Will. Should she keep pushing or back off and give him space? Last time he had ghosted her like this, it had taken about a week for him to cool off and come back to her. Maybe this stint of night shifts where she would struggle to contact him was good timing. It would allow him time to hopefully indulge Poppy's anxiety. Surely, he would eventually understand her fears? Really, what she wanted was reassurance. Reassurance that he had a moment of insanity rather than a destructive need hiding under the surface of his relaxed exterior. She didn't want to go behind his back and ring his sister, but if he still wouldn't return her calls at the end of her night shifts, she might have to.

Thankfully, whilst her head was trapped in this vortex, the first night shift was fairly relaxed. No one died, only one patient needed to be transferred to ICU, and most of the work was scut work. Poppy and Josh spent some of the time sleeping and even played a couple of games of pool in the Residents' Lounge.

'So, once this lockdown is over, you'll be going back to Cardiology?' Poppy asked Josh whilst they were playing pool around midnight, holding her cue in front of her.

Josh eyed the table, deciding on his shot then bent forward over his cue to take it. 'That's the plan,' he said before smacking his white ball. Standing back up after his shot, he said, 'And based on the latest COVID update this morning, I think we are likely to finish lockdown at the end of next week, so maybe after that I can get back to the cath lab.'

Poppy nodded as she made her way to the table, stretching the cue out in front of her. 'And Olivia is supposed to be back next week, so you can see the back of me.' She lifted her eyebrows at him as she bent over the cue before dropping her eyes to the ball in front of her. She would much prefer to keep working with Josh than have Olivia back.

His lips lifted quickly, his eyes bright. 'They'll probably make me help out in ED or something even worse next week. I think I'd rather stay keeping an eye on you.'

Poppy immediately felt that familiar wave of heat rise up her neck. She turned away and walked to the end of the table, buying time for the blush to fade. Once she was confident she could speak without turning scarlet, she turned back and changed the subject.

'This might sound weird, but what was Olivia like with you?'

His head tilted at the question. 'How do you mean?'

Poppy shrugged. 'It's just… I had trouble reading her. She was quite distant and not particularly warm.' Poppy couldn't believe she was being this honest with Josh and really hoped he wouldn't use it against her down the track. But she had to believe that their friendship was stronger now and he wouldn't betray her. And if he did, then that would have been his last strike.

Josh gazed intensely into Poppy's eyes before responding. Poppy didn't know if he was trying to think of something diplomatic or wondering why she'd changed the subject. 'Well, as I said before, we only went out a couple of times and it was pretty casual. She was… chatty.'

'Chatty?' Poppy couldn't help dropping her jaw in surprise. Chatty was certainly not an adjective she would use to describe Olivia.

'Overly friendly?' he suggested next, lifting one shoulder and then focusing on the pool table.

Poppy tipped her head back. 'She must be very different around you than me.'

After his shot, he came and stood next to her. Their bodies were under the mandated 1.5 metres separation and Poppy was very aware of her limbs, which were awkward and wrong, suddenly.

'Well, it's not surprising, I mean you're bubbly and vivacious,' Josh murmured, watching her mouth. Poppy wondered what he was thinking looking at her lips. Did he want to kiss her? When the pause was just becoming awkward, he turned his head back to the table. 'Olivia seems like the kind of woman who would see other women as threats, so she would want to distance herself from you.'

Her arms and legs were heavy and glued to the spot. What did his look mean? 'And why would she be chatty with you?' Poppy asked, knowing she couldn't deny that she was now flirting.

Keeping his gaze forward, on the table, he replied. 'Well, to her I might seem quiet and mysterious, and the overly friendly behaviour would be to draw me out. To try to get me to talk more and be more open.'

She nudged him with her elbow, her hands still clasped on the pool cue. 'That's surprisingly insightful of you, Josh.'

His expression was intense when he turned toward her. 'Are you suggesting, Dr Mason, that I might not always be insightful?'

Poppy noticed his blue eyes were twinkling. How could he be smiling with his eyes but not his mouth in this way? Her body was heating from the inside and she could feel the pool cue clasped in her hands almost vibrating from her energy. She knew he was playing with her and she wanted to play, too. It was fun and it distracted her from thoughts of Will. In fact, it was the lightest she had felt in a long time.

'Well, Dr Hunter, there may be times when I have noticed a propensity for lack of insight.'

He brought a hand to his mouth. 'Me? I am shocked. You will have to give me an example.' His smile teasing the edge of his lips, flicking in and out.

'An example, you say?' Poppy tipped her head to the side like she was thinking.

'Yes, you must provide evidence or rescind the comment,' he said in a mock serious way, his eyebrows coming together but his lips still hinting at a smile.

'Umm,' Poppy said, rubbing her chin in thought. *This Feeling,* by the Chainsmokers, had just started playing through the speakers in the lounge. 'Well, there was that time you got cranky at the acting NUM on red for picking on me and said how you hated it when people picked on the junior staff, and yet you do have a habit of doing that yourself.'

'A scandalous allegation.' His hand was now covering his traitorous mouth. 'When do I pick on the junior staff?'

'How about every time you got a consult from ED last year?'

This time the comedy was gone. His voice was low and he closed the space between them even more. 'Hmm. That was mainly just me flirting with you.'

Goddamn this man was sexy when he wanted to be. Heat shot through her. He was close enough that she could smell the spicy aftershave he always wore. Desire continued to stir within her, but she forced jocularity and snorted. 'You think putting me down and making me feel like crap was flirting?'

Voice even lower, his head mere centimetres from hers, he said, 'Poppy, I've been flirting with you in one way or another for over a year.' He reached a hand up to run a finger from her temple to her chin. The touch was electric and, finally cradling her chin, he tipped her head upwards, forcing her to look once again, into his eyes. The dark blue in stark contrast from his lightly tanned skin and mahogany hair. Staring into them she remained intrigued that they, too, weren't brown. Short stubble dotted his face and Poppy had a sudden desire to touch him and feel that roughness.

Josh continued, 'I know this is terrible timing, but I can't stop thinking about you. No one else I have ever dated has stuck in my head like you have. You're—'

Poppy put a finger to his lips, tipped her head up further and stood on her tippy-toes. Their lips met in a kiss that was gentle at first. Neither one of them knowing if the other wanted it as much as they did. Cues still in their hands but thrust to the side, their bodies connected as the kiss deepened, their tongues searching. Desire fizzed within her until Poppy's brain suddenly put on the brakes, extinguishing the heat and replacing it with shame.

'Josh, stop.' Poppy pushed him gently in the chest and stepped backwards, breaking the contact between them. Josh's hand, that had been cradling her face, fell to his side. His eyes, which moments ago had been full of hope, were now unreadable as if a cloud had passed in front of the sun. 'I'm sorry. I shouldn't have done that.'

She clasped her cue in front of her like a barrier.

Why did I do that?

Josh's head had been hanging, but now he raised it. 'I know you're not happy with Will. I've been here with you every day.'

She knew he was right. 'That doesn't make what we just did okay.'

'Then break up with him and give me another chance,' he pleaded.

A crack opened in Poppy's chest. He was so raw and honest right in this moment. This might be the most vulnerable he had ever been in his life and she didn't want to quash it as it could further reinforce those walls he had up, keeping everyone out.

'You're not ready for a commitment, Josh.' She said the words quietly, gently.

'How do you know I'm not?' A petulant pout on his lips almost mocked his response.

She tried to make things light again. 'Don't forget I've been here this last year. You're a serial dater. Often more than one person on the go at a time.'

'I can change.' There was a desperation that sat beneath his words.

The subtlest of head shakes and her voice almost a whisper. 'I can't be the person you practice on. I'm sorry.'

'He doesn't make you happy.'

Poppy still couldn't deny it, so she tried to make excuses. 'Being apart is hard. Lockdown is hard.'

'I make you laugh.'

She nodded, 'You do. But that's not enough.' He did make her laugh and the chemistry was still there, too. Had she kissed him to subconsciously get back at Will? She wasn't sure. It would certainly be easy to blame it all on Josh, but she had wanted to kiss him in the moment. She was the one who reached up and met his lips with hers. She had to accept blame.

Josh turned and walked away, putting down his pool cue and heading to the couch. He looked broken. His broad back hunched, his confident walk reduced to a shuffle. Poppy didn't want to end the conversation like this. This was only their first night shift. They needed to find a way to be comfortable around each other to get through this.

She sank down onto the couch next to him.

'Josh, I have thoroughly enjoyed the last month or so that we've been stuck together. I really feel we've developed a friendship, and I feel like I finally know you better than I did last year. I don't want to give that away. I like spending time with you, and I like working with you, and I never thought I would say that last year.'

Poppy watched Josh's jaw tick, his eyes resolutely fixed ahead. She gave him time to absorb what she said, letting the silence hang, hoping that he would do the mature thing, and agree to friendship. But she knew he was a guy used to getting his own way. Used to winning. Used to being the best. And as an only child who had never learnt to share, she wasn't sure he would be able to accept friendship over the possibility of something more.

When no response was forthcoming, Poppy moved to get up. But Josh tugged on her arm, pulling her back to the couch. Poppy's heart raced, worried he was going to kiss her again, and how much more awkward the rest of their night shifts would be if he did. Despite knowing it was wrong and feeling ashamed, her body was alert and willing, just in case.

But he didn't kiss her. He held her arm, looked at her and said, 'Okay. Friends it is.'

A flicker of disappointment flared but Poppy pushed it down. She stood up. 'Great. Now it's my shot, and I'm going to kick your arse.'

This time it was Josh who snorted. 'I doubt it, Mason.'

As Poppy walked with her back to Josh, she allowed a moment of reflection. She was relieved it had only been one kiss and that Josh had acquiesced to friendship. But, she couldn't deny the anticlimax too. Taking things further might have been a relief for her body, even if it was the wrong thing to do. This, however, was the better outcome. It enabled both of them to keep working together. She just needed to maintain this upbeat banter until they got back into a groove.

'Alright, Mason, show me what you got.' He'd joined her back at the pool table, but he was now observing the social distancing spacing of at least 1.5 metres.

Calling her "Mason" was new, Poppy thought as she lined up her shot. Maybe it was his way of distancing himself from her. She was okay with that.

She had already decided that she was not going to tell Will, or even Gemma about any of this. Will could not handle the information right now and Gemma would judge without the full picture. Maybe she could lock it down like she did her memories of Lulu. Hide it deep inside so the guilt wouldn't plague her.

Chapter 27

Walking into the hospital the next night, Poppy felt a knot tie in her guts. Not about Will for a change, but about Josh. The rest of the previous shift had gone smoothly, but Poppy didn't know how he would behave tonight. Would he go back to the bastard Poppy knew he could be? If he did, the rest of these night shifts could be a nightmare. They were hard enough on the body without being anxious you would be ridiculed at every step, or left to do all the work alone without support. So, she dawdled in the theatre changing rooms, taking her time putting scrubs on and finding a locker for her clothes, keeping her bag with her. As she rode the elevator to the eleventh floor, her pulse quickened in time with her thoughts. Time to find out how the next three shifts would be…

'Evening, Mason,' Josh said as she took the seat next to him. 'Did you sleep?'

So he's continuing with this Mason business. She could live with that.

'Got about four hours. Not the best. You?' Poppy watched his body language while they talked, looking to see how tense he was. But he was comfortable, relaxed. It was like last night hadn't even happened.

'Pretty good. Probably five. And I went for a run, so feeling okay.'

'A run! I'm impressed. I've barely exercised all term. Twelve-hour shifts are just a killer.'

'You've got to make time, Mason. It's good for you.'

'I know. But it's hard.' Her body slumped in the chair at the thought of trying to add in a run or a workout. She was getting so little sleep as it was.

'No excuses.' Poppy immediately thought of him as a drill Sergeant in some Navy Seals movie. 'Tomorrow, when you wake up from sleep, go for a quick run before you eat. Even if it's only twenty minutes. You'll feel better, I promise.'

'I'll think about it,' Poppy said, unconvinced. But she was glad he was in a good mood and hoped it would last.

Night two was not as quiet as night one, but certainly nothing like the last set of night shifts Josh and Poppy had done together. The Premier's daily updates and worldometer had predicted that Australia was now over the peak of the COVID wave of case numbers and Poppy hoped they were right. They hadn't had any new COVID-positive admissions in the last twenty-four hours, which was a first. But the existing cases were a mixture of minimally symptomatic patients and those that were really sick. The geriatric patients were still the most difficult to manage. They tended to get sicker from their COVID symptoms than younger patients and their other underlying co-morbidities often exacerbated things.

One of the Geri's patients took a sudden nose-dive and Poppy and Josh tried to stabilise them on the ward, but they rapidly deteriorated and died before they had even had a chance to call ICU. The double whammy of respiratory failure and underlying heart disease and renal failure just too much to overcome.

On a brighter note, one of the patients whom they had started the non-invasive ventilation on the previous shift was doing well and had not needed to go to ICU. When they reviewed him, they found him looking brighter, his oxygen saturation improved and they hoped he would be able to wean off the ventilation by the morning.

Sitting at the nurses' station together, Poppy said to Josh, 'I don't want to jinx things, but it feels like the patients aren't as sick as they were a few weeks ago. Don't you think?'

'You will jinx us with a comment like that, you know.'

'Sorry. But seriously, don't you think things are improving?'

Josh looked out and down the ward, clearly considering what Poppy had said. Finally, he nodded. 'You could be right, Mason. We have certainly called our friends in ICU less often than the last set of nights.'

'Maybe the antivirals are working?'

He paused again, then looked at her. 'Or the virus is mutating and becoming less aggressive.'

Poppy nodded. 'Well, either way, if we get through this and out of lockdown, life will be better again.'

Josh just mumbled and nodded. Poppy wondered if he liked the idea of prolonging their time together. Maybe he thought he'd win her over if they remained isolated in their weird COVID bubble together. Poppy worried it was possible. Immediately her body reacted and her guts clenched. She'd still not heard from Will. Guilt weighed on her, but mostly she was just anxious he could be using again. The lockdown had to end so that she could physically see him and make sure he was okay. She would will it into being if she had to. Focus all her positive energy into the antivirals continuing to work and the COVID wave continuing its new downward trend. Her head down she kept this mantra going while she completed blood test request forms.

By the final night shift, Poppy was desperate to talk to Will. She sent a final text on her walk into work and decided that if she hadn't heard anything by the end of her shift the next morning, she would call his sister.

> Hi Will. I'm heading into work for my last night shift. I really want to talk to you and clear the air. I'm sorry if I upset you. I really miss you. It looks like lockdown is going to end soon and I was thinking I might fly to Dubbo to visit when it does. I really want to see you. I love you, please text me, ok? P xxx

Head down and thoughts on Will, she entered the handover room on red ward and was startled by Josh calling out, 'Mason,' by way of greeting.

'Hunter!' She smiled and thoughts of Will receded. Josh and Poppy had an epic *Call of Duty* battle the previous shift and Poppy was looking forward to resuming it tonight. They had used their surnames as their avatar names and Poppy kind of liked it. Felt very military. She was Corp_Mason and he was Sarg_Hunter. And night shifts often had that battle mentality too. Thankfully, her back was holding up and the ointment she was using on her ulcer was finally making a difference. It was getting smaller and shallower and no longer giving her that horrible pain. Somehow, it was like her body was reflecting the horrors of the term and now as they were approaching the final stretch, she was on the mend. If only she could mend the fracture in her relationship with Will, and the world would be right on its axis again.

'There's a couple of sickies to review first, then we might be able to get back to our battle,' Josh said, looking at his list after handover.

'Yep, sounds good.' A flutter of excitement crested like a wave and then receded.

Poppy didn't notice the text ding alert with all her PPE on, and it wasn't until a couple of hours passed and they were finally on their way to the Residents' Lounge to resume their game of *Call of Duty*, when she checked her phone and saw, to her surprise, a text reply from Will.

She stopped walking and Josh turned back. 'What's up?'

'Just a text.' Poppy shed her mask and wrapped it around her wrist. 'You go and get set up. I'll be there in a sec. I just need to read this.'

'Okay,' said Josh, but Poppy noticed the single eyebrow raise before her eyes went back to the home screen notification.

She stared at it, her legs suddenly unsteady, not sure whether she could open the message.

What if he says it's over?

After pondering how awful that would be for a moment, her brain then threw up the opposite; what if it's not?

No, don't think like that, Poppy. You love him, you want to be with him. He's always been there for you. Now, you need to be there for him.

Poppy took a deep breath, unlocked her phone, and clicked on the message.

> I know you probably won't get this for a while, you're probably busy on your shift. I'm sorry I've been a dick. I love you too, and I'd love you to visit when you can. I

> miss you and can't wait to hold you in person. Everything is going to be ok, I know it will. Xxx

Poppy finally let out the breath she'd been holding. They were okay. The triple knot inside her loosened somewhat. She checked the time and then hurriedly sent a reply.

> So good to see your reply! Are you still awake? Quick call if you are?

Poppy waited in the middle of the deserted corridor to see if Will would call. She stared intently at her home screen, biting her bottom lip.

Come on, Will. Call me.

She just wanted to see his face, to know that they would get through this. Was that too much to ask? But no call came.

Dammit, he must already be asleep.

She gave up, put her phone back in her pocket and continued on to the Residents' Lounge.

Sitting on the couch, Josh turned his head toward her when Poppy entered. 'All queued up and ready to roll.'

'I'd rather a stiff drink.'

Josh looked up and saw her expression. 'What's up?'

'I was just hoping to talk to Will. We haven't talked in a few days, but he must already be asleep.'

'Oh well, call him in the morning. No stiff drinks now, I'm afraid. But shooting the enemy is on offer. Get your butt over here, Corporal Mason.'

Poppy laughed in spite of herself and took the proffered controller from Josh as she sat on the couch.

'I'll catch you later, okay?' Poppy said to Josh as she raced down the internal stairs.

'What's the rush?' he called out after her.

Without pausing, she replied, 'I want to try to call Will on my way home.'

'But—'

'I'll text you later!' Poppy said before Josh lost sight of her. She was in such a rush that she almost collided with Dr Hennessy, who had just stepped into the stairwell at the sixth floor. 'Whoops—'

'No harm done,' Dr Hennessy interjected as they narrowly avoided collision.

Poppy stopped on the landing, but her feet were still itching to move. 'I'm so sorry, Victoria, I've just finished nights and I'm in a rush to catch someone before their shift.'

'Well, I'm glad I ran into you. Literally!' She laughed at her own joke and Poppy smiled politely whilst her heart still raced. She really liked Victoria, but she just didn't have the time right now. 'I wanted to let you know that Katrina and I are working very hard on the situation with Professor Pilson, and we are very close to a resolution.'

'Oh, that's great.' She was desperate to scoot past Vitoria and continue down the last flight of stairs.

'Yes, so there should be an official announcement soon.'

'Okay.' She was jiggling from one foot to the other and looking past Victoria, down the stairs.

Victoria nodded, putting a hand on one jutted hip. 'I can't say exactly what's going to happen until the announcement, though.'

'Okay,' said Poppy again, not wanting to draw out more information from her, despite her suspicion that that was exactly what Victoria wanted.

'I'll let you go. But it should be within the next week or two.'

'Great!' Poppy gave a slight wave as she took off again, without looking back.

'Be careful, Poppy!' she heard Victoria call out as she opened the door to the fifth floor where the operating theatre changing rooms were located.

Finally, Poppy was back in her normal clothes and out on the street. She hadn't bothered with a shower before donning her street attire, it was probably overkill anyway. As she left the hospital, signing out of the QR code, and began her walk up Missenden Road she rapidly left the company of other people. That was the one good thing about lockdown, there was no one on the streets or pavements. No hustle and bustle and no one to listen to phone calls in progress, so no self-consciousness from Poppy as she put in her earbuds and called Will's number.

In that last hour before handover, Poppy had made a decision. She needed to let go of her fear and anxiety and just be there to support Will. Her fears would only increase his vulnerability and could even push him back into risk-taking behaviour. He had always been a calm and safe support for her. She needed to be that for him now. He didn't need her judgement, only her love. And that was the only way they could move forward.

'Hi,' Will said as he connected to the standard phone call rather than FaceTime.

'I'm so glad I caught you before you started work!' She wanted to rush straight into telling him she was ready to move forward, but he spoke before she could.

'I'm just walking up the path.' Poppy heard the sound of his bag rubbing on his legs as he walked.

'I just wanted to hear your voice. I texted when I saw your message, but you must have already been asleep.'

'Sorry. But I'm glad you called. It's nice to hear your voice too.'

There was still some stiltedness in their conversation, but that was okay. Getting started was the main thing right now.

'I love you, Will. I miss you so much.'

'I miss you too, honey. I'm desperate to come home.'

'At least it looks like lockdown will probably end soon. And hopefully that means the term will end soon too.'

'I hope so, but there's been nothing official yet.'

'I think they're just waiting for the official end of lockdown, then they'll announce it.'

'Probably, but they'll need to give everyone at least a two-week warning, particularly for country terms, so that people can sort flights or travel.'

'I hadn't thought of that. You're probably right,' said Poppy, losing a bit of her enthusiasm once again.

'So, it's probably still a few weeks minimum.'

Poppy was up on King Street now and she knew Will must be basically at the hospital. It was only a fifty-metre walk from his accommodation.

'Then I should definitely come up when the lockdown ends. For the weekend, if I can wangle one off.'

'That would be awesome, see what you can do.'

'I'll email Melissa O'Brien and see if she can help.'

'How many hours are you working at the moment?' he asked. It sounded like he'd stopped walking. Poppy could no longer hear the bag scraping like Velcro against his legs.

She stepped to the side to let a lady pushing a toddler in a pram pass at a safe distance. 'Don't ask, it's crazy. At least I've got the next couple of days off. I just wish you were here to share them.'

'Me too, baby. Now I'd better go. I'll text you later in the day, when I get time. Are you going to try to stay up?'

'Yep, till nine o'clock if I can.'

'I love you, talk later.'

'Love you too.' She disconnected and the second knot loosened and released.

He sounds better.

Poppy continued her walk home happier than she'd been in more than a week. She put a playlist on and increased her pace as *Exit Sign* by Hilltop Hoods came on. The end is near, she thought. Lockdown is almost over.

Poppy spent most of the day trying to stay awake. Books were a no-go as they made her sleepy, so she started with a movie. But lying on the couch induced a semi-slumberous state, so she pulled over one of the dining chairs, hoping that sitting up straight would help, but soon found her body slumping again.

A ding alerted her to a text and she looked at her phone and saw it was from Josh.

Hey, Poppy, want to go for a jog?

Poppy was now wide awake. She needed something to keep her awake, but was spending more time with Josh a good idea? Poppy tapped her foot up and down as she thought about it.

Poppy: I'm not much of a runner, but I am struggling to stay awake.

Josh: We can just take it slowly. Meet you corner of Eliza and King in 20? We can start from there and run through the park.

Poppy rationalised that anything to keep her from sleeping was a good thing. Hurriedly she typed out "OK" and pressed send before she could change her mind.

When she made it to their meeting place, she found Josh jogging on the spot. He'd obviously jogged over from his apartment, which was much closer to The Bennelong campus.

'Hi,' she said as she came up from behind him.

He turned around, still jogging on the spot to stay warm. 'Do you want to do some stretches before we start?'

'Probably should,' Poppy said, thinking how unfit she had become and how this was probably going to be really embarrassing.

She stretched her hamstrings, quads, and calves, and did a quick neck roll. 'Let's go. But not too fast.'

'No problem, I'll take it easy.' He took the lead on the narrow path as they headed toward Camperdown Memorial Rest Park.

Poppy started to get into a rhythm, watching where she placed her feet and keeping an eye on Josh's heels so that she didn't trip herself (or him) and he didn't get too far in front of her. Her knees and ankles initially protested at the jolting of each cadence, but soon that discomfort settled. He was taking it easy, and Poppy managed not to pant too much. Josh was far less punishing than Lucas had been.

Once they made it into the park, the path was wide enough for them to jog side by side and Josh started a conversation.

'Why did you rush off this morning?'

'I told you, I wanted to call Will before he got to work.'

'Everything alright?'

Her eyes flicked to him and then back to the path in front. 'Yes, it's fine.' She took a breath, then added, 'I just missed his call last night, that's all.'

'Okay,' he said and then silence descended. The only sound that of their feet as they hit the pavement, and their heavy breaths.

Eventually, Poppy wondered if Josh was annoyed with her for some reason. She didn't want to talk about Will with Josh. So, she stuck to more neutral ground. 'When do you find out what you'll be doing next week, when Olivia's back?'

'I'm not sure. Hopefully today, I guess, with the weekend and all.'

It irritated her that Josh could talk so easily while running. She found herself inexplicably noticing the strain of his pecs against his singlet as they ran and, hauling in a harsh breath, she returned her focus to the path.

They continued to do laps of the park, but it was quite a small circuit, so Josh suggested they continue on down to Parramatta Road and then loop back up to King Street. Back to single file, their conversation stopped again and Poppy returned her focus to her stride and breathing. He wasn't pushing her as much as Lucas had the other week, and she wasn't puffing and panting yet. She was still comfortable enough, but she suspected that by the time they made it back to King Street, she would be ready to stop. Especially as the route back from Parramatta Road would be all uphill.

They took Australia Street back up and at least this was a straight line direct to King Street and only one street over from where they started on Eliza Street. When they made it to the end, Poppy bent over, hands on knees and took deep, laboured breaths in and out. Annoyingly, Josh barely looked to be sweating Poppy noticed as she looked up at him. He was still jogging slowly on the spot, whilst she was panting, red-faced with her hair plastered to her forehead and neck despite the cooler weather.

Lifting one hand up in surrender, Poppy proclaimed, 'I think I'm done.'

Josh looked down at his Apple watch. 'It's pretty much lunch time. Do you want to grab some food and take it back to the park to eat? I've got nothing else to do today.'

Again, Poppy looked up at him from her hunched position. She was worried he was going to make another move on her, but when she analysed his expression, she couldn't see any lust in his features. He just looked normal, for want of a better description.

'Sure. I guess we only have each other to hang with as everyone else is at work.'

'Exactly. And I don't want to fall asleep. If I go home now, I'll be asleep by three o'clock.'

Poppy stood up and stretched her back. 'Alright then, Dr Hunter, where do you want to grab food?'

'Given we've been good and had a run, we should eat something relatively healthy. So, let's walk up until we find something that's open and go from there.'

'Okay.' Poppy felt a slight drag on her lower back and did a couple of extra stretches to loosen it before they walked on.

They settled on some Vietnamese soldiers and when they sat on Poppy's favourite seat looking down over the park, she felt happy. Not for any particular reason, it was just a nice day, and she felt good again. Her perioral fissure was healing and her sciatica settling. There had been less angst about Will since his text last night and the call today, and that was a relief. She didn't feel any particular pressure to make conversation with Josh, but she was comfortable in his presence. How funny that was, she thought.

'Why the smile?'

Poppy laughed. 'I was just thinking that I feel comfortable with you now.'

She couldn't read his expression. 'And that was funny?'

'Just surprising,' she said, looking down over the park as a breeze lifted the bottom of her ponytail.

A gentle silence descended like the breeze in the trees above.

'You know, Poppy, I've been thinking about the other day…'

Oh no, don't ruin this moment. Not when I was just thinking how comfortable we've become with each other!

Poppy clenched internally, held her breath, and turned to look at him.

His eyes left her face and looked out in front of him. 'And you're probably right. Maybe I'm not quite there yet. Not quite ready for "the one"…'

Poppy released her breath and noted that it was cute he'd used his hands to form quotation marks.

He was still looking ahead 'But… I think I want to get ready.'

Poppy waited, suspecting he had more to say.

He took a deep breath and turned towards her. 'And if… things don't work out with Will, maybe then I'll be ready.'

She gave him a brief smile and squeezed his hand. His words had definitely had an impact. Her heart felt fractured. One side committed to Will and ready to fight for their relationship, but the other now had a growing affection for Josh. She couldn't ignore all they had been through since COVID started, and how close they had become. It was no longer just sexual chemistry between them and Poppy could see the change in Josh and the openness for a meaningful relationship. It was there in the slightest elevation of his eyebrows betraying his fear of being hurt. It was there in the hand that anxiously played with the napkin while he made his declaration. This was not the arrogant, superior Josh of last year who liked the chase, but a gentler, more vulnerable version. But what could she say to him, when she didn't know how she really felt about either of them?

She left her hand on his and looked down over the park and hoped he would interpret her silence as uncertainty and not cruelty.

Chapter 28

Poppy was sitting on the living room floor with Gemma. Spread out around them were multiple bridal magazines. Lucas was nowhere to be seen, off running most likely. It's not like there were a lot of options in lockdown. Gemma was busy making a spreadsheet on her laptop of dress designers and styles she liked, flowers, table arrangements, photographers, colours, themes, and basically anything wedding-related. She was even starting a Pinterest vision board. When Poppy had laughed at her extreme attention to detail, Gemma had said, 'It's important to stay organized. Otherwise, I'll have random cutouts from magazines and no real idea of where to start.'

Poppy was flicking through a magazine and paused on a page, showing it to Gemma. 'What about this one?'

The image was of a simple heart-shaped neckline with spaghetti straps and a tapered bodice and skirt with only a small train. There was some beading across the bodice, which was quite detailed but subtly done.

'Yeah, that's nice.' Gemma took the magazine from Poppy to get a closer look. 'I like the skirt, it's not too over the top.'

'Exactly. You don't want to end up looking like a meringue.' Their eyes caught and they laughed. They'd always criticized movies where the bride looked like a head stuck on a voluminous bell-shaped dress with multiple hooped skirts, like something from *Gone with the Wind.*

Gemma handed it back and buried her face in her laptop. 'Where's it from?'

'Mmm,' Poppy said turning the page the right way up. 'Karen Willis Holmes.'

'Does it list a price?'

Poppy bit her lip and searched the corner of the page for more details. 'No,' she eventually concluded after scouring every word on the page and the one following.

'Let me look it up.'

Poppy dog-eared the corner of the page and kept flicking through the magazine while Gemma's fingers clicked on her keyboard.

'Yeesh, it's almost five thousand.'

'Wow.' Poppy screwed up her face. 'That's a lot… Because of the beading, I guess.'

'Everything is just so expensive,' Gemma complained, placing her laptop on the floor. 'I don't know why I'm even torturing myself with all these magazines. We'll never be able to afford what's in here.'

She looked defeated. Poppy scooched over and patted Gemma's leg. 'But you don't need to spend that kind of money, Gem. You just get ideas from here, then get the style you like done by a dressmaker. Or buy off the rack. I'm sure it'll be half the price.'

'Maybe,' Gemma replied, picking at her T-shirt. She looked crestfallen.

Poppy picked up some of the loose pages they'd pulled from magazines. 'And you definitely don't need these table arrangements and gifts,' she said, throwing them to the side. 'Keep it simple. Remember, the important thing is you are marrying Luc. That's what matters.'

Gemma looked up and nodded. 'You're right. Thanks, Pop.'

Poppy squeezed her knee and went back to flicking through the magazine.

Later, when they were having a cup of tea on the balcony, Poppy broached the subject of moving out. 'So, I've been thinking that maybe I need to start looking for somewhere else to live.'

Gemma turned to study her before saying, 'There's no rush.'

'I know. But once you guys are married, you'll want your own space. And you guys should keep this place; it'd be great for the two of you.'

'Are you sure? What about you and Will?'

Poppy dropped her eyes to her cup of tea, steam spooling out in a spiral. 'We might move in. We'll see.'

Gemma looked at her over the rim of her cup. 'Have you talked about it?'

Poppy knew if she looked at Gemma she'd crack and spill the beans on everything that had happened. 'A little. But there's been a lot of other things to talk about lately.'

'How's all that going?'

How could Poppy answer this without giving things away? 'Better,' she said, pausing to find the right words that would be honest without detail. 'Not perfect, but better. I'm hoping to get next weekend off, if they end the lockdown, and go up to Dubbo to visit him.'

Gemma put down her cup and turned to her. 'That'd be great!' She was so enthusiastic it made Poppy wonder whether she'd been worried they were breaking up and too scared to ask. 'I reckon they will end the lockdown this week.'

'I hope so,' Poppy said and sipped from her cup to avoid saying more.

What would Gemma say if she knew it wasn't just the kiss that Will was guilty of?

As Poppy trudged toward the hospital entrance on Monday morning, she thought about Olivia's return. She wondered if she would be any less frosty. They'd had a lot of time apart, maybe that was a good thing. Maybe she'd be easy to work with and they'd work more like the team she and Josh had become over the last month? She didn't want to start off with a negative attitude and preferred to be optimistic about it.

'How was your last set of nights?' Alex asked as she sat down in the handover room.

'Not too bad. When do you do yours?'

He took his glasses off and held them up to the light to see how dirty they were. 'End of this week. Just the Friday through to Monday morning.'

'Well, hopefully we'll be out of lockdown by then.' Poppy was hoping all this positivity could effect change.

Now cleaning his glasses with a cloth, Alex said, 'It's certainly looking that way, isn't it?'

As an afterthought, Poppy added, 'And, actually, we had less new COVID admissions on those last couple of shifts.'

'That's good.' He folded the cleaning cloth and put it into his scrub pants pocket. 'Maybe they'll stop the twelve-hour shifts after lockdown ends too?'

'God, I hope so.'

Glasses back on his nose, Alex looked toward the door where more people were filing in. 'I'd even be happy doing a fifteen-hour shift once or twice a week, than continuous twelve-hour shifts.'

Now Poppy was nodding agreement. 'I know, right? Doing one long day in amongst a bunch of standard days is so much easier.'

'Yep… Ooh, Olivia is back.'

Poppy turned toward the doorway and saw Olivia entering and taking her seat near Maria and immediately starting a conversation. She didn't even look over at Poppy, or say hello. Poppy's shoulders slumped.

'Weird that she didn't say hello,' commented Alex quietly, his body leaning closer to Poppy's.

'Mmm,' was all Poppy said. 'Maybe she just needed to talk to Maria.'

Yeah, right.

After handover, Poppy went over to Olivia and caught her before she left the room.

'Hi, Olivia. How are you feeling?'

'Fine.' She turned away and continued out the door.

'Well, it's good to have you back,' Poppy said to her retreating back, putting as much cheer as she could into the sentiment.

Olivia stopped suddenly and turned back to Poppy, forcing her to stop as well. 'Well, it sounds like you've been spending a lot of time with Josh.'

Ah, I see, she's worried I'm moving in on Josh. That's the problem.

'He was just covering for you.' Poppy didn't want to get caught between the two of them. She had enough of her own love life dramas, she didn't need more.

Olivia just stared at Poppy, then turned and continued to the donning/doffing station.

Poppy had no idea how to navigate her in this state. It was hard enough before she knew that Olivia was interested in Josh, now it might be ten times worse.

Poppy kept her eyes on the ground and saw this twelve-hour shift stretching further out in front of her. It was going to be a long day.

At the nurses' station, Olivia picked up her list. 'We've got a lot of patients, so we should get started. I'd like to start on the Geri's ward then head back here to red.'

Poppy raised her head. 'Oh. Josh and I found it better to leave the Geri's ward to the end, otherwise we'd be tripping over the Geri's team.'

'Quite the little team, were you?' Poppy chose to ignore the snide comment. She didn't want to make things worse. 'Well, I want to go to the Geri's ward first.'

Poppy agreed, thinking how silly Olivia was being, digging her heels in for no good reason.

Things started off okay because the Geriatrics team didn't start until eight-thirty, but once they did, Poppy's prediction came to fruition. They kept having to wait or backtrack as they ran into the Geriatrics team on their rounds. She could see Olivia getting increasingly frustrated but refusing to accept defeat. They soldiered on, taking more than two hours to review only ten patients due to all the stops and starts.

When they'd finally completed the ward, Poppy suggested they take a break and have a coffee.

'We've still got two more wards to do, Poppy. There's no break until we finish the round.'

It was at that moment that Poppy wished for Josh. She wondered where he was and what he was doing, as they took the elevator back up to the red ward. Again, appreciating the strange turn of events the last month had taken.

'Come on, Poppy, hurry up,' Olivia admonished as Poppy took her time at the PPE station.

'Sorry,' Poppy apologised, picking up her pace.

Once they were back in PPE and Poppy was wheeling a COW over to the end bay, Olivia asked about how Josh was. Poppy felt side-swiped by the sudden gear shift.

'Good, I guess.' She purposely kept her answer brief and lacking any detail. She really didn't want to encourage a conversation about Josh.

'I just wondered, because he hasn't really been responding to my messages.' Olivia's voice was low and she was right beside Poppy, breaking the social distancing rule.

'Oh,' Poppy answered awkwardly, staring straight ahead. 'Well, we did just finish another set of nights… maybe he's just tired.'

'Hmph.' Olivia was clearly not happy with Poppy's answer. 'Tell me about bed two.'

Poppy updated Olivia, who at the end of the briefing, said, 'Okay, you can examine them on this ward, and I'll keep the record, seeing as you know them all so well.' She pulled the COW away from Poppy, almost pushing her at the same time.

Poppy stumbled, raising an eyebrow as she turned away from Olivia. She had no idea what game Olivia was playing now, but she supposed it best just to go along with things.

'Hi, Mr Bennett, how are you feeling today?' Poppy asked as she came up to his bedside.

'Like… crap…' Mr Bennett wheezed between laboured breaths.

'I'm sorry. Okay, I'm just going to listen to your chest, now. I'll help you lean forward.' Poppy offered her arm for Mr Bennett to pull himself forward on. 'Just breathe normally for me, now, okay?' she said as she placed the diaphragm of the stethoscope on his chest.

Once she'd finished examining Mr Bennett, she came to the end of the bed where Olivia was standing with the COW and said, 'He's not moving much air, his sats are low and he looks tired. I think we should think about non-invasive ventilation.'

'What do you mean by "he's not moving much air?"' Olivia sneered. 'Describe what you hear.'

Poppy took a beat to look at Olivia's eyes, which gave nothing away. They remained unreadable, mirrors back to Poppy's mask and shield. Normally, both Olivia and Josh would just transcribe decreased air entry into the notes. Why did she want more info today or was she just trying to assert her authority even more than usual, Poppy wondered.

'I guess it sounds empty, like there's no air exchange at the bases, particularly.'

'And why do you think that is?'

Was she serious? Olivia wanted to turn this into some sort of teaching session? After showing no interest in teaching her all term?

Does she not appreciate how many more patients we have to see before we can take a break?

'I think if we did a chest X-ray we might see inflammatory ground-glass changes, which we are seeing a lot of in these COVID patients.'

'Okay,' Olivia said primly, clearly disappointed that Poppy had answered correctly and could not push the point further.

'Would you like me to get another chest X-ray?' Poppy asked, pointing to the COW.

Holding on firmly to the keyboard, Olivia answered, 'No.'

'Should we start HFNP?' Poppy knew Josh would suggest humidified high-flow nasal prong therapy in the first instance.

'Okay.'

What's with these one-word answers? And why is she just standing there looking at the computer? Why isn't she doing anything?

Poppy left the bed bay and almost threw up her hands in frustration. She had no idea what game Olivia was playing but she didn't want it to go on all shift. In the equipment room, she gathered the machine and special mask and tubing for HFNP. Poppy expected Olivia to have moved on to the next patient so they didn't get too far behind, but was stunned to find she was leaning against the wall in the hallway, looking at her phone through its snap lock bag.

What the actual fuck? She's not even going to see one patient by herself?

Poppy was now starting to get mad. She returned to Mr Bennett and hooked him up to the HFNP machine, entering the settings as she had been shown by Maria.

'Do you want to check the settings?' Poppy called out to Olivia, who was still standing against the wall outside the room.

'What settings did you dial up?' Olivia asked, her head appearing around the door frame.

Poppy read them out and looked up toward Olivia. When she finished, Olivia's head just disappeared behind the wall again.

Poppy had had quite enough. She left the machine and went outside into the hallway where Olivia was once more looking at her phone. Hand on her hip, eyes level with Olivia's, she said, through clenched teeth, 'This won't take long, Olivia, why don't you start with bed six and I'll be there in a sec.'

Without looking up, Olivia replied, 'No, I'll wait for you.'

Pointing at the mobile computer beside her, Poppy suggested, 'Well would you mind charting the HFNP?'

With a snort, Olivia looked up briefly. 'Poppy, I'm sure you can manage that.'

Poppy took a deep breath then returned to Mr Bennett's bed bay. She raised her eyebrows at Terry, who had just come into the room. What the hell was going on, she wondered. Was she not prepared to do any work now? She'd done the usual Registrar tasks on the Geri's ward, but here, she didn't seem inclined to do anything. Poppy's blood pressure was high and she was feeling increasingly resentful.

Once Mr Bennett was hooked up to the machine and Poppy had charted it in the electronic record, Terry said softly, 'Don't worry, I'll keep an eye on him for the next ten minutes. I'll grab you if there's a problem.'

'Thanks, Terry,' Poppy replied, feeling relieved that at least her favourite nurses, Terry and Mel, were on today. And Susan, too, was back, so at least she was surrounded by good people who would help her out if Olivia's slave driving threatened to pull her under.

The rest of red ward continued in much the same fashion, until they reached the last patient, Mrs Papadakis. As soon as they walked into her single room, Poppy saw she was in trouble. She was lying back against the pillows, her brown eyes open and staring, her chest faintly rising. Poppy rushed into the room, and quickly squeezed her shoulder, calling her name as her own heart rate spiked suddenly. The patient made no movement toward Poppy and no response to suggest she heard her.

Poppy looked up to where Olivia was standing idly at the end of the bed.

'Push the arrest buzzer!' Poppy demanded, as she used the controller to lower the bed flat and moved the patient's head gently toward a neutral position.

'What's happened?' Mel asked as she flew into the room, Terry closely on her heels with the arrest trolley, pushing Olivia out of the way, who was still showing no signs of taking charge.

'Unresponsive, barely breathing,' Poppy managed to get out.

Terry dialled up the oxygen to twelve litres without needing to be asked, and Mel proceeded to hook Mrs Papadakis up to the obs machine to get blood pressure, heart rate, and oxygen saturation results and called them out to Poppy. Terry was hooking up ECG leads and placing defibrillator pads so they could get an ECG reading and be ready to defibrillate if needed. Poppy was trying to assimilate all the information, whilst Olivia stood motionless at the end of the bed.

'Okay, she's not breathing up enough to move the oxygen. I'm going to put in a Guedel's,' Poppy said acutely aware of the sweat breaking out over her body. 'And then, Terry, I'm going to get you to bag her.' She measured then gently inserted the Guedel's airway into the patient's mouth and attached the bag that Terry passed her.

The team of three worked together with Poppy in the lead.

Poppy stood up, removing the cheap stethoscope from Mrs Papadakis' chest. 'Yep, chest sounds very wet. Mel, what do her legs look like? Any oedema?'

Mel pulled the sheets and blanket up to reveal legs full of fluid.

'Okay, she's overloaded. Grab me some Lasix.'

'On it,' Mel replied, quickly rummaging through the arrest trolley to get the Lasix, as Susan and Sylvie came into the room.

'Arrest team just getting on PPE,' Susan said.

'Sylvie, can you print out that rhythm?' Poppy asked.

Sylvie did as asked, then brought the sheet over to Poppy to look at.

'Looks like AF,' Poppy said aloud. She knew the patient needed a rate-controlling drug to slow her down, but knowing the arrest team was moments away, she thought she would wait and let them take over. She delivered 40mg of Lasix into the cannula in the patient's hand when Mel returned with the drug, then the arrest team was barging in, pushing Olivia out of the way.

'Who's in charge?' the team leader asked, and all heads turned to Poppy.

Olivia still said and did nothing, so Poppy stepped forward, 'I am.'

'What's happening?' the leader asked as the rest of his team took their places around the bed, taking over from Poppy's team.

'COVID-positive patient in her sixties, admitted two days ago with mild symptoms, managing on low levels of oxygen via nasal prongs and steroids.

Entered room today and patient was unresponsive, respiratory rate of eight per minute, BP 95/60, chest sounded wet, ECG looks to be in AF and extensive peripheral oedema. We started bagging and masking after no response to high-flow oxygen. I've just administered 40mg of Lasix.'

'Thanks, we'll take over. Let's push noradrenaline.'

Poppy stood back and watched while they attempted to resuscitate the patient. After about twenty minutes the patient was intubated and her heart rate and BP were stabilised enough to be transported to ICU.

'Thanks,' the ICU Registrar said to Poppy as he was leaving the ward behind the patient's bed. He looked over Poppy's shoulder toward Olivia, an unasked question in the lift of his eyebrows. Poppy shook her head and followed them out of the room, discarding her gloves in the bin at the door.

Terry, Mel, Sylvie, and Susan all gathered around her as the ICU team left.

Looking pointedly through the window at Olivia, who remained in the room, Susan said, 'Well done, Poppy. You handled that really well.'

'Thank you,' Poppy replied, a gentle blush creeping up her neck.

They were all still watching the patient's progress toward the lift when Olivia emerged loudly from the room behind them.

'I'm done!' she yelled, shedding her gloves in the middle of the ward.

'What do you mean you're done?' Poppy asked, startled. 'What are you doing?'

'I didn't have COVID, Poppy,' Olivia hissed. 'I'd just had enough.'

'Had enough of what?' Poppy asked, incredulous, as more nurses emerged from other bays to form a circle around them in the middle of the ward corridor.

'Of this!' She twirled on the spot with her arms out, pointing to the ward around her. 'The COVID patients. I don't want to get sick. And our Consultant is so scared of getting it, he hasn't even entered the hospital in more than six weeks. So, if he doesn't care then why should I? I'm done!'

She walked purposefully to the doffing station, shedding the rest of her PPE along the way like a trail of breadcrumbs.

They all stood in shock for what felt like minutes, but was probably only seconds.

'I did say it was the quiet ones you had to keep an eye on,' Terry murmured.

Poppy and Mel laughed, and then the rest were joining in.

'Alright, you lot, we've got patients to look after. Back to work,' Susan called them back into line, shooing them forwards in front of her. 'Poppy, why don't you come with me.'

She led Poppy to her office, shutting the door behind them.

Poppy wondered what was going to happen next. After the day she'd had so far, she no longer had any idea.

Susan sat heavily in the chair behind her desk and looked up at Poppy. 'I'm really sorry about that, Poppy. I had no idea that Olivia was faking COVID. And I'm really sorry you've constantly been so unsupported with us.'

Poppy could see how low Susan was feeling. 'It's not your fault,' she said, not wanting Susan to take the blame for all the shit that had happened this term.

'I know, but I do want you to know that I'm proud of you. Despite everything that's been happening, you keep turning up, working hard, and not complaining. And look at you today – running the ward round and the arrest. You're an excellent doctor, Poppy.'

A fire crept up her neck as she accepted Susan's praise. 'I'm just lucky I've had such supportive and experienced nurses to work with. And I've been lucky with Josh filling in, too. He's taught me a lot.' A flutter erupted in Poppy's chest at the thought of her time with Josh.

'Well, I'm going to call Dr Anderson, Prof Pilson, and Maria, and let them know what's just happened. Will you be okay on your own for a little while whilst we sort something out?' Susan picked up the phone and looked down at the touchpad.

'Sure. I'd better go back and check on Mr Bennett now, anyway.'

Poppy turned toward the door and heard Susan say on her way out, 'Thanks, Poppy.'

Walking back down the ward, Poppy noticed heads turn as she walked past. She hadn't yet really processed what had just happened, it had all gone in such a flash, but knew she'd want to analyse it more later. Right now, she had a job to do, and that was to keep Mr Bennett alive. In the midst of the medical emergency and Olivia's flip-out, she'd forgotten about him. But now it was up to her alone, to make sure he was okay. If he wasn't, she'd call ICU and get them to come and review him. Her steps were purposeful and she held her breath, hopeful that he was still okay, when she stepped into his room. Her only focus in that moment was on her job.

Chapter 29

By the end of the day, the gossip around Olivia and Prof Pilson was spreading through the hospital and Maria had studiously checked in on Poppy multiple times and Alex had offered to take on some of Poppy's scut work.

Gemma's text came in around three o'clock when Poppy was finally able to take a break.

> I just heard Olivia completely freaked out on the ward and resigned! And news of Prof Pilson's absenteeism also making the rounds of the wards. Tell me everything!!

Poppy laughed as she read it walking up the street to get some much-needed food and coffee. She punched out a reply, grateful how much easier it was to do out of a snap lock bag.

> Will have to give you the full run-down tonight, but she completely flipped and stormed out. Don't know if she resigned.

She took her food and coffee into the park and sat on a bench opposite her favourite one as it was closer to the hospital. The breeze and sunshine were a salve after the hectic day. She had just scrunched up the paper bag her sandwich came in when her phone dinged a text alert. Josh's name was visible and that flutter erupted again as she picked her phone up.

Just heard the news of Olivia. Are you ok?

That's nice, Poppy thought. He wasn't asking for all the details and was more concerned about her well-being. She smiled to herself as she texted back.

I'm ok. Thanks for checking. Where are u 2dy? Mbe u'll be back with me tomoz.

Josh: Most probably. I'm in ED today (sick face emoji).

Poppy: You sick? Or vomit job?

Josh: Vomit job - I told you they'd have me doing something worse

Poppy: True - but you didn't predict Olivia.

Josh: No def didn't see that coming. News of Prof also making the rounds.

Poppy: What are they saying?

Josh: That he's too scared of getting COVID to see patients.

Poppy bit her lip. This is what Olivia had said, but was it true? She didn't know. Maybe he had some health issue that she wasn't aware of?

Poppy: I guess they're prob not wrong.

Josh: No, guess not. On the bright side, Olivia's freak-out may lead to some resolution to the Prof issue too?

Poppy: Dr Hennessey did say something would be announced soon, so maybe.

Josh: (Fingers crossed emoji)

Poppy watched her screen but no more texts came through, so she placed it beside her on the bench and looked out at the park from this different view. She contemplated the bench they had eaten lunch on only a few days ago. That bench had been witness to a number of emotional scenes between her and Will, and now Josh. She recalled the feel of Josh's hand beneath hers. It was warm and soft and felt solid. Him messaging her now also made her feel good and she was confident he truly cared for her. But what would it be like to be in a relationship with him? Would he go back to the transactional style that had happened before? Or would he continue to open up? She didn't know.

Her thoughts moved on to Olivia. While she had been prickly and occasionally rude to her, Poppy had never suspected she was dishonest or would fake having COVID to get out of work. That was unthinkable. But now that she had admitted what she'd done, it made Poppy angry. Some of that anger was directed at Prof Pilson as well, but only a small amount as Poppy still didn't know what the truth was behind his absence. When Poppy, and Josh, and so many others were working tirelessly and without complaint in this difficult time, it was painful to think others were shirking their duty.

Lastly, her thoughts rested on Will. She knew he would be proud of how she had handled herself and the ward today. He was usually her biggest cheerleader. In the past, thinking of Will had made her feel light. Now it made her feel heavy. So much of her thoughts and emotions this term had been wrapped up in what was happening with Will. Her pager vibrated against her hip and thoughts of Will, Josh, and Olivia evaporated. She unclipped it from her waist, looked at the readout and stood up from the bench. Her rubbish was tossed into the nearby bin and she called the extension as she began the walk back to the hospital.

As predicted, Josh was pulled back to helping out and relieving Olivia. They were sitting in the Residents' Lounge, eating lunch, when their phones both pinged with new email notifications. Poppy reached for her phone and opened her email app to see a new email from the hospital administration.

'Whoa!' She glanced over at Josh. 'You should look at this too. They've just announced Prof Pilson's retirement.'

Josh pulled his phone toward him, and they both read the email, silently.

When she finished reading, Poppy looked up. 'I guess this must be what Dr Hennessey was referring to.'

Josh put his phone down and looked at Poppy. 'I guess so.' He rubbed his chin in thought.

Before he said more, Poppy continued, tucking one leg up underneath her so that she could face him. 'They must have pushed him out. I'm sure Dr Anderson will be glad, I sensed she disliked him.'

'She dislikes everyone,' Josh suggested, and Poppy laughed.

She thought how rarely she had seen Dr Anderson smile, even before everyone was required to wear masks. 'Do you know his replacement, Dr Biddle?'

'Yeah, I do. He trained here, was maybe four years ahead of me? He was an advanced trainee when I was an intern. Went overseas to do a fellowship, I think, then I heard he was locuming at Prince of Wales, maybe?'

'Was he nice?' They had continued to face each other on the couch, the energy companionable rather than sexual. Poppy liked looking at his eyes. The blue dark and almost smoky, like the edge of a storm cloud.

'Yeah, he was alright. Does it say when he's going to start?'

Poppy looked down at her phone breaking their contact. She picked it up from her lap and opened the email again. 'At the end it says to welcome him next week, so I guess, that soon.'

'That's good.'

Without breaking eye contact, Poppy replied, 'Yes, it is.'

Then Josh's gaze moved to her lips and she was suddenly acutely aware of them. Were they suddenly swelling? Engorging like they'd been pumped full of fillers? She dropped her head and swivelled back to the TV. What was she doing? This was nuts. She shouldn't be encouraging him. Her half-eaten sandwich was where she left it on the coffee table when the email came through. She picked it up and took a bite, not tasting it, just needing an excuse to move out of his spotlight. Josh, too, returned his attention to his half-eaten lunch. The Premier appeared on the screen at a briefing podium and Josh reached for the controller to increase the sound.

'Thank you, everyone. And thank you, Dr Chant for that update on the COVID situation.'

There were multiple flashes from photographers and Poppy found her attention glued to the screen. Would they announce an end to lockdown?

'As you've just heard from Dr Chant, the new COVID-positive cases are far reduced from where they were a few weeks ago and new admissions to hospital are also down. The ICU numbers are fairly stable. So, we are planning to end the Sydney lockdown and stay-at-home orders this Friday, the 13th of March, at 3pm. We still would like residents of Sydney to only travel within the state and only as necessary. We will be maintaining a "no congregating rule" and social distancing. Everyone will still need to use QR codes to check in and out of venues and there will be maximum restrictions for numbers of people in indoor venues based on size. We would like everyone to remain cautious and vigilant.'

Suddenly Poppy had mixed feelings about lockdown ending. She'd been so desperate to see Will for most of the period of lockdown, but now that it was likely she could travel to see him, she was unsure if it was still what she wanted.

'Yeah, but it's a bit vague isn't it?' Josh said, oblivious to what Poppy was really thinking.

'I guess there'll be more information on the NSW Service app and online. Maybe I can visit Will in Dubbo this weekend.' Poppy kept her head on the screen. She didn't want to see Josh's reaction to this news; afraid his disappointment might make her doubt her feelings even more.

'Hmm.'

She tried to turn it back to something positive for Josh. 'And it means they should be announcing the term end date as well. Hopefully it'll be in two weeks. You'll be able to get back to Cardiology.'

She chanced a glance at him. His jaw was clenched and he didn't look at her when he spoke. 'I don't want to get my hopes up just yet. The terms will change and things might die down for a while, but I suspect we'll be back where we started before we realise it.'

'Don't be such a pessimist, Josh. We got through it!'

Poppy let that sink in. They'd got through the worst of COVID. Surely things would get back to normal now? A sudden fizz of excitement about the future simmered in her gut. Maybe this was a sign. A sign she should stop messing around with Josh and focus on Will. She picked up her phone and opened Webjet to see if flights were listed to Dubbo for Friday evening. It was time to push forward and rip the Band-Aid off. She might see Will in only three days.

Friday came around quickly and Poppy's mood continued to improve, buoying her along the rest of the week. This continued to be the sign that moving forward with Will was the right thing to do and she avoided any more lingering glances with Josh or thoughts of whether he could really manage a relationship. Poppy even went as far as locking the memory of her brief kiss with him deep inside her and refusing to indulge in examining or enjoying it again. She'd booked a flight for seven o'clock and Josh had promised to cover the last couple of hours of her shift alone so she could get to the airport.

Once she was at the gate, her excitement started to phase into exhaustion. All the adrenaline powering her through the week was subsiding and the reality of she and Will being together in a little over an hour was sinking in.

How would she really feel when they were reunited? Would she rush into his arms, kissing him and forget about everything that had happened in the last few months? Or would they move toward each other awkwardly, consciously aware of their limbs? What if the broken bits of her heart failed to mend at first touch? Then what would she do for the whole weekend? Sit around talking, feeling increasingly uncomfortable? She was certain she wouldn't be able to hide her discomfort from Will, if that was indeed how things panned out.

Whilst these anxieties were building, and Poppy was starting to feel sick, Gemma texted.

> Hope you and Will have a great weekend! You deserve it!
> And don't forget (eggplant emoji + umbrella emoji,
> laughing emoji)

The feeling of wanting to vomit waned, and Poppy smiled in spite of herself. It's funny how Gemma always knew the exact right thing to say or text.

> Not sure about (umbrella emoji, eggplant emoji), feeling sick & not sure how things will go all of a sudden

Poppy watched her phone as the three dots appeared. It felt like an age before Gemma's reply came through. Her stomach continued to twist and churn.

> Don't overthink it! Just see what happens! Call/text whenever, I'm here for you! (heart emoji, kiss lips emoji)

Poppy took a deep breath, Gemma was right. There was nothing she could do now. She just needed to see him – her body would tell her what to do from there. Things had been improving between them these last weeks and Poppy was now much more confident that his mistakes were just a blip. A minor wiggle on the horizon, distorting the light. So really, she had nothing to worry about. She banished any thought of Josh from her mind. It had been a minor flirtation at a difficult time, she told herself.

After months of gruelling work schedules, Poppy surprised herself by falling fast asleep after takeoff. Her body jolting awake only as the plane touched down. A little snort escaped as she jerked awake, but there were so few people on the plane, she hoped no one noticed. She removed her mask surreptitiously and wiped away the drool that had pooled in her healing ulcer at the edge of her lips and felt her stomach rumble. There'd been no time to eat at the airport once she cleared security, and she'd missed the paltry tea service on the plane. Hopefully, there would be somewhere to pick up takeaway on their way back to Will's place.

Walking her heavy limbs across the tarmac toward the terminal doors, her heart rate began to quicken and those anxieties that had plagued her at Sydney airport started to return.

Stop it!

She consciously remembered Gemma's text and her plan to wait to see Will's face and trust in her body to lead her response.

The sliding doors opened as she approached and she gripped the handle of her bag as she wheeled it beside her. She saw his shape before anything else and held her breath…

Her eyes sought Will's and she realised, in the moment their eyes connected, that he was as anxious as she was. His hands were shoved deep into his jeans' pockets, and his shoulders hitched around his ears. In that moment, her heart melted, and they walked purposely toward each other.

'Poppy—'

'Will—' Their worlds collided as they approached with arms outstretched and reaching for each other.

As they embraced, Poppy began to cry, her tears soaking his shirt. 'I've missed you so much,' she mumbled into his chest.

'I love you, Poppy, I'm so sorry I hurt you.'

She realised, with a jolt, that Will was crying too. They stood holding on to each other for what felt like an age, and as they finally pulled apart, they saw they were standing alone at the gate. Even the staff had left, the gate fully locked down for the night.

'Do you want to get out of here?' Will said, somewhat shyly.

Poppy placed a hand in his and together they walked from the airport.

Chapter 30

Will drove them away from the airport. Poppy kept a hand on his leg, her eyes out the window, watching the landscape as it passed by. She looked up at the tall gums with their grey branches reaching out to each other across the road like friends embracing in the night. The rustle of the wind in the leaves she could imagine as their convivial chatter over mugs of tea or glasses of wine. It felt welcoming to her. She felt optimistic about the future again. She and Will could weather this small storm. Maybe they'd even be stronger and closer for it.

'Did you get any food?' Will interrupted her thoughts, his eyes darting her way before joining the road again.

'No. Actually, I'm kind of starving. Can we stop on the way?' Suddenly the emptiness of her stomach was the only thing on her mind.

'Sure, what do you feel like?'

'What fast food can we get?' His face was all sharp lines in the low lighting. He'd definitely lost weight while he'd been away. Poppy wondered how much of it had to do with his mood and what had happened between them.

'Usual suspects; Maccas, KFC, Opporto.'

'Ooh, I haven't had Opporto in a while, that'd be great. I love their chips.' She looked back out the window as they approached more buildings getting closer to town. The houses were closer together now and interspersed with some shops occasionally. Once they crossed the river, they were into the town centre.

Poppy was hungry and exhausted. At Opporto, she ate quickly. Will watched her eat, not interrupting the fast pace of chips to mouth between bites of burger. He relaxed in her presence, casually sipping his drink, his shoulders relaxing away from his ears. Finally, when Poppy was sated, she sat back and took a better look at him. Will's unruly hair had grown long, hanging over his ears and starting to make some curls at the nape of his neck. Every so often his long fringe would obscure his vision and Poppy watched him flick it back from his eyes.

'You need a haircut,' she said, taking the last sip of her drink.

He ruffled his fringe. 'Yeah, it's looking pretty grungy. I'll probably get it done before I come home. Did you see the email this afternoon about the end of term?'

Poppy leant forwards. 'No, what did it say?'

'Two more weeks, as predicted, then I'm home.' He beamed and his eyes crinkled the way Poppy remembered.

'That's awesome.' Poppy reached across the table to grab his hand and entwine her fingers in his. It felt so good to hold his hand and feel him close to her.

'What?' Will asked.

'I've just missed your face.'

'And I've missed yours,' he said, leaning across the table to place a soft kiss on her lips.

The kiss was light and quick, but it was enough to send a shot of heat into Poppy's pelvis. His face wasn't all that she'd missed.

'Let's go,' she said, still not letting go of his hand. Relishing the warmth building between them.

The drive to the back of the hospital, where Will was staying, was short, and they were pulling up behind a series of squat 1960's red brick bungalows in no time. Will got Poppy's bag from the boot and then opened the front door.

'Brendan's away for the weekend. When he heard you were coming up, he decided to go home, that way we'd both have a good weekend.'

'Excellent,' said Poppy, heat building again in her pants. Despite her exhaustion, she wanted to have sex with Will tonight, and not wait until tomorrow. Partly it was the notion of getting over the awkwardness, and partly it was from genuine desire. She'd been watching his face, a face she'd grown to know so well, and noticing the small crinkles at the corners of his eyes, the soft smattering of freckles over his nose and cheeks, and the fullness of his kissable lips. That delicious citrus scent was there, minus the usual salty undertone he must pick up from the beach, and his lean frame looked stronger than usual. She could definitely detect more bulk in his biceps, even if his face was looking thinner.

'Have you been working out?' Poppy asked as Will was turning on lights and putting his keys on the kitchen bench.

'There hasn't been much else to do, and there's a little gym and pool at the back of the hospital for students and staff.'

'You look good.'

'You do too,' Will said, advancing towards her. He tucked a strand of loose hair behind Poppy's ear and bent down to kiss her. Poppy lifted her chin and returned his kiss with increasing enthusiasm. She ran a hand down his back and over his butt, squeezing him toward her more so that she could feel the outline of his growing cock through his jeans. Will wasted no time and started unbuttoning Poppy's shirt without breaking their kiss completely. He pushed it off her shoulders, letting it drift to the floor and then pulled his own T-shirt over his head.

Ooh, he has been working out. His pecs are bigger. And those biceps!

Poppy now kissed down his neck and chest while her hands found his belt, unbuckling it, and unzipping his fly. She felt her clit pulsate and she pushed Will's jeans and undies down over his lean hips and to the floor. Her hand found his cock easily and rubbed it as Will quickly unbuttoned her bra and pushed down her skirt.

It had been so long since she'd had sex and Poppy was so wet and desperate to feel his fingers inside her. Knowing just what she liked, Will slipped a hand in her undies, found her clit briefly, then went for the sweet spot. Poppy let out a groan of pleasure.

'You're so wet,' Will whispered in her ear as he gave it a tiny nip.

'God, I want you,' she moaned.

'Let's go to the lounge.'

Poppy removed her undies, and Will hopped out of his jeans, holding onto his cock to keep it hard. Poppy shamelessly sat back on the couch, spreading her legs, as Will crouched in front of her. His tongue licked from opening to clit backwards and forwards several times before concentrating on her clit as he inserted two fingers into her. Poppy moaned and arched her hips in time with the flicking and gentle nipping Will was doing, all thoughts gone from her mind, only the pleasure she was feeling in this moment. Poppy continued to arch her hips with his finger thrusts and was soon close to climax.

'Ooh, yes… yes…' Poppy called, 'don't stop…faster…' and then the crest of her orgasm created ripples of jerking movements throughout her body.

Will sat back, rubbing his cock again to return it to its previous state of attention and then rolled the condom on that he'd brought with him to the lounge. He must have had one in his jeans pocket ready to go. Cheeky bastard.

Before her orgasm could disappear completely, Will thrust into her, his full length crushing against her cervix and she took a deep breath in. She'd forgotten how good it could feel to have his dick so deep inside her. Then Will pushed one of her knees back toward her chest, adding more depth and Poppy began to moan again.

'Oh, that's good,' she purred.

'You like it deep?'

'Yes, don't stop, I might come again.'

And Will ground into her over and over again. Poppy was getting close, but Will pulled out.

'Wha—'

'Roll over,' he demanded.

Yes, I like what he's thinking.

Poppy complied and before Will put his cock back in, he licked her again from behind.

'Oh my God,' she said, almost weak with the pleasure.

'You taste amazing... but now I need to keep fucking you,' he said as he shoved his cock back inside her once more.

Poppy reached a hand down to her clit, finding her little bean and running rapid mini circles on it as Will fucked her from behind. She was soon shouting with pleasure as she came again. Will followed immediately after and collapsed down onto her back. They both sucked in air and then flopped onto the couch.

'That was so good,' Will said between ragged breaths.

'Yep, it was,' Poppy added, laying an arm across his chest.

Once they'd caught their breath, Will rolled toward Poppy. 'Come here.'

He embraced her and tucked his legs up beside her on the couch, so that they were spooning lengthways. Poppy felt her eyelids and limbs becoming heavy. It was a struggle to stay awake. Her breathing slowed, and she gave in to the pull of sleep.

Sun was warming the side of Poppy's face, waking her from deep sleep the next morning. She woke disoriented, blinking a few times, not recognizing her surroundings, before she remembered where she was. On the next pillow, Will was still asleep, his jaw soft. She was naked in the bed next to him.

He must have carried me here from the couch last night.

Suddenly aware of how full her bladder was, Poppy eased herself out of the bed, trying not to wake Will, and tiptoed out of his room. They'd been in such a rush to have sex last night, that Poppy hadn't had a tour of the place, and wasn't sure where the bathroom was. As she came out of his room, she saw the lounge room in front of her, and to her left was a corridor and two more doors. She hoped one of these was the bathroom, otherwise she might piss herself. Scurrying to the first door, she was grateful when she opened it to find a toilet. What a relief. Now she shivered as she realised how cold she was. It looked like the whole house was tiled. Probably a good thing in the heat of summer in the west of the state, but hard on the feet in the cooler months. She pattered quickly back to Will's room and slipped back under the covers. With the sun in her face, she knew she wouldn't be able to go back to sleep.

'Morning,' Will said opening one eye only then shutting it again.

'Hi,' Poppy said, wiggling her body in closer to his and kissing his lips.

Will reached an arm up so she could get in closer and cuddle. 'How'd you sleep? You were dead to rights last night. You didn't even stir when I carried you to bed.'

She tipped her chin so she could still see his face. 'I slept like the dead. I'm just so buggered.'

'I'll bet.'

They lay in bed for a while, talking, then Will got up to make them breakfast.

'I might just have a quick shower, if that's okay?' Poppy sat up, holding the sheet over her still naked torso.

Pulling on briefs, Will said, 'Of course. I'll make bacon and eggs, so you've got time.'

'Great.' Poppy threw on one of Will's T-shirts that was hanging over his desk chair. She found her bag where they left it next to the front door and her discarded clothes from last night. Taking everything back into Will's room, she found what she needed and headed to the bathroom. 'Do you have a spare towel I can use?'

'Yep, there's a cupboard opposite the bathroom that has linen in it, just grab what you need from there,' Will shouted from the kitchen as she continued down the hall.

Poppy felt dirty after the long day at work and the flight, as well as their nocturnal activities, and was glad for the hot water coursing over her cold body. She turned her face up to the shower rose and relished the warm water massage. For crappy hospital accommodation, the water pressure was surprisingly good. But she was also hungry, so she didn't stay for too long.

Dressing in jeans, a T-shirt, and a navy-blue loose jumper, she emerged from Will's room with wet hair, that she was still trying to dry with her towel.

'Thanks, Will, this looks great,' she said as he placed a plate of scrambled eggs, bacon and toast in front of her.

'No coffee, I'm afraid, but we can go into town later for one. Do you want some juice?'

'What have you got?' she mumbled through a full mouth.

'Apple?'

Poppy swallowed the bacon she'd been chewing. 'Sure, thanks.'

She watched him as he scraped the last of the eggs and bacon onto a plate for himself. He looked relaxed and like the Will she fell in love with. His limbs fluid and unhurried. Still watching him unnoticed, he tucked a strand of curls behind his ear, picked up his plate and glass of juice and walked around the kitchen counter toward the table. Poppy dropped her eyes back to her own plate but felt that final knot of anxiety in her chest let go. This was right. This was where she was meant to be and who she was meant to be with.

After a few more mouthfuls of food, she looked up at Will. 'So, what are we going to do today?'

'Whatever you like. Do you want to go to the zoo?'

Poppy wasn't sure she was up to walking for hours in the sun. 'Umm, maybe.' She swallowed the last mouthful of egg and then said, 'to be honest, I am so tired, I'd be happy just to watch a movie and have a nap.'

'You're on. We've got Netflix, so I'm sure we can find something to watch. Maybe you'll be up to going out for dinner tonight?' He reached out and ran a hand over the side of her face.

Poppy leant into his hand. 'Sure. As long as I get a nap?'

'I can deal with that.'

After breakfast was tidied away, they went to the shops for coffee and supplies and returned to watch a movie. By lunch, Poppy was already flagging, so she had a quick snack and then went for a nap in Will's bed while he went for a run. Despite the saggy mattress and starchy sheets, she fell asleep almost as soon as her head touched the pillow.

'Poppy,' Will whispered close to her. 'Sorry, baby, but you've been asleep for a couple of hours, I thought maybe you should get up now?' His voice was soft and tentative, like he didn't want to upset her. Clearly, he was still unsure of this new territory they were in.

'Mmm,' Poppy mumbled. 'What time is it?'

'Almost four.'

'Gee, okay,' she said, blinking her eyes open. 'I think it's a relief to be out of Sydney.'

Will was lying on top of the sheets next to her, his head resting on his crooked arm. 'It's been a horror of a time for you.'

'Mmm,' Poppy said, her brain finally waking up more. She sat up a bit in the bed, pushing the pillow up behind her. 'So, what did you do while I was out of it?'

'Run, shower, then just watched some TV.'

He didn't look disappointed, but Poppy still felt bad. She reached out a hand to his face. 'I'm sorry, I haven't been good company.'

Will kissed her fingertips then held onto her hand gently, tucking it against his chest. 'Don't be, it's fine. Anyway, I've organized for some of the others to meet us for dinner.'

'That's a good idea. I'd like to put names to the faces of the people you've been working with.'

'Excellent.' The way he said it, she realised they'd both been a bit tentative and cautious with each other.

They lay silently for a beat. Poppy wondered whether she should ask him about how things were going with his calls to his sister. She didn't want to break the good vibe they had going, but she was curious as to whether they were still talking.

'You're biting your lip. What are you thinking?'

'Oh,' Poppy said and consciously stopped biting her lip. 'Nothing.'

'Come on, out with it,' he said, scootching closer toward her and smiling in a teasing way.

Softly with her eyes on the sheets and not on him, she asked, 'I was just wondering how things were going with your sister?'

'Oh…' He rolled onto his back, letting go of her hand. 'I figured you'd want to talk about it at some point this weekend.'

It was like the air shifted around them. Only moments ago there was warmth and comfort, but now a chill crept in between them. Poppy patted his arm, tentatively. 'I'm sorry, you don't have to if you don't want to.'

Still looking at the ceiling. 'No, it's okay… we've been talking every few days, and it's been great. We've talked through a lot of issues around my ex. And I think that's where this has all come from…'

Poppy kept her voice soft and low. 'How do you mean?'

Will sighed heavily. 'Well, she hurt me so badly with her betrayal. And I guess, I never really worked through that. I was still angry about it… And then when I kissed that girl when I was drunk, I really shocked myself…'

He fell silent for a moment. When he spoke again, his voice was low and raw. 'Like how could I hurt you, like she'd hurt me? You know?'

Poppy didn't answer, she didn't think he was really asking her the question. More like he was questioning himself. She waited, keeping her body separate to his, until he continued.

'I was so shocked that I could do something like that. So angry at myself. And scared.'

'What were you scared of?'

'Scared that if I could kiss someone else, did that mean I could sleep with someone else, or have an affair for months, like she did? Maybe I was just like her, just as callous as her?' Now his head turned to look at Poppy and she saw the fear in his eyes. Was he afraid that she wouldn't be able to forgive him?

Poppy reached out, touching his chest again. 'But you're not her, Will.' She patted his chest, hoping he believed it.

'Yeah, I know. Because I felt awful. The betrayal and the keeping it from you was eating me up inside.' He pulled at his hair. 'And maybe that's exactly why I'm not like her. Because the guilt from just one kiss was horrendous.' Will cupped Poppy's hand against his chest once more. 'And then, I lied to you about it, making the guilt double, and then I just felt like I was drowning, you know?'

Poppy nodded, not because she knew how he felt but just to give him the reassurance that she was here, listening.

'And I stopped eating, and just couldn't stop thinking about you, and how I'd hurt you, even though you didn't know. And then you started getting worried about me—'

'I thought you were depressed.'

'Yeah, I figured. And that made me feel worse. You were trying to help me. And then I was obsessing about it, and I had the discarded fentanyl vial and I was about to put it in the sharps bin, but I just slipped it into my pocket… Like I wasn't even thinking what I was doing at the time, it was just there… And then I hid it in my locker in the theatre changing rooms. And I kept thinking about it. And you. Then I just… took it.' His eyes drifted down to the bed and he finished almost in a whisper.

Poppy was holding her breath. She didn't want to move or make a sound. She needed to hear the rest.

He looked back at her now the hardest part had been admitted. 'Of course, that made the guilt even worse, and I started spiralling even more. Until I came clean. And now… well , now, I feel like before. Before the kiss, before any of this.' He used his arm to indicate the house, and Poppy assumed, Dubbo in general. 'I'm ready to come home. What do you think?'

His eyes were searching hers, looking for any hesitation or doubt.

What did Poppy think? She certainly believed everything he'd said, and she could see that his mood was better, and he was more like the Will she knew. Maybe he was right, maybe this was all just a consequence of not dealing with the emotions of his ex's betrayal. Not grieving that betrayal? Poppy hoped so.

'I think it sounds like being isolated hasn't helped,' she said.

'Absolutely… if I'd been in Sydney, with you, this never would have happened. But in a weird kind of way, I'm glad it did.'

Before she could even ask what he meant, he reached out a hand to her. 'I don't mean that I don't regret what I did, I promise. It's just given me time to really think about my ex and what she did, and also really look at myself and who I am and who I want to be.' His hand was warm and heavy on her shoulder. 'I know now that my love for you is really strong. It's not just new love and lust. Although, don't get me wrong, the minute I saw you come through those doors at the airport, I wanted to tear your clothes off.' His smile broke the tension in his face. 'But it's more than that… you're my person, my soul mate.' He ended with the upward inflection of a question, as if begging her to confirm this.

Once more, Poppy reached her hand out and rested it on his chest. 'I love you too, Will. It's been terrible being separated from you and worrying so much about you but being unable to help.'

'But you did help. You listened and you made me talk to my sister. That really made a difference.' Will leaned in and, slowly, his eyes never leaving hers, ensuring the move was not unwanted, let his lips brush hers.

Poppy felt a flush of overwhelming love for this man in her arms and she deepened the kiss, gently parting his lips with her tongue and then feeling Will responding in kind. Poppy rolled on top of him, shedding the bedding as she straddled his body and continued kissing his mouth and then down to graze his collarbone. Their kisses continued as they shed their clothes and their bodies united in sex again. Slower and more thoughtful than the previous night, but just as hot. Their bodies committing once again to their partnership. Accepting the past and moving forward. When they finished and Poppy was staring at the dirty ceiling, she finally let the last knot in her chest unravel. She was finished with second guesses and "what if's", it was time for the next stage of their lives together.

'So, what do you think about moving in together?' she asked, turning just her head to check out his reaction.

Chapter 31

The last two weeks of term Poppy found herself counting down each day, knowing that Will would soon be home and they could start flat hunting. Gemma was relieved to hear how well things had gone in Dubbo when Poppy came home, and they continued to make wedding plans. Occasionally, Lucas, too, would join in their planning sessions. Josh was still filling in for Olivia and the shifts were still twelve hours, but their new Consultant was young, enthusiastic, and present, so their days felt shorter and the COVID admissions became fewer. With the weather getting colder, they were starting to see some of the usual respiratory admissions like pneumonia and exacerbations of emphysema. Things were starting to feel closer to resetting.

The lockdown orders had eased, so there were more people on the roads and out and about in general, but masks were still required, takeaways were the norm, and strict QR check-ins and limitations on the numbers of people gathering together were still enforced. But the 5km radius had also eased, meaning Poppy could surf again. She and Josh had a random day off in the middle of the week as they were going to be doing the weekend, so he had offered to come to the beach with her.

'Do you surf?' She raised a sceptical eyebrow.

'Not well.' Poppy could see it was hard for him to admit this failing.

'Hunh… I didn't think there was anything you did poorly, Josh. This I am going to have to see. Do you have a wetsuit and a board? It's going to be cold.'

'I'll borrow Charlie's.'

'Can you pick me up at ten?'

Scraping a hand low in front of him in a bow, he said, 'I am at your service.'

Poppy laughed at his grandiosity.

Getting ready at home, Poppy wasn't sure how she felt about surfing with Josh. It was her thing with Will – he'd taught her after all. But she didn't really want to go by herself, and it might be fun to tease Josh, if he really was as bad as he said. She knew Will probably wouldn't like the idea of Josh being so physically close to her and sharing this with her, but she had no plans in telling him about it, not unless something weird happened. In fact, she hadn't shared with Will any of the more intimate conversations she'd had with Josh this term, the brief kiss they'd shared, or the fact that he'd basically said he would still want to be with her if she and Will didn't work out. She didn't feel guilty about keeping this from him as she knew Will would not handle the information well and it would hurt him, and them at this fragile rebuilding point. Poppy found she was far better at compartmentalising than she ever imagined.

The water at Bronte was like glass. Crystal clear and reflecting the clear blue sky above. There was only a slight offshore breeze which kept the windchill down as Josh and Poppy paddled out on their boards. They sat upright waiting for a swell to line up, Poppy looking out at the horizon, happy to be out on the water and in the sun. She was thinking how good it was that work was getting easier and the end of term was imminent.

Josh nudged her leg to get her attention. 'You've been pretty happy since coming back from Dubbo, so things are good now with you and Will?'

'Yeah, we're good again,' Poppy replied, not looking at Josh, letting her fingertips glide through the water beside her, and not stopping the smile that formed so quickly when she thought about Will. Poppy's board was gently rocking up and down and her left knee knocked into Josh's again, forcing her to turn and look at him.

'I'm happy for you,' he said and Poppy saw that he was being sincere. 'You deserve to be happy, Poppy.'

'Thanks, Josh.' She was relieved that he wasn't going to make things awkward between them. They hadn't even discussed Dubbo since she got back.

'But just know… if there comes a time when he stops making you happy again, give me a call.'

Poppy just looked at him. She didn't know how to respond, she'd only just been relieved he hadn't made things awkward, and now this. A glimmer of steel had entered his eyes. Was he saying he would beat Will up if he hurt her again? Or that he'd be there to pick up the pieces and potentially move into his vacated position?

Before she had a chance to respond, the swell was upon them, and Josh was turning his board to face the shore and catch the first decent wave. Maybe it was his arrogance, always needing to be first, but Poppy suspected he rushed onto this wave so that she couldn't question him over his true meaning. She watched him push off the board to stand as the wave was cresting but then focused her attention back on the swell to pick the next decent wave for herself. The rush was pure as she popped up on the crest and she relished the subsequent drop-in. It was so smooth she even surprised herself by carving back up the face of the wave in a nice manoeuvre before gliding back down and eventually bailing out before the chop.

Not as rusty as I thought.

Surfing was so seductive. The thrill of the ride and the elation and endorphin surge that occurred was so addictive. All thoughts of questioning Josh's meaning were gone, Poppy just wanted to get back out and line up the next set.

'How'd you go?' she asked Josh as they paddled back out together, her arms propelling her through the water and over the waves. Sea salt spray providing sudden bursts of refreshing chill to her face.

'I wiped out pretty much straight away. You looked good, though.'

'Thanks, I was worried I'd be really rusty. I haven't surfed since the beginning of the term.'

'If that was rusty, I need lessons.' He swept his wet hair off his forehead as he sat up on the board.

Poppy laughed, and Josh joined with a smirk. 'I think you might need lessons, but probably from someone better than me.' They were sitting side by side again.

'How long have you been surfing?' Josh didn't seem to be in too much of a rush to find the next wave, happy letting their boards and legs bump into each other.

A breeze lifted Poppy's wet hair and a shiver ran over her scalp. 'Just since last year… It was actually Will who taught me. He's a really good rider.'

'I didn't know that,' Josh replied and their conversation fell flat. A seagull dove in front of them, plucking a small fish out of the water and carrying it off in its beak before another one chased it, squawking and trying to steal it. It was enough to break the tension and Poppy suggested they turn and get ready for the next set.

Josh had a few more goes, but never really got the hang of things and gave up, paddling back into shore with a scowl on his face. But Poppy stayed out and made a few more rides before taking pity on Josh and coming in. He was shivering on the beach when she ran up, her feet sliding in the cold, dry sand.

'That last one was pretty impressive,' he said, standing up as she approached and handing her towel up to her.

'Thanks.' Poppy dropped her board and took the proffered towel, immediately drying her face and trying to take some of the excess water out of her hair. 'I was trying to get into the barrel but didn't quite make it.'

She was still warm from her efforts but she could see the mist forming with Josh's breathing. There was no one left on the beach and the clouds had come in sometime in the last hour, blunting the sun and plummeting the temperature. In a groove out on the water, she hadn't even noticed.

'It still looked good.' Despite his bulk, he looked small in the wetsuit and somehow vulnerable.

Poppy slung her towel around her shoulders. 'It was a nice break today. Shall we get a coffee, you look cold.'

Picking up his board, he said, 'Good idea.'

When Josh dropped her home and he was getting her board out of the boot, he said, 'I meant what I said before, you know.'

He placed the board in front of her but held onto it, looking down at her.

'What about?' Poppy asked but knew he must mean his comment about Will.

He sighed and Poppy noticed he didn't have an anxious tell – he didn't run his hand through his hair, or look down at his feet, or wring his hands. He was still a very confident human being. And even though it was at times as annoying as hell, it was also a turn-on.

'I know you think I'm not ready for something serious, Poppy, but if Will doesn't live up to what you deserve, then I would be very happy to take his place.' He didn't move in to close the space between them or touch her in any way. The tic of his jaw was the only sign he was anxious about her reply.

'I'll keep that in mind,' she said lightly, picking up the board and turning toward her building. At the entrance doors, she looked back. 'I'll see you tomorrow, Josh.'

She raced up the stairs, refusing to check if he was still standing there, her heart jumping as she went. Did she mean to leave the door open for him in her heart? Is that the way he would have interpreted it? Second-guessing herself, she paused before putting her key in the door at their apartment.

Poppy decided not to tell Gemma about Josh's comment that night. Ever since she'd gotten back from Dubbo, Gemma had been singing Will's praises, and it was starting to get annoying. She knew that if she told Gemma what Josh had said, she'd be jumping to Will's defence, even though she didn't know the full picture. Gemma didn't know how close she and Josh had really become over the term or how Poppy's feelings toward him had changed. When she thought about it in the bath, it felt reassuring, in a funny way, to know that Josh wanted to prove to her that he was worthy enough. It meant that she was right in thinking his arrogance was often bluster, masking the insecurity that underlay his confident exterior. A deep-seated need to not be hurt by someone else, the way his father's absence must still hurt so much. Josh wasn't the bad guy he pretended to be, and the vulnerability he'd showed her meant she would keep him in her heart. Tucked down low. Just in case. She didn't question whether that was fair to Josh, feeling confident he would have no trouble keeping himself occupied with others.

The final week of term brought with it the fear of end of term reports. Poppy knew that Dr Anderson would be writing hers due to Prof Pilson's early retirement, and she had no idea whether it would be fair.

'Don't get so worried about it,' Josh said as they were walking back down the road with coffees on their morning break. 'It's really not a big deal.'

'Says the man with the highly coveted Cardiology advanced trainee position. I bet you never had a bad end of term report.' Poppy took a sip of her coffee. Her right hand was already getting hot from the cup and so she switched it to the other side.

'True.'

'And you know how much Dr Anderson despises me.'

'I think "despise" might be taking things a bit far. I'm sure she rarely thinks about you.'

She nudged him with her hip and chuckled. 'Thanks, that's helpful.'

He lifted his coffee cup higher in the air to avoid spilling it, then stopped, causing her to stop too. 'I'm sorry, that was thoughtless.'

He sounded so earnest, Poppy was surprised. This was more of the new Josh and each time she received this version she had to let go of more of the old wounds.

'What I meant was, you are a Resident. And, yes, it wasn't long ago that I was in your position, but I'm sure she doesn't think about you as much as you do her. She'll give you a fair report. You've worked very hard this term, made no complaints about all the shit you've had to do and the hours you've had to work. She should be thanking you.'

'Thanks, Josh.' She smiled at him, tilted her head to the side and sipped her coffee.

'You're welcome. Now stop stressing about it.' Josh resumed walking and she followed suit. 'You heard there's no end of term ball, right?'

'Yeah, but I knew that was coming. The capacity restrictions were never going to allow a big function.'

'I know, but it's still disappointing. After everything we've been through this term, it would be really nice to let loose.'

'Can you imagine if everyone who attended got COVID, though. What a disaster that would be.' Poppy laughed. 'Are you getting excited about going back to Cardiology? Has it been confirmed yet?'

Josh scoffed. 'Finally. Got the email last night. It is a relief.'

'That's great, Josh. You deserve that, too. You've really helped me this term, and barely complained.'

'Hmph.' But his lips betrayed him, quirking up into a mischievous smirk. Their eyes connected and Josh's were full of warmth and fun. Maybe they could manage a friendship after all.

Dr Anderson came to the ward late in the afternoon. 'Ah, Poppy,' she said, striding toward her with elegance as always, despite the PPE. 'Do you mind if we have a word in the conference room?'

'Ah… okay,' Poppy said, her neck taking on familiar heat and her pulse elevating automatically.

They shed their PPE at the doffing station, Poppy noticing Dr Anderson had the highly coveted personalised FIGS scrubs, and kept their masks on as they took seats next to each other in the conference room where they'd had their first Monday meeting at the beginning of the term. Poppy pondered how much had happened and changed since that first week. She had no idea why Dr Anderson had sought her out, but she didn't want to be the first one to talk.

'Poppy, I wanted to thank you for your resilience, this term,' Dr Anderson said. It was the second time today that Poppy had been surprised. She reflexively sat back in her chair, as if the shock of this statement had pushed her back. Luckily, she didn't think Dr Anderson noticed this change, as she continued without a pause. 'This whole situation with Prof Pilson, Adnan, and Olivia has been completely unacceptable. But you've not complained, you've just got on with the work and done as much as you could. I really appreciate that on behalf of the entire Respiratory service.'

Poppy knew Dr Anderson would expect a thank you in response and she stammered, 'Ah… thank you, Dr Anderson.'

It had been delivered fairly stiffly, but the sentiment was still the same. Dr Anderson was complimenting Poppy. The others were not going to believe her when she told them.

'You should get a copy of your end of term report by tomorrow. I made sure to make it clear that you had really gone above and beyond what would be expected of a first year Resident this term. We really wouldn't have gotten through this COVID peak without your dedication. And I wanted you to know that it was noted.'

'Thank you,' Poppy said meekly. Like most junior doctors, she was unused to compliments in general, but multiple in one sitting was unheard of and she felt awkward and uncertain what was expected in response.

Dr Anderson then sat back herself as if she'd done what she came to do. But it was clear that their tete-a-tete was not over. Poppy saw the wheels turning behind Dr Anderson's eyes and waited.

'There will also be an announcement that I will be taking over as head of Department.'

And there was the extra information Dr Anderson wanted Poppy to know.

'Oh, congratulations,' Poppy said dutifully.

The slightest simmer of a laugh came from behind Dr Anderson's mask. 'You know, last year I never would have thought it would be you who helped me push him out.'

'What?' Poppy's guts clenched. What did she mean? 'I never wanted Prof Pilson to go. He's lovely.'

'Yes, but he needed a push to get off the merry-go-around. Now some of his more antiquated notions can be modernised.'

Poppy felt dirty, like she had been complicit in Prof Pilson's demise. Whilst she was grateful to Dr Anderson for ensuring she now had a Consultant on a regular basis in these last few weeks of term, she didn't like the feeling of being used to further Dr Anderson's own agenda. Yet again proving what a pragmatist she was, and that Poppy was thankful she would be moving on next week.

'Anyway, thank you. Your contribution has been noted and will not be forgotten,' Dr Anderson said as she stood and made her way to the door.

But she turned back before walking through and Poppy had to stop abruptly in her tracks. 'You know, Poppy, I never forget who I owe a favour to.'

With that she walked through the door and left the ward, leaving Poppy still stranded in the conference room, a chill running down her spine.

Chapter 32

Poppy stood at the gate waiting for Will to disembark from the plane on Saturday morning. The final days of the term had been uneventful, and she'd just been treading water waiting for Will's return. With no end of term party and limits on where and how many people could congregate, Poppy, Lucas, and Gemma had gone to the Marly last night as a mini celebration. They were allowed outside in the beer garden in maximum groups of four, with tables well separated and all food and drinks had to be ordered at your table via a QR code to ensure limited interaction. Poppy had toyed with the idea of inviting Josh, to thank him for his help and support during the term but decided against it. Ultimately realising that both he, and Gemma and Lucas, would be uncomfortable and then Poppy would be forced to do all the talking whilst pretending that everyone was having a good time. It would just have been too exhausting. So, their trio had eaten burgers and chips and drunk beer and cocktails, and Poppy had felt a lot of the stress of working through the COVID wave dissipate.

Now she saw Will's tall frame and newly tamed hair come through the doors at the gate and she rushed over to meet him. His eyes were all crinkly at the edges, just the way she liked, and they moved to the side and wrapped their arms around each other, pulled down their masks, and kissed long and deeply.

'Hey, you,' Will said when their lips eventually parted.

'Hey, you,' Poppy replied, kissing him again and ignoring the stares of those around them. 'Welcome back.'

Will placed a hand on her butt and Poppy scooched in close as they walked slowly toward the baggage claim area. When they were waiting for Will's stuff, they resumed their kissing, their lips hungry for each other's. They didn't care that they were surrounded by random strangers, they were just glad to finally be together again. Glad that they wouldn't be parted now for many months. At least not until Poppy's country term later in the year.

Poppy had borrowed Gemma and Lucas' car and, on the drive back to Will's place, they talked about Dr Anderson and what her final comment had meant. They'd talked about it off and on all week and still had different viewpoints. Poppy felt it was vaguely threatening but Will held strongly to the belief that she was telling Poppy to call in a favour when she needed it.

'I just don't see how you can read a threat into those words,' Will said again, for what felt like the tenth time.

'The way she said it didn't feel like she was saying she owed *me* a favour. I guess you had to be there.' Poppy had her right arm resting on the door, the window partly open, her hair blowing in the breeze.

'But you said her exact words were "I never forget who I owe a favour to."' Poppy could hear the frustration in his voice and could tell he was getting sick of discussing this.

'But it felt more like a threat, like I owed *her* a favour for writing the glowing end of term report.' In her peripheral vision, Poppy saw Will shake his head.

'No, I really think she thinks you helped her get rid of Prof Pilson and make her head of department. So, she owes *you* a favour.'

They were stopped at the lights and Poppy turned to him. 'But I had nothing to do with either of those things. She did those on her own.' Poppy didn't want to be guilty of orchestrating either of those events.

Will looked out the window, turning his head away from her. They were clearly never going to agree. Poppy didn't want to start the weekend fighting, so turned back to focus on the traffic.

After saying hello to Penny, Will's flatmate, they retreated to his room. Poppy flopped into his comfortable reading chair and watched him unpack. Even though he'd been out of Sydney for the entire term, he had very little to unpack. Either he'd done a lot of washing, or he wore his clothes for days before washing them. Poppy wrinkled her nose up at the thought and Will caught her.

'What?' He paused, with a pair of jeans in his hands.

'You didn't take a lot of stuff with you, and I was just wondering how often you washed it?'

'Are you suggesting I have poor hygiene habits?' he teased. 'I'll have you know that I have excellent hygiene standards. I was planning to bring some more things when I came home that weekend, but when that didn't happen, I made do mainly wearing extra scrubs from the hospital.'

'Oh. I didn't think of that,' Poppy admitted.

He flicked the jeans at her leg, and she pulled them away, laughing. 'But I'd be happy for you to inspect my hygiene status in a mutual shower?' He raised his eyebrows provocatively and came closer to lean in towards her, resting his hands on the arms of the chair. 'What do you say, Poppy?'

His face was only centimetres away, his voice low and hungry. How she loved this face, she thought as she put her hands on either side of it and kissed his lips, closing any distance between them. He pulled her hands, lifting her off the chair, then trailed them behind him, never letting go as they walked toward his bathroom.

Epilogue

October 2020

The day was clear. The relentless rain of the last few weeks had finally abated, and the sun was out. Poppy thought it was a fabulous day for Gemma and Will's wedding. She was so excited, they were finally able to get married. They were taking advantage of the government's decision to ease restrictions on gatherings, now allowing up to fifty people for a wedding. Still, fifty people meant a lot of Gemma's extended family were missing out, but they were happy.

After they returned from getting their hair and make-up done, Poppy helped Gemma get into her dress. It was ivory silk, figure-hugging and cut on the bias, accentuating her long limbs. Spaghetti straps and a heart-shaped neckline with crystal beads stitched delicately into the bodice added subtle bling to the simple design. The dressmaker whom they'd chosen to copy the Karen Willis Holmes design had done a really fabulous job and it had been about half the cost of the original.

'Gem, you are stunning,' Poppy said once she was zipped and buttoned in at the back.

Gemma looked at herself in the mirror and Poppy saw her relax.

'Are you happy?' she asked her.

'Yeah,' Gemma replied, a smile refusing to stay quashed once she saw herself in the full-length mirror.

'But no tears, okay? You'll ruin your make-up.'

Gemma smiled up at Poppy's reflection in the mirror then glanced at the beside clock. 'You'd better get dressed too.'

Poppy quickly slipped into her own dress of turquoise blue. Hers was to the knee and flared from the waist with a halter neckline, accentuating her moderate bust and lengthening her average height. There were a few crystal beads sewn into her waistline to tie in with Gemma's gown. Whilst turquoise wasn't a colour Poppy would normally choose for herself, it certainly complemented her blue eyes and she was happy enough.

'Oh, my darling girl,' Gemma's mum gushed as they emerged from the bedroom in their dresses.

'Don't cry, Mum,' Gemma said as her father came over, two glasses of champagne in his hands.

'You look so beautiful,' he said as he handed Gemma the drink and the photographer snapped a picture of them both.

'Thanks, Dad.'

'You too, Poppy,' he said as he handed her one too and winked.

'Thanks, Mr Winstead.'

'We've got to go,' Gemma said, hurrying them along.

Poppy quickly skulled most of the champagne as Gemma passed her the round bouquet of lisianthus, delphiniums, and freesias. 'Cheers.'

'Okay, get to the car, people.' Gemma pushed her parents in front of her and chuffed them out the door, the photographer's protests ignored.

When they arrived at the church fifteen minutes later, Gemma's father opened the door for Gemma to get out of the vintage Rolls-Royce with the classic white streamers at the front, while Poppy and Gemma's mother got out of the Mercedes behind them.

The photographer scurried over. 'No, wait!' He gestured for Gemma to stop. 'I want to get a picture of you in the car and then coming out.'

She agreed but Poppy noticed the frown line that flickered between Gemma's eyes again. The photographer was already getting on Gemma's nerves.

They took some photos at the car and then on the stairs, Gemma's frown deepening even more.

'Don't worry, I can Photoshop that frown out,' the photographer said.

Poppy pursed her lips to prevent herself from laughing.

'I think that's enough,' Gemma said, turning to open the church doors.

'No, Gem, you wait.' Poppy barred Gemma's arms. 'We don't want anyone to see you. Just let me open the doors and signal the boys, okay?'

Gemma immediately relented and stepped back.

'You look beautiful, and you're marrying Luc, who loves you more than anything. It's going to be wonderful,' Poppy reassured her.

Gemma's frown faded and a smile replaced it, slowly warming her whole face. 'I love you, Pop.'

'I love you, Gem.'

'Now let's get me married!'

Poppy nodded, peeked in the doors and signalled to the best man that it was time.

Poppy sought out Will's eyes as she walked down the aisle, finally spotting him near the front on the left, his eyes sparkling as he mouthed to her, "*You look hot!*"

Poppy beamed in response, holding his gaze until she got close to the front. Her eyes flicked to Lucas, who was anxiously searching the back, waiting for Gemma to enter.

'You got this,' Poppy whispered as she got close, before taking her position opposite him and leaving space for Gemma.

The music changed and then Gemma and her dad entered the church, the organ vibrating through Poppy's spine as a shiver of happiness for her two best friends engulfed her and a tear threatened to fall. She found her eyes tracking between Gemma and Lucas, and the pure love and adoration in Lucas' face as he watched his almost-wife walk toward him almost broke Poppy. Gemma, too, looked strong, at peace, and ethereal. As Poppy's eyes returned to Will, she found his glued to her, and full of emotion.

"*I love you,*" he mouthed at her and Poppy's heart swelled. They were in such a good place now after such a tough year.

The rest of the ceremony went by in a blur. Poppy would only remember feeling light and on the edge of tears of joy throughout. After location photographs at Oak Park, they headed to the reception at The Founders Room.

After the main course and speeches, the DJ started Lady Gaga's *Shallow*, and Gemma and Lucas took to the dance floor to have their first dance. Everyone formed a circle around the dance floor, and Will's hand slipped into Poppy's, squeezing gently. But Poppy's eyes were glued to Gemma and Lucas, lovingly dancing, their eyes lost in each other. Poppy wanted what they had. A love that was so strong, the rest of the world faded into the distance. Was that what she had with Will? She turned and looked in his eyes as he leaned into her and brushed the faintest of kisses on her lips. Might she have found that one true love?

The music changed and Christina Perri started singing about loving someone for a thousand years. Poppy tugged on Will's hand and led him onto the dance floor as other couples joined Gemma and Lucas. She wrapped her arms around his neck and rested her head against his chest as they slowly moved to the music. A deep sense of contentment embraced her as she listened to Will's heart beating in time with the music. Right in this moment, Poppy was content.

Caught in the Undertow Playlist

This city by Sam Fischer

High Hopes by Panic! At The Disco

Medicine by Robinson and the Romantics

Rushing back by Flume

Thank u, next by Ariana Grande

Goodbyes by Post Malone

Happier by Marshmello ft. Bastille

Bad Liar by Imagine Dragons

Before you go by Lewis Capaldi

Born this way by Lady Gaga

Just Dance by Lady Gaga

Shallow by Lady Gaga

This Feeling by The Chainsmokers

Exit Sign by Hilltop Hoods

A thousand years by Christina Perri

Acknowledgements

Thank you for reading, *Caught in the Undertow.* I hope you have enjoyed Poppy's second adventure. The last twelve months have flown by in a whirlwind. I've met so many wonderful readers and writers and learnt more about my craft and the indie publishing world. Thanks to all of you that also read, *The Swell*, and came back for the second instalment. And all those that connected with me on social media and shared their impressions of *The Swell*, or pictures of the book out in the wild. All these connections have been so meaningful for me and are the biggest reward to sending my stories out into the world.

But whilst writing a story is a solo effort, publishing a book takes a team. Thank you first to my alpha readers; Joey Houghton, Angie Black, Nicole Gower, and Caileen Cachia. Your feedback is so vital and I hope you will be willing to do it again! I'd also like to offer my sincerest thanks to Professor James Burrell and Dr Baerin Houghton for reviewing my medical scenes for accuracy. I have to acknowledge that both these esteemed doctors commented that arterial blood gases are performed less commonly now and that CTs and Radiology services or interventions were kept to a minimum during the COVID period to reduce potential for transmission of the virus. For the purposes of the story, I kept these in to a certain extent to aid in building tension, both within Poppy, and also the plot. Thank you to my editor, Kelly Rigby, for your effort and support in getting, *Caught in the Undertow*, into its best possible shape. I've learnt so much about novel structure from you and I look forward to putting these lessons into practice for book three. Thank you to Belinda Mark, my amazing cover designer and friend. She is incredibly talented and has outdone herself again! Next on the list is Ian Hooper and his team at Book Reality Experience for all the finishing touches and getting the book publication ready (especially with such a short turnaround). You've been a fabulous font of knowledge for me over these last twelve months, and always kind and patient, thank you.

Finally, thank you to Carrie Clarke, author, mentor, and friend. Everyone needs a Carrie in their corner!

I started writing the first draft of, *Caught in the Undertow*, in 2020 in the midst of the COVID pandemic. It was a very challenging time to be a doctor and I wanted this story to capture some of the fear and hardship that frontline healthcare workers faced. I used a number of resources to assist in my writing but ultimately I chose to adjust the timeline to suit my story and exaggerate and accelerate the death toll that Sydney experienced for the purpose of building tension in the plot. To that end I also ignored the fact that on Monday, January 27th, 2020 this would have been a public holiday for Australia Day and therefore the Respiratory team's Monday meeting would not have gone ahead as it would have been skeleton staffing only. Please forgive this and other adjustments that were intentionally made in making the story as streamlined and interesting as possible for readers. It is, after all, a work of fiction. Any mistakes, of course, are my own.

Australia was lucky during the COVID pandemic from a numbers perspective. Our physical isolation helped stem the tide of transmission and preserve our healthcare resources. However, the lockdowns particularly in Sydney, and even more so in Melbourne, were some of the toughest and longest in the world and these brought their own set of problems. Humans are naturally social creatures and lockdowns had negative effects on people's mental health and wellbeing. It also had significant impacts in the development and wellbeing of children who missed out on crucial socialising and milestone events in schooling. Nursing home residents were also severely affected by being cut off from friends and family members. We may not truly appreciate the flow-on effects of this for some time. I felt writing about this period was important for preserving the human experience in an unprecedented time. Let's hope there isn't another one for a while!

Thank you for all my friends, colleagues, and patients who supported and were cheerleaders for, *The Swell*, I hope you've got your pom-poms ready for this one! Last but not least, my thanks must finally go to my family; James, Alexander, Lachlan, and Isabella for all the love and support they give me and for just being in my life each day. I am so lucky!

Also by C. E. de Gzell

The Swell (Poppy Mason series book 1)

About the Author

Dr C. E. de Gzell is a Radiation Oncologist who specialises in the treatment of patients with brain tumours. A period of burnout in 2019 reignited an old passion for writing. Her debut novel, *The Swell*, was published in 2025 and is the first book in the Poppy Mason series. She lives in Sydney, Australia, with her husband and three children, and a goofy sheepadoodle, Fudge, who likes to escape and go on her own adventures. Dr de Gzell is a big fan of weekend naps, delicious desserts, and sweet cocktails. Check out her website- cedegzellauthor.com, or connect with her on Instagram @ ce_degzell_author, or Facebook @ C E De Gzell.

www.ingramcontent.com/pod-product-compliance
Ingram Content Group Australia Pty Ltd
76 Discovery Rd, Dandenong South VIC 3175, AU
AUHW020207230226
423694AU00003B/14

9 781764 069120